The BOOK *of* FIRES

JANE BORODALE

The

BOOK *of* FIRES

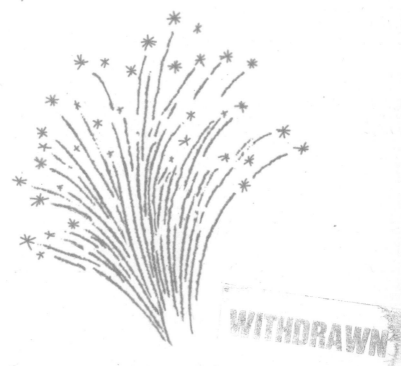

Pamela Dorman Books

VIKING

V I K I N G
Published by the Penguin Group
Penguin Group (USA) Inc., 375 Hudson Street, New York, New York 10014, U.S.A.
Penguin Group (Canada), 90 Eglinton Avenue East, Suite 700, Toronto, Ontario,
Canada M4P 2Y3 (a division of Pearson Penguin Canada Inc.)
Penguin Books Ltd, 80 Strand, London WC2R 0RL, England
Penguin Ireland, 25 St. Stephen's Green, Dublin 2, Ireland
(a division of Penguin Books Ltd)
Penguin Books Australia Ltd, 250 Camberwell Road, Camberwell,
Victoria 3124, Australia (a division of Pearson Australia Group Pty Ltd)
Penguin Books India Pvt Ltd, 11 Community Centre,
Panchsheel Park, New Delhi – 110 017, India
Penguin Group (NZ), 67 Apollo Drive, Rosedale, North Shore 0632,
New Zealand (a division of Pearson New Zealand Ltd)
Penguin Books (South Africa) (Pty) Ltd, 24 Sturdee Avenue,
Rosebank, Johannesburg 2196, South Africa

Penguin Books Ltd, Registered Offices: 80 Strand, London WC2R 0RL, England

First American edition
Published in 2010 by Viking Penguin, a member of Penguin Group (USA) Inc.

1   3   5   7   9   10   8   6   4   2

A Pamela Dorman Book / Viking

Publisher's Note
This is a work of fiction. Names, characters, places, and incidents either are the product of the author's
imagination or are used fictitiously, and any resemblance to actual persons, living or dead, business
establishments, events, or locales is entirely coincidental.

Library of Congress Cataloging-in-Publication Data

Borodale, Jane.
The book of fires : a novel / Jane Borodale.
p.   cm.
Includes bibliographical references.
ISBN 978-0-670-02106-2
1. Women—Fiction.   2. London (England)—History—18th century—Fiction.   I. Title.
PR6102.O76B66   2010
823'.92—dc22   2009027163

Printed in the United States of America
Set in Fournier
Designed by Francesca Belanger

For Sean, Orlando and Louis

With thoughts spared
for all those condemned to death by hanging at Tyburn

Fixed Suns

*T*here is a regular rasp of a blade on a stone as he sharpens the knives. The blade makes a shuddery, tight noise that I feel in my teeth. It's November, and today is the day that we kill the pig.

I am inside the house, bending over the hearth. I lay pieces of dry elm and bark over the embers and they begin to kindle as the fire takes. A warm fungus smell rises up and the logs bubble juices and resin. The fed flames spit and crackle, colored jets hissing out wet. A column of thick smoke pours rapidly up the chimney and out into the sky like a gray liquid into milk. I hang the bellows from the strap and straighten up. Fire makes me feel good. Burning things into ash and nothingness makes my purpose seem clearer.

When I stand back, I see that the kitchen is full of smoke. My mother is busy and short of breath, flustering between the trestles and the fireside, two blotches of color rising on her cheekbones. This fire must be a roasting blaze, one of the hottest of the year. It has to heat the biggest pots brimful with boiling water to scald the pigskin, and later will simmer the barley and puddings, fatty blood and grain packed into the washed guts, moving cleanly around in the cauldron of water. I go to the door and step out into the yard to fetch more wood. The weather is not gasping cold yet, but the chill is here. It is already not far till Martinmas, though the frosts have not set in like most years, and my breath is a white cloud ahead of me. A low sun has risen over the valley, pushing thin shadows into the lane. The damp air smells of rotting leaves and dung and the smoke from the chimney. I can hear rooks making coarse-throated noises over the beech trees on the hill. And my brother Ab is whetting the blades by the back door, scraping the metal over the stone away from him. As I cross the yard to the wood stack, I see the knife catching the shine of the orange sun as he works, a sharp flash of blinding light.

I whisper a list of things into the wood stack as I pull out logs and branches and pile them up against the front of my dress.

My name is Agnes.

I live in a cottage on the edge of the village of Washington, at the foot of the Downs where the greensand turns into clay. The lane that leads past the cottage is narrow and muddy, and floods with a milky whiteness when the rain pours down from the hill. Above us the scarp is thickly wooded, up to the open chalk tops where the sheep graze. My father's family has been in Sussex for years. I am seventeen, we are quite often hungry, I work half of the day weaving cloth for the trade. And for the remainder, I do what girls do: stir the pots, feed the hens, slap the wind from the babies, make soap, make threepence go further...

His knife has paused. There is an unsteadiness on the air, something that does not add up to what I say. I stop myself talking and balance the armful of logs up on my shoulder to carry in.

The earth floor of the kitchen is a clutter of borrowed pots. We collected them from Mrs. Mellin days ago and are scalding them clean. My mother is counting out onions and shallots ready for chopping. She reaches up to the salt box over the mantel.

"Mother! Hester's grizzling," I say to her loudly over the confusion of children, as though she were deaf, and she leaves the hearth and ducks into the back room, bending her long uncomfortable body over the truckle bed to pick up Hester. Her back is like a twist inside her clothes as she jigs the baby up and down on her hip to make her quiet. Her patience wears a little thinner with each child that comes.

We have debts in the village. My father's work pays less since enclosure started, and he has been looking for any hiring that he can get. There is no more hedging work in the district. Last week he came home with six blue rock doves that we hid in a pile in the brewhouse until he could take them to Pulborough for the fair. My mother had been angry all day and when he came back after dark they fought for hours, using up rushlight. When we came down from the chamber in the morning I saw one of the jugs was cracked but put away tidily at the back of the shelf. This is the third full year we have not had a strip to grow a crop, and even the common land could be gone by the next, so this is the last pig.

Through the door into the back room my father's feet are just visible at the end of the other bed under the blanket. He will be up soon, before my uncle arrives.

"We are doing the pig early this year, but we owe and this will sort us out," was all that he said when he'd made up his mind which day was for slaughtering. His face was flat and there was a bad quietness at the table. I stirred my soup round and round with my spoon. "There will be enough left over," my mother said as she stood up and returned to the weaving, but it sounded more like a question, as if she were asking for something. Her hands rubbed up and down her overskirt before she picked up the shuttle. I fear that any day now we could come downstairs to find large men in dark clothes blocking the light from the open door: one writing notes with a long plumy pen and the other pointing directions while the rooms are emptied and our belongings piled outside in the lane.

But I am not myself. The sickness and bad temper that has been causing me trouble for the last few weeks is rising as usual and will last for hours. I squat by the hearth, laying the logs over the spitting hot brash without burning my fingers. Hester is fretting. Her mouth is sore as her teeth push themselves up in her gums, and she is still missing her sister. Ann began to work at Wiston House two months ago and she has not been forgiven for leaving us here, but only Hester is allowed to voice her feelings. My own fury is absorbed into the house by other means.

I know that Mother can't manage with the children the way that she is. Her body is giving out. Last year two children came too early like small undressed poppets and we buried them at the back of the house wrapped in cloth, but more keep coming, and now her old woman's body is big with another weight.

The fire is taking.

Long yellow flames build up the heat, for a hard day's work. I send William to fetch more water from the pump at the end of the lane, and I occupy myself with rubbing at the pots.

I am covering it well. I won't even let her see that I feel sick, or she will think I have an ague and make me swallow a mush of herbs or a live spider rolled in butter. I can tell no one what is happening to me, not even Ann, and now she is gone there is nobody to notice. I have only missed two bleedings and yet the small storm inside is changing me within these months. My girl's nipples ache with a new weight and my hair feels different, as though it grew from another girl's head. Sometimes, keeping this disaster to myself makes me feel as if I should explode, and I begin to beg myself to tell someone. And then, after those moments of weakness, I make myself imagine the day that my mother notices, the burst of her anger stiffening to shame as she turns her back. My father would take on a rage lasting long after he had staggered two miles from the alehouse. I never imagine what would occur after that. Even the thought of it causes a rickety panic to rise up inside me, making my heart rush around in a tight chest. My head is light with complication. I spend hours awake in the dark lying rigid in bed while I try to change things with the violence of thought that comes in the night. *It's a mistake. It wasn't my fault.* It was all my fault, and my mistake is made flesh, and will swell up inside me. Perhaps I will die in childbirth and they will have to forgive me, standing around the coffin they could never afford as I'm lowered into the earth in St. Mary's churchyard.

How dark it is when I try to sleep. It is as if I were breathing in the night itself: not just the air but the sense and smell of darkness. Every night I listen to my sisters' breath rising and falling effortlessly there beside me, until I am too tired not to sleep. On pig-killing day we have to rise before the sun, as the morning comes so late this time of year.

We will boil up Mrs. Mellin's pots one by one and my father and my uncle will kneel their weight on the pig so they can stick the knife in at the heel of the throat. It is hard not to run away. I remember how I ran away one year, out into the lane to get away from the sound. The pig roared and roared, an ear-splitting agony of held-down terror, the back legs scrabbling and squealing out the last drops of panic, even as the knife went in. Then the squeal bubbled and stopped. The quietness was a shock. Out in the lane I held my elbows tightly in the emptiness that followed and then on the far side of the copse a woodpecker drilled holes into the silence. My feet slapped loudly on the muddy path as I ran back hastily before they saw that I was gone. This year the pig is smaller; a spayed sow with a black patch at the back of her head. Her eyes are very small, as though she were willing to let enough light in but will give nothing away through her stiff, pale lashes.

I shall hold the pot up to catch the bright burst of blood rushing crimson from the slit. Steam will rise from the warmth of it as it pours into the cold earthenware. It will be a slow thickness, cooling and darkening as I stir and stir, lifting out the threads and clots, tipping the cooked barley in to make up the puddings. Later we will pour scalding water over the pig's coat and take turns to pull the candlestick hard over it the wrong way to take the bristles off without breaking the skin. There is always a strange smell, and rooks and other scavenger birds hang around the orchard. William scares them off, running on his short legs and waving the broom that is almost as big as him over his head, and they fly heavily above, circling the chimney with their black wings fanned out like leather gloves. Lil says they are the kind of birds that give you bad dreams.

She knows nothing of the sense in my belly; none of them do.

It is a small fat heat that began to grow two months ago, after the last of the beans were down. That last quick crop had been a good one; all the others previous were blighted with mold, June and July having been so damp and wet. Our hair smelt good in the late sunshine as we split the fresh pods open with our nails until our hands were green, spreading the tender beans out on the mats to dry. Our hands smelt of broken leaves. It was warm for September, almost like a St. John's summer. We rested at the edge of the field upon the bank. I remember that Ann stood up and moved her shadow so that it fell across my face as she took the empty buckets back to the outhouse. The last drops of the midday ale were gone and my mother was way back at the house where the weaving was behind for the week, bulky hanks of unwoven yarn piling up by the loom. There was so much work to do; I cannot truly say why I was so lazy on that afternoon. There were no clouds in the dusty sky, just a milky blue space stretching up and up. A long way above the beech trees, black specks of swifts and martins were moving about, almost invisible. It was still. I can remember the flighty look of the seeds at the top of the grasses, and the tiny purple vetch twisting in the hedge beside me. The sun beat down. I heard the squeak of wattle as Ann closed the gate, and fell asleep.

I don't like to remember most of what came next. His face was up close above me and blocked out the sky; his neck smelt like a warm stone. I remember the feel of him as he rubbed his hands about like he some-times did if he could catch me. His fingers inside me felt like a goat kick-ing out. At first it almost felt good. I opened myself wider and shut my eyelids red against the sun. The weight of the sun on me was like a bless-ing. Then he pushed my knees apart wider under my skirts and put his length on me. I had to bite into his hand as it pressed my mouth. His hand was salty and full of muscle. I was blinded by the sun, my head pressed into the soft bank. It was intolerable. The discomfort made me choke out loud. Then it was finished and he rolled off me and sat there with his eyes narrowed in the sun like a man leaning against Chantry Post up on the hill, taking in the view.

And then he'd just said, "See you Tuesday, then," whistled for his grubby dog to come and leave the rabbit holes alone, and sauntered up the lane. It was as if I were not there at all. My legs shook under me as I stood up, and I spat into the hedge to get the feel of him away from me.

Did I cause that to happen? Surely it was something that I did. I'd thought he liked me.

I waited for an hour or more, until the signs of tears were gone from my face, and then left the field for home, closing the gate behind me as I went.

I was sure that they would see my guiltiness and shame, somehow smell my difference or see some sign of it. I was too afraid to go inside. I kicked my heels against the granite of the trough by the back door until the last of the sky was slipping down all brightly concentrated behind the thorns in the field below the house. Bats flew overhead. Inside the cottage Lil and Ab were bickering between the hall and parlor. I saw Ann walk into the back room and put a flame to the rushlights, her face lit from beneath with a wobbling glow as she came close to the window. A chill grew out there and settled in me as the darkness seeped into the valley, and I waited, shivery, for my father to come home. Then I could see his bulk approaching through the half-light in the lane. He was made taller by the sticks strapped to his back and the sticks were the clearest part of his shape against the white walls as he rounded the corner toward me. I held my breath that he was sober.

"Ag, your mother back?" was all that he said when he saw me there. He knocked the clay from his great boots against the step and lowered his bundle to the ground. Then he ducked under the lintel before I could answer and I followed him in.

My mother put down the baby and stood up to serve the supper as he entered. She was tired of mending and her mouth made a hard line when she saw that my skirt was torn at the side.

It was September, the busiest time of the year.

"Agnes!" she is shouting. I forget myself, am nearly spilling the blood out onto the stones in the yard. I level the pot. There is so much pig's blood, perhaps eight full pints of it. There are red splashes all over the ground, and my feet ache with the cold.

"What is the matter with you, dreamy girl?" my mother scolds. Her breath is white all round her in the cold air, so that I can hardly see her mouth.

My uncle slits and empties the pig in a rush of dark bowels. It is washed. We are all there watching when he pulls out the heart. It is marbled with a fan of yellow fat, like veins over a leaf.

Then he hangs the pig from her back legs, big in the outhouse, and two days pass for the flesh to become firm.

Its presence is everywhere; a twelve-score weight pulling at the hooks between the tendon and the ankle. The head hangs straight under the spine although the throat is cut, and pink fluid runs down the snout and drips into a pot upon the ground.

When I go to the outhouse to fetch soap for the laundry, William is there scolding the cats away from the bucket of soft parts that we have not yet eaten. He picks up a twig and pokes in among the wetness.

"What is that?" he asks. I look, and tell him that it is the stomach.

"The slippery stomach, the slippery stomach, shall we tickle it, shall we?" he says, and shrieks in horror at his own joke and runs away.

I take my turn at the loom.

It is a quietly complicated object, causing nothing but a runnel of thoughts to slide evenly through my mind as my hands follow their task at the shuttle and threads, in the same way as a horse will step along a familiar route without heed or guidance. When my hands are engaged in this way, the thoughts of trouble that rankle inside do not take me over. It is when the racket of the loom ceases abruptly that the twisting panic returns and plunges a kind of darkness through my head, as though a sharp wind had gone through a house snuffing out candles and leaving space for fear. I arrive at that point early in the day when I have sat out one hour at the loom.

"Agnes!" my mother shouts suddenly into the back chamber, making me jump. "We are short of a skillet!"

So I leave the house to get the pot, my ears buzzing with the silence of my stopped work, and head out on the lane as I am bidden. My mother's voice, muttering instructions to Lil as they prepare the stew, dwindles and then vanishes as I walk. The sun is out, and sparrows flit and whirr between the hedges.

Mrs. Mellin is our closest neighbor and her house lies in the opposite direction to the village, along the muddy white road that leads to the chalk pit. She lives declining and alone; her son was taken away by the press-gang in a port on the coast three years ago, and was said to have died of drink or bullying. Her husband has been dead for as long as any of us can remember. He died on a Sunday; Mother said he was a thoughtless man who had left his wife little but bad habits.

It is a pleasant day, and for all our troubles perhaps the winter may not be so bad. There is a blue sky above the top of the ridge of the Downs, and sunshine is shivering patches of brightness through the trees by the side of the road as I walk. But the sun is getting old now for the year. Sitting lower in the sky each day, it hardly warms the ground at all, and my feet walk along the lane in shadow.

Her cottage sits tightly into the base of the scarp, the steep coppice threatening to swallow it. I call loudly as I approach, and hear how her chickens make a fuss and clamor at the side of the house. The door at the front is shut and I lift the latch and push it open, bending straight into the coldness of the parlor. A brown cat rushes outside.

"Hello!" I call. "Good day, Mrs. Mellin!"

Mrs. Mellin is deaf, and she doesn't answer my greeting as I clatter about, choosing a skillet. The pots are loud and hollow on the worn brick floor as I stack them into their habitual places behind the dirty cloth stretched under the shelf. I go into the kitchen, where she is always. She has her back to me, sitting in front of a stone-cold grate. "Oh!" I say in concern. "Why is your fire out, Mrs. Mellin?"

And I am shocked. Mrs. Mellin is dead in her chair. Her purple tongue is sticking out and her eyes are rolled back in her head. Her arm lolls down over the edge of the chair. On the floor, as if it has rolled away from her, is a small china jar, the jar that usually sits on the left of her mantelpiece. The lid is further away, almost out of sight, right under her chair. My mouth is dry.

"Oh, Mrs. Mellin." I am afraid and sorry. My heart beats very fast. I talk to her as if she were asleep as I prop her head and push her eyelids closed. I expect her body to be stiff but she is soft and limp. I don't look at her tongue and I hear myself talking giddily to her in a way that I don't recognize. She doesn't need me to be foolish, but I talk and talk. I pick up her fingers between my own and fold them into a sensible arrangement in her lap. She looks more ordinary now, although I still don't look at her tongue. Her hands are neither cold nor warm; they are the same temperature as the wooden chair that she is sitting on. Mine are still warm after walking fast up the lane in the sunshine; I see I still have black blood under my fingernails. I sit down on the settle at the other side of the hearth to gather my breath and ask myself to whom I should run and ask for help. It is a long way to the rectory. I stand up again. My mother will be working without me, thin and tired after the long day boiling pudding and preparing to salt the new pork flesh in the big trough. When it is done we will wash off the salt and hang the sides from the iron hooks at the back of the hearth in the smoke. I should go home again. I am ashamed to think of eating, but a sudden thought of the taste of meat makes my mouth flood with water.

I do not know how much time has passed. I lean forward. Perhaps I have made a mistake and Mrs. Mellin is just asleep or ill. Perhaps she needs help. She is not much liked. I lift her eyelid back up, gingerly. Her eye is yellowish blank and I notice that there is an odd smell about her, as though she were already changing into another substance. No, I have been around dead things enough now to know that Mrs. Mellin has been gone for some days. I stand back; I must send a child to tell the rector she is deceased. He will come and he will say some words and let her fingers touch the cover of his Bible and then they will bury her and that will be that. I bend down to pick up the fallen jar beside her chair and glance inside.

And there are the bright coins.

They spill out and roll and clatter on the floor in my surprise. They gleam and flash astonishingly as I bend again to pick each one up and turn it over in my fingers. I count a guinea; a half-guinea; one, two, three, four, five crowns and a handful of foreign gold, perhaps from Spain. The burnish on them is high, as if she had spent time polishing each one. They are so bright: brighter than rosehips in a dark hedge, than birch leaves in October, than celandines or toadflax, than stones still wet from the riverbed, than yellow fungus in the coppice, than the yolk of a hen's egg. They are like . . . fire. Like the sun.

And then the coins change as I am holding them and begin to show their value to me. My heart begins to beat so fast that I can hardly hear the plan taking shape inside my head.

2

*T*he half-mile home along the lane seems a great distance. It is bright out here, and hurts my eyes, my crisp shadow bouncing along ahead of me between the bank and the hedgerow.

There are no flowers, save some tight, worn heads of black knapweed, although matting caps of toadstools like soft flaking eggs are pushing through the moss and grasses. The ridge of the Downs is a great bulk above me, like the darkness of an animal waiting for the sun to set. At the bend by the place where the stream curls inward and almost touches the lane, flooding it over during wet times and washing the bones of the road smooth, I meet a traveling man. He comes along from Steyning way, with a tall pack on his back that makes him stoop sideways with the burden of it. The shadow he casts is stretched out and misshapen on the bank.

"Will not persist," he says, implying the sunshine, halting for breath and glancing awkwardly up at the sky. He cocks his head backward as best he can, to the east beyond the line of beechwood on the hill. His voice is thin and weaselly.

"A great weight of fog rolling in off the sea is pressing in over the scarp, down there. No doubt we'll be near to choking with it," he adds with a gloomy relish, "before the night has encroached itself upon us." He has a curious manner of speech; his eyes are very keen and they look me over, taking in my shape, my hands, the skillet. He blocks the way. I pull my shawl closer about me, and ask what it is that he has in his pack. It is bound up with strips of fabric, all grimy with dirt from the road.

"Sellings," he replies inscrutably. "Buyings and sellings." The man looks down at the road and passes me and rounds the bend, but the thought of him grows like a canker in my mind as I walk on. I see that my shadow is already fading in the road ahead of me, and that the man's footprints are deep in the mud all the way back to the house. Clots of blackberries are finished and moldering in the hedgerow, and the undertow of a loamy smell of rot and fungus hangs in the air.

Inside the house I see that my mother has unstrung the pig, and struggled it onto the bench. It is heavy on its side, and judders with fat when William rocks the plank to show me. "Mother's cross. She's shouting," he whispers at me plaintively. I touch his upturned face and wink at him to stay in the kitchen and guard the pig from dogs and rats. My mother is pouring the hot kettle over a board. She doesn't look up from her cloud of steam.

"Did she spare the skillet then, nor mind us asking?" she says. A strong smell of scalding wood fills the room.

"Why did you not wait for the men to move the pig, Mother?" I say. I wish she would look at me. How I wish I could beg her to glance up now and notice me, to see how things are wrong. Standing there I count to four inside my head.

"Oh, I must get on, Agnes," she says, slamming the kettle back on the black hook over the fire. The hook shakes with the weight. "The skillet!" She holds out her hand. "Your father'll not be back before midday if I know him." Her voice is flat and tense. "No, Hester!" she shouts abruptly. "Put that down!" And I reach out hastily and take a bowl away from the baby before she breaks it on the floor.

My mother sits down then and rubs her sleeve over her forehead, and I see that her face is long and gray and tired, which makes the disquiet twist about inside me like a worm. How would she get by, were I not here to help her in the house? But of course from the back room the noise of Lil working the loom comes regularly hissing and clacking like a mechanical breath.

"Where is Father?" I ask.

"Where do you think, Ag?" she says shortly.

Hester begins to crawl to me, gurgling with effort, her baby's gown dragging at her knees through the dirt as she crosses the floor that wants sweeping. I wait again for my mother to ask me why my errand took so long, but she does not, and so I blink and turn away. Perhaps the fire needs to be stoked; I bend over the hearth, pushing the logs closer together to coax at the heat. I wish that color wouldn't rush so readily into my cheeks. I begin to talk up cheerfully about Mrs. Mellin's skillet.

"She did mind, the old witch, but I promised her a bit of meat after the curing was done," I explain lightly. It is my first lie of such proportions, and it comes away from my tongue with an ease that I don't much like. The tended flames gather and spark brightly from the wood.

When my uncle arrives with his boots crunching on the path, and the butchering itself begins, I go straight to the trestle to cut up the onions, and turn my back. I find the smell of the pig is too strong this year for me to stomach. The blood is too red, the skin too much like my own. I have to swallow over and over to go on with the cooking.

My uncle is good with the butcher's knife. Not like my father, who has not the patience. When I was smaller I liked to watch him cut up the carcass. There was a kind of miracle to the ease with which he separated the sides from each other, as though this were the way that nature had intended after all, it being so neat. I liked how the meat shrank away behind the cut of the knife as he worked, as if he had only to touch the meat in the right places to make it part of its own accord. Not the bones, though, all splintery rasping and sawing with blades to break them apart. Nor the fibrous caul that is beaded with fat around the stomach where the belly is flatter; he had to tug and rip at that to take it away to put into the larding pot. There should be six pints of lard to render and boil and strain from this pig, and some left to beat into flour to make flead cakes.

"Oh, the fat smells good!" William is excited and jumps about, holding the spoon. When he skims off the scum as it rises his little mouth is opened up with concentration.

The whole pig's head boils whitely in a deep pot at the edge of the fire. I always set the pot so that the snout faces inward to the flames, as though it were warming itself and cannot see what we are doing to the rest of the body. I keep it covered to the ears so that it cannot even hear what we are saying, until it falls softly apart in its own juices. When it is done and taken away from the heat and cool enough to touch, William will sit and pick the head bone clean. He has a way with being careful, although he does not skin the tongue himself.

I am thinking, thinking.

At first in Mrs. Mellin's kitchen the thoughts had flung themselves from side to side in my head, like water does in the pail on the walk from the well. I'd paced about. My heart had beat so fiercely that I was afraid for it and pressed my fingers at my chest bone. All the time the coins were winking brightly at me, a yellow pile upon the wooden table. I had hardly dared to touch the coins again, although my fingers left the place over my heart from time to time and hovered near.

Are they a sign from God? I'd thought.

Shall I leave them untouched? Are they a check upon my honesty? Are they a gift from Providence? Are they tainted by death? Do they belong to God now? How much is a burial? Is gold the Devil's property? What is the punishment for stealing from a corpse?

The hens were fighting outside in her yard.

I'd scooped grain from a bushel sack and stepped outside. It was somehow surprising that the same sun was still shining. I took a breath. The leaves on the beech trees and the birch were vivid and they caught at the light, making many shades of yellow against the blue sky. Two finches swayed on thistle-heads, plucking out seeds. The air was fresh and clean, a cold, scouring kind of air, making the world seem washed and bright. It could be hard to conceal a secret in such an atmosphere of clarity, I'd reasoned.

I flung handfuls of grain and they drummed the ground firmly, as heavy rain does when it strikes baked earth at the start of a summer downpour. The hens strutted and flustered. It was extravagant to give good wheat to the birds, but Mrs. Mellin would not be needing flour where she had gone.

I almost laughed at how the world had changed so sharply.

The yellow coins had made my head feel light and free, quite a separate feeling from my bigger quandary.

Only six of Mrs. Mellin's hens were left. A fox had taken the rest in October when the ground was hard with the second frost, creeping low out of the edge of the wood like a living shape of fear. The chickens that were spared the slaughter sat in the lower branches of the ash tree for two days until hunger drove them down again to scratch at the earth as if nothing had happened.

I brushed my palms together to get rid of the wheaty dust and the feel of Mrs. Mellin's dead skin against my own. I took a breath. How cold and clear it was. Outside in the yard the world felt calm and ordinary. I counted some beats of my heart, eighteen, nineteen, thankful that no one could hear it.

And I realized that if I were gone from here, nothing would change. Any space I left in the world would fill in quickly, as earth closes in when you pull beets up from the ground.

I will take my disgrace elsewhere, I'd thought. *I must run from here, until my shame is over or changed.*

Quickly I'd gone inside and bound the top of the sack of grain closed to keep out rats. I took up most of the coins and gathered them flatly into a coarse piece of cloth. I put one to my lips as I did so; I could not help but touch my tongue to it, and bite. It was cold and hard. The metallic taste was almost like blood, and a ball of my white breath puffed out into the cold air of the room. I folded the cloth tightly and tucked it between my stays and my skin. When I breathed in, I could feel the lump of the coins pressing my rib cage. My ears strained for any sound of footsteps on the path, and I glanced again and again through the dirty glass of the window facing the lane. I replaced the china jar on the mantelshelf neatly

THE BOOK OF FIRES 29

with the chipped part facing the wall. Inside I'd left two pieces of Spanish gold to pay for the burial, this being only seemly, and knowing as I do how one should never cross the dead unduly.

"Mrs. Mellin." I nodded to her body sitting there, and then left the cottage. Just in time, I had remembered the skillet.

How long ago that seems already, though it was only this morning.

"Two days per pound, salting," my mother calculates, "which takes us to one month on Thursday next." She eyes the powdering tub.

"I'll do that, Mother," I say. The cut meat is a bright, deep red in the flicker of firelight.

I feel dizzy. By a month on Thursday next, I will have been gone for so long. Lil will brim with sadness and rage for weeks. She will cry. William will cry. Hester will be puzzled and then she will not. My mother will be eaten up with anxiousness, and then her baby will come and she will have enough to do without worrying after me. I do not know about my father. Unburdened partly by my absence, he may say to my mother, "She is a big girl, Mary," as he takes up his coppice tools for his walk to the Weald to find work again, or as he clenches his large, toughened hand around the handle of his flagon at table. Or he may not. A girl can never know a father.

I know, though, that the sense of change that they will feel by my desertion might be dispersed by a short-lived sense of better eating. *One less mouth to feed. Less feet to shoe. Less laundry. Less water to carry.* When my mother hisses and claps at the cat to get outside, it is not hard to think that it is me her irritation is directed at. "Good riddance!" she shouts, and the door shudders on its wooden latch as she slams it shut. My thoughts run on as though I were already gone and I feel my heart hardening inside me like a stone as I watch them busy in the room without me. Often on the Downs you can find a fist-sized round of chalk that seems too heavy for itself, and when you crack it open on the path you find it has inside it the dense glassy darkness of flint. Lil will have more space in the bed for a while till Hester grows.

And how a full belly will take the edge off things.

One by one I take the four flitches and lay them heavily in the powdering tub. Evenly I salt the flesh, turning the pieces and rubbing the rough mixture in handfuls into the taut meat as it drains, until my hands are sore and my arms wet up to the elbows with the pink briny liquid that comes from it.

My father, returned at last from the village and smelling of drink bought on the strength of promises, comes up to the tub and holds up a piece by the bone. "Will you see that ribbon of fat about the back and collar!" he exclaims. "As thick as my thumb and forefinger together. That's good eating! That's worth months of scraping the beer wash out into a bucket. Didn't I say so!" He looks at my mother. My mother, picking up Hester from the floor, does not even seem to hear him. Her belly is huge.

"Is there plenty of pepper, onions?" my aunt nags from the back room, picking up this and that and turning things over in her hand. She means for the sausage: the bits and pieces, the scrapings and leavings, crusts, herbs. There is no waste. Lil has gone out to the stream with the stinking guts looped up in a bucket, where she washes and washes them until they are clean, and until her fingers are so frozen cold she can hardly push the guts inside out.

My mother ignores my aunt nosing about, as she always does. She has had too many years of it to care. She takes Hester to the truckle bed and lays her down under the blanket for her sleep, then comes back to the kitchen and begins to chop the heart and kidneys into dark pink pieces on a board.

"Oh, there are always onions," Lil cries despairingly when she returns, holding her wet red fingers out before the fire. She hates the taste of them unless they form but a tiny part of something good to eat. "Should we be starving to death, our legs sprouting bony from the hems of our skinny ragged dresses, there would still be onions to feed upon." Lil has the sweetest tooth of all of us. She seems to suffer most from the plainness of our diet, becoming pale and drawn and falling asleep if she has carried fresh water all the way from the well. "Soup made with onions, for days on end, gives people a bellyache," she always complains, as though my mother chose to make it on purpose to vex her.

My aunt comes out holding a pail in front of her. "You should cover your butter, Mary," she says accusingly, and tips it up so that the soaking pat of butter in the water bobs against the side and threatens to spill out. "Mice will be having that, leaving their evidence all over it. Get a good lid, weigh it down. A heavy thing will do, a tile, a rock. Go on, Elizabeth!" She has always chivvied us. My mother says that at least it is a good thing that she married our uncle, as his natural state is patient to the point of indolence. *Lucky that she didn't wed our father then*, I'd thought when she said that, as his temper wouldn't stand for nagging.

Lil rolls her eyes as she goes to the door.

She is right, of course; mice will eat anything. I have found tallow candles nibbled down to the wicks before, and green scrubbing soap ridged and pocked with teeth marks. Their droppings get everywhere, like big seeds of dirt. In summer we cut lengths of water mint and rue to strew over the boards in the upstairs chamber, in the hope that mice will not climb up and eat our hair in the night or make nests in the straw of our bedding.

"If I was choosing," William had said, watching us from the doorway, "I should make my whole nest from herbs and feathers."

"If you were a mouse, you mean," I'd said to him.

"If I was one." And I'd laughed at his earnest look and scooped him up and buried my face in his hair out of merriment. How things have changed.

I knock the mud from my boots at the back door, then sit down in the corner to clean them. There is a quietness in the room, under the chat and the noise of the knives chopping. The cat mews once outside the closed back door, then goes away. My uncle whistles something through his teeth.

"Why are you greasing your boots, Agnes?" William asks suddenly. He has come and sat beside me. Everybody stops talking, and looks around at me. There is a silence. Or perhaps I have imagined it, as they are talking again.

"They are so dry, William," I reply in a low voice. "I had to catch them before the cracks set in, before the wetness of the puddles began to soak through them too easily. Shall I do your boots for you?"

He unlaces his boots, which are too big for him, and takes them off, then sits down beside me on the floor in his woollen stockings while I again warm the grease, which has cooled and stiffened. His feet look small. He watches me work the warm liquid evenly into the leather with a piece of rag. When I have finished, our two pairs of boots are dark and shiny.

"Thank you, Agnes," William says, and the face that he turns to me is pleased and trusting. I get up to put the greasepot away on the high shelf, so that he cannot see my eyes filling with tears.

Traitor's tears, I think.

Crying is no good. I remember the time that my mother, enraged at my wallowing over some squabble with Ann, cried out, "Upset? There is no place for upsetness before a pot over the fire, my girl." And my slapped cheek stung in the heat of the flames, the salt taste of my tears mingling with the smell of scorched soup overboiling and hissing into the hot wood ash on the hearth. No, tears are uncommon in this house.

That was the year the cold was so bitter at pig-killing time that even the running stream froze at the edge where it touched the bank; swollen icy webs clung about the stems of reeds like boiled sugar.

At the hearth I watch my mother slip Lil another piece of kidney when she thinks my father cannot see, in the same way that she keeps a brown crock of honey in a secret place behind the barrels in the outhouse, and gives a spoonful of it to Lil to make a difference to her bad days, when she has them. My father does not know; it might stoke his wrath unnecessarily. My mother thinks I do not know about the honey either, but when Lil comes close with her breath smelling of sugar and flowers it is hard not to notice. Once I took a spoon out there and prized up the sticky cork to help myself when no one was home. The honey was like metal and blood and summer all together in my mouth, but the guilty taste was the one I remembered, day after day for weeks. I didn't do it again.

We sell the honey from the hive if there is enough. Hive money, egg money, bird money when my father has trapped larks and snipe. "The wealthy suffer from their fancy palates and inconstant appetites," he says. "So we must offer something delicate, and should it tempt the shillings from their silky purses when they pay off the butcher, so much the better." That thought made him wink at me. It all goes toward the important things we need: flour, salt, twine, the mending of pots and boots.

The day draws on.

Later we sit at the trestle table together and eat, although I can taste nothing but the smell of the raw pig everywhere, and I find I cannot swallow the rough bread at all. William leans over, still chewing at his own, to grab my bread and press it eagerly between his little teeth. Nobody scolds him, as nobody notices, they are so occupied in being well fed. I do not enjoy the thick stew made with pig's liver and pig's kidneys that Lil ladles out to all of us from the blackened pot. Instead I watch my mother's bony hands spoon gravy into Hester's open mouth until her bowl is empty. "This is good," we all say, trying not to seem too hungry before my aunt.

I go to the loom.

I am thinking hard and yet not thinking at all. It is as though my mind were all in pieces.

It had almost happened once before, I remember, when I was sat with John Glincy on the bank, one time in spring. I'd let the pig go on slowly down the lane, snouting at roots all by itself. I would have been in trouble if they'd caught me doing that, just letting a weaner go wandering off.

"It's nothing but playing, is it, Ag?" he'd said, as his hand was inching up inside my underskirt. I didn't mind, I told myself.

His face took on a strange shape as he was talking, as though it had a lot to concentrate on. His hand was rough and didn't stay still. I didn't think much on it either way, and no one ever saw, so what harm was it? In truth I did not know what I should have said to make him stop. Like I say, no one saw, and besides, old Mr. Jub came shuffling over the brow of the hill and John Glincy slid his hand out quick enough then, and touched his hat, if you please, to Mr. Jub as he passed us by; Mr. Jub who leaned so heavily upon his stick it looked as though he were punishing the ground at every step. Then he went off.

That afternoon I saw John Glincy beating at his dogs on his walk home with a viciousness that made me catch my breath. His father is angry like that, too; we heard there was a working dog at Gallop's Farm, over Findon way, that he killed by kicking at it until it fell down. My mother says there must be some kind of ill-luck in the earth under their dwelling house, they have had so many troubles there. Yet John Glincy is blessed with a head of thick yellow hair, the color of straw, so that it is his head that stands out brightly against the darkness of the field when the men are driving the plows and the sun shines down on them. That makes him hard to gainsay or refuse in any way; he is so unyielding, and goes at a matter until he has it, like a hound after a hare.

"Are you sickening now, Agnes?" my mother asks impatiently as I sit working the loom in the corner, and I realize that my feet have paused over the treadles. I shake my head. I can't tell her that I am full up inside and that there are coins hard on my skin wherever I go and that they feel already like a great weight. I fling the shuttle backward and forward through the warp with a vigor that I muster from a wretched part of myself.

Yet I am certain that my aunt stops in the doorway to stare at me before she goes home to wash. I do not turn my head, but I can hear her rustling and breathing and the creak of the basket over her arm. It is as though she hesitates, then does not say a thing. I wait till I have thrown six more rows before I look around, but I find the doorway is empty; there is just a darkness as the sun goes behind a cloud.

I have made up my mind.

he next day passes. By afternoon the light is failing more quickly than the approach of sundown, and the sparrows stop piping in the hedge outside. When it is too dim to work at the loom, I go to the window and see that there is not a breath of wind and that the sky has thickened into low cloud. Even as I watch, a gray November sea fog begins to roll in over the hills and down the scarp slope through the woods, like a vast, damp smoke engulfing the house. How cold it is.

"When you were up at Mrs. Mellin's yesterday," my mother says, "I hope you told her that I said she is welcome to walk to Mutton's Farm with us tonight. She can hardly come alone, the weather like this, can she?" I turn away from the window.

"Oh, but must she walk with us?" Lil grumbles. "She creeps along like an ailing badger dragging its toenails, always moaning that her back is an agony of humpiness and that the baker won't deliver to her anymore from the village. Small wonder, I say. She spoils the day."

"Elizabeth!" rebukes my mother, sharply.

"Oh, where's all the fun gone?" Lil adds under her breath to no one in particular, and provokes my mother's quick and stinging palm across her cheek. We are well practiced in the art of ducking now, whether we deserve a slap or not.

"That's what happens when you spoil a maid." My father's unwanted comment comes from the settle, where he has his boots off before the fire. It is a good thing that he does not know about the spoons of honey. He was displeased enough when the rector's wife told me I should have an education.

"Schooling?" he'd shouted. "That'll feed us nicely, will it? You'll go to no school I know of!"

And so instead the rector's wife helped me to read after church on Sundays, or when she had a moment on a Friday. I liked the kind of words I found inside the newspapers she lent me, and in the Bible, the way that words could tell things properly. "You must learn to write next, Agnes," she'd said. "You are a quick and clever girl; you could train to be a teacher." And then the rector's wife was expecting a child at last, after five long years of waiting and hoping, and there was no time to help me anymore.

We wait for Mrs. Mellin a little, but of course she does not come, and by the time we are walking to Mutton's Farm for the Martinmas feast, it is dark and quite impossible to see more than yards ahead. The lamp that my father carries casts light poorly before us, the damp air giving it a halo made of mist and light. The sounds of our talking bounce back strangely at us. Lil and I cling together as we walk, with our free hands outstretched into the murkiness; it is as though we were walking in our sleep together. William's voice chatters on and on somewhere behind us in the dark.

Once a year Mr. Fitton gives a great feast to keep us sweet, to keep the rents flowing in pleasantly and the pool of ready labor there to hand. My brother Ab says that Mr. Fitton has his inner eye undyingly to Lady Day and Michaelmas, when the benefit of letting land is apparent in the easy shape of gold and guineas. He can afford to get the butcher in to brown a fat sheep over a blaze of fruitwood and to stuff us with spice cake and have the prettiest girls pour out a froth of ale into our cups, Ab says. He wants to butter up his workers and his tenants, holding us over with some lurking, ancient sense of gratitude we should be feeling. My brother Ab will take a look at the people pegging away at the victuals when we get to the great barn and he will spit on the ground.

"Fill the belly and the will sleeps," he always says.

My brother Ab is a knot of rage these days. He is like a horse-winch straining at its strap and on the point of breaking loose. A breaking strap can cause a grievous injury to those in its vicinity. But the village girls appreciate the strength of his opinions and the broadness of his shoulders. Myself I find some truth inside his arguments but often cannot hear the content of them through his fury. My mother says he was born big and angry, that he fought his way out of her belly crimson with rage. But it is hard to work at ease when your boots are mended so many times that their lumpen shapes are mainly composed of glue and stitching.

The great barn is a blaze of light. It looms suddenly out of the mist as we round a corner, lit up like a great ship. The double doors are flung wide, and flaming torches flank the entrance, burning at the tallow greedily, quick black smoke rising and curling from the tips of the long orange flames like a hot, stirred fluid.

We are quite late. Inside the barn the air is warm and sweet and close. Lamps hang from the beams. There is a galloping, churning fire in the central hearth, smoke twisting up to the holes in the high ceiling. Jim Figg and Jim Hickon from the village are sawing at their violins and Mr. Tucker's little boy beats at the skin of a drum. Girls younger than myself are dancing, their shoes kicking up a chaffy dust into the air. Disturbed by the smoke billowing about beneath the trusses of the roof, a bat flutters up and down the length of the barn. It cannot get out.

He is here of course, John Glincy. When he sees that I am here, he picks up his jugful of ale and sidles over. I hate it when I feel like this. I hate him and his rough hands on my shoulders in front of my father, and his dog that shoves its nose between my legs. I shrug him off.

"Could do worse than that, Ag," John Glincy shouts over his plate on the bench opposite me when we sit down at the trestles to eat, and I wish that he wouldn't, his beer slopping over the slats. He is a drunkard and a lech. He is not to be trusted. How could I trust him? I do not even look him in the eye at first. Worse than what? I do not understand him. So much is bad. I am bad, my badness multiplying. And it is now too late anyway. If I stay here my fleshly crime will remain, growing under my skin by increments till its limbs push at my belly, and the results of my thievery will stay pressed to my skin from the outside. I will be found out. It is too much to think otherwise.

The cooked meat tastes of nothing to me. I just chew and swallow. Even now I am watching the door in case someone should enter with a warrant for my arrest, crying out before the assembled crowd, *"Agnes Trussel . . . for the dishonest purloining of twelve pieces of gold from Susan Mellin, deceased, with other coinage, the suspicion of murder of the victim aforementioned falling upon her . . ."*

"Jumpy tonight, Ag." He grins as he reaches around from behind me, but I don't like it at all and push him off. I don't want to be touched, and I tell him so.

"I should prefer to run to the post bridge over the river Arun and throw myself in, and I shall not do that either," I spit out at him. He does not know I am with child, nor will he ever.

"But the law is binding in that respect," he says mockingly. "You envowed yourself to me. I can use that, see, and ensure your bindedness. You will find it's up to me." He finds it funny. He takes a pull of ale from his jug. Wetness glistens at the corners of his mouth.

"What a lie you would have employed then for your own bad uses, John Glincy," I retort. "I have made no such vow, nor will I ever." I am sickened by the very thought of it. I am near to tears in my confusion.

"Aye," he says, and then he bends and speaks quietly inside my ear. His mouth is hot. "But I've had you, Agnes." He has stopped smiling.

And he is right.

"See"—John Glincy thrusts his foul face up to mine—"that's where the difference is, your lie against mine." And he walks away from me across the room and turns his yellow head about and raises his jug to me and grins again, wider.

What a twist and tangle it all is. I am lost in it; how I wish that I could shut my mind tight and make it vanish. The music reels on, making me dizzy. When I open my eyes again after a moment, I go straight to Lil and shout that I am tired and not so well, that I shall go home to lie down. She nods as though she has not heard me; her cheeks are pink and flushed.

"Whatever's the matter, Miss Misery-Me? Dance! Dance!" She tugs at my arm till I get up and dance a quadrille with her, though my heart is not in it.

"Mrs. Mellin did not come." She leans and shouts to me above the noise, pushing some hair back into her cap. Her breath is sweet with ale.

"No," I say. "She said her leg was bad."

Lil's face is thoughtful for a moment, and then, because she is young and the music has started again, I can see that she has forgotten all about it. In some discomfort, I feel the yellow coins are working loose inside my stays, and slide about.

I tell her to take care and she takes no notice, but how could she know exactly what I mean? She is twelve years old, and has pronounced that she will not lie with any man till she is three-and-twenty. She thinks that I have drunk too much, no doubt, and am leaving because of it.

I see my bootlace is untied. And, as I bend to tie it up, the coins slither in my stays and to my horror one bright round of gold tips out and falls spinning on the chaffy floor. Quick as a flash I snatch it up and push it back into my bosom.

"Lucky find, Miss Agnes Trussel!" John Glincy's voice booms in my ear. I clap my hand to my chest.

"Don't creep about like that," I shout guiltily. My breath feels unnatural. "Sixpence, it was a sixpence and no more than that, none of your business."

"I'd say that it could well be my business what you keep in there. Nice and cozy, I'd say. Nice place for a good little sixpence to nuzzle up. And one so shiny. Any room left over?" He tries to bend into my neck. God, how he smells of liquor. I push his head away and wish that he would leave me be. Could he see the glint of metal of the coins against my skin? Surely not. John Glincy mistakes the grimace on my face for a smile.

"You should ease up more, Agnes Trussel," he slurs, encouraged by this. "I'll show you how." His hand sidles around my waist and he tries to pull me to him, so that I stagger.

"Don't touch me," I hiss, looking about. I pray that no one sees him groping me like that.

"Well, well, you are a bashful maid today, not like I have seen you be, with your legs spreading for me so readily," he says. "Weren't so bashful then."

"I'm warning you, John Glincy, get your hands off," I say, and wrench myself free. Why can't he just let me alone? His leery face is undeterred.

"I wish you would drop down dead," I say.

God help me if I stay and my belly swells so that it is clear what my trouble is. They will make me swear the father before the parish men, and if I comply they will force John Glincy to marry me so that I and my unwanted bastard child will not prove a burden of charity upon the parish. If I keep my mouth shut tight and do not say they may find out anyway, as he will know, and besides the shame upon my family would be too much to bear. But I will not be made wife to that man. Not if my own life depended on it would I lie with him a second time.

He presses his face close again so I hear him distinctly, and he pinches my thigh so forcefully it hurts.

"You can only taunt a man's cock," he mutters thickly, "for so long." And with that he leaves me there, and takes his empty jug back to the barrel for more. Though he has his back to me I can hear his coarse bellowing laughter even as I am doubled up and retching onto the damp grass outside the barn door.

An owl hoots.

"Oh God," I say beneath my breath, "what have I done?" There is a shuffle of footsteps and Mrs. Peart, the cordwainer's wife, is looming over me. Her shape casts a long, flickering shadow onto the path, onto the shifting fog out there, with the firelight behind her.

"Don't drink so swift," she croaks in sympathy, when she sees who it is. She must have heard me whimpering. Mrs. Peart who always smells as if she were stuffed entirely full of loose tobacco, and with her fingers as yellowed as parsnips.

"It's a fearsome brew this year they have, fearsome strong," she says, staring out at the night. "It will have done some men a deal of damage come a few hours' time." She puts her pipe back in the gap between her teeth to go on smoking. "Let's pray that nobody sets hisself on fire this year at least," she says, and gives a dirty chuckle. "After all, Mr. Tuke still has those scars." She pats my shoulder a little in mindful, unsteady friendliness and then ambles back into the revelry.

"What shall I do?" I whisper when she is gone, but the night says nothing. There is just the fog out there, shifting its uneasy formless bulk about, obscuring any sight of stars.

At the door of the barn I hesitate and turn around. I cannot see John Glincy now. Through the smoke, I see my mother is there, on the other side of the barn, her foot tapping in time with the drum. There is a warm smell of sweat, and new rushes on the floor and the smolder of wood on the fire, which has settled into a steady blaze, burning with large branches cut and dragged down from the copse where the beeches fell in the great storm. Hester is lying awake across her lap, her little legs kicking at the air. I cannot see my mother's face; there are people in front of her. As I turn away a huge burst of laughter comes out of their mouths like a red explosion. It rings in my ears as I hurry away, the sudden quiet and the cold outside making me deaf for a moment like a clamp over the ears. Nothing feels right.

The flares along the misty path outside have burnt down almost to the quick. I step back along the dark lane, my hand up before my face, and I think my trouble over: the twist and tangle of my life like a wattle fence, holding itself together with to-ing and fro-ing, and yet having some order in a certain direction, and making a boundary between one state and another. And somehow it helps to think of my troubles interwoven like this. As I walk homeward, I become quite clear in the resolve I've made.

At the empty house I tie some things inside a piece of oilcloth, in haste lest someone should have followed me home. The house feels desolate and fixed suddenly in time, with things strewn about just as we left them, like an ordinary day. I cannot choose this moment to depart, of course, as all of drunken Washington would be engaged in searching for me as soon as my absence from the cottage were discovered. They would think me murdered or ravaged, or both. I must wait until the break of morning and slip out then. I carry the bundle in readiness out of the house, taking it a short way down the lane through the fog. The fog is wet and penetrating everything. The entrance to an empty field looms up suddenly upon my left, and I push the bundle under the hedge behind the gatepost. If I didn't feel so sad and muddled it would be almost ridiculous, hiding my belongings under a bush like a vagrant or a criminal.

"I am going to London," I say into the mist, to try my idea out. My voice is like the voice of someone else; it sounds thin and flat in the dark field. This is how felons feel. They feel small and lonely, as they should. I have stolen money from a corpse. The short tubes of stubble crunch under my soles. I stand still, with my hand to the gatepost for a long time, and breathe in the cold smell of night in the cropped field, hear the small sounds of night creatures finding their way along the new hedgerow. There is a dripping as the mist collects in droplets on the underside of things; on the limbs of trees, on twigs and leaves. Each drop gathers water slowly to itself, becomes fat with heaviness, then falls pat onto the dead leaves below. I find this dripping strangely comforting, as though it were the noise of the earth nourishing itself. As I turn back and step out blindly to the lane, the cry of a wood owl quavers out of the copse behind me.

That night I hardly sleep for fear of waking late, or for fear of shouting something in my sleep. The straw ticking is lumpy beneath me and I turn and turn, trying to lie easily. Once the others have come home, filling the air with the reek of stale beer breath even when their chatter has ceased,

I turn my face to the wall. And then I dream horrible dreams about my shape; my body going thin and stretched out for miles and miles across a brightly lit landscape, till I am nothing but an empty skin. Then I dream I am solid once more and curled under one of the ancient grassy mounds at the top of the hill, piles of flinty soil pressing me flat into the darkness, growing dry as the old bones the Wiston hounds uncovered there and dragged about, two years ago, after a week of strong rain had weakened the tamp of the soil and caused a collapse on the south side of the barrow that is exposed to the wind from the sea.

Of course when I wake I am none of these things.

Already a pale quantity of light has begun to seep through the patterned calico hung across the casement; a piece of the dress my mother wore at my uncle's wedding when I was tiny. I did not mean to sleep so long. There is a sour smell in the room as I rise, take up my cloak and boots and pick my way across the creaking boards. I'm sure the anxious hammering my heart is making must be loud enough to wake them all. I pull the leather strap and open the door onto the stairs.

Down in the kitchen my father is asleep in a sideways position on the settle with his boots still on and the hem of his overcoat pushing ashes on the hearth into a ridge. His head is thrown backward and his mouth has dropped open, and a crackling, wet breath is rising out of it slowly into the silence of the room. I turn my eyes away as I creep past him in an agony of caution, and my feet in their woollen stockings make no sound at all on the smooth clay floor. My mother turns over in bed in the back chamber, and I see that Hester begins to stir and suck at her fist in the truckle bed beside her. I dare not cross the room to kiss her white face quiet, and her dark eyes watch me to the door.

I touch my stays where the coins are. Out here the fog has weakened and gone and the chill air is thin and rushing to my head. I am dizzy with escape, with stealing away. With an effort I do not run as I walk down the short path and turn out onto the lane. Above me the stars are fading pinpricks in the blue sky. I can just make out that the Plow points to the North Star, as it always does. I think of the city of London, vast to the north over the next line of Downs. The sky is huge, and when I look back over my shoulder I see that the house looms pale behind me in the early light.

I look back again, and my heart almost stops when I see a glimmer of movement at an upstairs window.

I wait for the casement to be flung open and someone to cry out, "Agnes! Where are you going? Get back this minute!" But there is nothing but stillness. It was a trick of the light or the dark, reflected. Nobody knows I am gone and I feel bleak with sadness as I turn away again between the dark passage of the hedges. The rutted lane makes me stumble.

I am ashamed. How Lil will sob and sob when she finds that I am gone, and then she will rage at me for weeks and then she will slowly forget. When I pull my bundle out from under the elder it is sopping with dew from the night, and it makes a cold wet patch on the front of my clothes.

No smoke rises from the huddle of dwellings around the green, only from Mr. Reekes the baker's chimney at the end of the village. His smoke is white and curling, spooling upward toward the dwindling stars as though his morning fire was freshly lit. I cannot smell the baking of loaves; the hour is too early even for that. He will be kneading and pummeling dough by lamplight with his hands as big as dinner plates, hands that I once saw squeezing inside the bodice of Alice Mant when she went in for loaves, when they thought no one was looking. I cross the pastureland then skirt the common, taking the path at the edge of the Wiston estate. I think of Ann.

It was she who had observed John Glincy following me about one day. She is the kind of girl to notice everything. She'd said that it would be my brown hair having the shine of a ripe cobnut that drew him in.

"You haven't got blemishes," she'd added, standing back to get a look at me. "You have a good-shaped chin, neat wrists and ankles and your belly isn't gone soft with eating too much butter. Watch out for that one, Agnes Trussel," she'd said. "You know that family is trouble all round." She could see from my face that I was a way from pleased about this and so she'd gone on talking. "Just keep your bonnet on before him. Just put your head up high and say, 'No, I don't think so, I'm really far too busy now,' or some such. It's very easy." Of course this was all too late, I remember thinking, watching her lips go up and down as though I had never seen them before.

"Oh, don't sit there looking like a misery." She had laughed. "It's not so bad! You are a sensible girl with manners, that knows how to behave."

But of course it was bad, it was very bad indeed. I didn't like to think of her jolly face clouding up with shame and disbelief if she found me out. I would be someone different to her suddenly, not like her sister that she knows at all.

"Where are you, Ann, when I need you so much?" I whisper in the darkness, over the damp fields to Wiston House.

I have four miles by foot along the back lanes and over the fields before I reach Steyning, or I will beg a lift on a passing cart or dray, till I get to the place called The chequers where the lane joins the road, and there I shall wait for a carrier to London. I picture it drawing toward me, hooves mashing the skin of the road, towering wheels whirring and grinding over the grit in the yard of the inn as it comes to a halt. I feel sick. The journey will cost me two days and more than a guinea, and if all goes as it should I shall be long gone from the county of Sussex, up through the county of Surrey and into the great city by the time they find dead Mrs. Mellin in her cold house.

The lane reaches the edge of the copse and sinks down into a dip at the base of the scarp, where the mud deepens and becomes more sticky with the clay. My boots make a sucking noise with each tugging step I have to take, as if the land were but reluctantly letting me pass. Red cattle are clustered together in the gloom under the beeches; they wake and shift their hooves uneasily in the thick mud as I go by, their breath rising in clouds. How dark it is under the trees. Even the early-rising blackbirds are asleep, and it is hard not to shiver with sleeplessness and the newness of what I am doing.

4

*T*he carrier pulls jerkily away and up the lane. It is a low wagon smelling of sacking and poultry, and I am sat at the back, on a bench furnished with a bolster of woven horsehair cloth, shiny with use. Besides the four other passengers, the carrier is heaped with bales of raw wool, three crates of pullets and some closed baskets into which I cannot see. The oily smell of fleeces makes it hard not to think of home, it is so strong.

I am a thief, a disgrace and a deserter. I have a pain high up in my lungs that I deserve; it rises till the misery is a choke in my throat. A fat woman sitting to my right is staring sideways at me. I hate her for this. I have to look down at my lap and swallow over and over, not letting a tear fall. It is as though I were moving along in a swaying kind of sleep led by the horses, knowing nothing of what I am at, nor where I am going. I fold my arms tightly over the fear in my stomach, look about and breathe the air.

I had pulled my cap low over my brow as I passed through Steyning to the inn. I do not know so many people here, but there are those who know my family well enough, and I prayed to God I would not see a soul who knows my father.

Yet sure enough, as we passed out of the village I saw Mr. Benter ahead with a pack on his shoulder, going out to the sawpits. I froze. I scarcely breathed. *Dear God, may he not catch sight of me*, I thought. As the cart swayed past him, he stepped onto the bank and greeted the coachman. His breath was white about him in the chill. Richard Benter has been my father's drink-mate since better times were had between them. He was so near I could make out the pockmarks on his cheek and smell the tobacco smoke leaking from the clay bowl of the pipe he sucked upon. It was nothing but a wonder that he did not see me, but I could not drag my gaze away. Then at the moment that we rounded the corner he seemed to return my look directly even as he disappeared from view behind the shop. My heart thumped.

The picture of his puzzled squint and half-raised hand comes to me over and over. Did Mr. Benter see me perched upon the carrier to London? How could I know? And if he did, what will he do?

"Was it one of yours I saw this forenoon?" I could hear him say. "On the up-cart for town?"

My father, who could never bear to give away what he has no knowledge of, would keep his mouth buttoned up at that suggestion.

"May have been," he might say, and shrug.

Only later would he mutter that, if it was so, then it was without a by-your-leave. My father would not ask to borrow Mr. Fitton's mare to ride behind and bring me back.

It makes no difference if they know where I have gone. At least, if nobody knows about my thieving. And of course they do not. How could they know? No one would have thought that Mrs. Mellin had a quantity of money. For we did not, and were we not her nearest neighbors? I have a flicker of doubt. Surely it was just her mean little secret that she hoarded away—and for what? She had nobody left.

The woman beside me makes me jump. "Sawpit does well from the need for fencing these days, don't it," she comments. Of course, she must know Mr. Benter. Perhaps it was her face that had caught his eye.

I cough, as if I did not hear her properly.

And the terror ebbs away, but some miles on a trickle of disquiet continues chuckling and babbling inside my head, willing the horses' progress to be faster, faster. Pressing at my stays, I make sure that the coins do not clink or rattle up against each other. I eye the road behind. When I get to the city I will be swallowed up, I reassure myself; all traces vanished.

We go through Ashurst, past Blake's Farm and Sweethill Farm.

A way after Godmark's Farm we have to wait in the road to cross the river. I make myself eat dry bread from my pocket, my fingers stiff with cold. I make myself take notice of the way the road goes on, opening a distance up between some portion of my troubles and my circumstance. I see a man drinking from a wooden flask, his head strained back to take the liquid in. I see a hawk. I smell the tang of horses, and the straw of the fat woman's bonnet. I see a team of oxen opening earth behind the blade of a plow. I see three new, pale wheels in a wheelwright's yard, and hear the hiss of a spokeshave peeling at wood. I see the orange carcass of a fox.

And over time the motion of the carrier steadies me and makes me sensible. Taking the chill air deeply keeps the sickness at bay. In truth there is nothing to do but observe the world unfolding behind the carrier and to the sides of the road as we progress. I see how the mud in the road behind us changes from a pale clay to a darker brown of silt, and then to clay again.

The mud is shallow and white with chalk as the wagon heaves uphill to a gibbet on the crossroads. The man beside the driver cries, "Burnt Oak Gate!" But no one gathers up their bags in readiness to leave. As we approach, I see a glistening crow push itself away from the gibbet's crossbar and fly heavily upward. It catches a breeze that we cannot feel here on the ground, and stays almost motionless on the movement of the air, skillfully floating, like a malevolent thought. It waits for our arrival. Its head turns as it surveys the landscape; we draw up alongside and inch slowly by. I don't like to look, but somehow my head turns toward the gibbet anyway. I feel something prickle over my skin, as though spiders were crawling there. I grip my forearms tight with my hands.

One of the irons has the last bits of a man's body hanging in it; the head has slumped in the top cage and the rest is tarred bones held together with very little. Some threads of fabric hang down from what remains of his breeches. The other irons are empty and swing more loosely in the cold air. A creaking is just audible. There are some small dry yellow bones on the ground beneath, and white splashes of bird droppings. The fat woman nudges me, smiling with triumph.

"See how they deserves it," she declares. "A dreadful crime, no doubt." I cannot find a thing to say, but another woman nods and points her finger toward the scene in case her daughter sitting beside her hasn't heeded. The daughter's head swivels round as we pass, drinking in the detail.

"It's a man, Mother." Her childish voice is satisfied and lazy. A chill has settled in me, although I make myself nod faintly in agreement. I must appear an honest, law-abiding creature, even to myself. The fifth passenger in the back seat takes no notice of the scene, nor of any other passing by. He alternates between a dozing state and being occupied in eating something crumbly from a brown packet on his knee; a cascade of pastry falls down the front of his greatcoat.

As we gain sufficient distance from the gibbet, the crow behind us drops and settles on the irons again, twisting its head sideways to reach its black beak through the bars. Another crow flies down, and I look away. They say that crows and rooks mean trouble, and there are always plenty of them.

Lichfowl, my mother calls them. Corpse birds.

And beyond here I am plunged into unknown country. Burnt Oak Gate marks the edge of what I know. How rapidly the world is changing; everywhere we pass new fencing and altered boundaries. Thorny hedgerows of quickset and blackthorn slice straight through the sensible, ancient lengths of land, taking no heed of the curve of running water or the shape of a hill, just spanning the breadth of the stubbled fields to form vast, unreasonable squares that make no sense of the terrain they apportion. We see a quantity of people walking out on the road, with packs and babies and pieces of furniture strapped to their backs. They have the shifting, dogged look of people uprooting and leaving behind them all that they know. They are looking for labor in towns, in the city.

A woman looks up as we go by, and stares at me as she moves to the edge of the muddy road, making way. We pass so closely I could reach my hand out and touch the thinness of her jaw. I can hear that she murmurs a rhyme over her shoulder to the child tied to her back.

Jack, he was nimble, Jack, he was quick,
Jack, he jumped over the candlestick.

"Which Jack is that, Mamma?" the child asks, twisting its little fingers in her hair, and there is a pause and then the woman replies bitterly, as if to herself, "Any man jack with an ounce of sense left in him."

And she is right. I can hear the words, even after the carrier has rounded a corner and she has gone from sight. We should all be snatching our chances if they show themselves to us. The old ways are gone now. The carved-up countryside is filling fat men's pockets with more than they need, while working men like my father are broken down and weakened and made small as their choice and independence are removed from their reach. Enclosure is a tightening around their necks, making slaves of them. It is a length of cord held only by some men of wealth. Enclosure drives them into corners like rats. My blood starts to boil with fury, and I clench my thumbs inside my fists. For my family there can be only misery ahead. For my family next year there will be no pig. There will be little but trouble, I fear, for them and so many like them, hunger making their bellies tight, day after day.

Good men like my father, feeding his family, taking what dismal employment he can, to pay off the baker, the shopkeeper, the miller. Bad men like *him*; all in the same sorry plight. What is a good man, though, I start to think, or a bad one? As the carrier rattles on these thoughts begin to open up and drift about like smoke inside my head.

As I say, I am not myself, and I can hardly pronounce on morals or goodness. I picture myself entering St. Mary's Church with my belly swollen, round as a mare's in the very shape of shame, and my face flushes with humiliation.

I will not think of these things.

Instead I make myself notice that the sun is a flat disk of white light, more like a hole in the clouds. I see that the hedges are filled with berries and drupes of ivy. I notice the twist and crook of the road. And then, gradually, my fists unclench and I slip into a drowsy state with my head nodding forward onto my chest, until the cold wakes me again. The clouds thicken as the morning passes. It is a long journey, in countless ways.

Halts occur at intervals to water the horses, to take up a passenger or set one down. Uneasily I eye my bundle, strapped with the rest of the baggage, at every stop. Mrs. Mellin's coins are tucked inside my stays securely; I feel them there against my ribs when I lean forward or breathe deeply. All that I have, I could lose, I remind myself.

On the heath before Horsham, two men hail the carrier and ride the tailgate. They thump their boots on the floor of the cart so that it shakes and they are loud and troublesome and smell of liquor. I am relieved when after a mile or so they are forcibly turned off. A quarrel ensues and then one of the men falls to the ground. I can hear the growl of the driver's terrier at the front of the wagon for a long time afterward, and I fall asleep to dream of a man with a chafed, red neck walking along the edge of the road, alongside the carrier. His strides are purposeful and angry. I awake with a start to find he is not there.

The hedges wind along beside us until my eyes are glazed with staring. A young rabbit bolts across our muddy wake and disappears into the undergrowth. I see that the light is beginning to fail, and there is a stillness to the cold air, our white breath rising as though we were all smoldering, quietly on fire.

After the bustle of Horsham the afternoon dies quickly around us. We pass lit windows in the walls of dwellings, and men returning from work on foot, their faces caught in the carriage lights as they stand aside. I hear the thump of wood being split with an axe. We go by a low cottage with a taper burning in the kitchen where a woman bends forward at the waist; she is raising her hand and shaking something at a man seated by a table. It is a curious matter, the seeing of things and yet not understanding.

We halt for the night some time toward Dorking. The Red Lion is a dingy place. I order broth that comes in a broad swilling plate of pewter that makes it cold upon arrival, and I cannot tell what meat has given it its flavor. I finish it as best I can.

"Cheap beds?" The woman in the taproom repeats my words too loudly, as if to feign offense, then calls an older woman to take me to the back chamber. The woman has brown spots over her neck like the burnt parts of a griddle cake. When she reaches out to take the payment her eyes widen just a little at the sight of all my yellow coins together. I push the rest back into my stays, and look about. There are other beds in the room, but it would seem that I am the only lodger here tonight. A musty odor of old upholstery and unwashed bedding hangs in the air. There is no fire. The woman lights a dripping candle for me from the one that she holds, and turns to leave.

"I should sew that gold into your skirts, young woman," she observes from the doorway, her spotted hand on the latch. I look at her.

"I should?" I say.

She pokes her head back into the gloom of the chamber, and lowers her voice to a conspiratorial rasp.

"Tuppence for the use of a needle and thread, and three shillings for the excessive trouble I shall be put to in not telling a soul," she says. "My mouth does run away with itself sometimes, about tidy, shiny sums tucked up in warm corners, here and there." Her eyes glitter as she casts a meaningful glance round the empty room. "I *knows* individuals, and what they can thirst for." My heart sinks, and I nod in dismay.

Later I sit and pull uneasily at the needle she brings me; the thread is red and garish and looks out of place against the weave of my plain fabric, and my fingers are clumsy with cold. The woman had bitten the coins that I gave her and chuckled horribly to make her point all down the corridor until a door closed somewhere and the noise was muffled.

When the sewing is done, the needle lies on the sill in the candlelight like a sharp little knife.

I do not sleep at first, there is so much din and clatter from somewhere nearby, so that when sleep comes to me eventually I dream of rats the size of dogs chewing at something I cannot see. It is cold all night. When I wake in the morning I see that the needle has gone. Though I look to see if it has rolled away onto the dirty rug or between the floorboards, I cannot find a trace of it.

5

*I*n the morning I try to swallow bread to quell my sickness, and when the bell rings at eight I take my bundle outside and join the carrier. The passengers have swelled in number, and I find I have to squeeze my way up onto the bench at the back of the wagon. When we leave the town the morning light shows a countryside choppy with hills, dotted with brightly golden copses and small farms and hamlets. Spiders' webs catch at the damp between the stems of dead hemlock and milk parsley. Plumes of smoke climb into the air from abundant chimneys and we see many people working the fields and driving goats and oxen. We stop for carts more frequently, even at this hour. The land seems teeming with its population.

One of the new passengers sits very upright on the bench. There is a glossiness about her. She has a fine, fancy patterned shawl over her shoulders, and her mantua is made of silk bearing woven sprigs of flowers and birds. She seems tall and narrow, with a head of brown curling hair under her bonnet. Her face is pale as a china cup. High on the cheekbones two luscious spots of blush are painted on like raspberries. She is fresh and bright. I cannot stop watching her, until her eye catches mine and she smiles directly at me. I look away hastily, my own cheeks flushing in ordinary patches on my face.

Her hands are long and bony, and she knocks them together through her white kid gloves from time to time as though eager to reach her destination, or as if she is filled with an impatient kind of song or energy that must escape by any means. Under her boots is a small leather case. I have a feeling that her eyes are on me, but then she turns and begins to listen to the fat woman talking to the unpleasant woman with the daughter. I fold my arms carefully across my stomach and do not hear them. I pray no one will speak to me. I am bad, spoiled. I am best not spoken to; I am like an apple rotting slowly away once the worms have got in. A rotten apple touching the skin of a good one in the store will taint the others till they fester together.

The day is milder than the day before. There is no sunshine, but the clouds are high and pale, and the air has about it the nameless sweetness that earth gives off before the great frosts begin.

After some time the woman pulls off a glove and eats some fruit with her bare hand, swallowing quickly and not letting juice drip on her dress. I am startled when she leans across to me, her long fingers reaching out to offer me a plum. I take it gratefully and bite. It is late in the season for such a good one, sour and pleasant at once. The bloom on it is like a mildew on its perfect skin. "Thank you, ma'am," I say.

She pulls on her glove.

"My name is Lettice Talbot," the woman says, as if to set up conversation. The voice she has is light and coaxing, like a child's. "Some people call me Letty." I spit out the stone of the plum and throw it onto the road.

"What an uncommon name," I answer, out of manners.

"I like it very much," the woman replies, which is a strange answer, and makes me think somehow that she has chosen it herself.

I cannot think of any other thing to say to her. A curious smell comes away from Lettice Talbot's clothing when she moves about; as sweet as beeswax, or the dusty odor of roses that have been kept to dry inside a cupboard, or something else I cannot place. It is a good, intriguing smell that makes me want to sit a little closer to her.

At noon we roll over White Down Hill and descend into the village of Leatherhead. The inn is adjacent to the blacksmith's, and as we pass I look into the darkness of his shop and see white-hot coals flaring and dulling with the roar of the bellows. From the yard of the inn we can still hear the regular metallic clang and ring of a hammer on hot iron against an anvil. In the silence that follows I know well the hiss of a horseshoe going into cold liquid, and the smell of a scorched hoof as the warm shoe is nailed on.

The jolting slows and stops.

"We can take something to eat here." Lettice Talbot gets down immediately over the tailgate and calls up to me, brushing dirt from her palms. The harnesses clink as the ostlers unbuckle the horses. The horses are sweating and breathing heavily.

"How stiff we become on the back of this cart, our legs stuck out over the road like a crate of dead fowls!" She looks doubtfully toward the pullets at the front of the wagon, and then laughs, as though something wicked had occurred to her. A dog barks.

"Are you not hungry?" she asks. I suppose I must eat. "I'll bet your last fair meal was another life ago. Am I right, sweetheart?" She beckons me to descend.

"There is abundant time for an inn-dinner at the Rose and Crown," she reassures me, as if she traveled frequently this way, and the sun breaks through the clouds as we cross the yard.

Inside, my eyes accustom to the darkness. There is a fire blazing in a broad hearth, and a savory smell of woodsmoke and ale. Two men glance up at us and then back to some papers spread out on a table. The girl drawing ale from a barrel at the hatch directs us to a bench. We have our backs to the sunlight that falls through the leaded window, blue with smoke from the fire. The brick floor is swept. The miserable man wearing the greatcoat takes a solitary seat on the far side of the room, opening his mouth to order something made with beef, then rubs his belly. He keeps his coat on. There is loud laughter from the porch and then the room seems filled with stir and levity.

How has my life changed so quickly? I feel small away from home. I feel dizzy with it.

"What shall we have?" Lettice Talbot says brightly. "Why not oysters!" The girl wipes a cloth over the table and brings some for us, with hard sallow cheese and bread. There is a lot of greasy red hair escaping from her cap. She looks at me as she puts them down, then goes away. The food is salty and good, and we eat hungrily without conversation. The girl comes back to remove the dish of empty shells, and Lettice Talbot claps her hands.

"Brandy!" she suggests.

"Brandy?" I say doubtfully. I don't mention that I have never tasted it. The girl brings a jug and pours out one glass. The liquid is a bright brown as it catches the sunlight. "Drink up," Lettice Talbot coaxes, pushing the glass toward me and smiling kindly.

"But you have none," I say.

"No, no," she says, "it is for you—you look as though you need it!"

So I swallow it down. It is hot, as though it had within it something of the fire itself.

"Where are you headed, sweetheart?" Lettice Talbot asks. I cannot think at first of what to say. As she leans forward, I see a little locket is tied at her neck on a piece of yellow velvet, flashing in the light. The gem set upon it breaks up the brightness sharply into separate colors, as a drop of water might, catching the sunshine after rain. Her neck is smooth and white above the ribbon. She sees me looking and her hand goes to the locket as if to hide it with her fingertips.

"How did you come by such a lovely thing?" I exclaim.

"It's not real," she says quickly. "Not a proper diamond." And then she smiles and asks again where I am going. She stares at me when I do not answer, and so I have to embark upon the story I have been making up inside my head.

"I am traveling at a day's notice up to London," I say, "to stay with an aging cousin suffering from an illness of some gravity." My voice sounds like it is reciting lessons.

"Where does she live?" Lettice Talbot asks. I think quickly.

"Within the city walls. She has rooms in a small house, and the servants do not like her and all of them have left her service. She is quite

alone." I make my face look sorry and anxious as I talk, which is not difficult. My fingers touch my lips as though they know that I am telling lies.

I add with effort that she needs someone to carry water from the pump
and cook up broths and sago, and take the slops away; in short the heavy,
bending, stirring tasks she cannot do.

"What sickness is she suffering?" Lettice Talbot asks, and pours
more brandy for me from the jug.

"Bronchitis," I say without a hesitation. I know about bronchitis; my
grandmother died all curled up with coughing up dark slimy matter, suf-
focated by her own lungs when they failed within her, the doctor said.
Dr. Twiner was a costly body to have stepped inside the house. It seemed
scandalous to me that he gained his guineas whether his patients lived or
died. The regretful countenance he fixed upon his shiny, well-fed face
was glib and practiced, and melted away as he ducked his head out of the
threshold toward the lane. I watched his diminishing form swinging his
polished cane all down the track until the rowans hid him from my view.
My mother propped his bill behind the salt box before she sat down suddenly in front of the fire as though her legs were broken, and sobbed there
for a week. She was different in those days; it was still possible to guess
a little of what she thought on any matter. For one whole week she was
too loose and grieved to cook, or clean the babies. Then on the seventh
day she set her lip straight and stiffened quite perceptibly throughout the
funeral, as though the cold draft that was blowing in under the door of
the church was freezing her in more ways than one. The framework of
her manner became a shape to hold her feelings in, and from that day on,
her outward disposition did but rarely alter.

The room in the inn has darkened.

It occurs to me how, once the lies have started, it should become both
easier and more necessary to go on fabricating a pretense. I must con-
struct the lies quite fully, like a makeshift house, and live inside them.
Lettice Talbot taps her long fingers on the tabletop, then unbuckles her
case to take out a little bottle. She tweaks out the stopper, puts her finger

to the hole and tips it up. She presses the wetness lightly to her neck, and an intense, giddy scent the color of pinks and creamy whites and oranges envelops us. I am almost dazed by it.

How can I tell whether she is listening to me if she does not answer? And yet it is discourteous, I think, to be deceiving her like this. Her eyes are roving around the room as I talk; she is taking things in. I will have to check myself. It will not be long before my conscience has become quite fat with secrets.

I hold my glass up by the stem and tilt the drop of brandy that remains, and, feeling a sudden, foolish need to share a truth and not a lie with her, I laugh and say that drinking it is like drinking fire. I regret my words immediately, but this is no matter because Lettice Talbot does not hear. She has stood up and begun to wrap her patterned shawl more closely around her for the next stage of our journey. How clean and new her clothes are. She pulls on her gloves, and with unease I catch a glimpse of what has happened to her wrists.

6

We go out into the open air to find the weather turning. My cheeks are hot with liquor and I find that something of the world is changing and unsteady. The sky has darkened and clouded over and the unpleasant woman and her daughter are fussing that it might begin to rain and turn their ribbons limp. The fat woman shifts about on the hams of her legs and makes a great scene out of exchanging her bonnet for a large ugly hat that covers her features and obscures some of the view to my right. At the final bell the greatcoated man appears and hauls himself into the wagon. A sour, unclean smell of pipe smoke and urine leaks from his clothes. I am dismayed to see him leer at Lettice Talbot as he pushes by her rudely, and to see him smirk as he rubs against her legs. He wipes some spittle from the side of his mouth with the back of his glove, lurches heavily as he sits down, and goes to sleep under his hat. Lettice Talbot does not remark at his behavior; it is as though she has not seen it.

The horses strain and gather speed as they pull away from Leatherhead.

I ask Lettice Talbot why she would not let me pay for what I had eaten at the inn. I was too confused by brandy to protest as she counted out coins and left them on the table as we left. But she shakes her head vigorously when I try to repay her and raises her hand as though it is a trifling matter.

"But I have money!" I insist, too loudly, and she puts her gloved finger swiftly to her mouth.

"Shh! Quiet!" she says.

So I am indebted now, and the heat spreading out from the spirits inside me has made the world seem vivid and too much to bear. I am unable to stop thoughts from welling up and I am sorry that some tears spill out, making the road behind us seem wobbling and indistinct. There are too many troubles to think of at once. I have been struggling to keep some thoughts quite separate in my head, as if letting them touch each other could unleash havoc in there, as flints would, knocking together on a dry day and sparking, making fires on the heath. I cannot stop the thoughts from jumbling about now. But I don't make a sound, and then the tears cool quickly on my face in the open air.

Sometimes a fire on the heath is good for the land, I think. The blackened plants find a refreshment in their ordeal and so grow green again.

Lettice Talbot doesn't speak a word, but she leans over and brushes my hand with her own, then puts it back onto her lap. Her gloves are made from soft, new kidskin. There are pricks of holes in the kidskin, where the hairs of the animal grew out. The leather made from kid is very fine and supple, and easily torn. Inside the inn I had seen how white her fingers were, as though she had not touched grime or drudging tasks for a long time. Uncomfortably I remember also how the whiteness of her skin was discolored at the heel of her wrists by a rim of broken purple bruising that had seemed quite fresh.

Finally I sleep, and when I wake I find her hand is resting over mine again, so gently that I can hardly feel her touching me. Her eyes are fixed on the jolting horizon as though she had been watching it for hours.

"Have you napped yet?" I ask, taking my hand away from hers, but she shakes her head.

"Where do you come from?" I ask, and she smiles at me as though she has not heard, or as though she is thinking hard about something different and cannot leave that thought alone. Her face is serene. "I have"—she looks about—"an acquaintance in this county. I was here to do business." That is all she says for a long time.

The clouds keep gathering and thickening in the sky, but no rain falls.

"Mild day it is, for November," the other women nod and comment hopefully, as though by that wish alone they can forestall the rain, their heads bobbing and quaking with the roll of the carriage going over the ruts. The unpleasant woman and her daughter break a cake between them on their laps and share it. The daughter chews dreamily, and I catch the fat woman eyeing the cake, her mouth turned down a little at the corners, as though by rights the cake were hers and they had stolen it from her.

Lettice Talbot yawns and rubs her narrow shoulders. "It is not so far now," she says to me.

Stretched out on our left we see the marshes. Smelling of low-tide, salty mudflats, these marshes and hamlets seem a desolate beginning to a city. Shabby tufts of reeds and sedges give a green-gray color to the wet-land draining to ditches. I see birds like snipe and redleg. I see a heron, trailing its untidy legs beneath its flight. We go through another hamlet and mount a rise. The houses are made of brick instead of flint, and many have neat gardens around them. And suddenly, as the road climbs and takes a turn to the right, the city comes into view below us. I am amazed. I stand up unsteadily, grasping the rail, and try to see ahead of us over the load of the carrier.

"I can hardly believe it!" I exclaim aloud, turning to Lettice Talbot.

"It is nothing more than a great stinking town," she says, amused.

"And that river is the Thames!" I breathe. Shimmering water like a snaking sea reflects the sky, its surface wrinkled with tiny swarms of boats and ferries. I stand on tiptoe to see more clearly, though the wagon jolts and rocks along. There are so many houses that on the far bank the city is clustered down to the edge of the water. Thorny spires and domes rise up from its mass.

The orange sun flashes on the water.

I am impatient. We enter Southwark, and our progress along the high street is impeded by the crush of traffic around the butchers' shambles. I see a butcher wipe a bloodied cloth over a cleaver as we pass. I see an-other butcher pressing his fingers along the length of a dead pig's spine as he looks for the soft place to put his knife between the bumps. I have never seen such a quantity of meat hanging together at one time: rows of pigs, yards of limp poultry slung from their own tied feet, the head of a calf with its eyes wide open, a brown bucket of livers. One gutter is red with blood where a washing has happened.

"This is London Bridge! Bridge!" the driver's voice shouts at last from the front of the carrier. The other passengers begin to shift and talk in their seats. The fat lady daubs something white from a small pot onto her face. London Bridge is wide and chaotic, like no bridge I have ever seen. It is as broad as a street and lined with shops, and men are working in gangs between the premises among piles of rubble, where broken bits of building stick up into the air like blackened ribs. I stare astonished when I see that, in a corner between two walls, an unkempt man has made his habitation. He is squatting before a hearth, feeding a small, fierce fire with sticks. Smoke drifts a thin choking column into the traffic's path. It smells tarred and bitter, making my eyes sting, and as the carrier passes, the man struggles up abruptly from the flames to turn his head toward us, as though it were his duty to observe all entries to the city. His coat is dark.

Below us the river smells of low-tide weed and mud and foul waste.

The road crackles with the noise of iron wheels turning over cobbles. Traffic knots and unknots itself in all directions. I have never seen so much at once: horses, carts, coaches weighty with passengers, quick squeaking gigs and traps, boys running with sedan chairs on handles, even one man driving two white heedless oxen down the very middle of the street. I am deafened by it and hold on to the side of the carrier as if it were a pitching boat on a rough sea.

Lettice Talbot shouts out the names of streets as we drive on.

"Fish Hill Street, Gracechurch Street, Cornhill, Poultry," she says, above the noise. Cheapside is a broad, fine street lined with shops, where the afternoon light gleams on the glassy fronts, and shoals of people pour in and out. I see the ghoulish whiteness of so many of their faces, and their grayish powdered heads.

"They wear so many clothes!" I exclaim to Lettice Talbot.

I am startled by the noise of breaking glass beyond us up the street; there is a roar of drunkenness and the pound of running feet.

"A hanging," she shouts. "There was a hanging today. Most of the crowds go off calmly when it is over, but there is always disorder left in the districts along the route, and fights break out in taverns and on street corners. It can be very unruly." She turns her head away. "The smell of sudden death infects a violent man with bloodlust."

"What?" I say, trying to hear her.

"Violence!" she shouts. "Make sure you head swiftly to the safety of your relative."

"Along what route?" I ask, trying to get nearer to her so I can catch her words. The carrier lurches. "Where is the trouble?"

"The way the condemned cart goes between Newgate Prison and the gallows tree at Tyburn."

"To where?"

"The gallows tree!" She laughs merrily. "Justice, my sweetheart!" And I shiver and pull my cloak about me.

We turn into a dingy lane, and draw into the great yard of the Cross Keys Inn. I am alarmed to see so many people jostling to reach the carrier. Lettice Talbot leans forward.

"Have we arrived?" I say.

"Disembark here, Agnes," she advises kindly. "This is where I get down." I shrink from the idea, wishing I could make myself small as a mouse or sparrow-sized, and go back at once to Sussex on the dusty floor of the carrier under the horsehair seats, by people's shoes. But of course I cannot, as my journey is the kind of journey that cannot be undone, and so I find myself descending with difficulty over the wheels, and my feet standing on London cobbles, my lungs breathing in the tarry smoke that hangs over the yard. It is as though I were quite another person arriving in another place called London, in a dream. I keep imagining that someone might call out, "Cease that, Agnes!" but of course they do not.

I can hardly believe it. I clench my jaw to keep my teeth from chattering in agitation while I wait for my bundle to be untied from the rest of the baggage by the loaders and flung down onto the pavement.

Lettice Talbot draws me gently aside and speaks low in my ear with a sudden urgency.

"You cannot trust a soul, Agnes," she says. Her eyes are serious and blue in her thin face. A man is thunderously rolling empty barrels out of a hatch and up onto a painted cart. There is a strong smell of stale beer coming up from the cobbles.

"You should not let your guard down, Agnes. Always presume that there is no one to trust. You must look out for tricks all of the time," she whispers, watching my face. "People taking advantage."

"Tricks," I repeat. I am so tired suddenly.

"You have nowhere to go, do you?" Lettice says. She is still standing close to me. Fine soft hairs on the side of her cheek are catching the light behind her. And now I see that, although she speaks with such assurance, she must be young, perhaps almost as young as myself.

I shake my head. "I do not."

Lettice Talbot reaches into her bodice and takes out a crumpled little piece of paper that she gives to me. She speaks quickly now.

"This is the address of my lodging house toward St. Giles. Follow these directions, and begin to look for number twelve after the sign of the bootmaker's shop. The landlady is Mrs. Bray; she is a decent woman. Tell her you are one of my acquaintance, no, you are my particular friend, and there will be room for you. Make sure you do that. You must find your own way as I have business to attend to, for the while. If they should ask, be sure to say that you have had the smallpox."

"I must find work," I say. Lettice Talbot smiles.

"There will be plenty," she reassures me.

"What kind of work?" I ask hopefully. Lettice Talbot looks at me. "Priceless," she murmurs. "Priceless." The gem flashes at her neck. "You are a darling," she says softly, and touches my skin. "There is profit to be made from what you are." I nod at this, not knowing what she has in mind, but understanding that she knows how to behave in London.

Her teeth are good and wide apart. Her arm is light about my shoulders.

"We are going to be such friends," she says, and squeezes me tight.

"I have never had a friend, not really," I say. "Only sisters."

And so I am persuaded, as I have no other plan, and am tired of thinking. When I have pulled out my homely bundle from the dwindling pile before the tailgate, I turn to Lettice Talbot to bid goodbye to her, but she is gesturing with someone at an upper window of the inn, shaking her head with vehemence, and does not see me waiting. I brush the dirt from the front of my dress with my hand, and when I look back again, she is gone. I cannot see her anywhere.

By the front of the coach when I go to pay my passage I find an argument is under way between the driver and the greatcoated man about his fare.

"I cannot help the nation's lack of coins!" the man bawls, puffing with righteousness. "Your nuisance shortage then just means your loss, not mine! Here, you'll take my double-guinea piece and give me the change that I am due!"

The coachman's boy holds out a dirty hand for my own guinea, which he takes and bites. When he holds it up and looks closely at it in the gloom, his face changes and he glances sharply back at me. I am gripped by the idea that he knows it is stolen. *How could he know that?* He could not. My face goes hot, even though he shrugs and drops the coin into a bag inside his waistcoat and turns to pull the coachman's terrier away from someone's legs. The dog barks and strains at the collar, and when I turn to look again, I find the coachman's boy is standing still and staring after me, as though he has something to say. I hurry off. I cling to my bundle in the crush and leave the yard. And yet, as I reach the gate, instinctively I have another sense of someone watching me, and I look back quickly to the balcony. I cannot see a soul up there, only a movement flickering behind a window, behind the crisscrossed panes of glass, which dips out of sight.

My bundle is an awkward shape to carry.

I start to make my way through the crush of people outside the yard, and hold the thought of the yellow coins protectively inside my head. *If I can keep it there without distraction, nothing will happen*, I say to myself. It is difficult, like holding a large slippery plate of meat above the clamor of a pack of animals.

The noise of the crowd is huge and judders in my ears, and I find it hard to keep my balance. It is a hundred times worse than any market day or fair that I have been to. Since the child began to grow inside me, odors are so much stronger, and here the street is swimming with stenches that I am fighting to move through without gagging. Stale bodies inside unclean garments press around me, giving out foul exhalations as they walk, of sweat, rotting teeth, disease. I have to hold my breath until my lungs are almost bursting, until I am a fair way past a tavern called the Boar's Head, and on the other side of the street I see a burial ground pierced with the uprights of headstones and memorials, where my feet seem to take me. In its midst stands a towering plane tree, its scaly broad trunk rising firmly between the grassy mounds. The branches are dark with rooks gathering, like a crop of black fruits.

Carrion birds do irk me. Their cawing and rough hacking chat is like the sound of death. Here there are so many rooks that they are like a terrible smoke billowing and settling about the tree. The ground is littered with black feathers, droppings and bits of twigs beneath their nests, which cluster on the branches.

I linger here, too long. I read slowly from an engraved tablet at the side of the street. *Old Site of St. Peter's, Before the Fire*, the tablet says. And nearby on the iron railings at the corner of Wood Street I see a likeness of St. Peter, whose fingers hold his keys comfortably upon his lap.

It is Lil who is good at the names of saints. She loves to take William on her knee and make up stories, and her mind wanders easily while she is working. I've heard her say that a thief has a fishhook on every finger, because a fish caught by St. Peter was found to have a shining piece of money in its mouth. My own thief's fingers are blue with cold. I blow upon them to warm them with my thief's breath, and turn my back on the likeness of St. Peter with his judgments.

I take a deep breath, step across the sea of Cheapside and turn down Bread Street. The likeness of St. Peter puts me in mind to mutter something from St. John. *Walk while ye have the light, walk while ye have the light*, I say inside my head, keeping a rhythm with my footsteps on the cobbles, and the familiar words are something of a comfort to me. I have always liked these chapters of the Bible best. I say it a few times more until I am past the church door of All Hallows, when with a start I find a beggar lurching along with me in the shadows.

The way he strains with effort to keep up fills me with remorse. And then he plucks at my arm with swollen fingers, and as he turns his face toward me, I see that one eye is closed and weeping a stickiness. It is as much as I can do not to shout out and fling my free arm to stop him touching my body.

My coins: they are the only things that truly separate me from him, and I am horrified by my difference. His seeing eye is a hole of misery that is hard to stomach, as though there were something crawling in there, already eating him up from his gut outward. It is the nothingness of him that is frightening me. I dare not shout, "Go away! Away!" or move as if to strike him, as I would at home if I had discovered rooks eating the soft parts of a lamb in the field behind the house. I grip my bundle.

He comes after me, persistent. Perhaps he can smell my coins, his jaws working away as though he were chewing on the stumps of his teeth. Why does no one come to help? There are people all about.

But then he speaks to me, and his voice is mild and croaking.

"Got a drop, love?" he asks. "It's just I got a thirst on me. Thought you might."

I shake my head shamefully and then he spits on the ground, a kind of black, bronchial spittle, and shuffles away. As he goes, he calls out something to me that at first I cannot hear, then with a shock I catch his words.

"Lest darkness come upon you," he is saying. Walk while ye have the light, lest darkness come upon you.

It will soon be late.

7

*N*earby a church bell strikes. The noise is short and harsh, like a stick beating a cracked pan.

Uneasily I put my hand on the outside of my skirt over the place where the money is sewn, and as I do this, an old woman selling oranges from a crate on the filthy paving catches my eye. Her pale face stares directly at me even as she hands oranges to a woman bending down, and pockets her payment. I shiver and hurry on, and as I pass I see with a shameful relief that she is blind, that her eyes are milky right through, like the eyes on a cooked fish.

The lodging house cannot be so far.

I stop again and study the instructions that Lettice Talbot gave to me. *Turn right, take the long thoroughfare until the church, then turn the corner.* But my sense of distance is becoming muddled. It is hard to measure, with no tree on the horizon, nor any silence on the road between strides. I cannot hear my steps amid the clamor of the crowd. I am invisible. The street noise is as loud as a river in full spate in winter after a week's worth of rain. It is too much, like hearing all the songs you've ever known sung at once inside your head.

I am jostled and ignored. There are hatches gaping open to kitchens and cellars deep in the ground below the pavement, filled with glimpses of casks and barrels, smells of meat, steam, the sourness of drink, slops. I see some fingers wiped on an apron, someone carrying a brimming pot of something heavy up some steps and a squealing infant put to the breast. Through another hatch I see a bent, bearded man making a shoe at a bench, and his quick hammer as he knocks tacks into the leather sole sounds already like a footstep on the cobbles.

Another church bell rings the quarter, or the half hour.

I smell a butcher's shop and see strings of songbirds: brown larks and thrushes, hung from hooks on shutters opening out onto the street. *Saul Pinnington, purveyor of game and preserved meats to the nobility*. A single hand freckled with dark spots of blood stretches out of the window very close to me, to unhook a shining brace of pheasant. When I peer inside I can hear the splintery chopping sound of a cleaver going through flesh and bone. I should enter the white marble darkness of the shop and ask here for directions.

I take a breath of butcher's air.

And then a plain-looking woman comes out abruptly from the doorway, and I walk on.

I pass a smoky wax-chandler's and a ballad seller bellowing from sheets of music, and still I do not ask directions. It begins to rain, and I duck into the porch outside a draper's shop. *Holling's Fabrics. With flowers raised or satined. All sorts of best Spitalfield silk, water silks, galloon, chintz and Persian*. Ann would be enthralled by these.

Inside the shop a thin, smart man striped like a reed looks up and glowers on seeing me, his large draper's scissors paused mid-cut across a stretch of velvet. I am not invisible at all, I think, and move away into the street.

The pavement is uneven and poorly made, with loose slabs that squeeze out a pulp of puddle water when I tread. The hatches have been closed and the cries of the sellers are gone from the thinning crowd. I cross the kennel gutter in the middle of the street and see a dead rat lying long and draggled, its tail stretched out. Carriage wheels flick mud behind them. The smell in the air is choking now, as though the force of the rain has stirred up unspeakable things. It is getting darker.

My bundle is wet and heavier to carry with every step. And when a sedan chair sways by, I see the hook of a finger lift the curtain flap inside and a powdery white face glances out. It is as white as a corpse, as if death itself were riding by. I shiver and try to hum something.

I have plenty of time yet to find the address before dark, I am certain that I do. And, turning a corner again, I begin to look for the sign of the bootmaker's shop beside the railings, which will show that I'm nearly there. But there are no shops at all in this street except for a place that sells liquor, where a man is slumped. The crowds have dwindled away.

This cannot be right.

The houses here are older, closer together, sometimes almost touching across the street or leaning sideways on each other for support as though they could fall down at any moment. There is a sour stench of urine and rotten things that closes the back of my throat. Along the road a woman with bare feet and a short, dirty hem is leaning inside an open doorway, her toes curled over the front of the threshold. She watches me fixedly as I approach.

"What district is this?" I venture to ask, but I see that her stare is glazed and blank.

"Is it . . ." I put my hand into my bodice to check the address on the paper again, but with a little lurch inside I find I do not have it. Where is it gone? I must have lost it farther back. And the woman doubles over suddenly at the waist, clutching at her grimy stays, and spits something dark out of her mouth onto the pavement. And as she turns inside she staggers and steadies herself with a hand on the wall and the peeling door. There is a great stain on the back of her skirt. I hear a baby crying through the crack in the door that she leaves ajar, and my heart clenches. The wailing is a newborn's weak, persistent noise that latches onto me as I retrace my steps back to the corner.

I take the next left turn to shake it off.

I am almost retching when I breathe in. My feet are sore from stepping again and again on the uneven street. I think the Hell the Bible speaks of must be quite like this: that baby growing in so much noise and filth. At home our hunger has never been as bad. Here the ground seems tainted with it, a malignant oozing worse than the dung and waste I am stepping through. A man hisses at me, a drawn-out wheezy threat. I do not run, though I am stiff with fear, and although he does not follow I hear a jug or bottle smash behind me.

Out on the main street I take another turning in despair, knowing now that I am wholly lost.

The air is becoming murky with the approach of dusk. I see a row of broad, new houses with exact rectangular windows, and I see inside the nearest room a servant laying out glasses at a table. She holds a glass up against the light from the window and as it turns in her hands for a second it looks like silver. My chest is tight with misery. I tell myself twice over that I will not cry until I have tried just one more turning. I am so thirsty. The ringing *clip-clop* of a shoed horse walking on the street makes me close my eyes and think of the lane at home to Storrington, where Ann and I would sit on the flint bridge over the stream and watch the carts go by, kicking our heels.

The first time John Glincy spoke to me was on the bridge.

"Not got much to do then, Agnes Trussel!" he'd called out, and winked; he was sat on the tailgate of Mr. Fitton's cart all piled with brassicas and greens from Hasler's Steading, with his felt hat pushed back upon his yellow head. My stomach twisted up with good surprise, and nerves. I'd thought it over all the way home, not heeding Ann's presence there beside me, nor the fresh spring blooms she'd picked from the bank to give to Mother; one thinks too little of these things till they are gone. I'd thought about John Glincy's wink, though, when I couldn't sleep that night; the recollection was like a lump or a disturbance pushing at my ribs and I did not know if it was agreeable or not. I turned and turned, trying to lie comfortably on the straw ticking in the moonlight until Lil woke up and asked me crossly to be still, and then I'd pushed it from my mind as being a childish fancy I would do well to be without.

A church bell strikes again.

The rain gets up. I walk because I cannot think what else to do. I shift my bundle from shoulder to shoulder. I am light with being thirsty. I need to rest. And without a thought I take a left turn through an archway wide enough for just one carriage at a time to pass through, and I am in a smaller cobbled street. It is a dead end. The noise on the thoroughfare outside is swallowed up and quietened behind me. The buildings on both sides here seem old, but they do not have that stench of collapse and decay about them. They are broad, with timbers crookedly spaced and small windows crisscrossed in lead punctuating the plasterwork. One house is set back slightly from the street, as if making way for the fair-sized walnut tree growing up through the paving slabs before it. I am surprised and glad to see a tree and I put my hand on the smooth cracked bark of the trunk to lean and catch my breath.

Over the front door of the house behind the walnut tree, I see that a curious sign is squeaking from an iron bracket: a painted picture of a squat man covered in leaves holding a bright star. It shines, wet with rain and catching the light. The faint squeak it makes is regular and soothing, like a bird. When my eye lights upon a small board with handwriting on it pinned to the door, my heart skips a beat. I come away from the tree and tread up onto the stone steps to be sure of what it says in the gloomy light.

J. Blacklock. Required—housekeeper for small household.

An anxious hope expands rapidly inside me, though I can just see how faded the letters are, as if they were chalked some time ago. I try to decide through the sickness if I might be suitable. Am I sufficiently old for such a position? What experience is needed? I can keep house well enough, I think, and after all I have lost the directions to Lettice Talbot's lodging house.

The sign of the wild man creaks louder as a breath of cold air blows down the street and pushes the rain sideways for a moment. I pull my wet cloak closer about my shoulders. To walk farther seems impossible, and it is effort enough to lift my hand and rap as hard as I can on the door, with my knuckles all white as they grip at the knocker. The door is wide, with large iron studs holding it together. The sound of my knock is like the thump of an axe on wood a great distance away. Surely no one will hear it.

And yet I hear someone coming, drawing the bolts back.

I swallow in readiness. Somehow I expect a maidservant to answer, and so am startled to find the door is opened by a tall man in working boots and jerkin. His shirtsleeves are pushed up on his broad forearms as though I have interrupted him at work. Spread out on the side of his face is a raw, red mark where his skin has been burnt. He is wearing a dark wig, or perhaps his own hair, tied in a disheveled tail, and he has a long, alarming face with high cheekbones. He glares at me, then past me into the street. He is perhaps as much as forty years. I swallow again.

"I'm looking for work, sir." I point in the direction of the notice. "I am quite used to housework and I think, sir . . ." It is hard not to be short of breath. "I've had the smallpox," I add, as Lettice Talbot told me to. I have told so many lies these past few days, a lifetime's worth.

"You *think* you've had the smallpox," he replies sarcastically. His voice is deep and has a rough, strange flavor to it.

"I mean I have, sir." My voice dries up into a tight swallow. "I mean, I've been with cows, sir, and couldn't catch it if I tried." I have a sense that someone is watching me and turn quickly round. A rat skitters along a drainpipe and disappears into the shadows behind some barrels, and outside on the street I hear someone shouting angrily. I realize how close it is to nightfall. The tall man in the doorway reaches out and unhooks the notice.

"The work is gone now," he says curtly. "Yesterday a new house-keeper was engaged."

My insides tighten up with disappointment. I can see that he is irritated to be disturbed. He has already begun to close the door, but fear and thirst give an edge to my voice.

"Are you Mr. Blacklock?" I call swiftly at the narrowing crack. "I am a good worker, sir. I'm used to working hard at weaving, and I can turn my hand efficiently to most things you could conceive of."

The crack in the door opens again and he takes a step forward to lean out into the rain toward me. His face is older than I thought, or is made so by the lines and shadows round his eyes.

"But what *qualities* do you possess?" he asks. His voice is dark and the words come out abruptly from him. I don't know what he means, and hear myself say anything that comes into my head.

"Firm fingers and quick fingers, sir," I say. I hold them out dizzily before me in the rain as evidence. My plain cuffs are dirty, and limp with water. His eyes inch over my hands and back to my face.

"Today I could have made use of some spare quick fingers," he says, gruffly. "God knows they are hard enough to come by. I was pressed to finish what I'd planned."

I try to return his gaze steadily and to stand with my back straight, though the bundle drags at my shoulder like a dead weight. Still he says nothing. I want to turn around and walk the whole way back to Sussex, but I cannot.

Where will I go? I am tired. The rain that drips down from the sign above is seeping into the nape of my cloak, and suddenly a boy is rushing toward us holding a flickering light ahead for two men in coats, their voices strained and angry. A smell of burning tar comes away from the torch, and their shouts echo in the empty street. They are going to fight, I think, trying to step out of the way as one of the men starts to shove at the other, but I am roughly jolted as they pass. We hear the boy's voice saying thinly, "It's this way, sirs," and they duck down an alleyway. When the brightness of his light has gone it leaves the beginning of a thick and terrifying dusk.

And then Mr. Blacklock moves his head once.

"I will decide," he says bluntly, "how much you shall be paid after one week of working." I am amazed. He holds the door open a little wider and stands back to let me pass.

Dead Fire

8

*T*here is a strange smell inside the house. The place becomes dingy as Mr. Blacklock closes the door on the noise of the street and goes ahead of me along the corridor. He has broad shoulders that tilt slightly to one side, as if carrying a weight. Another door is standing ajar, on our left, and the smell seems stronger as we pass: a disturbing odor of many notes.

"You will bring me items I need from traders and shopkeepers," Mr. Blacklock says, coughing heavily. "You will prepare the equipment and observe closely what I do, in order to be of use to me." There is something about the way he says the words that makes me think that perhaps he is from another country, but it is hard to be sure. I can make out that the corridor is dark with paneling and tapestries. It is an old house, perhaps as old as the manor house at Steyning. We go into a kitchen, which is dirty and cluttered.

As I stand beside him, he seems even bigger than before. His tallness is stark, like a tree in winter.

"Sit down," he says, jerking a finger at a chair, and as I do so a sleepy cluster of flies rises from a pot upon the table. An oil lamp casts a circle of light upon the pages of a large book lying open. A low, unkept fire is dying in the grate. Along one wall there is a high dresser with plates and pots upon its shelves. I blink in the lamplight and look about.

"I cook but plainly, sir," I say in haste on seeing the hob grate, which is huge and complicated. "I can stew a good wet soup and make pies, and cook an egg in the wood ash of the hearth." I look doubtfully at the reddish cinders as I say this, but continue. "I can churn butter, and press and salt it; I can bake a tasty loaf of quality, and prepare a pot of porridge as you like." But Mr. Blacklock interrupts me with a raised, impatient hand. The burn is an open wound on his face. I see it glisten in the light, and his shadow is huge on the wall behind him.

"Well, that is something, but we do not need a list of virtues at the moment! I cannot abide chatter," he stresses curtly. "I do not need the debris of your mind to furnish mine. Excessive vocal activity within the throat causes the stomach to bloat with air and nonsense. And hearing such causes unnecessary discomfort in the ear of the listener." He leans toward me and stabs at the air between us with a blackened finger. "Clarity! Accuracy! Think of your words as a key to fit into the lock of your meaning. Cast them with precision. That key should then be swift and perfect in achieving its aim: well-shaped talk at its best is a release from the indefinite. It is explanation. Preparation. Nothing more." His gaze is severe.

I look at him confusedly.

"Sir," I say, and then squeeze my mouth shut. I dare not even lick my lips in nervousness. His requirement, I understand, is for the presence of a quiet character that does not fluster. Inside myself I vow I could be that.

He picks up a tub by the hob and shakes out pieces of black coal onto the embers, and the fire begins to hiss. I have seen coal before, but never burnt or cooked upon it. Perhaps it is coal that makes the atmosphere smell so strangely bitter. I glance at the book upon the table. I can see dark pictures and words stretching over the yellow pages, but even when I frown with concentration the swarming letters make no sense at all.

"Italian," he says, suddenly towering above me, and presses at the page. His hands are lithe and knuckly, with long spreading fingers, though with a jolt I see that on the right hand he has only a damaged stump where the forefinger should be. Without warning he reads aloud, fiercely, ". . . this power alone makes metals grow and revives half-dead bodies. Half dead!" He snorts. "Perhaps."

I look up and his black eyes are fixed on me. He has an intent, seeking kind of look that is hard to hide from.

"What is your name?" he asks abruptly.

"Agnes, sir, Agnes Trussel."

"They are all making claims, Agnes Trussel. The world is awash with claims for knowledge." He smiles grimly. "Knowledge is like time: it forges a way forward but must look back over its shoulder to remember where it has come from. The only certain way to forge new understanding is to carry out investigations for oneself." I jump as he snaps the book shut.

"Where have you come from, Agnes Trussel?"

I hesitate before I answer. "Sussex, sir," I say. The room has a chill to it despite the fire, and I am trying to conceal from him that I am shivering. I can barely hear, I am so faint and tired now.

"And what are your *circumstances*?" he asks, sharply.

I think rapidly of what to say. A hot piece of coal falls with a tick through the grate onto the stone flags. It glows fiery red and then cools and fades.

"I have no family," I reply. "They . . . died in a fire, sir, just a few months ago." It is the truth indeed that they are lost to me now, I think, as though this makes my lying any better than it is.

There is a silence.

"Do you need a bite or drink?" Mr. Blacklock asks.

"I am as parched as tinder, sir," I say. He nods and stands up. Our interview is over. Somewhere in the house a clock chimes into the stillness. I don't add that my clothes are wet and an ache in my head is mingling with the ache in my heart, making a sickness.

Mr. Blacklock takes the book under his arm. "I will call for housemaid Mary—Mary Spurren," he says. "Good night."

"Good night, sir," I say.

He leaves the room, and I hear him talking in a low voice to someone outside in the hallway. Then the door opens again and Mary Spurren enters the kitchen. Her gait suggests a girl possessing some ill-humor: drooping shoulders over a long, bony figure bent into a shape resembling a kind of pothook. Clearly she is not pleased to be roused, and mutters to herself while she cuts at something in the meat safe and slaps a slice of cold boiled beef onto a plate for me. She looks suspiciously at the floor by my feet while I try to eat as she waits to clear the table. Her neck is drawn out and hangs forward, as though the weight of her head were too much to carry. Her mouth is large, and makes a tutting noise from time to time. The meat she has served has an unpleasant flavor, but I am more than glad of the ale, which helps a small warmth grow back into the pit of my stomach. My ears buzz with strangeness and traveling. Then she takes a new candle out of a box and lights it for me with a spill of wood at the hob.

"Keep it upright as you walk upstairs and blow it out as soon as you're in bed; it'll need to last all week and there won't be another." Her mouth is a ridge of disapproval.

Out in the hallway she points up to where I am to sleep and then she leaves me, her disappearing back making a thin shadow briefly before she turns the corner. I carry my juddering ball of candlelight and my damp bundle into the chamber, and the latch flicks shut behind me.

I hold the candlestick high to see about the room. There is no bolt on the back of the door. The room is full of the kind of still, slow cold that builds when no one has been in it for a long time, and has a sharp odor of mice. When I open the cupboard under the washstand I see a pile of chewed cloth and droppings. The bed looms solitary in the corner; it must have been made up months ago, and the sheet and blanket are damp and dusty under my fingertips. There is a hole where moths or mice have nibbled away at the wool. The bed creaks as I sit on it heavily to remove my wet boots.

I take off my outer garments and my stays, and spread out the rest of my belongings over the furniture in the hope they will dry in the night, but it is shivery cold in here. Perhaps tomorrow I will hang them in front of the grate downstairs. I nearly cry when I find that my second petticoat is quite dry, having sat at the bottom of my bundle under the other things, and I press my face into it to breathe in the smell of home.

"*No*," I whisper aloud, and put it aside.

I will not think of home.

There is a plain chair by the bed. I am in a strange house with strangers; I could move the chair before the door to stop intruders coming in while I am sleeping, but what use would it serve? It is flimsy and light. Instead, I climb into the bed half-clothed and lie uneasily.

The journey spins around in my head like a jolting sickness still, as though it were not quite over yet, as though my spirit were still out there traveling along the turnpike, straining to catch up with me. How disappointed the lovely Lettice Talbot will be to find my absence at the lodging house, and what a shame it is to lose a special friend so soon. What would she think of me for walking into any stranger's house upon the street, and going to sleep there when I had promised to be careful? At the earliest prospect I must go to look for Lettice Talbot. I shall seek her out and tell her where I am.

What is this place?

The flame of the candle bends and flickers in the draft. Outside, the rain is drumming at the windowpane. The curtain shifts.

There is a noise above me, and some powdery dust falls down from a crack in the ceiling and onto the bedcover. I pull up the cover and squeeze my eyes tight shut. I pray that my mother won't work herself into an illness without me, now I have left her, and that Lil is not fretting and crying the night away. I can't pray, though, that the trouble I hold inside me now will dissolve away and leave me be. I can't even think of that. I won't. And I can't help that tears come out and run down the sides of my face into my ears. The coins are a lump in my underskirts as I turn in the bed to blow out the flame.

Later I dream that John Glincy is pushing gold into my mouth with his dirty fingers, and I am choking on it: choking on the waste it is to swallow Mrs. Mellin's coins.

9

I go down at first light and the kitchen is empty, though the coals in the hob grate are smoking briskly. Through a small window at the back of the house I can see the rain streaming over roofs, pouring and splashing into the yard. The glass of the panes is thick and greenish, like ice lifted from ponds in winter, but I can make out weeds growing through cracks in the brick paving, and a spindly tree that might be a linden. The thick glass makes these things far off and crooked. High up, a bird stands hunched and small by a cluster of chimney pots. How sick I feel. I look down at my familiar hands in these strange surroundings. The curious smell pervades the house; it is everywhere. I see that my fingertips are blackened with grimy circles from touching the sill; the dirt is an odd, gritty layer on the furniture, the banisters, the cups and plates.

Mary Spurren comes into the kitchen with a dustpan and broom.

"Late for breakfast, you are, but you can take small beer from there." She points and clatters. "I'd get on. Mr. Blacklock will be shortly in to fetch you. There is a loaf. Mrs. Blight is new here and is gone to make her face known about with shops and traders. I've told her Saul Pinnington's for beef and mutton. Spicer's always for soap and grocer goods. She said she'd see the worth and value before she'd buy a thing." Her voice is clogged and hard to understand, as though she is not used to speaking much.

"What kind of business is it here that Mr. Blacklock has?" I ask her timidly, pouring from the jug.

"Fireworks, he makes," she says.

"Fireworks!" I am astonished. "He *makes* them?"

She rubs her nose on her sleeve. "That's what I said. All kinds of pyrotechnicals. Exotic fires. Godless explosions for the summer is what I calls them. For the pleasure gardens, and assemblies for the quality. What I think about it I don't know, but it makes dust and as long as there is dust there is a place for me. Even burning money makes ash, and what is ash but dust?" She shuts her large mouth tight and glances at me doubtfully as if I might disagree.

So fireworks are made by hand, in the same way as hurdles are, or pipes or horseshoes; they are not freakish works of nature nor of witch-craft, as I'd thought when I was little. I have read of fireworks in the yellowing, thumbed newspapers that pass about the village after the rector has read them through himself. And my brother Ab saw some himself, once, as he was passing Wiston House.

"I have heard how they are like fizzing, white blossoms, a cold kind of devil's fire," I say eagerly. She shrugs.

"Never seen 'em. Close-up, properly. Nigh on three shilling it is to get into most gardens for the night. Better drains there are to pour your wages down, such as they are."

"So Blacklock is a chemist then, or alchemist?" I press.

"Just a maker of fireworks. Pyrotechnist. Never heard of such a thing before I got here." She looks at the kitchen floor. "Dirtiest place I'd ever seen." She puts a cloth in a bucket and swills it about.

"And now there's Mrs. Blight to take the load off, not to mention Mrs. Nott to do the laundry, when she turns up, that is." She scowls, as if a thought had come to her. "Why are you here?"

"I don't know," I begin to say, and Mary Spurren makes a noise of disapproval through her teeth and scrubs hard at the table. Her cuffs are rolled up, showing how bony and red her wrists are. She scratches a lot, though whether from nervous habit or because her lice are very bad I cannot say, and her round face has no color to it at all, like a plant that has been sprouting accidentally inside a cupboard for a long time.

The coals splutter. By the hot grate, the clothes from my bundle steam damply on the rack.

"I'll tell you what," she croaks under her breath, cracking the back of her brush against the step to loosen the dirt from the bristles. "He has a temper that you may not like. He's inconstant in his habits. He can go this way or that way in his needs and wants." She looks defensively at me, her mouth open a crack.

"Have you been here for quite some time?" I ask, swallowing the beer. She nods her big head.

"I've been constant here, four years in all," she says. "I goes along with it. When I were ten years old my mother said, 'There is a steadiness to you, young lady.' I stuck to that—I'm here for good." She laughs with a hoarse, difficult wheezing sound that is alarming and I prefer it when she stops. Her mouth is so wide when she laughs it seems as though her head were split in half. Her tongue is pale, like a sheep's.

Mr. Blacklock summons me from the hall.

"Come!" he barks, going ahead of me down the corridor. He unlocks a door.

"The workshop runs perpendicular to the lie of the house," he says. "This in case of fire means the workshop is as disconnected from the house as it could be in this situation. I do not need to stress the perils of a blaze beyond control. This you know." The door is thick and swings open heavily. "Fire has no conscience, none at all."

Behind my back I cross my fingers, and don't say a thing.

The darkness shrinks away as he creaks the shutters open, one by one, and soon gray morning light shows me a long high room with a sloping ceiling hung with a variety of strange tools and loops of threads. Faintly, I can hear rain drumming on the roof. The smell of substances I do not know is so strong in here that something flickers in my head. The windows facing the yard cast a fair quantity of daylight onto two broad workbenches ranged with further tools and apparatus; implements that Mr. Blacklock proceeds to identify at random, straightening articles and boxes on the benches as he strides about.

"The beamscales," he says. "The spigot. The file. The pestle. The filling-box. The burette for liquors." He points. "Alembic, pelican, condenser, retort, roller, funnel, nipping-engine, pipkin, nipperkin."

"A nipperkin?" I ask.

"A measure for liquor a half pint or less. I am hoping that your mind is as quick and firm as your fingers claim to be," he says. "I do not care to have to say the same thing twice."

He goes to the side of the workshop, his legs moving stiffly as if talking makes him uncomfortable. The shelves are ranged with quantities of bottles and canisters of differing heights and thicknesses: a disorder of great glass tubs that bend each shelf with weight, a mass of dusty jars as big as my fist, vessels as squat as the tea caddy at Mrs. Porter's, and tiny corked phials.

He reads some labels out, his back to me.

"Sulfur, antimony, orpiment, charcoal, ambergris, oil of turpentine." His voice is dark and rough with coughing. "Brassdust, steel filings, niter. Gum resin, pitch." He reaches the end of the first shelf and then turns sharply to make sure that I am paying attention.

"I can read, sir," I say, trying to be helpful. The jars are filthy, and many of the labels are faded and hard to read in the gloomy light, but I say some aloud to show him—*cadmia, red bole, camphor, crocus of Mars.*

"The words come slowly, sir, but once learnt, I find I do not easily forget them. Though I should be ashamed to say I do not write," I add. He nods, and seems strangely satisfied with this. He stares at me intently for a moment. His eyes are unblinking, and I see there is a yellow ring about the darkness of his pupils, like a hawk's. I look away quickly, at the shelf.

"What is crocus of Mars, sir?"

"Powdered calx, a reddish solid," he says.

"There are so many jars," I breathe, gazing at them. It is clear from the grime and the cobwebs that many have sat untouched for quite some time, their waxy seals unbroken, as if the contents had no purpose here. "But you don't use them all," I add.

"What?" he says abruptly.

"Unopened, sir. What are they for?"

"Six years ago I had objectives of a different kind," he says shortly.

"And what did you use them for?" I ask, but he seems not to hear. "A waste!" he mutters angrily, as if to himself, and I am sorry that I mentioned it.

"Until this day I have had *no* females in my workshop. They bring friction and trouble. Their emotions are liable to set off sparks. They have a chemistry that goes against the smoothness of my practice." He clears his throat. "My attendant must be tranquil and nonplussed by nothing, at all times."

I grasp at that. *Attendant to Mr. Blacklock, pyrotechnist.* I have a flush of excitement at such a thing, and narrow my eyes to hide from him the sudden leap I feel inside.

"The atmosphere must be as still as pond water in here," he says, and it is a good thing he cannot see inside my head.

"No flighty, sudden movements. It has been a male domain. But still, most rules are there to be unmade." He coughs again, into his fist. "Tie up your hair and make a habit of keeping your clothes tight about you." He hands me a leather apron. "Fasten this, always at the back. No trimmings. No lacy bits or ribbons. I want no tools from this bench to be mixed with tools from the bench over there. Only ram with wood, never copper."

Clearly these are the rules that are not to be unmade, and I imagine with good reason. The very air itself in here could probably explode without a moment's notice. I vow never to generate a spark by so much as feeling strongly. Then I undo this hasty thought; vows themselves being dangerous things.

He is beginning to cast about for things to say when I see a movement in the darkness at the back of the workshop. A scrawny, ill-clad boy with dark or dirty skin sidles almost noiselessly out of the shadows and comes to stare at me. His eyes are huge in his head.

"Joe Thomazin sweeps and keeps a presence here when I am absent," Mr. Blacklock says. "He does not speak, or rather, he has not been known to. Not quite an apprentice yet, but perhaps one day."

He is about the same height as William, though as thin as a deer.

Joe Thomazin does not smile back at me. There is a look about him that makes me think so far his life has not been filled with warmth. It is not a slowness or a hunger that I see there, more a stiffness, a halt in what he gives away, although his great dark eyes are wide open, getting the size of me, so that in the end it is I who drop my gaze and he edges back to the end of the workshop and begins to ready the stove for lighting.

"You will commence today by oiling tools and replacing them precisely where you found them and, when you are done with that, by observing what I do," Mr. Blacklock says. "I am behind in preparation of Mr. Torré's urgent order for his display at Marylebone, which should comprise four hundred rockets, Roman candles and maroons, if I have so much in stock, and I expect a silence, now, to work in."

And he turns away and begins to consult a piece of paper.

I do not like to ask another thing, so I embark upon a long search for oil and rags. It is a good thing that I know what to do, having watched my father oiling his coppice tools every winter that I can remember.

It is quiet and still in the workshop. I find a sticky, dirty bottle of linseed oil among the chemicals, and take it down. Mr. Blacklock counts out package after package into crates spread out upon the floor, crossing off the items on a list. I notice he uses his left hand more readily than his right. *Devil's fist*, my mother would have said. His fingers make black prints on everything.

The woody smell of linseed fills my head as I rub at the metal tools and wonder what their purpose is. Some I can guess, like the steel shears that hang beside the cabinet stacked inside with paper. Others are evil-looking riddles, more like instruments of torture might be.

Outside in the yard the rain falls ceaselessly all morning.

Mrs. Blight is there in the kitchen when we dine at twelve. Her large brimming form is bound together capably with enormous stays, like a roll of pork tied up for roasting. She bustles about, too busy to notice me.

"I am aggrieved I cannot cook a decent meal until all this shocking mess is quite in hand, Mr. Blacklock, sir," she declares, picking up a fork and wiping it pointedly on a corner of her apron before she sits down to eat. Her hands are very large and fleshy. "Took half the morning just to find my way about the place. No order at all, sir, not yet."

"Not enough pepper, Mrs. Blight," Mr. Blacklock grunts, chewing the meat.

"I cannot abide food hot in that way, Mr. Blacklock," she says breezily, as though there was nothing to be done about it. Mary Spurren glowers from the table's end.

Mrs. Blight does not speak to me until Mr. Blacklock goes into his study to drink the coffee that Mary Spurren takes to him.

"Ship-smart we wants it here, my girl," she says, breathing noisily as she watches me putting plates on the stack of dirty crockery beside the wooden bowl for washing. She smells of drink.

"If I asks you to get down on your whirlbones and scrub and this and that, I shall expect as such. Standards—that's my indication all is well within the body of a house, and there's a sight to be done here, I must say, before we've reached that particular state of bliss." And then she pushes her sleeves over her broad white forearms, takes up a sack of potatoes propped at the back door by the barrow boy, and bears it to the kitchen table as if it were no weight at all.

"And by the by," she adds, "there's one other thing I'll not abide, and that is thievery. D'you hear?"

"Of course," I say meekly.

It rains all afternoon. In the workshop, while I oil the tools, I cast my eye occasionally, as I was instructed, to see what Mr. Blacklock does. His long, tough back is bent over his work in silence. I have never seen a man from eastern Europe, but I imagine he might look like that; tall and lean, like a hunter. I feel safer when he is not looking at me. His gaze is sharp and goes on for too long.

It is cold inside the workshop, and increases in coldness as the evening draws near. The dirty boy Joe Thomazin brings a lighted lamp into the gloom. Mr. Blacklock does not seem to feel the draft at all, but when I rub my fingers together to try to warm the stiffness out of them, he glances up at me.

"You may go to the stove to warm yourself from time to time but you must not wear your apron by the fire lest it harbor combustive matter of some kind, and you must brush your sleeves of chemicals. Never shake a substance from yourself with overbriskness. Entire establishments have been lost in blasts caused by such small errors."

As I go by he appears to think of something and bends abruptly down. "Let me see the sole of your boot!" he barks. Obediently I raise my foot and show him in the yellow lamplight. I am ashamed of the holes and patching there. "Too many tacks!" he says to my surprise, so that I do not drop my foot immediately but instead look baffled at the nailheads flashing in the pitted leather. They were Ann's boots before they were my own and have been mended so many times over that the original fabric of the boot is largely gone.

He turns back to his bench. "However, you cannot work in stockings so you must continue as you are until you can afford to purchase another pair. The shoemaker at Aldersgate will tack them very deeply so that they do not strike a spark. It is not a hazard here upon the boards, but in the outhouse the floor is brick." He gives a brief dry cough. "Therefore, until that day arrives, you will step cautiously. In this business one must remind oneself that it is not *if* an accident will happen but *when*. Never forget that."

I nod gravely.

Inside my head I picture smoky bursts of fire as harsh as gunshot caused by something that I did unknowingly, and wonder how it was that Mr. Blacklock came to maim his hand and have the purple mark of a burn across his face. It is not a disfiguring mark, but it looks painful and provokes unease to look at it. Holding my hands over the heat of the stove, I think how the day I can put on a pair of new-made boots unworn by any but me will be a day worth waiting for, if it should ever happen. Joe Thomazin, his scrawny elbows showing through his coat, stares at me blankly until I move away. I keep my footsteps mild back to my bench and watch Mr. Blacklock binding what seem to be empty tubes together into blocks until the church clock somewhere close strikes six, when we are done for the day.

"If you have silk," he finishes while fastening the thick door on our way out, "you cannot wear it; it, too, can create sparks." There is no trace of humor in his voice; his face is alarming in the lamplight when he catches my eye.

"Remember that," he says again. "In here there will be no silk and no bare candles."

I do not laugh aloud about this as we go down the corridor to take our supper of cold beef and pudding in the kitchen, but smile later to myself in my dark cold bedchamber, taking off my outer clothes before I climb into bed. I do not think that I have so much as touched a scrap of silk in all my life. The candle gutters as I look about. My thick useful petticoat hangs dry from the hook at the back of the door. My other belongings look small in the chest at the foot of the bed: my Bible, with a blade of grass between the pages of St. John to keep my place, my good dress that was my sister's, my small linen.

I am so tired that I forget to pray. On the brink of sleep I have a sudden thought of Lettice Talbot going away from me down the street, holding the hem of her fine tabby silk gown up high above the dirty pavement; but then I do not dream at all that night.

*O*n the second day there is no rain. A patch of cold sun falls through the high casement beside the kitchen fireplace. Mary Spurren does not speak at all at breakfast, which is bitter tea and rolls. Mrs. Blight bemoans the lack of moral spine among the young in general, spreading the salty market butter abundantly and talking as she chews. Even at this hour she smells of liquor. This morning when I came into the kitchen, I spied her sipping at her hip flask, which she stoppered and put away quickly enough when she saw that I was standing there.

"Indulging in cuckoldry," she is saying, midway through a tale of shame and recompense. "Like some brindled hog in heat."

Mr. Blacklock puts down his bread half-eaten, abruptly pushes back his chair and leaves the room.

"You must understand the purpose of good grinding and consistency," Mr. Blacklock says, as I follow him into the workshop. He pulls out two small barrels, each tightly capped with leather.

"Mealpowder, and another fine grade of gunpowder that we purchase from the powder merchants. Coarser black powders are of little use to us, except sometimes for maroons and loud reports. But taking scoops of powder ready from the tub will teach you nothing of its composition. Grinding is dangerous, but necessary if you are to learn."

He looks up and pins me with his black gaze as if giving me due warning, then shows me in the light to take up a pinch and rub it in my palm.

"Niter, charcoal, sulfur," Mr. Blacklock says. The meal is a powdered substance not quite as black as soot, like a heavy dark flour. The gunpowder is grayer and gritty, like coarse seeds against my skin. I sniff at it cautiously.

It smells of eggs and earth and metals, and gives me a curious agitation in the pit of my stomach that is not unpleasant. "What does it do?" I ask.

Mr. Blacklock takes a measure of powder and tips it into a small open dish. He motions me out of the back door into the yard, where he puts the dish upon the low brick wall and lays a length of grayish cord so that its end within the dish is touching powder and the other end is hanging free. He goes inside. Up on the roof of the house a flock of starlings are whooping and cackling in a liquid crowd, flexing their speckled, oily heads in unison as they whistle in the sun.

Mr. Blacklock brings out a lighted taper from the stove.

"Stand back!" he barks, and touches the taper to the cord's end. In an instant the flame sizzles up the cord to the dish and an astounding crack shakes the world about us. A cloud of thick bluish smoke has shot upward, and drifts sideways over the yard. I press my hands to my ringing ears. My heart is beating fast. I cannot be sure if it was noise I heard or light exploding in a way that made it seem like sound was made. The smell of the smoke is very strong.

"That is what gunpowder does," Mr. Blacklock says dryly. "It is a powerful beast. Treat it with respect and you will find there is much you can achieve." His dark face is alive, like that of a man who has been walking briskly uphill. "In due course you will make up coils of quick match and learn to cut and paste the cases. You will charge rockets and gerbes and tourbillions until you could do it in your sleep as easily as taking breath. But you must begin with basic comprehension of the materials you work with. Nothing good was learnt too swiftly. Knowledge should be a purposeful accumulance of observed experience, applied and tested to the full."

"It is like a storm," I say, watching the smoke rising to the gutter and dispersing above the roof where the starlings took flight. "All concentrated to a moment."

It is calm now in the yard. But one strike of lightning is never enough in a storm to clear the air of thickness at the base of the Downs. I long to see the blast again but would not dare to ask.

The back door from the scullery opens a crack.

"Exceeding disquiet, Mr. Blacklock!" Mrs. Blight shouts out indignantly, shaking dirt from a cloth, and the door closes again, but Mr. Blacklock makes no sign of having heard.

I like the bench. I like measuring the chemicals in the scales, with tiny weights of an ounce or less. I have learnt that one grain troy has the same weight as a single grain of wheat taken from the mid part of the ear at its moment of ripeness.

I like the feel of the great pestle crushing wettened chemicals inside the smooth deep hollow of the mortar. As it can while working the loom at home, my mind is free to gather up thoughts and fancies, and roll them about without disturbance. I think how the wheat harvest was not so good this year, yet not as poor as the year of the drought, when the patchy crops could not reach full height and the ears were dry and empty on the stalk. I think how my uncle can stand in the field and know by the feel of the grain in his mouth if it is ready to cut.

"What are you doing, Uncle?" William asked when he first saw him stood there chewing with such concentration upon his face.

"I squeezes the grain between my teeth," I remember him saying, after a pause while his jaw worked up and down, looking into the blue distance toward Steyning as he spoke. "And with my tongue I finds the necessary bit of it, and I chews it up cautious." The air was hazy with warmth and dust.

"What for, Uncle?" William asked, picking a grain carefully from the ear with his little fingers.

"I considers it," my uncle said. "And knows when it is done."

"But what do you tell?" William asked, earnestly chewing. "Gummy bits and hard bits. It's not tasty."

"Try grains from time to time each August that comes; in a ten-year you'll have it," my uncle said, walking away, his breeches all pale with chalk from the dry ground. I remember William's little head standing above the wheat on the edge of Mr. Fitton's field.

"But is it ready, this wheat, then?" he shouted after him. "Is it done?"

"It's done," we heard my uncle say, and he went into the barn.

William looked at the field, still tasting it. The swallows twittered and skimmed for flies across its surface as though it were a yellow pond. "Next year is a long way," he said plaintively to me later, when we were home again and boiling a broth before my father got back.

"It is not so far," I reassured him, stirring the pot. "Time is always less time coming than you would expect." And how true that is. Swiftly life changes and moves along.

Grinding composition is arduous work at first; I find it difficult to get the texture as it should be.

"Finer, it must be finer," Mr. Blacklock says sternly, looking into the mortar's cavity to see what I have done. "I cannot work with a finished mixture less fine than the soft particles of flour: between that and pounded sugar. It must be mixed more intimately, more evenly."

"But it is wet," I say. "How can I tell what fineness I have reached?"

"Experience will teach you when your pounding is enough," he says.

He puts more into the bowl of the mortar with a little water from the flask, and grinds evenly for many minutes. The sound is small and regular as his arm works. I would like to please him, I am thinking as I watch his sleeve. I would like to take pride in reaching an evenness of texture every time.

"You may find it helpful to imagine that the purpose of your action is not to break these fragments up," he says as he works, "but to conjoin all three substances more forcefully yet intimately together."

"I should think of their separate properties pressing together?" I ask.

"Not just pressing," he replies, "but becoming intrinsically combined."

"I see," I say. "Like a marriage of three."

Mr. Blacklock seems to flinch. He is a striking man for his age. Why does he have no wife?

Later he shows me how to wash out receptacles once he has finished with them. I watch him stroking the dirt away with the flat of his big hands, the warm water scooped up in his palms. Then he takes me into the yard, and shakes a light dusting of mixture onto a board.

He cups a flame with his large hand against the air as though it were a living creature, touches the edge of the mixture with it and stands away as the lick of flame passes smoothly across the board. I feel a small clutch of pleasure as it moves.

"That is a clean and satisfying burn," Mr. Blacklock confirms. "An even powder. There should be no agitation in its progress. Every pounding should bear that result. If you are unsure, test your mixtures in this way until you know by sight and by the feel of the ingredients under your pestle. Even the sound made by the particles as you grind will become familiar to you." He puts down the tools and leaves me to practice out in the yard.

"This could take days," I call anxiously, calculating drying time. Mr. Blacklock turns and looks at me.

"It will," he concurs. "A lifetime could be spent in less productive occupation." He coughs. "A rocket that is badly mixed will smoke and show a poor quality of fire. We strive for better. When engineers order works from Blacklock's they know their quality is unsurpassed in London."

The winter sun shines down upon the bricks. Inside the house I can hear Mary Spurren humming tunelessly as she washes something at the sink. A dog barks.

And I think of how there is something else I have not much dwelt upon these last few days. The thing inside me that I cannot name has begun to flutter and nibble at me like a shoal of fishes: tiny fishes in my belly, like minnows or young sticklebacks. It pulls me up short when it occurs, it is so occasional and so surprising, and then there is nothing for hours and hours. For three nights now I have found myself holding my breath and waiting for these moments with certainty and wonder, much as one waits for a shooting star to fall from a dark sky prickling with light. I am afraid to like it, but it is so briefly gentle, so wondrous, it is hard to reconcile the anger brewing in me with the cause itself. I am afraid instead that I am growing soft to it. Growing soft will make a ruined woman of me.

On the seventh day Mr. Blacklock makes no mention of my leaving, so I suppose I have employment. He hands me four shillings for one week's work. When his back is turned I count the shillings out again with some relief, and later I hide them under the washstand in my chamber. Mary Spurren will not go in there; she says she cannot stand mice. Perhaps I will find a way to send what I can save to my family, my mind running ahead to the end of the winter months when provisions are low. And then I remember why I am here; and that it will not last.

I must find Lettice Talbot.

The reasonable place to begin my search would be where I saw her last. She is the only person who can help me when the inevitable happens and I can no longer stay at Blacklock's. She said there would be work, that she is my friend.

And so one day when I find that I have woken very early, before the morning has fully shaken off the darkness, I pull back the bolts, slip out into the chilly gloom and walk as best I can remember back to the Cross Keys Inn to look for Lettice Talbot. I have to ask the way from time to time, but it is not so far. The streets are humming with the footsteps of laborers and shopkeepers going about their business, and there are few carriages. The church on the corner of Wood Street has not yet struck eight o'clock, but I try to relay a message for Lettice Talbot to a dirty child I find outside in the shadows of the inn's yard, rinsing bottles and stacking them to dry over the drain. The child's hands are red with cold. She looks blankly at me, then runs inside an outhouse, returning presently with a man who comes out wiping his hands on a piece of cloth. He does not seem to know who Lettice Talbot is, so I describe her curling brown hair and patterned shawl and leather case as best I can remember. He shakes his head and shrugs.

"What makes you suppose her to be here, wench?" he says, rudely. His voice is hoarse, and a smell of strong drink comes away from him. "There is a quantity of travelers pass through the Cross Keys any day you care to name." He jabs his thumb at the busy yard as though I were slow-witted.

"But this is all I know of her," I say, at a loss to describe her any further. Then I touch my neck above my collar.

"She has a gem here; not a diamond," I say, and something like a grin goes over the man's face, and he bends and says something that I cannot hear to the child, who giggles and runs away unsteadily into the street. Then he goes inside. Did he mean me to wait while the child went to find her? I sit on the mounting block in the freezing, bustling yard and pull my cloak about me; I wait until I am almost fainting with the cold, and still there is no sign of the child. Nobody speaks to me, and St. Dunstan's clock strikes nine before I realize that she will not come. I am late for work now.

As I pass out of the yard, I look into the stables. It is rank and musty in there. I hear a whinny and the ring and clip of hooves. A boy is grooming a great coach horse, reaching up to pull his brush over the bulk of its flank. And as he glances up and meets my eye I see it is the coachman's boy who took my guinea here before, and to my amazement he seems to recognize my face, and halts his brushing to shout for someone I cannot see inside the stable.

"Mr. Haines! Mr. Haines!" he calls, and shakes his hand out urgently as if to try to stop me.

In alarm I turn and hasten from the yard and then do not stop running down the street till I can go no farther. The air is so sharp that my quick breathing gives me a pain in my side. I look about, and thank God that no one has followed.

On my way back to the house I have a sense that I am watched, but when I look up I see only the fanned-out shape of a red kite hovering high in the sky above the streets, and I can almost feel its shadow crossing over me. There are so many eyes in the city.

I have missed breakfast, and how hungry I am, but there is no time for it now. As Mrs. Blight is not looking, I run my finger around inside the porridge pot and lick it clean.

"Lateness is an irritation I do not tolerate," Mr. Blacklock says coldly, without turning around, when I try to slip into the workshop unnoticed. "You will not appear so tardily tomorrow, nor the next day, nor indeed any day henceforth in my employ."

"I will not, sir," I say. My heart pounds with awkwardness. I try to explain. "I was looking for . . ." Mr. Blacklock raises his hand.

"Spare me," he snaps.

At the bench my ears strain for the sound of knocking at the door.

Why has nobody come looking for me?

Perhaps they have. My brother Ab? John Glincy? Or the headborough of the parish of Washington, having wind of the theft of Mrs. Mellin's coins? I must be alert to any danger of discovery. But I fear I shall not know it when it comes.

Mrs. Blight is a talker. She fills the kitchen with noise as she works. Her teeth must be loose from the acid of her stream of words; it is a wonder that they do not fall out more readily. It is a relief when she nods off beside the fire in the early part of the afternoon. Her mouth drops open and I can almost hear her teeth rattling as she snores. She is quite fat, but like dough that has been proving for too long and sunk back into itself. Her chin hangs from her jawbone and has a life separate from the remainder of her face.

While we clear the plates, I ask Mary Spurren if she knows why Mr. Blacklock isn't married.

She gives a slow blink.

"Mr. Blacklock had a wife four years ago." She doesn't look up from the sink. "She died."

"She died!" I say.

"He had the doctors to her."

"What did she have?"

Mary Spurren shakes her big head slowly. "There was blood, so much blood. I rinsed it away down the drain out there." She nods into the yard. "At the end he was holding her up over the sheets and crying so loud it made your toes curl to hear it. Her arms was loose and hung out over the bed. I left the room until he stopped." She sniffs and wipes her nose across her cuff. "When my mother died we just covered her up until the body could be buried." A coal spits in the fire. "My father went to work the same as usual and then after a year or two had passed he married Alice Ebbs, who was next door a widow."

I can't help wondering whether they have discovered Mrs. Mellin's body yet, sitting all cold in front of a cold grate. Perhaps she has flopped forward onto the floor. I swallow.

"I'm sorry that your mother died," I say. Mary Spurren doesn't reply; she swills the water over a pot and turns it upside down to drain. There is a silence, and then Mrs. Blight's chair gives a little creak. When I glance at the shape of her beside the hob I see that her breathing is shallow and too quick for someone sleeping. Her eyes are open a slit and watching our movements around the kitchen. I must be careful about what I say in front of her. She is like a lizard, a fat cold lizard wanting gossip and particulars to feed on. I am glad to go back to the workshop when we are done, away from her nosiness.

"Completed fireworks are kept in the safe," Mr. Blacklock says as I go in. "Come!" he barks, and I follow him out across the yard to a low brick building behind the spindly linden tree. Mr. Blacklock opens the door with a large key. It is gloomy inside. "Step carefully," he warns.

"The safe is lined with lead," Mr. Blacklock says, and unlocks a huge cabinet as tall as myself. The door is like a well-oiled jaw dropping wide. At first I do not understand what I am peering at. It is as ordered as a bee's nest: lined with rows and rows of square compartments like a honeycomb and filled with packets. He opens another safe with the same great key.

"Rockets," Mr. Blacklock says. It is bristling with sticks.

"A bouquet can be as much as six hundred rockets in a display, or even more for royalty or particular occasions. In Green Park three years ago, the Ruggieris' pyrotechnic show to celebrate the peace sent up flights amounting to a figure greater than ten thousand rockets." I am amazed, although I do not fully understand what it is a rocket does.

"In favorable conditions, a six-pound rocket will reach its apex at two hundred feet," Mr. Blacklock says.

"Does it burn as it goes?" I ask, trying to picture it.

"A sudden upward rush of sparks and flame," he says. "Which eases to a coasting to the high point of its flight, then, dependent on the garniture within it, a break of common stars with a report, or tailed stars, or fiery rain, and then a natural fall to earth, as all things fall, sparks fading and winking out: the equilibrium of the propulsion and burn demonstrating a remarkable balance of forces between release and tension." He coughs.

"The gunpowder lies in the third safe. We receive delivery of powder from Soul and Tibbet about twice a month. There is not much; powder should be fresh." He returns to the first safe and reaches for a large, tubular package.

"This is a Roman candle," he says, placing it upon my palm. "A Roman candle does not leave the ground when fired, but breaks into a plume of sparks and is charged with stars that spit out like vivid balls of fire into the sky."

It is twice as long as my hand.

"See how neat and perfectly it is bound," says Mr. Blacklock. "How every work should be. The innards, too, the garniture, are flawless: precisely measured and evenly packed, whole stars layered with bursting charge and blowing powder and dark fire, which is a fire that burns invisibly to give pause and space within a burning time." I don't say a word, but I nod when he looks at me. The packet is curiously light for such complexity. It is dry and dangerous, like touching the body of a very large dead wasp: a papery crisp cylinder with a sting in its tail.

I look closely at the small printed image in an oval shape placed on the outer paper of the firework, about as large as a florin. The figure of a woman holds a prickling light like a bright thistle up against an inky darkness.

"Who is this?" I ask Mr. Blacklock as he shuts the second safe.

"Barbara is the patron saint of firework makers. It is judicious to acknowledge her." Smoothly he turns the key in the lock.

"Do you go to church on Sundays, sir?" I ask.

"I do not," he replies brusquely. "St. Barbara comes from the printshop by the thousand, to be glued onto each packet with a dab of boiled rabbit skin, sealing it up at the very last."

How many times has she been propelled into the blackness, I wonder, with a tail of sparks behind her before she is burnt up or exploded apart? Perhaps there have been times when she has stayed undamaged, fluttering to earth like a printed petal. Mr. Blacklock motions me to put the firework back. "There is much to do," he says. As we cross the yard to the workshop, a striped cat runs by with a damp rat stuffed into its jaw.

"Tell me," Mr. Blacklock asks suddenly, later that day. "Do you find the smell in here disturbs you?"

I am measuring sulfur into the beamscales as I have been shown. I let weights drop out of my fingers and click into the copper pan until it balances and swings free. Six ounces troy. "I'm not sure, sir," I reply, with hesitation. I try to find the words to say just what I mean.

"It is like that particular smell of boiling a hen's egg in a pot on the fire," I suggest. "No, it is almost like that, but more powerful." I am thinking hard. The sulfur is a dirty, sharp yellow against the polished warmth of the copper and the broken-up lumps are uneven.

I have explained it badly, and he is looking at me as though my answer is not enough.

"The smell in here leaves a dark, backward taste in my mouth," I say.

I don't try to add that the smell sets off ripples on the hairs on my arms, that it makes my mouth into a cavernous place where whole shapes of tastes explode and fade as I breathe in.

I realize that still he is looking at me. Why does he look at me so hard? His eyes seem to burn right through me. What a stupid thing I must have said, and my fingers go hot and big with clumsiness as they tip the sulfur out of the pan and into the mortar. Some of the pieces fall over the rim and onto the bench. He turns back to his work and his face, when I glance at it again, is flat with concentration.

Mrs. Blight comes to the door of the workshop and peers in.

"Mr. Blacklock, sir?" she warbles. "Can I borrow Agnes to run to the shop for me as I needs butter and with Mary being out all afternoon I'm up to my elbows, sir, quite frantic, and I shan't want supper to be late." She refuses to step inside.

Mr. Blacklock scowls. "Be quick then." He jerks his head at me. "But don't make a habit of it, woman."

"Oh, thank you, sir," she simpers.

Spicer's Grocery is just across Mallow Square and around the corner, but the weather is cold and I am glad of my cloak. The shop is busy and crammed with goods.

"Just butter, please," I ask shyly, looking about. Mrs. Spicer is large and neat, with reddish, webbed hands, like a goose.

"Working at Blacklock's, aren't you?" she says, friendly enough, waddling to the slab to cut the butter.

"I am," I say.

"Half a pound?" she asks. I nod.

"Always spot a new face around here, we do," she says, wrapping it up. "See everyone going by and hear all the gossip. No chance for tedium! On account for Mr. Blacklock, and bought by . . . let me see if I can remember . . . Agnes!"

"That's right," I say uneasily, taking the packet. I am surprised that someone knows my name already.

"Eccentric, that man," she says, wanting to chat. "Though talk has it he was an ambitious man four years ago, then when his poor wife died like that, so sudden . . . the spark seemed to go right out of him."

It is true there are many eyes in the city. But as I turn to go, something occurs to me.

"Do you know a girl called Lettice? Lettice Talbot?" I ask, hopefully. "I am looking for her."

Mrs. Spicer frowns. "Lettice Talbot. No, I don't think so, love. Wait a minute. Spicer!" she shouts out suddenly, and a small man appears from a door at the back. "Do we know of any girl called Lettice Talbot?"

Mr. Spicer pushes his spectacles further up his nose and shakes his head. "Not Talbot, no," he replies. "There's the Tallets, up by Cripplegate, but they haven't got daughters."

"I thought not," Mrs. Spicer says. "More than a ten-year we've been here, and know most people roundabouts. Never heard that name, love." She smiles at me and turns to serve another customer.

"Good afternoon," I say politely then, and leave the shop.

At the end of each day I am exhausted. My right arm aches like a heavy load from my shoulder as I spoon the supper into my bowl. Sometimes Mr. Blacklock prefers to take his evening meal after we have brushed the crumbs away and left him by the fireplace. He reads his heavy, leather-covered books, often without turning the pages. Once, as I stood up to leave, he looked up as if startled to see me there. The hallway seemed a lonely space outside as I walked through it to the stairs. Sometimes he stays in his study and we do not see him.

In the night I am often woken from a deep sleep by the sound of his footsteps creaking the tread of the stair outside my room, a weak circle of candlelight stretching under the gap in the door as he passes.

Other noises wake me, too. I hear the church bells about the house, each of their various clamors becoming known to me now.

But I freeze with terror when one night a strange deep bell tolls out above the others as they begin to chime midnight. It is like an omen. *God help us*, I am muttering as I scramble from bed and pull my shawl about me. What can it mean? At home when the church bell tolls unexpectedly at night it can only portend disaster of one kind or other. I rush from my chamber and fly up the crooked attic stairs to rap at Mary Spurren's door.

"What is that bell?" I say, breathless, when she opens the door a crack.

"Bell?" she says stupidly. Mary Spurren rubs her big head. I have woken her up. We strain our ears, but the bell's horrible clang has stopped. Her shift is pale in the spill of moonlight.

"Is it midnight?" she asks.

"It is," I say.

"That would be St. Sepulchre's bell, most probably. We'll likely find out tomorrow who's to swing." Her head breaks into a great yawn.

"It is not a disaster, then?" I say, uncertain of what she means by this, and shivering now.

"Not for us, no," she says grumpily, and pushes the door closed.

I tiptoe down.

As I round the corner I hear the sudden creak of boards. Mr. Blacklock's figure is looming before me in the corridor, and I almost shriek aloud in fright. I blink in the dazzle of the guttering candle that he holds up.

The yellow light is bright in my eyes. He stares at me and does not speak for a moment before he clears his throat, and lets me pass. "Goodnight, sir." My voice comes out in a whisper. I grope for the latch and in the darkness of my chamber I go hot and then cold again with shame. What must he think of me, creeping about in the shadows like that, wearing only my shift and shawl, with my hair all loose and tumbled about my shoulders, in my bare unstockinged feet? I must have looked wild. It was almost as though he had never seen my face before, he stared so fiercely, blackly, at me. I must have startled him.

And then I wake to the early street noise, the clattering carts, a dog barking, St. Alban or St. Mary the Virgin or St. Stephen's striking the hour. The brown blanket is rough on my cheek. The water that I splash on my face from the jug makes me gasp with cold. It comes from the pump in Mallow Square, tinted with the orange of rusted iron, and it tastes of mold and metal. I emerge from this sleep with a longing for home, and my legs ache as though they had been walking for miles, taking me there.

Down in the workshop, I mention the bell to Mr. Blacklock.

"Why did it sound so strange, sir?" I ask. "It was eerie."

"It means there is a hanging; it is intended to strike fear into the hearts of men."

"A hanging," I say, swallowing.

"At Tyburn. You can go if you are inclined to do so. I have no reason to stop you."

"Go?" I say, puzzled. I cannot see his face.

"To the hanging. It is a spectacle, there to be seen."

Joe Thomazin is at my side. Though he could know nothing of the coins, he reaches out and touches the stitched patch on the outside of my skirts where the red thread shows through, and looks up at me in query.

His earnest look is so like William's that I feel a sudden rush of tender confidence and lean and whisper to him, "I keep my secret there!" And of course he does not reply, but his fingers lightly touch the place again. Not probingly as if to find out what is underneath, but more as if he were reminding me that he is good at keeping secrets. For the rest of the day he follows me about like a shadow, so that if I turn unexpectedly I almost trip on him. Once when I smile as he hands me the sash-brush I have dropped under the bench, I am almost sure I see the glimmer of a smile in answer.

I am glad he is not in the kitchen later, to hear the turn our conversation takes.

"Dead bodies. I've seen a few before," Mary Spurren says, wiping her nose upon her sleeve. "Have you, Agnes?"

I am clearing the plates from the table after the meal.

I think of Mrs. Mellin with her purple tongue sticking out. "Oh no, never," I say, pretending to shudder.

"What would you do if you saw one?" she persists. I think of Mother's dead babies come too early, their mild, bloodied little corpses small as pigeons. I think of the tarred and blackened body swinging from the gibbet high on Burnt Oak Gate. "What would you do?" she says again.

"I would turn and run away, perhaps," I say shortly. I do not know why she needs to ask me.

"Run for the constable, you should, more like."

"Perhaps." Why does she keep on so?

"But if the death were not natural causes. If it were crime, say!" Mary Spurren's face is pink. "You'd need the law on your side!"

"The law is not always enough," I say, uncomfortably. A thought comes into my head, and I hear myself declare, "The law is man's poor answer to irregularities of fate." My brother Ab would speak like this.

She blinks at me.

I realize my mistake. My mother would say that that is the kind of talk to raise up trouble. I quickly add, as if to justify my unguarded words, "I mean that God is the authority."

"God?" She scratches her head in confusion. "Sweet Jesus!" She wipes her nose again, looks sidelong at Mrs. Blight and sniggers. "She's never seen a body."

"On my way up to London I did see a man hung up from a gibbet," I say, as if I had just remembered it. "Just the bits of him left, hanged by the law. Later I dreamt of him walking along by the carrier," I add. "At least, I think that's who it was. He was angry, and he had a red, chafed neck."

"Most probably did have," Mary Spurren says, gloomy now. "The unsettled dead will travel the old roads in search of something."

"In search of what?"

"Dunno," she says. "Peace for their guilty souls, most likely. Something restful to latch on to." And I shiver.

"I saw my first body when I were but a slip of a girl," Mrs. Blight says, from her chair by the hob. "They sat me by him laid out all through the night, but more in terror I was of my grandfather in life than the mere corpse of him." Mrs. Blight goes on. "A great gangling bully of a relative, with pinching fingers if he had a mind to it, like when his mood should take an unexpected dip upon hearing my catechism recited wrongly." She snorts. "Wouldn't catch me in church on Sundays now. Regular passive sinner, I am. No prayers, nothing! No point in going on poking yourself in the eye with a sharp stick, unless you needs to, is there?" And she laughs more loudly than she need do, as if she had a point to prove, or as if she hoped that God might overhear.

"Churchgoer, are you?" she asks me.

"No," I say, looking away. "Not anymore." But I would like to go into the church of St. Stephen, I think, the one behind the house. It looks peaceful in there.

That night I do not blow out the candle immediately when I retire to my chamber, but sit shivering on the edge of my bed as I unpick the red thread from my skirts turned inside out. How the hem is becoming dirty. There is something about the red thread I do not like; it is too thick, too insistent, like the worms we found last week in a piece of white fish that Mary Spurren bought at Billingsgate. I pull the last wriggling strand out away through the weave with some relief, and push the coins back into my stays again. They feel safer there, less evident.

In the morning Joe Thomazin's eyes search my skirt's fabric for the red thread, over and over, and he puts a look upon his face as if to ask, *Where is the secret gone?*

I shrug lightly and then turn away, so that I do not see his hurt.

As the days and then the weeks go by, I begin to slip into some kind of working pattern. And it is almost December when, for the first time, I am left alone in the workshop. Mr. Blacklock has gone out on business up to

Threadneedle Street, near the Exchange, and Joe Thomazin is running errands for him all afternoon.

I am stood at the mortar, grinding a mixture with antimony and boiled oil added to the powder. For every ounce of dry ingredient I must add twenty-four drops of linseed oil. My grinding skill is improving daily now, I think with a little outward breath of pleasure. I stop and take a look about me. The fed stove glows at the back of the room. On Mr. Blacklock's bench the jar of antimony sits with its cork half open. On the boards under his stool there are dust and footprints, where charcoal was dropped and trodden on yesterday and has not been swept up. Out in the street a horse and cart pull up by the back door of the workshop, and the room darkens. There is a hubbub of laughter, and someone shouting.

And then abruptly the back door opens and a lean man enters without knocking, blocking the sudden gray light from the street. I stand up hastily. Cold air swirls in.

"Blacklock!" he shouts out, and doesn't see me. The man bends and puts down a tub onto the floor, goes out to the cart and comes back with another. My boots scrape on the boards, so that he turns around and sees me in the shadows.

"Mr. Blacklock is out," I say, keeping my back straight. "He won't be back before three o'clock." A brief look of curiosity opens up his face as he sees the tools in my hand. I put down the pestle and tuck my stained fingers into my skirt. "I am Mr. Blacklock's assistant," I say stiffly, in case he thinks I am doing something that I shouldn't.

"So it is true, then!" the man exclaims. "There was talk about his new subordinate being in skirts! I heard it, and thought it must be idle chittle. There we are." He looks closely at me.

"I have the samples he expects." The man's speech is quick and pattering. He indicates the wooden tubs that he placed so carefully upon the floor. "Our supplies are changing, for the better is the truth of it, and these are what we have to choose from. The mills are a farther drive, but every mile is worth the horses. The mealpowder is as good, I feel, or better, and the grain is even and reliable."

I look at his boxes, and back at him.

"Cornelius Soul on your premises, madam," he says with a sudden change in manner, and he bends at the waist, bowing his trim figure mockingly toward me. "Seller of gunpowder and explosive accoutrements to the gunnery and blasting trades." He likes saying that; he enjoys its satisfactory ring. There is something of the brashness of the city in his intonation, as though he is accustomed to making himself heard above the noise of busy streets and taverns and markets. He wears no wig. Although he is a young man, his hair is as fine and white as zinc, and tied in a tail. His eyes are blue and bright and move fast in his head, and his nose is small and sharp. There is a gleaming, vigorous paleness about his person, and he wears a gray velvet frock coat that gives his movements as he speaks a kind of silver sheen. Only his hands, I see, show any traces of the blackness of his trade.

"Not a stranger to irregular and small deliveries for the artisans in this field, within which your good man Blacklock holds his own so admirably." He turns and bows again and grins. Mr. Blacklock has returned and takes off his hat as he enters the workshop.

"Stop talking like a weasel, Mr. Soul," he says, putting his hat down.

"I have introduced myself to the new and striking element in the establishment," the man says. His eyes dart between us. "My invoice," he adds.

Mr. Blacklock picks up the paper that Cornelius Soul has flourished on the bench before him and narrows his eyes at it. "That gold tooth glinting in your skull indicates your dealing cannot be so bad this year," he says dryly. "You have a shrewdness when it comes to business matters. Still, there is a promptness that I like about your service." He pauses. "If a certain—flashiness—about your distribution methods." It is the first time that I have heard him make a joke. Cornelius Soul chuckles, his gray coat shimmering.

"You are referring to my fine new cart you passed out there. Just a short spell at the sign painter's for a lickabout with a fresh coat of color and the old is young again. And that mare you see before it, who pisses yellow in your gutter there, ahem, with no respect for your stretch of pavement, is now also mine to thrash." He draws a breath.

"I have at length and after deep deliberation purchased every ounce and morsel of my partner's business. We no longer trade as Soul and Tibbet but Souls alone. Which means I am a free man now to make my own advancements."

Mr. Blacklock's dark eyebrows rise. "Then you are to be congratulated upon your liberation. I wish you luck, and caution with it." He counts out and pushes a small stack of gold toward him. "Tibbet was a mouse of a man, to be sure, but he had a nose for the place where sense and money meet."

Cornelius Soul drops the coins into a leather pouch tied about his waist beneath his coat. "Spanks and rhino, what a rarity! These days of shortage, one may never bank on who may not drop dead or be snapped up in the debtor's prison." He turns and says to me, "What a marvel! Can there be a sweeter sound than the click of coinage?" He looks up at the ceiling as if in thought. "Ah, but I omit one sound perhaps that is a little sweeter even still." He lowers his voice to a dramatic whisper. "That of a good woman at the peak of her fulfillment!" I do not understand him; indeed I am confused by his direct manner.

He pats the cloth of his gray coat and grins and turns to wink his blue eye shut at me, then he ducks out of the doorway and is gone, rather in the way that a bird within one's sight will take flight suddenly. When his horse pulls away from the window, a strip of late sunshine falls in upon the bench. I see dust spinning in the brightness it makes.

"Mr. Soul is a scoundrel and a dramatist," Mr. Blacklock says, as if in irritation. "Pay no heed to him at all."

I take up the pestle and return at once to the work on the block. I bend over the mortar and fix my attention to the task before me until my neck aches. Joe Thomazin is back from his errands. The noise of him sweeping the floor at the back of the workshop is quiet but insistent, like the sound of a light wind blowing through dry beech leaves in winter. He sweeps for an hour until the boards are clean.

*T*onight I dream of an overcast sky waiting to rain. I am walking down a long white track between two hills. The air is warm and thick; flies swim about on it and bother the cattle. The endless road seems to dissolve ahead of me in the far distance, where the clouds are heaviest. I bite into a good apple and chew. The fruit is crisp and sweet as summer in my mouth. And then I look before I take another bite and see the worm, dark in the wet flesh.

I wake with a pressure on my chest and a trouble niggling inside, and the sickness is worse than usual this morning, so that I have to breathe deeply when I stand up and go to the basin.

Downstairs at breakfast I find Mrs. Blight and Mary Spurren muttering agreement about this and that. Their voices drop when they look over at me, though I can hear them still, as if that were intended. I have begun to sense that they talk about me behind my back, though I don't know why. I do not understand people very well. They are perplexing.

"I'd had enough of her malapert sauciness," Mrs. Blight is saying. I know they do not mean myself, but still I am uncomfortable. "Ended up over Seven Dials way among the gin shops, she did. Drunken discharged soldiers and seamen. Lots of trade there. Hardly of the kind she had expected. Though even among the cream of society you find the murkiest of morals, making games of what should be left twixt man and wife."

Mary Spurren snickers.

"Like after their goose and gooseberries, after the cards and the white brandy has been put to one side . . ." Mrs. Blight pauses for effect. "Then they starts up! Best amusement east of the bathing houses? Debauched, I call it." Mrs. Blight rattles the teeth in her head with a succulent indignation. "The things girls has to do for money now," she laments.

"What do they do?" I interrupt, unhappily.

Mrs. Blight leans over, her bosom quivering over the floured pastry, and inside her pocket her little hip flask clunks against the chair.

"In company! Not a stitch on!" she hisses. "She's trussed up, on her back on a huge silver platter! Like a great juicy chicken!" My mouth drops open. "Spun round and round she is, a plump little whirligig on the table, in the middle of the jostling." She wipes her mouth with the back of her hand. "And the winner, blindfold, gets the lemon right in!" She is beside herself. Mary Spurren snorts, her white cheeks flushed.

There is a sharp click as the door opens suddenly and Mr. Blacklock enters the room. I see how Mrs. Blight and Mary Spurren slip so easily into a semblance of work.

"Yes, Mr. Blacklock, your coffee will be along in just a moment. Agnes will do it." Her voice is bland and occupied with kitchen affairs. I keep my face turned into the cupboard and bend about as though I were looking for something small and tucked away. Could he have heard us? I am mortified. The door bangs as he leaves the room. I pour a handful of beans into the mill as I have seen Mary do, and begin turning the handle.

"I have a grievous headache," Mrs. Blight says plaintively, dabbing at the edge of her forehead with her sleeve. She lifts the pastry up on the rolling pin, then lays and unfolds it over the plate of chicken. She slices at the edge and it drops away in slow, fatty loops onto the marble top. Her skill makes her quiet for a moment, and she breathes heavily as she seals the edges of the pie closed with deft pinches.

In the silence, as I turn from the hob to pour water on the ground beans, I distinctly hear my coins clink against each other inside my stays. I stand stock-still. Could Mrs. Blight have heard it, too? That unmistakable, slithering click of metal, letting slip the certainty that I have money hidden on my person. And even as she is looking up at me, I burst out absurdly, "I like it!"

"Like what?" Mrs. Blight narrows her eyes.

I point at the pie. "The . . . fresh kind of leaf smell of pastry, before it's cooked."

"Leaf smell? Leaves! Listen to her!" Mrs. Blight's mocking laughter rings in my head. She lowers her voice.

"More like a man's fluids, that smell is," she breathes, with a wink at Mary Spurren.

"A man's what? A——" My cheeks flush. "I don't know what you mean," I say. Mary Spurren snorts again. And Mrs. Blight looks triumphant, as if she is on the way to catching me out.

She is a coarse kind of woman, and it is a relief to take up the coffeepot and escape across the corridor into the study. I set out the cups and sugar, then pin the shutters back so that the cold sun falls in across a corner of the desk. I look about. On the far wall there is a cabinet, bearing a range of books upright on its middle shelves. I look more closely, and see the volume that Mr. Blacklock was reading on the evening I arrived. Perhaps I have spent too long in here already, but I pause, just to touch the spines and look.

I make the letters out on each. *Pirotechnia. Metallurgy. De Re Metallica. The Book of Fires.* I spell out the strange and lovely words, and then, holding my breath, I reach out and take a volume down. It is so heavy. The leather binding is pale and shiny with use, and the rag corners of the pages are softened and dirty from being touched. It is a workingman's book. Within are stiff drawings of contraptions and devices that have been sliced through to show the inside of processes and apparatus. Short men in long boots and old-fashioned breeches work at flames that look like wriggling blades of grass, and smoke that is drawn streaky, like the grain of elm.

I freeze.

Mr. Blacklock's footsteps are coming down the corridor. I can hear voices at the door as his client greets him: the Italian pyrotechnic engineer called Mr. Torré, who does not take his hat off when he goes into a room. I push the volume swiftly onto the shelf and leave the study as it should be.

After their meeting I hear them in the hall.

"A pleasure to be working with you on this performance," the hatted man is saying. "You're an oddity, Blacklock, neither trader nor gentleman; or rather both." And he slaps Mr. Blacklock on the shoulder as he turns to leave.

Mr. Blacklock barks out a short laugh. "Throw any insult, call me anything, but do not call me *artificer*, Mr. Torré."

"True, your mind is too innovative for that, signor. Delighted to sign a contract with you."

"I was preparing to join forces with your fellow countrymen."

"The Ruggieri brothers?" Torré laughs easily. "One day I will outstrip them! Despite their claims that they will make pyrotechnic splendor for us, the like of which we have never seen before."

Mr. Blacklock holds the door ajar.

"We are all searching for something new, Mr. Torré," he says, quietly.

Soon after this I am bitten by an earwig, and Mrs. Blight, on seeing me sucking my finger like a child, thinks I am putting currants in my mouth.

"No, no!" I protest, and try to show her, but she is too busy to pay much heed to what I say.

"I've warned you afore, no helping yourself, no greedy-gutsing," she says. "No liberties! Thieving little miss, you are." She bends over, panting. The sickly sweetness of liquor on her breath is everywhere, but at first I don't retort. I have noticed that the level inside the new bottle of Madeira wine—bought from the housekeeping money so that, she said, she can make up a tolerable sauce for boiled duck—has been dropping over the week like the line of high tide when the moon is waning.

Mary Spurren comes in. "Doing it again, she is," Mrs. Blight says savagely.

"I took nothing!" I say, taken aback at first, and then indignant. "Besides, how can you say that, drinking Mr. Blacklock's wine!"

Mrs. Blight smirks. "What wine?"

"The Madeira."

"Oh no." She denies it flatly.

"It's going down quite steadily," I say, my face flushed, and I go to the dresser and point at the half-filled bottle for her to see, my fingers shaking, but she doesn't miss a beat.

"Evaporation, that is," she agrees. "These foreign wines are misreliant." She sucks in her teeth regretfully and shakes her head so that the crop quivers under her jaw. "Terrible waste it is, terrible, all that good spirit leaking out into the atmosphere without effective stoppage," she says. "No man has invented yet the cork that will bring to bear the containment of these foreign liquors." She picks unconcernedly at her teeth. "Haven't touched that bottle since Tuesday last," she says. There is a wet runnel of liquor about its neck, and even as we look, a drop slips down its length and makes a sticky patch on the surface of the shelf.

And I look sideways at Mary Spurren, but she does not catch my eye.

As I go to bed that evening, something causes me to forget this disagreeable dispute.

"Agnes!" Mr. Blacklock shouts out, looming from his study into the corridor. His face is stern in the poor light cast by my candle. I swallow. Mrs. Blight must have told him that I have been thieving from his kitchen.

"Yes, sir?" I say. My voice is an anxious whisper. But it is worse.

"You have touched my books!" His displeasure glares down at me.

I nod, ashamed. How I wish I could vanish.

"Should you touch them in future you will ensure that your fingers are clean," he barks.

I blink in surprise.

"And you must bring your reading matter to discuss further with me," he goes on. "There are inaccuracies in those volumes that would need to be identified." He returns to the study. Of course I will not do such a thing; he must not be bothered with trifles, I think, turning away. Yet the idea of the books is stored inside me like a pleasure that I go back to just before I sleep. *Your reading matter to discuss.* So much I could learn.

But pleasure is a weakness, and I guard against it where I can. I have begun to reason that receiving unkindness should make one grow harder, which is in turn a fair protection against being foolishly soft and vulnerable. But when by chance a person says a gentle thing to me, my heart does an undue gallop, like it does on the day that Mrs. Spicer looks at me over her counter as she weighs out raw chestnuts.

"Remarkable pale, you are," she says, folding the packet over and passing it to me.

"I do not sleep so well," I begin to confess, then check myself.

"Do they treat you proper at that house?" she probes. "Or should I say, in those infernal regions, God only knows!"

"Oh yes," I say hastily. "It is only that I sometimes do not sleep so well, as many don't indeed." She puts her head to one side in sympathy. I hold the packet to my chest.

"Still, your cheek is whiter than it should be, than it was when you first came." She will not let up. "The consequence of being apart from home, no doubt. Unnatural, it is, to be so far from native soil, poor love."

"It is nothing," I reply, and my voice does not shake. I go quickly from the shop into the rain on the street.

When I get back to the house there is nobody in.

I go to the scullery and sob and sob. I am wanting my mother, like a child does. I long for home; for the woods, empty of leaves, and the wind rattling the sound of winter around among the trees. I long for open space and for a good flat breeze blowing across my ears. I long to see how the dangling sycamore seeds are stiffening into winter at the ends of the branches. "Kit keys! Kit keys!" I can hear in my mind William's delighted voice, running toward me with a bunch held up tightly in his little fist.

Then I hear the front door opening and Mrs. Blight's footsteps marching unsteadily all down the corridor as I rush to dry my eyes and scold myself for behaving with indulgence. She stares at my hot face suspiciously when she comes into the kitchen.

"Short of something to do?" she demands. "Why is that fire nearly out when I am about to cook that neck of veal upon it?"

"I did not notice," I say feebly.

"There are plenty in town these days that are not from here," Mrs. Blight says harshly, as she rakes out the dull coals. I can smell the liquor on her, which means that she must have come past the Star on her way back from market. "No point whindling for what is gone and nevermore. Mostly life is suffering what's dealt to you, and red-eye weepy sorrowing will get you nowhere, my girl, unless your aim is to achieve an ugliness as bad as persons maimed by inveterate distemper." She slams the hod on the hearthstone angrily and picks up the bellows. She is right, of course, but I hate her for this.

"I know that," I say, gritting my teeth. "Best to let time swallow up the worst of any suffering."

"Life is all suffering, my girl, and time does not eat up anything," she says bitterly, puffing with the bellows. "You'll find that out."

The coals redden.

And of course I do not contradict her, or explain why she is wrong. I do not trust that woman one little bit. She is waiting for my mistake to show itself to her, to everybody, I am certain of it.

"Arse-prickle," she adds, the syrupy smell of liquor all about her. "A contagion of arse-prickle I am suffering from, and do I get sympathy for such affliction? I do not." She bangs the spoon against the stewing pan.

London is not so vast a place. Lettice Talbot's lodging surely cannot be so far away? Why do I not encounter her upon the street in the normal course of errands, while carrying packets of antimony back from the apothecary, say, or going with a basket to the herbwoman's market barrow near the Leadenhall for swedes or turnips? I glance at the clock. Mr. Blacklock will be here any moment.

"Do you read?" Mrs. Blight asks, thickly.

"I have no time, Mrs. Blight," I say, setting the cups out in a rush, and I think of Mr. Blacklock's books of science standing upon the shelf in the study, crowded with knowledge. How I would like to!

"Good reads can be had for fourpence if you're down by the Globe," she says regardless, and she picks up a printed pamphlet and waves it about. "*The Proceedings of Justice*," she declares importantly. "All the good bits of the *Gazette*, only better, all squeezed into one." She adds more salt and smacks her lips. "They writes up every session of the Old Bailey, most meticulous—they do not spare the details." And I have to listen to her halting drone as she reads out, "*William Crofts . . . indicted for stealing two Gloucestershire cheeses, property of John Curtis, cheesemonger. 'I was in my parlor and had full view of my shop. I saw the prisoner enter and take up the cheeses . . .'*" The riddled coals draw the heat more forcefully.

"*Verdict: guilty. Transportation.*"

"So harsh a sentence!" I say, shocked.

"They gets what they deserves," she says. "*Anne Fox, for stealing one gold ring, one pair of silver buttons, two guineas and a half, the goods of . . .*" She trails off and reads on in silence for a moment. "It seems she pawned the ring and buttons as her own. '*I was a hired servant to them for half a guinea for half a year. I went to demand my wages when my time was up, and he said, if I did not hold my tongue, he'd lay me fast in Newgate.*'"

"We are late with dinner," I interrupt, swallowing. I do not want to hear her going on with it.

"And also, though it's tuppence dearer, after hangings there's the account of dying words as they're said to the priest—that's most reveal-ing." She adds, "You should have a loan of 'em when I am done. I'll bring 'em in. Get cozied up by the fire with your feet up on your half day. Do you good, getting a glimpse of the wicked world like that."

"No thank you," I say faintly.

"Suit yourself," she sniffs.

It is not as though I were walking quite oblivious out there. Time is slipping along and I need a plan to turn to, as circumstances will become more pressing every day. I am looking, looking for Lettice Talbot all the time.

"What was the sentence meted out to that poor woman wanting wages?" I ask Mrs. Blight later, despite myself. Mrs. Blight picks up her horrid pamphlet and opens it at once, as if she had been waiting for my curiosity to rear its ugly head. She hiccups.

"Anne Fox? For greedy thievery?"

And she recites, triumphant: "*Guilty. Death.*"

Cornelius Soul has begun to deliver powder every week, until we have so much in stock that Mr. Blacklock is forced to tell him that we have no need for any more consignments for a while. "Your new business is too profuse in its release of goods," Mr. Blacklock says with an irony I do not understand. Mr. Soul takes no offense, and he winks at me, as he always does.

"I hear the company you keep is of a coarser quality these days," Mr. Blacklock says as he sits down at the block, his jaw tight with displeasure. Cornelius Soul looks keenly at him.

"Where do you hear this gossip, sir?" he asks, taking a measuring stick from the shelf and flicking it up into the air. "At your coffeehouse? Something muttered by a thin-lipped merchant used to taking refuge behind his hat to dodge the pointed bradawl of his wife's long tongue?"

"Slipped standards are rarely regained once lost," Mr. Blacklock replies. "You will do damage to your business lest you keep an eye fixed on your horizons. The city's gutter is always but a step away, as your bear-garden acquaintances may know already."

"The gutter! What kind of damage can be caused by simple bouts of pleasure due to any man that works as hard to earn his living as I do?" Cornelius Soul demands.

Mr. Blacklock does not respond.

"You would do worse perhaps than to sample some of that yourself!" And Cornelius Soul laughs loudly.

Mr. Blacklock turns and glowers at him. "There is no *time* for this," he says impatiently, and then winces, putting his hand up to his face but not touching the burn. "Are you not done yet with your ferrying in and out, man—the draft is irritating."

Mr. Soul stops to look at what I'm doing as he passes. "And what qualifies you to be so strangely employed on such a premises, Miss Trussel? They say a woman's atmosphere will slow the powder, or rile it up with pique and petulance." He grins.

"No special qualities," I say, very quietly, so I do not disturb Mr. Blacklock. "But my fingers are nimble enough for the task."

"And what kind of fingers are they?" he says, and I am sure that he would have grasped at my hand if I had not thrust it away from him.

"Weaver's fingers," I reply, my face flushing.

"A weaver!" He flings his arms wide. "My father was a velvet weaver! A journeyman of twenty years standing, with an unmatched quality coming off his loom you'd touch as soon as clap your eyes upon. I was his drawboy as a youngster." He beams with pride.

"And what do they weave down there in the seaside hills?" he teases. "Rough fustian? Do they even trouble to shear the sheep, or do they leave the fleece attached to the beast before they spin the yarns up!"

"It was good woollen stuff that we worked," I say.

He bursts out laughing again, then looks at me and stops.

"I beg your pardon, madam," he says. "The finest fowling powders for gentlemen's shooting parties in the country come from down that way, their quality unmatched."

"I am not offended," I reply, mildly enough, never stopping my work. And then he winks at me as he ducks out the door onto the street.

Indeed, against my wish I find my thoughts returning to that wink from time to time.

His eye is too bright.

13

*S*ometimes I cannot sleep for hours, and lie there in the dark. I hear shouts of drunken troubles in the street outside, or cats fighting. On a still night I can hear the watchman crying the hour outside on the main street. "Two o'clock!" "Three!"

My sister Ann at Wiston House is sixty miles from here. From this safe distance I whisper some things to her about my day. I tell her of sulfur, of charcoal, of saltpeter, and how they combine in extraordinary ways. I tell her how much I have learnt in the month I have been here already, and how, when my fingers are occupied with the tasks I am managing more thoroughly each day, I feel a kind of lightness in my head. *My quick weaver's fingers serve me well, Ann. Yours would, too, if you were here.* I do not tell her anything about my belly, how it increases in roundness like an uncooked loaf. I do not say how my belly is white and perfect and dreadful to me, though there is nothing to see when I put on my clothes. I do not mention any aching inside, where my heart lies.

Occasionally I invent another conversation in my head, with Lettice Talbot, explaining to her the things I did not tell her on our journey, things I have never told anyone. I do not even whisper them; I mouth the words into the dark.

I tell her how I have never loved a man.

I tell her how, on the fourth of September last, a man took a chance of love from me and twisted it up viciously, like twisting the neck of a chicken before the plucking and boiling, but with less cause.

And I think of the way that there was a change in the calendar, so that the fourth of September, along with ten other days, was quite swallowed up when the nation moved to the new style of calendar to keep abreast of time in other places. Mrs. Blight is surely wrong, I think; time can swallow anything, in certain circumstances.

We did not take note of such a change until it was already in place. Four days we went, by accident, into the portion of the month that should have been removed immediately. Removed like deadwood, or unwanted cloth outside the pattern, cutting away at the year to make it fit its new shape cleanly, but we were taken by surprise. On Sunday at St. Mary's, the Reverend Waldegrave told us of it. Long and thin, like a spoon wearing a cassock, he read solemnly from Psalm 104 to smooth anxieties that we may have harbored.

"He appointed the moon for seasons: the sun knoweth his going down. Thou makest darkness, and it is night . . . ; the sun ariseth . . . ; Man goeth forth unto his work and to his labour until the evening," he intoned.

"Nothing has changed," he assured us from his pulpit. I clung to that thought gratefully; my shame was growing inside me, though I did not know it then. "Look about you," he urged. "God's world is unalterable in certain ways." I loved the way he held the Good Book to his chest as though it gave him warmth.

And so we leapt with little query toward the midst of the month, going directly from the second to the fourteenth of September. Some particular days were displaced: the Nativity of the Virgin Mary, the day of the Holy Cross. There were some in the village who thought they had been robbed of something, but most took no odds on it. It was a slow realization for me at first, but I tried to hatch a sense that there was a little blessing in the loss of days for me: the fourth of September, being the day of my undoing, was quite disappeared.

It was neatly done, I told myself, over and over. There was some kind of magic in that. Surely it was a single, inadvertent kindness done to me by Parliament, I'd thought at first, so that I did not think about the consequence of what had happened to me in the bean field till it was too late.

And I am shocked when my imagined Lettice Talbot turns to me one night and says, with her beautiful red mouth shaping the words clearly:

"That is all well, Agnes Trussel, but nonetheless you have the seed of that day lodged inside you. What will you do when this thing comes? What preparations have you made?"

"I cannot think of that now," I say to her angrily, clenching my fists, "I am asleep!"

Then I wake up. I must have shouted out, as I hear Mary Spurren stirring in her bed upstairs. I am shaking with misery. I cannot think, I will not think. I cannot. But the night outside is rolling on toward the morning, and what can I do to stop it? The graveness of my situation begins to dawn on me anew.

14

A spiny frost coats everything outside the house. The water in the jug in my chamber is frozen hard across the top, which I have to break to pour and wash with it. The freeze has made this place seem almost unfamiliar again.

Later, carrying a pressing message to a merchant's house in Cannon Street, I take a wrong turning and another and then find myself beside the Thames. My breath comes in clouds as I stand and stare. The wharves are heaving with barges and men landing cargoes into the warehouses and onto carts, hammering metal strappings onto barrels, cursing, working cranes. The water glints invitingly. I weave my way through the crowd along the bridge to a gap between the houses and the torn-down premises, and stand there with the chaos of the traffic at my back, looking at the great river pouring downstream till I am dizzy. I should be back at work, I think ruefully, while I have a job to go to. There are vessels gathered on the water, waiting for the high-tide bell to signal that there is sufficient draft of water to pass under the bridge.

"Don't do it!" jokes an old man in a wide hat, walking by. He stops to rest his elbows on the rail beside me. I suppose he means I should not jump.

"A suicide was washed up only yesterday, in the steelyard at Scott's Wharf," he says when I do not answer. "An unfortunate woman. They said she was not poor, by the clothes she had on her, or what was left of them. And the Lord knows, it happens often enough."

"I was hoping to see a fish, sir," I say. It is the first thing I can think of, and besides, it would be pleasant to see an eel or a shoal of forktails swimming down against the tide. We are a long way over the water. At the edge of the Thames, on the line of the reach, we watch a handful of children gathering scruff for fuel, piling the damp sticks and bits of coal into a basket strapped to the back of the largest child.

The man is smartly dressed in wig and waistcoat; he tells me he is out to gain some exercise before he dines. "Though an icy day it is." His voice is shaky and agreeable. "I'll mark it may be a sign the winter will be fiercer yet this year." I think how at home the rowan bush outside the cottage was red with fruit when I left, like a beacon. He points out the church of St. Magnus, Cocks Key and Lyons Key, and Custom House, and the Tower, and some types of boats: the colliers and lighters, a man o'war . . .

"The whole world is represented in the goods that unload at this shore," he says, pointing into the light with his polished cane. "Olive oil, silks, tobacco, cotton, wines."

"I would like to be on a boat heading out to sea, growing smaller and smaller until it rounds a bend and disappears," I say. The man smiles and shakes his head.

"It is a hard life at sea," he replies. The man thinks me to be an ordinary shopgirl airing myself on my half day, I suppose, and not one riddled with a shameful, swelling error that is not far from being apparent to anyone that cares to look. In some way I have betrayed his trust, his confidence in my respectability being so misplaced.

"Good day to you, young lady," the man says when our conversation lulls, tipping his hat at me courteously and making his way through the crowd toward Fish Hill Street. The bell in the church tower chimes three.

There is something about this encounter that strikes me: the small, chance politeness of it, the vastness of the world converging there, a pleasing contact between strangers.

I wonder on the hardness of the weather that we have ahead. And I remember how last year it was as late as mid-December when the flocks of winter birds came down the valley, stripping the berries from the hedgerows. Plump redwings and gray, gawky fieldfares settled over the rowan tree outside the cottage so that it swayed heavily beneath their weight. They ate the rotten orange fruit at speed, stretching their necks and flapping for balance, so that the trees crawled with birds and noise. They were incautious of the sparrow hawk that burst from nowhere and knifed its way abruptly through their midst and took a single bird midair.

All the rest of the birds melted away. The rowans, near bare of fruit, shook a little in the breeze of their departure and were still. It was a calm scene before the window, just the lane and fields, not a thing to show of any kill, save one soft feather drifting down toward the muddy lane: that and the sudden sharpness to the air, a quickening absence that made the blood run faster.

Mr. Soul came while I was out.

"Said he was thirsty, he did," grumbles Mrs. Blight, putting another kettle on the heat for Mrs. Nott, the washerwoman. "Come peering in, right into my kitchen, and said there was no one in the workshop and here was a note about supply. Fidgeting, he was. Kept looking round."

"Like he was looking for someone," Mary Spurren says, and a glance sidles between them. Mary Spurren sniggers.

"That glass of beer you give him got drunk that quickly when he saw it was just us in here."

"Only small beer."

"Hoping for something better."

Mary Spurren sniggers again, more loudly this time. "Then we couldn't get rid of him, hanging about, fiddling with the spoons, tapping his foot."

"Never stops moving, that one," Mrs. Blight says. "Gives me a headache, all that coming and going with his hands."

I take my cloak off and hang it up on the hook in the scullery. Cornelius Soul is like a wagtail, always dipping and turning, his coattails gray as cloud, as smoke, as gray as gunpowder. I turn to go back to the workshop.

"Seemed like he were . . . expecting something," Mary Spurren says, and gives another look at Mrs. Blight as if that had some kind of meaning that I'd missed. "How very frequent he seems to come these days," she comments to the air in general.

I pause at the door. The kitchen is thick with steam and the smell of soap. The washerwoman is going back and forth with kettles of water to the yard.

"Hello, Mrs. Nott," I say when she nods at me. She stops and puts the kettle down to show her swollen, cracked hands to me.

"Worst in wintertime, it is," she mutters, turning them over ruefully. Her nails are flaked and brittle as oyster shells, and the skin is pale to the elbow, and covered in an encrusting kind of scale, as though she had fallen asleep with her arms in a bucket of lye. Her skin's color is deadened to naught, except where the rawness of the red patches shows through beneath. She grimaces when she puts her hands into water at the start of her day, a hiss escaping between her teeth, but she rarely complains, and she sings like a jenny wren.

"Must get on," she says. "Lagging a bit. Should've been an' gone half an hour since, and they'll be waiting, up the road."

Out in the yard, squatting over the tubs, working the crown soap into the bedsheets and linen, pouring the gray, grubby water away into the drain; it is hard to believe that the great strong voice that pours from her mouth can be hers. Mrs. Nott seems as small as a badly fed chicken, yet on clear frosty days when she sets up her tubs on the bricks outside, the yard seems to throb with the strength of her voice. I like it when she comes. It is as though my spirit were feeding on her songs.

"Will you see to the fire before you go to the workshop, Agnes!" Mrs. Blight says. "Coal dust everywhere." She nods into the yard at Mrs. Nott. "I knew her sister Lizzie Beal last year over near St. Paul's. Now there's a miserable tale." She sorts garments from a pile of last week's dry laundry, holds up a crumpled petticoat and casts her eye over it in the light from the open door.

"See you got that bloodstain out, Mary." She smirks. "Told you that bucking would work a treat. Never would've got it out with that useless ordinary boil you'd started. Can't think where you learnt your cleaning." Mary Spurren scowls and says nothing in reply. How Mrs. Blight likes to be right, I begin thinking, and am quite unguarded when she turns, mid-cackle, her hand over her mouth, and looks at me sharply, as if a thought had come to her.

"Haven't had any rags from you yet, have we, Miss Trussel?" Mrs. Blight says.

"Rags?" I ask, puzzled. *Oh God!* My stomach churns in alarm.

"Your morbid flux. You've brought nothing down for the bucking pot since you was here, and that is surely more than four weeks now." I cannot see her mouth.

"No," I say, and my voice is too loud in the horrible pause that seems to grip the kitchen as at the back Mary puts down the scrubbing sticks and doesn't appear to be working at all. "I . . ."

"Bit proud, are we?"

"Oh no," I say again, and with a struggle I add as quickly, lightly as I can, "I am waiting, of course, but I can feel it not far off. I have a bad ache here." I give a vague prod at my apron. "It was probably the journey, the jolting of the cart, that set me out." I bend over the hearthstone and sweep up the dust as she asked me to.

Mrs. Blight's lizard eyes are still upon me, but I can't look up. "No need to be made so red-faced by talk of women's stuff, is there?" she says. "We're all big girls here, aren't we, Mary, after all!"

"I'm accustomed to being inside a family," I mutter, my cheeks burning. "Not speaking of private things out loud like that to just anyone that asks. I don't like to."

"Needn't be so touchy, neither," Mrs. Blight says, turning away. "Quite the precious little hermit, aren't we! Probably the sort to go around in half-washed rags done in cold water in your chamber sooner than muck in with others. I'm right, aren't I? Could do with a bit of humility, your sort, considering." Mary Spurren snorts. And Mrs. Blight goes on, "Jack-in-the-cellar was all she had by the time he'd done with her."

"Done with whom?" I say faintly.

"With Mrs. Nott's sister, Lizzie Beal—are you not listening to anything today?" As I stand up again she gives a sideways glance at my belly. Wretchedly, as if I were feeling the cold air coming in, I pull my shawl tightly about me. *Mrs. Blight surely cannot know my trouble. It cannot be that plain to see.* "And the man in question but a baker-legged tanner with no intentions of marrying her, as he rightly should've, despite the chit she was bearing to term. Disgrace, it was." She flicks a shirt savagely. "Spent his time telling great whisking lies in the tavern on the corner of Milk Street, and all the time carrying on as if nothing was changed. Ran off, he did, of course, before the parish could put demands on him for money."

She spits on the flat iron.

Intentions of marrying her. And quite suddenly an idea comes toward me in pieces, a collective swell like a rush of droplets brought down in the wind from trees above.

It is a half-formed plan, yet ingenious in its simplicity. Not a trap, I make clear to myself when later I have a flicker of doubt. Not a trap, but morsels of bait set up along a certain path. I plan to lay that bait with all the cunning I possess. Which is why, on Friday next, when Cornelius Soul brings a tub of powder, I ensure that I meet his eye a little, and, as he takes his leave, I give him just the slightest glimmer of a smile.

Nothing more than that. I do not find it difficult.

Mrs. Mellin is in the dream I have tonight.

She has looked up from polishing her coins, her fingers black with a paste made from ashes.

15

*T*here was a girl on a farm at Thakeham or Chiltington, I forget which. She arrived from nowhere, it seemed, to work in the April of the previous year. Her belly grew as the year swelled and grew older, and she ate more to show off her appetite, taking large pieces of cheese at the table when everyone ate. Her mother was fat, she declared; how like her she was becoming. Her stays became tighter. A particular day came.

After the milking she returned to the dairy and churned for two hours. From time to time her knuckles whitened over the wooden handle, but she kept the cream churning. She scrubbed out three pails after the butter was done, fetching the salt from the back of the dairy. She became unwell; she said her head was beating and beating and making her sick. To prove it, she vomited into the gutter outside the dairy and rinsed the vomit away. She put the pails to dry and took off her apron and hung it up on a hook. She went up to the attic. Someone heard furniture scraping heavily over the floorboards as she wedged the door tight. She was not down for supper and the cook put the meat on her plate back into the meat safe. Night passed. The sun rose and she came down from the attic pale but better. Her headache was gone. She went out to the cows and hulked the brimming pails back into the dairy. She churned the butter, drained it, pressed it into the molds and salted eight pats of butter. She worked more slowly than usual, blinking uneasily from time to time. At eleven o'clock she clutched at the side and tipped up a setting bowl, spilling ounces of cream. The skimmer fell to the floor with a clatter. At three o'clock she dropped quietly down on the floor as though the bones had gone from her body, and lay in a heap until somebody came who knew what to do, pulling her loose limbs aside so they could press on her heart. She let out a red pool of blood between her legs that spread out over the flagstones and darkened quickly as it cooled. The blood was the brightest thing that had ever been seen in the dairy, which is in general a pale, white place. After an hour they agreed that her heart had become too cool and still to revive, and laid her down on the marble slab by the cheeses until Dr. Twiner could come and confirm this for them. When later they went to the attic and searched through her baggage for items of value to send back to her family, they found a dead blue baby folded up under her petticoat, a bruised stripe around its tiny, flopping neck, like a collar.

I have gone through this story again and again. And today, for some reason, it rolls around my head all the time like a fruit in an empty barrow, although at last Mr. Blacklock is to show me how to charge the rocket cases.

"Listen hard to what I say," he barks. "The method is complex and I shall not show you twice."

I see how the case sits over a spindle in the box, which penetrates it deeply, so that the composition is compressed about what will be a hollow cone-shaped space when the rocket is done, which gives air to the burning.

"Twelve light blows with the mallet to consolidate the dry clay powder at the choke, which is the constricted mouth at the base of the rocket," he says. "Then fusepowder, with further blows on the hollow rammer or drift. Continue with scoops of powder, using first that drift with the large hollow inside it and then the medium, and, nearing the top of the spindle as it fills, use the drift with the smallest hollow inside it." Mr. Blacklock turns his head away to cough. "Then the solid rammer above the spindle, with dry clay, until the case is full, then twist the rocket from the spindle. Finally push a length of quick match inside the rocket's hollow core and paste it at the mouth.

"Manufacture and attachment of a rocket head, with a variety of appended garnitures of stars and fiery rains and so on, we will cover on a further occasion," he says. "Likewise the stick, which is necessary for balance and guidance in flight like a rudder or tail." He holds up the half-finished shape. "This is an honorary sky rocket, which carries no head; small and plain, with strong composition.

"The smaller the case, the quicker the mixture used to fill it." He passes it to me. I hold such a remarkable thing gingerly.

"Quicker?" I ask.

"Fiercer. More instantly combusting. Smaller rockets will contain mealpowder, which you will remember to be gunpowder ground exceedingly fine." He gets up and motions me to sit before the filling-box.

"Do not mistake the degree of roaring of a rocket upon ignition to be an indication of the fierceness of its powder," he says. "The loud roar depends upon the quantity of surface that is available to burn. And a rocket that is insufficiently rammed will simply explode upon ignition. Indeed, any poorly made firework is in danger of explosion if held in an ungloved hand, for instance."

The filling-box is deep with washed river sand and stands securely on a block of oak.

"Brace yourself," Mr. Blacklock says, clearing his throat. "You must put your legs apart." He demonstrates.

I try. "No, wider," he says. "You must be braced and comfortable. You cannot charge a rocket ill at ease."

He stands back and considers my posture. "Adjust your skirts above your knee."

Obediently I tug at the woollen fabric until my legs are free to move about unencumbered by my skirts or petticoat.

"There!" he exclaims.

I do not believe that he is looking at my legs above the ankle, which are naked now, inside my stockings, but know it must be possible, should he choose to do so. My cheeks are flushed with the thought of it.

"Make your back long and upright," he suggests. He is looking at my face, I am sure, though I do not turn to look at him. He does not take his gaze away. I can hear him breathing.

I try to sit up straight.

"Are you at ease?" he demands at last.

"I am, sir," I say, sitting there with my legs apart. "It feels . . . natural like this."

"Then, so stationed," Mr. Blacklock says, "you can begin. Soon you will be adept at filling rockets, lances, gerbes."

"Gerbe?" I say. "What is that?"

"It is the French for *sheaf*," he replies.

"Oh!" I say, with a start of recognition. "Like a sheaf of corn, a sheaf of wheat?"

"Precisely so," Mr. Blacklock says. "It burns like a spray of ears of wheat, and is named accordingly—"

"Stooked up in the field, the shining ears spurting out, like a fountain of gold," I interrupt eagerly, a smile growing inside me.

"You can picture it now?" he asks.

"I can picture it very well," I reply.

My first attempts are clumsy. I am left alone to make mistakes with quantities of powder, spilling the scoops as I tip them in. The hollow rammer jams with compacted powder, so that I have to beat hard to loosen it and much is wasted. It is impossible to strike the mallet with even, satisfactory beats. I hold the tools so tightly in my anxiety that my bare hands chafe and become sore.

After paying so much attention to my person, Mr. Blacklock barely seems to notice me for the remainder of the morning. I am so afraid the rockets will explode in front of me I hardly let my breath come naturally.

"Do not rush," he says once, without looking up from his bench. "The flow of work will come when eventually you manipulate the tools adroitly, but it should never be a frenzy."

And because the orders are fulfilled he goes off to Child's coffeehouse to talk of business matters, and is not back to take the midday meal with anyone.

The tool sits uncomfortably in my hand and my back aches in a new way.

At the end of the day, when the gloom becomes too thick to properly see what I am doing, he returns to check what I have done.

"It looked so simple when you showed me," I say. I am disappointed with my progress. I remember the first time I was permitted to milk a cow at Roker's Farm, when I was six years old. I took the teats expectantly and found that they did not behave at all as I imagined they would. It took days of practice before the milk drenched regularly into the pail, my fingers using a movement that was neither a tug nor a stroke, but rather something in between.

I am tired. My palms are stinging and blistered with effort.

"You will do the same exercise until you have it right," Mr. Blacklock says, with no further comment.

But the next day, he surprises me again.

"It is apparent that you have an aptitude for what we do here—and any energy that I expend in divesting specific areas of knowledge upon you may not be a waste." He stops to cough. "I will be frank: in the past I have not achieved much in the way of success with the training of assistants. But there is something receptive about your ear, which pleases me, and which indicates that thorough learning may bear good results."

A flicker of hope kindles something inside me. And then I think perhaps I should not flatter myself that this is due to any special quality I possess. Already I had been told by Mary Spurren about his last apprentice.

"Davey Halfhead was a squat youth covered in boils," she'd said. "With such a temper. I breathed more natural when he was gone. Ate a lot of fat, he did. Wouldn't touch loaves. Said they gave him a cramp in his leg." Mary Spurren had drawn breath at the very thought of it. "Mr. Blacklock's not a man to have assistants," she'd said.

"Are there other men like you, sir?" I ask.

"Like me?" He looks amused. "We are a various breed. Our compass ranges from plain artisans making batches by the ten thousand to impresarios like Torré who do not lay a finger in the mixture and are concerned only with spectacle. There are philosophers with ideas of *nature* to convey, and entire families traveling between cities across Europe with their fire-working mastery."

"And all these people make a living from this . . . trade?"

"The appetite for artificial fireworks cannot be sated, or so it seems. Once it was the private pleasure of kings, but now the common man is glad to pay to see these things we offer. And we all want to find the most novel, the most dazzling, the biggest, best, newest creation. Competition is rife. We are a cutthroat lot, among ourselves."

"But how does anybody ever learn anything then, sir?"

He looks at me. "A keen question. The knowledge is passed on strictly by word of mouth between interested parties. Neither formulae nor tricks of the trade are shared in the public eye. If anything is written down, it will be in manuscript form and locked away. It is a secretive business, pyrotechny."

"Do you write your recipes down, sir? How do you remember them?"

"I have never done so," Mr. Blacklock says. "They are safer inside my head than out."

"But what if something were to happen to you?" I am asking too many questions now.

"The world would manage, if it were deprived of a record of my labors," he says. For a moment his face is stone-still, and then a flicker passes over it. He clears his throat. "And there is much to learn," Mr. Blacklock says. "How can one know a thing about the quality of substances without an understanding or experience of how it is derived, composed, originated?" He uncorks a jar of flowers of sulfur and knocks a little out into a dish. "The same could be more broadly said of life," he says.

"Mrs. Blight says that life is all suffering," I find myself replying, without intending to at all. "*All suffering*, she says."

The sulfur is soft and yellow in the dish. Mr. Blacklock looks up and then back at the tool in his hand, turns it over.

"Indeed, there seems to be a quantity about," he says. His voice is quiet. Perhaps he is thinking of his dead wife. My aunt always said that my mother's raw grief for her mother was never healed because she would not speak of it, and left it trapped up inside her.

"What was Mrs. Blacklock like?" I venture, watching his face. He fixes his eyes upon me, unspeaking, for a moment.

"She was tiny," he says, turning around to the work on the bench. His jerkin is smooth and worn at the back. I wonder whether he is trying to reach her with fireworks. Or maybe not. Maybe he is trying to punish God; there is a violence in these devices. I have seen something like a black fire far back inside his eyes.

"And your own misfortune?" he asks me, unexpectedly. At first with a jolt I think he means the child inside me, and then regretfully I remember the fire that I claimed had burnt up my family in one night.

"You were at home?" he asks.

I nod.

"Did you try to put it out?"

"Oh yes," I say. What can I tell him? "It was early," I murmur, putting my hand to my face. "Some of them were still asleep upstairs. I expect it was a small fire at first. I had no idea. There must have been a spark . . ." I falter. "And the heaped wool caught quickly at the bottom of the stairs." Mr. Blacklock looks at me.

I stop. I can't go on, and I fold my arms over my stomach in a kind of agony of untruth and missing home. It feels as though I have killed them with my story.

Cyphers

16

*M*y weaver's hands are changing. The nails are blackening and the tips are sore from touching the dry chemicals. There are painful cracks beginning to open up between my fingers. At first I tried to work with the great leather gloves that sat upon the filling bench, but they are large and stiff, the size of a man's hand. They make me clumsy. And so instead I let my bare fingers do the work rapidly; I can fill twenty casings before the bell on the thin steeple of St. Mary the Virgin strikes midday. At night I rub yellow salve into my skin before I sleep. But I find I no longer suffer waves of sickness on rising each morning, as I had before. Indeed I begin to feel quite well again, as though a fresh kind of vigor had taken hold in me.

It is the darkest part of the year.

Christmas Day passes with little note, and although I hear the bells calling the faithful to church all over London, I do not go myself. Mrs. Blight cooks plum porridge. The fires draw quickly. At first it is too cold to snow heavily. Fine, powdered flakes fall outside the house, a bitter wind scuttering them about. When the wind drops, the snow ticks on the ground—as embers tick as they cool in the grate when a fire has gone out.

If we sit too far from the stove in the workshop our breath drifts in clouds about us.

"I know about charcoal, sir," I point out, when Mr. Blacklock lays some pieces on the bench. "Men take good green wood and let it burn slowly in a clamp of soil and on the fifth day or thereabouts, they stop the gaps and smother the hot coals where they lie."

"That is so," Mr. Blacklock says. "And it chars quietly by itself, the contained fire eating at the pithy underwood until it is as brittle and as strong as glass. It is the fuel in gunpowder."

"Up in the Weald the charcoal men use hazel from the coppices, also willow and sometimes alder," I say. I do not add that you can see small white-bellied birds, tree-creepers, inching up the alders by the Stor. The leaves of alder are stiff and make a dense kind of shade, so that a river beneath them flows without warmth or sunshine. The wind hisses through alders. The leaves of hazel are as thick and napped as cloth. But they are more sparse on the branches, and allow for sunshine to break through and dapple the woodland floor.

There is a big warren on the edge of the hazel coppice under Black-patch Hill. My father had been known to trap wild rabbit in those woods on his journey back from over Findon way, his sharp billhook strapped to his back.

And a thought comes to me: it is said that, at the rarest of times, a rabbit who has conceived of babies can absorb her young back into herself, when it is too cold, when food is scarce or conditions are too harsh for her to nurture them with adequacy. No waste. There is something clean about this, their tiny unsuitable souls dissolving back into the warmth and darkness of her body.

Outside the window the snow spins in dizzying columns, like icy dancing flecks of flies. When Joe Thomazin comes close to me to bring a box of cases, I see he is shivering.

"Are you cold?" I ask him, and put out my hand to touch his face. He winces, as though he expected me to hurt him. I look at him in consternation, but he has gone to the stove.

"He does not like to be touched," Mr. Blacklock says, though his back is turned. I remember what Mr. Blacklock told me, outside his earshot, when I arrived.

"His mother, no doubt being a tippler, a whore or an unfortunate, gave up Joe Thomazin to the whim and obligation of the parish," he says.

"And never returning for him, he was deserted. Or perhaps she is dead." Mr. Blacklock shrugs as he says this, although spreading his hands as if to bear the great weight of his not knowing. "Joe Thomazin knows about endurance. Most parish children do not achieve the age of six, but die a wretched, sickly death for want of milk or cleanliness."

I glance over to the stove, where Joe Thomazin squats on his heels picking up bits of fallen coals with his grubby fingers. How small he looks. And he has not forgiven me for hiding my secret from him.

"Stars, for instance," Mr. Blacklock says, breaking into my thoughts, "can be improved with charcoal."

"What are they like, sir?"

"Globes of light, little planets of sharp fire. Stars with far-reaching tails of lengthy duration are achieved with an excess of charcoal. They burn out slowly, gravity pulling them down in a trail of amber, making a drooping shape, like the branches of willows reaching toward water." He shows me some already finished.

"They just look like broken pastilles," I say, holding one up.

"There is much yet that you do not know about," he says, and his eyes glitter so blackly as they meet mine that I cannot look away. "Fire so white it hurts to look at it. Sparks like ice. Burning grains of fire, plumes, fountains. Our fire is like the noble metals at the very birth of their existence, the hot mouths of the gods spitting gold and silver into life. We can only make white fire, tinted with warmth or coldness as we please, but its range of purity is so rare, so transforming, that these limitations do not matter." His dark face flashes with joy. I have never seen him smile like that before. It must be because at last his burn is healing and does not give him so much pain. "Maroons! Gerbes! Metallic rain! Cascades! Bengal lights! Tourbillions! Serpents!" The thing inside me that I cannot name seems to move about in excitement as he speaks.

I know about serpents, though. Up on the Downs on a hot day the adders stretch out with their dry flanks panting as they soak up the sunshine. It is as well to be noisy as you step through the grasses, so that they slither away.

An adder's fat is the cure for its poisonous bite, they say.

We stop at twelve to dine. It is Mrs. Blight's day off, and in the kitchen Mary Spurren has let the fire go out, so that the sweep could clean the chimney, and he has just packed up his brushes and gone.

"That lowers my spirits," says Mary Spurren, staring at it gloomily. "Nothing colder than a fire that is out." She is right. It is a sobering prospect.

She cuts at the cold mutton she has taken from the meat safe.

A fire that is out is a desolate space in the grate. Mrs. Mellin's fire had been out for days when I came upon it. I don't know if the fire was a lit and blazing comfort when she died, warming Mrs. Mellin's body at the very point when her heart gripped her in a squeeze of its own choosing and clutched itself to death, or if she sat before a dwindling smoky heap, uncomfortable as the chill of winter settled already in her bones.

We eat the cold meat almost in silence. Mr. Blacklock's cough has worsened with the weather. Mary Spurren has relit the hob and it roars with a yellow blaze of kindling.

"Know the date?" Mary Spurren whispers to me when he has left the kitchen. "Epiphany was the day she died. 'Tis hard to say if he has taken note of it this year. Last year he drank a mortal quantity of brandy and slept in the study as he had no use of his legs. It's the snow out there, reminds me of it." She lifts the hod and tips on bigger coals.

"He has all her gowns and petticoats still." Her voice is hoarse.

"Says he does not know what to do with them, but I think he keeps them all for company. I hear the lid of the chest banging shut from time to time, as though he's been gazing at them in there, taking a look. Full up it is, that chest. Every bit of garment you can imagine, still there. All folded up flat, laid out regular with bits of herbs to keep out moths. A blue quilted petticoat. Stockings, hats, aprons, garters. Very neat, it is."

"Poor man," I say. Thick smoke pours up the chimney.

"I offered once I could package it up and take it to Queen Charlotte's

Hospital for charity. Plenty of folks would fall upon those things like they was starving for fabrics, good stuff like that. But he wouldn't. Just shook his head as though he was only hearing half of what I said." She shrugs her bowed shoulders. "None of my business, anyway. Got enough to do, no need to chaff away at other people's matters." She turns to the table and begins to scrape the bones and gristle from the plates into the stockpot.

Out in the hall Mr. Blacklock puts on his greatcoat and vanishes into the cold street for a good part of what is left of the day. An icy draft blows under the workshop door, and the coals in the stove glow red-hot. And Cornelius Soul, when he comes with his batch of mealpowder, does not seem inclined to leave. He warms his hands, then comes to lean on the bench beside me and fiddles with the tools.

"Saw Blacklock out there on the street," he says, chuckling. "In a temper, was he? Scarcely raised his hand, though he saw me clear enough!"

"Perhaps he did not feel like talking," I say. "Or he was thinking of something else."

"Bad-humored blood runs through his veins, more like," he says. "Never knew a man so coiled up by his own ill-temper."

"He is not a bad man," I say.

"Irritable, discourteous . . ."

"It is four years today since Mrs. Blacklock died," I say, to stop him.

"Ah," he says.

He moves away toward the window to glance out and up the street, as if checking for something.

"How long has it been since you lost your father? You said he *was* a weaver," I ask. If my plan is to work, I must be interested in everything he has to say.

He looks around. "Oh no, he is not lost," he says, after a moment. "It is only his pride in his workmanship has deserted him. Down on the dock now, lumping coal. There seemed to be no overlie between the need for ready labor and his long-standing aptitude with warp and weft. He took what he could, and sold up the loom to pay off his overdue rent."

He stills the tool in his palm, and adds, almost bitterly:

"Priced out by master weavers putting out to garner further income for themselves."

He scratches at his scalp, at his fine silver hair that must be soft as feathers, and shakes his head. "I do not like it. I do not like the way the wind blows lately so much in the money spinners' favor."

He seems to brighten.

"Which is why"—he rubs his merchant's hands together—"I am going to work the system. Employ what means I will to climb the ladder headed for the pinnacle. And if that means I bend the spine of the law a bit this way, a bit that, as I go, then so be it."

He picks up my mallet again, and spins it about on the bench.

"You are a good girl," he says, no longer serious. "You will think badly of me if I go on in this way!"

"It makes no difference how you talk." I shrug. "And will you leave that mallet! I do not like the order of my tools all jumbled. I like to put out my hand and know what it will fall on, without looking." I make sure he can see the smile I pretend to hide from him.

"You may be crisp with me," he says, laughing as he puts the mallet back on its head and out of place on purpose. "But I'll warn you, sharp Miss Trussel, that my soft heart beats on regardless. While you were at home, weaving your sackcloth with the cluck of chickens all about you, I was out there"—he sweeps a gesture at the window—"marshaling my certainty of freedom."

I am busy with my task and do not look at him. "Worsted," I counter. "It was worsted we made, a sturdy cloth."

And he laughs and bends close to me before he makes his way toward the door. "I hear that you have quite a talent for this pyrotechnia," he whispers in my ear.

"You heard that? Where?" I ask him, disconcerted, but he just grins and goes out into the snow.

It is dark so early at this time of year. By four o'clock in the afternoon Mr. Blacklock has come back, resuming his place at the bench quite cheerfully, and Joe Thomazin brings in the lighted lamp for us to work by.

Mr. Blacklock is almost jovial tonight, like a man who has been thinking out some bother and has arrived at a solution. He takes a shilling from his waistcoat with his blackened fingers and directs Joe Thomazin to run to the pie shop and back.

"Why should we not eat supper here where we sit, as we are peckish and an immediate sating of appetite is perfectly possible!" he says. He claps his hands together to urge Joe Thomazin faster up the street. The pies Joe Thomazin brings back are hot and full of pork and potatoes. He takes one out to Mary Spurren in the kitchen, and I sit with Mr. Blacklock before the heat of the stove in pleasant silence. The meat juices have bubbled and gone to black sugar at the edge of the crusts. I lick my fingers and consider my good fortune.

"Palatable?" Mr. Blacklock asks, glancing round at me with the glint of a smile in his eye. "The world seems a more congenial place with a hot baker's pie in one's hands! They are peppery enough, aren't they? Not like the bland, buttery rubbish that woman serves up." He is tall beside me. What can have happened to make him so lively?

"There is something in the work of a chemist called Hales that I find interesting," he says suddenly, as if reading my mind. "He measured the various airs he gained from the action of acid working on metals; he observed them carefully, though he has not concluded much from his inquiries."

"What is an air, sir?"

"What Van Helmont would have called a gas is known latterly as *air*, and there are many different kinds. Fixed air, for example, given off when a substance such as charcoal burns." He pauses, and then takes another bite. "This afternoon at Child's there was talk of a man from Edinburgh doing significant work in this direction."

I nod, and do not say a thing. A hopeful warmth that does not come from the stove is flooding through me. And looking up at him while he is talking, unexpectedly I see his neck, the skin beneath his jaw, and see it is firm and smooth above his collar. I realize that his age cannot be more than thirty-five; not as old as I had thought.

How he must miss his wife.

Up in my chamber that night I stare at the candle for quite some time, like someone in a dream. It is a round purple flame that rolls about, gathering itself inside the hot and waxy cavity. It is a little ball of purple flame that leaps up suddenly, like an idea, as it gathers strength and begins to suck the oils up from the wick.

I snuff the candle before I sleep. I am good at this, having had so much practice at it. If you lick your fingers and pinch the flame out quickly, there is no smoke.

17

*M*rs. Nott the laundrywoman has not come again, though she was due, and there is a great pile of crumpled dirty sheets to wash.

"Mrs. Nott is undependable, but so is everyone, I find," Mary Spurren grumbles, scrubbing at the linen, with her big head nodding. "Time and time again, turns out you can't put your trust in no one nor nothing. Except for death, that is," she adds, looking over at Mrs. Blight's new pamphlet lying on the table. "Wouldn't catch *me* sitting idle with my feet up on the fender."

I say nothing.

"Death always turns up in the end," she goes on. She works up the lather with a grim satisfaction. "No doubt better that we never see it coming."

"I would like to," I say. "I would much rather see my fate approaching."

"Not a chance of that," she points out. And despite the steamy warmth filling the kitchen I feel a shiver passing over me, as though her words presage something unpleasant.

Mrs. Blight does not eat heartily for several days. She has complained all morning of a worm in her tooth, holding her jaw from time to time between rolling the pastry and stoking the fire. "I needs seeing to," she grumbles.

"Mr. Blacklock will not have a doctor set foot inside the house," Mary Spurren declares.

"Not even if she pays for it?" I query.

She shakes her head with vehemence. "I know he won't."

So Mrs. Blight sends me out to the apothecary to buy some proprietary drops she thinks will stop the ache. I don't mind—perhaps today will be the day I catch sight of Lettice Talbot.

As I walk I think how Mrs. Blight's teeth are black and yellow at the edges. I am afraid of their looseness, that one day a tooth will turn up in the soup or under a piece of buttered sea kale; a tough, yellowing lump like a bad nut. Lettice Talbot's teeth were good and white, I think, pushing open the door. The air filling the apothecary's shop is pungent with chemicals, herbs, oils of plants and minerals, dried unrecognizable bits of things.

Mr. Jennet is busy standing on a step to dust big glass bottles on a high shelf. He peers through the rounds of his spectacles and grunts, and makes me wait. The shoulders of his frock coat are chalky with powder from his ancient wig.

On the counter I see something in a jar labeled *Liquid Bloom of Roses*. I remember Lettice Talbot's perfect rosiness and wonder whether this was how she made herself so beautiful. There is some part of me that would like to try it for myself; if only I could make myself a little prettier, Cornelius Soul's attention might be more keen. I must do all that I can, if I am to make sure that he becomes obliged to marry me. And as Mr. Jennet's back is turned I pick up a little gallipot and prize up the china lid to see inside.

He will not see, I think, and furtively I press my finger into it. A red paste, the consistency of goose grease, lines the inside. I rub a smear of it onto the skin of my hand above the knuckles; it does not smell at all of roses, but has a cheap fattiness to it. It is not how I imagined. Disappointed, I put the gallipot back upon the counter and try to rub the Bloom of Roses off. It is tacky and persistent; it spreads about until my stained hands look like the butcher boy's at Saul Pinnington's. When at last Mr. Jennet climbs stiffly down and turns to serve me, I tuck them into my skirts and put what Mrs. Blight owes to him upon account.

Walking home I feel branded like a strayed sheep marked with ochre, or as though I were sporting evidence of a careless, vulgar murder I had committed somewhere. It takes a great amount of soapy scrubbing to get it off when I am back inside the house, and even then faint dots of scarlet seem to be embedded in my pores like tiny, gory freckles.

Mrs. Blight's temper improves once she has swallowed twenty drops of what I bring, and her conversation becomes rambling and animated for some time.

"My husband was in the business of needles and pins." She leans on the mixing bowl unsteadily and makes sure I'm listening.

"Three children I bore him. All dead by four or five." The chicken sizzles on the spit. "By the third death I thought perhaps that is enough of trying now, and then Mr. Blight suffered an apoplectic fit and expired where he stood, so that were a dead loss all round. My father put the blame upon my marrying into unsound blood, and told me Blight by name means blight by nature." She looks oddly small, her fleshy hands pressed together.

"So I took the imbursement that the Guild had given out as Mr. Blight had overseen the drawing-out of pins and needles for twenty-seven years. He would have gone round the world seven times over should those pins have been laid end to end, but I may have recalled that figure wrongly." She shakes her head and hiccups sadly. "He had such a terrible fondness for the chocolate house on Lombard Street. Then I had attentions put upon me by a wax-chandler by the name of Thomas Veare, or was it Veasey? By then I was accustomed to putting the shape and shine and victuals back into other persons' houses, and had no cause to sit about amongst the deadwood of my own effects, knowing what glumness that can bring. He looked abjectly shocked at my refusal, and then a hard smile froze up his face, and he went away. My father said I was a wrong-headed fool, and then the next week, dying himself of a sharp blow to the back of his neck on the way home from trading, he could have no more to say on the subject. On my birthday that were, the eleventh of May."

"And they say it's the thirteenth that's unlucky for some," Mary Spurren remarks.

"But I'll not reach my dotage neither," Mrs. Blight adds. "My plan being to eat so many pies that I die comfortably of being fat." And she opens her toothy mouth wide and laughs loudly at the ceiling. "Don't listen to my tales, not without salt, nor common sense of your own." She glances at the little clock on the mantelpiece above the fire, slides the chicken from the spit with a flourish and lays it to rest on a warm plate. She claps her hands, "Knives, Mary, knives, knives!" Mrs. Blight cuts the bird up neatly until it is an oily pile of cooked meat.

"Life is brief, Agnes Trussel, and I spends it wisely," she says. I nod and swallow. Why do I feel that already I have squandered mine? The fluttering sound of the clock over the fireplace is like a creature caught in a trap.

But I agree because I have to keep her sweet, I am sure of it. I know that, on a whim, she could cause me damage.

I return to the workshop to charge rockets in the afternoon, and find that Mr. Blacklock has been making something while I was gone. He is not in the room, nor is Joe Thomazin. But there is a mess of spilt powder and chemicals left over the bench, as though something in the center of all the activity had been snatched away when it was done. I am put in mind of the ring of feathers about the place of a killing by a hawk: a perfect circle of plucked, blooded quills and under-feathers and plumage. What was he doing?

At the back of the workshop I see there is apparatus propped up on a trestle. A group of new glass vessels strapped together, bulbous and gleaming, and a clean pipkin. They have not been used for anything.

I set up the spindle and pick up the drift. My sides ache with bending and scrubbing. It is calm in the workshop, and my thoughts can roam freely. A draft blows in under the door to the street. When I knock at the drift with the mallet, the thing inside me flutters my belly as though feeling its strike. Surely it must be time for Cornelius Soul to come!

If my plan fails, what kind of life would this creature have, if I should carry it to term? I would lose my position here at Blacklock's instantly. I think of myself walking the streets, taking poor lodging in a St. Giles tenement or begging at Seven Dials. I think of a gray, dry scarcity of work, a thin suckling child strapped to my chest.

I make myself picture its big eyes hollow with hunger. The skin on its head as tight and as fleshless as the shell of a nut. Its brittle fingers too weak to grip at me. No suck in its mouth, nor maybe milk enough to suck at.

And then a bloodied cough would come, or flux, and it would ebb away in a tiny agony.

I put down the drift and rock back and forth as though this could make an ounce of difference to the thing inside me. That would be my doing, my weakness causing so much pain. I close my eyes tight shut and press hard upon the lids until I see stars and colors flashing there. Oblivion is surely better. Perhaps death in this case for something so small and helpless would be warm and dark. Not death, I think, just not being born.

That night my anxiety is tenfold in the dark when I blow the out candle beside the bed. I can hear mice gnawing at something in the cupboard under the washstand, and cannot sleep.

There is a place in the north of town, in the open fields above Gray's Inn, where some unwed mothers can desert their children. At first on hearing this from Mrs. Spicer in the natural course of conversation I grew hopeful and asked her more about it, tentatively, so as not to rouse suspicion.

"They say that the mother's character is scrutinized, so that no bad blood can unsettle the tidy atmosphere," she said at once. I kept my face turned away and put my hand into a sack of dried meal on the floor as if testing the quality. "They say that only one child in a hundred or more is admitted to this hospital, but when they are, that it is good." I brushed my fingers free of dust and went straight from the shop.

I walked up over Holborn Bridge and up Gray's Inn Lane, right to the new gates, and peered inside before the porter saw me loitering. A group of boys in brown serge coats were running on the grass. After a while I could not see them anymore, as my eyes were filled with tears that would not stop, and so I turned away. I could feel it in my bones that this would never happen to the child I carry. It is too great a risk to wait for. I am not of good character, as I have stolen money from a corpse. I am a criminal, and should that subsequently come to light, would they turn out the child? I do not know.

Thief, thief, a voice in my head whispers, over and over.

There is a glimmer of light outside, as though a scrap of moon were being blown about, and a breeze is twisting at the fabric of the curtains. Everything is unsteady. Sometimes it feels as though there were eyes at every crack. *You will be found out,* the voice says, an icy whisper. In the darkness I reach under my mattress and touch the coins where I keep them at night. They are still there, as hard as stones, as cold as death.

It is almost too late.

There is no time, no time for indecision. My head hurts with it.

I turn and turn on my bed through the night, trying to find rest. I hear Mr. Blacklock slam the front door when he returns. I hear the watchman on the street outside call three and then four o'clock before I sleep.

"Cease to be," I advise it in a whisper, rubbing at my belly over and over.

18

*M*r. Blacklock does not dine with us at noon today, but remains in the workshop for a reason that he does not choose to share. He has been in a grim mood all morning. Mary Spurren is boiling pickle at the hob.

Returning to my bench, I pull up short outside the closed door, my hand frozen at the latch.

"Bastards!" he is shouting. "Damn those bastards! Damn their . . ." and then his voice drops to an ominous murmur and I cannot catch what he is saying. I shrink from the door in shock. I can hear his footsteps crunching on broken glass. After some moments, my concern becomes anxiety that he may find me standing here, eavesdropping on his solitary rage.

I inch back to the kitchen and close the door again. The smell of vinegar is choking. Mary Spurren is wiping the rims of filled pickle pots with a rag.

She cannot think what might have caused his outburst, she says, when I tell her, her big head tilted loftily. "And yet, I knows his patterns. I knows he feels things more than a man should, and that this creates in him a confined storminess that must get out." She shrugs. "Daresay it will pass."

She begins stretching leather over the pots.

It is only later that I remember that Mr. Blacklock was not alone. Joe Thomazin was sitting there beside the stove at the back of the room, as he almost always is. Joe Thomazin must understand John Blacklock more than any other being does. He must know his moods, his habits, his breaking points, his wishes. He is like his shadow or familiar, always beside him, always silent, taking things in. If he could speak, how much he could say!

I do not know John Blacklock, not at all.

"It does not do," Mrs. Blight says, shaking her head so that her chin wobbles, "to talk unguarded in the company of your employer." She takes a handful of herrings left over on a plate and gobbles them down. "I've been hearing all sorts."

"Why should that be?" I ask, uneasily. I think of the time that I asked Mr. Blacklock about his wife, and I am sure he did not mind. "You have heard what sort of things?"

Mrs. Blight shakes her head and laughs, her open mouth filled with fish. "She who treats her words with a certain economy must also possess a mark of efficiency in household matters. Doesn't chatter: therefore doesn't waste soap nor candles. 'Tis logic." She stops chewing to push out a fishbone between her teeth.

"Don't overstep no marks nor boundaries. That's the rules. Right, Mary?" Mary Spurren looks over slyly then, and Mrs. Blight licks herring from the corner of her lips. "Though there are some who might find it of benefit to speak out a little more at table." I do not reply to this, though I know she finds my silence an irritation to her.

"A funny setup it is here," she goes on. "All together at noon like we were a family. It's not right. I gets uneasy over it." She lowers her voice and bares her discolored teeth.

"John Blacklock is eccentric," she hisses. "Only yesterday I was speaking out with Mrs. Spicer in the shop and she told me how she sees his lights just going on burning for most of every night." She taps her head significantly. "And what can he be doing! She sees it, she says, when she gets up to use the pot or fetch a compress for Mr. Spicer, who has his ailment still."

"What is it to do with her?" I ask hotly. "His business is his own, whatever time of night it is."

Mary Spurren looks up.

"Must be them chemicals," Mrs. Blight goes on. "Since I got here I've always said you should watch out with them, they was not healthy. Only have to look at the ends of his fingers to know that. And God knows what they does to his insides; just hear him coughing of a morning." She glances at my fingers suddenly. "Mind you, Agnes has got yellow skin, too, now. Look at that!" She grabs at my hand with her wet fingers and holds it up. "Devil's toys, those squibs and rockets! Not natural. Though I see you take to them well enough."

Mary Spurren slams the door when she goes out to the pump in Mallow Square, though I cannot see why. Without thinking, I press at my stomach in discomfort.

"Indigestion again, is it, Agnes?" Mrs. Blight says, but I don't reply.

"By the by, I brought 'em in for you," she adds, nodding at a stack of pamphlets on the high dresser.

"Thank you," I say. I doubt that I will read them.

19

*I*t is not far from springtime, even in London. I see in the yard the linden tree has new buds now, and the milder weather means great drenches of rain between the sunshine. The clouds roll over the rooftops.

At home in Sussex the great tit will be sawing at his endless, tuneless song from the edge of the apple tree. Spikes of bulbs will be breaking into crocus cups and the fingery spread of anemones. There will be the crack of squirrels in the dry branches, and the earthy sap smell of spring about, as distinctive as the scent of a small child: a smell that quickens the step and causes songs to loosen in the throat. The magpie and jay and jackdaw will be flying across open spaces with twigs in their beaks, or scraps of yellowing wool from the backs of sheep. The babies will be outside playing in the mud and dabbling wet fingers in the water trough. There will be eggs for cooking with again, and the prospect of fresh butter not too far away. The water in the pail will not freeze nor need to be broken for the pig to drink from it, though there may yet be some frosts.

And then I remember that this year there is to be no pig. And I begin to worry again. How I long for some word of my family, of Ann and Lil, of little William, who will be taller and advancing in his boyhood.

"At home we use saltpeter for curing pork, sir," I say, when Mr. Black-lock puts a dark glass jar in front of me. "One spoonful mixed into half a peck of common salt is enough to keep the meat from spoiling."

"Indeed, saltpeter, not a common salt, has many qualities," Mr. Black-lock says. "There are many kinds of salt; for instance baker's salt, salt of lemon, salt of hartshorn, salt of wormwood, Glauber's salt, Epsom salt, salt ash, salt of amber, salt of lead, salt of crab's eye, salt of oxbone, salt of lime, digestive salt of Sylvius." He stops to cough.

"Saltpeter, being potassium nitrate, is more usually known in the trade as niter."

I think of how my hands become sore with rubbing the salt on the meaty flitches of ham. Wet and fractious under the skin of my palms, the sharpness of the salt dissolves steadily into a briny, bloody liquor in the base of the trough. The kimmelling tub was what my grandmother called it, though I never knew why. That tub must be four times older than I am.

Excessive use of saltpeter turns a pickling salt green and the resulting meat will be dark and hard.

"Pig meat is fresh pork," I remember telling William. "But pork means salt pork, strictly speaking. Sometimes the meaning of a word can shift with what we say or how we say it."

"What a trouble it is then, not to make a mistake!" William had said. His face was thoughtful.

The hatted man called Mr. Torré comes to talk of business, and he emerges with Mr. Blacklock from the study after an hour, just as I pass down the corridor with a message from another customer. The empty study smells of coffee. Mr. Torré turns at the front door on his way out.

"By the by, Blacklock," he says, like an afterthought, "those Roman candles you supplied last week were of exceptional quality. Exceptional."

Mr. Blacklock sees me standing as I wait to speak to him and he nods his head in my direction. "My new assistant made that batch from start to finish," he says.

Mr. Torré's eyes widen, and he looks at me closely. "Those were good works, Blacklock, good works." I glance quickly at my boots to hide the small flicker of pride I feel. How grubby they are.

The wind makes the door shut loudly as he leaves.

"I am sorry for him," Mr. Blacklock remarks when he is gone. "It is hard not to take on something of his loneliness after a morning in his company."

I am puzzled.

"What do you mean, sir? He has a wife!" I say. "I saw him walking with her once on Sunday, toward the park. She wore a shawl under her hat, as though feeling the wind would give her an earache."

Mr. Blacklock coughs. "There are many different kinds of being alone," he says. "His wife is ill. They say she may not see another winter."

I look up. Mr. Blacklock is pasting seals of St. Barbara onto finished candles. Outside, the yard is flooded with the song of the wren. He looks critically at his work, squints at a case against the light from the window and then puts it in the half-filled crate. His chair scrapes the floor as he gets up.

"Do you still suffer from the loneliness of losing your family?" he asks me, without warning.

I hesitate.

"Blood is what ties a family together in hours of want, sir, and . . . sometimes that is all we have to share," I say slowly, not quite answering his question. I do not want to lie to Mr. Blacklock anymore. "I am not alone," I add. "I have my sister Ann, and she has me." The homely thought of Ann's face makes tears spring to my eyes and I blink down at my work. *How are you, Ann?* I imagine myself calling the great distance. *How are you all, so far, so lost to me?*

"And what of marriage?" John Blacklock says abruptly, sitting down before the filling-box. "What do you think of marriage?"

"Marriage, sir?" I say.

I do not know what kind of answer I should make. It is a strange question that I do not understand. Does he mean that he has seen through my plan to capture the hand of Cornelius Soul? Does he disapprove of it? My heart races at the thought of that. I wish that I could ask for his advice. I open my mouth and close it tight shut again. It is my own business. Why does it make me so uncomfortable? My heart beats faster still. I touch the skin above my stays and press at it. What of marriage? The puzzling question wavers in my head.

And then I realize that he is thinking of his dead wife. I do not answer then, as I cannot think of anything to say, and it would seem that he forgets to wait for a reply as he bends and works upon his rocket with deeper concentration and does not mention it again.

I would have said, if pressed, that new blood is forged by marriage in the making of children.

The tap, tap of his wooden hammer goes on all morning.

"I have a mind to show you the method for making a more complex firework, a rocket for which I hold particular regard," Mr. Blacklock says later. He goes out to the safe across the yard and returns with a strange double firework in his hands, like a cross.

"A Caduceus rocket must always be brilliant white. In ancient times, the Caduceus was a white wand, borne aloft by heralds declaring peace on battlefields," he explains. "It represents therefore the first stride toward the resolution of conflict. It is a powerful symbol that must be used respectfully and sparingly to preserve its magic." The cough rattles in his chest.

"I like a single Caduceus rocket to commence a display," he goes on. "Blazing its message across the sky as a sign that our explosives are not to demonstrate or threaten of destructive might or forces."

"Are you making your peace with the world?" I interrupt, without a thought before I speak. My face flushes instantly. I meant no disrespect.

Mr. Blacklock looks at me without smiling.

"Perhaps I am," he says.

"The construction of the Caduceus rocket takes the form of the *crux decussata*, or cross on the diagonal," he continues, holding it out. "You can see that a Caduceus rocket is not a single unit but two rockets fastened together at the waist in a shape like the letter X."

Yellow flax is twisted firmly about them in a solid, waxy binding.

"The propelling action of the rockets means that they proceed at variance with one another, and there is a remarkable tension produced by the counterthrust, which causes the whole to rotate fiercely and results in a beautiful screw of fire across the sky.

"It is not an easy rocket in any sense; neither to make, nor to fire, nor in motion. At no point in its arc can it coast smoothly on its own velocity. It is always endeavoring, always straining. Like two notes sounding a harmonious conflict, its balance is perfect, never slack or uneven."

Finally Mr. Blacklock tips the rocket upside down to show the foot of the cases. "It is fired by a conjoined length of quick match inserted in the end of each." Something occurs to me.

"When you say it must be white," I ask curiously, "what do you mean? Do you think that colored sparks and flames are possible to make?"

Mr. Blacklock seems to stiffen. He turns aside and waves his hand dismissively. "That is talk for another day," he says.

I want to make sure that I have grasped his implication fully, so I try as best I can to sum up what I know. "You have taught me how to make golden, silver, brilliant and ruddy fires with degrees of warmth or coldness or intensity within a range of hues lying between white and orange, sir. But you have never mentioned color before. Color is green, crimson, violet: rainbow colors. You have not said a word about colored fire."

"I would not have," he says shortly.

"But is it possible?" I ask, timidly. I would like to know.

"Enough talk, I said!" he barks, and he puts down the rocket and strides from the room. He is irritated by my questions.

"Imagine!" I breathe aloud to Joe Thomazin when I hear the door to the study slamming shut. "If there could be fire like a rainbow!"

Perhaps I did not understand him properly.

Outside in the yard the light becomes blue with approaching dusk. When Mr. Blacklock returns we speak of other matters. He takes a paper from his waistcoat and asks me to prepare two dozen rocket cases for a small, private order he would like completed within a day or so. He comes closer and stands beside me. His nine fingers spread out firmly as he leans them on the bench. I notice there is a neat packet by my tools that, now that I come to think of it, has sat there for days. Whatever it is, he must have forgotten to put it away. He tells me the bore of rocket he requires, and the strength of powder needed. "You have much to learn," he says. "And so, it seems, do I. Life throws up matters when you are least prepared for them." He looks at me, and then, as though he cannot keep it to himself a moment longer, begins to tell me something altogether unexpected.

"By chance I was in the Mitre Tavern near the Royal Society at Crane Court last night," he begins. "And a herd of men of science poured in, freshly puffed up from their lecture." He snorts with contempt. "The loudness of their superior knowledge was the only thing audible as they filled up the room with tobacco smoke and opinions. I was poked in the ribs in the crush and vowed to leave, but as I swallowed down the last of my drink, I caught an exchange that sharpened my ear at once." He leans toward me. "Hearing the words 'artificial fireworks,' I turned to see a man in a thick hat boasting of something that he had seen with his own eyes. I heard him say 'on my return from Moscow.' Then I distinctly heard him say 'a bright and spirituous green fire.' "

"Green fire!" I exclaim. "So it is possible!"

"I became rooted to the spot and strained my ears for more, but the hubbub increased, and by the time the man had finished his little speech he was so walled in by backslapping confederates I could not approach him."

"What can you do about it?" I ask. "How can you—"

"Do?" he interrupts. "Look for the precedents. I read that language well enough."

He turns to his work again, and there is no sound but that of the fire roaring softly inside the stove.

"Blasted Russian secrets," he mutters to himself.

And without warning, as though it, too, is listening to him, the child moves distinctly inside me, like a dark feather creeping about in my belly. There it is again. And a dread that he will despise me soon breaks over me like a flood coming down from the hills. I am awash with fear. I am quite cold with it.

The child is almost all that I have. And its existence will ensure that anything else will be taken away from me.

Later I have to go to him and ask him to repeat his instruction. He glances at me strangely then.

"The listening ear should always be left ajar to possibility," he rebukes. I look down at my yellowing hands.

"I am sorry to appear discourteous," I say. "It is only that . . ."

"You are thinking of your family?" he asks me unexpectedly.

And I hesitate before I say, "I suppose that I am."

"There is something for you," he adds, and I realize that he is pointing at the packet on the bench.

"Is there? From whom?" I ask. "From . . ." It must be something left by Cornelius Soul, I think, and my heart gives a leap. My plan is working.

"Myself," he says abruptly. He lifts on his greatcoat and then seems to hesitate, as if to watch me open it. Peeping inside the packet, I see that he has bought me a pair of brand-new gloves. I take them out, amazed. I pull them on and bend and straighten all my fingers one by one. Their supple creamy kidskin is like a second skin on me.

"Thank you, sir," I say, looking up, but find the door has shut and he is gone out already.

I am sorry I cannot work in them.

They look too perfect. It is disrespectful to dirty them with chemicals and paste and charcoal dust, though I do not want to seem ungrateful.

Mr. Blacklock seems disappointed when he returns and sees that I have taken the gloves off and laid them down on the bench. At first he does not say a thing. Later he asks me if there is something wrong with them.

"Are they too tight, too coarse?" he asks earnestly.

"Oh no," I say, thanking him. "It is simply that they make my fingers stupid."

His face falls when I say that. I suppose he must have spent two shillings on them.

The week is calm after this anomaly. For days I make stars, dry stars and choke rocket cases and then charge them. I work alongside Mr. Blacklock, watching him from time to time to see the skill with which he works, but we do not often speak. On rare occasions Mr. Blacklock leaves the workshop on some business. Today he has to meet with Mr. Torré in the coffeehouse, and then he is going south of the river to a large estate on the other side of Southwark. For the first time, he has left me with a list of fireworks to complete by the end of the day.

"I need mutton chops this afternoon," Mrs. Blight announces as we clear the breakfast. But Mary Spurren cannot go to the butcher's shop, as once again Mrs. Nott did not come this morning and Mary has to make a start upon the laundry. She is in a sour mood already, scrubbing the soap viciously into the weave of the linen, slapping the wet cloth into the bowl of water. Mrs. Nott seldom seems to come as promised, but instead a week later when nobody expects her and the wash is half-completed anyway.

"Indeed it may be expedient, Mr. Blacklock, sir, to look elsewhere," Mrs. Blight had declared at breakfast.

"No, no, woman!" he said roughly. "Be good enough not to waste time seeking a replacement."

"She is a low class of female," Mrs. Blight said, grumpily.

I could tell that Mr. Blacklock was irritated by this, but Mrs. Blight burst out, "Not as if she were one of your staff that you take it so badly; she is a woman as turns up to scrub at clothes. Turns up at her leisure, it seems to me."

"Enough!" he barks.

Mrs. Blight is quite put out, and at noon cooks the spinach to a pulp almost on purpose.

"She does not rinse to a point of clarity," she hisses, slamming the colander down. "Too much lye unrinsed between the threads of linen makes a body itch. Not to mention her being completely lacking in moral fiber." She glares across as though this were somehow to do with me.

"That's some folks for you," Mary Spurren says, sourly.

I have a mounting fear that Mrs. Blight thinks I should be made an example of. She has a way of looking at me that cuts right to the heart of what I'm hiding.

"Mr. Blacklock don't like too much change," Mary Spurren says, squeezing out a wet shirt.

"It is ridiculous," snaps Mrs. Blight mutinously. "No way to run a household."

"Too much change by far these days," Mary Spurren adds, the shirt dripping on the floor.

I scarcely know how Mrs. Nott manages to lug the quantity of water from the pump in Mallow Square, the tendons in her scrawny neck straining against her knuckle-grip.

"Perhaps he likes to hear her singing," I suggest. "It is so sweet and clear." Mary Spurren sniggers, looking sidelong.

"You'll go for the chops, Agnes," Mrs. Blight says. "And cook them up."

"But I do not know how," I say anxiously, thinking of all I have to do for Mr. Blacklock today, yet mindful that I have to keep her sweet. She looks bad-tempered, seeing her drinking time at the Star being cut by half if she has to go herself.

"Rarely we ate fresh meat at home in Sussex," I say. "That is why I am so fat now!" I exclaim, taking my chance. "We eat so very well here."

"I'll take a gamble," Mrs. Blight says sarcastically, "on what ability you have with meat and tell you again to fetch chops and onions before you go into that workshop this afternoon."

"But . . ." I begin to protest, but she jabs at the open recipe with her finger. As soon as she is gone I rush upstairs to relieve myself. I hope she has not noticed how often now I have to use the chamber pot.

I know that Cornelius Soul is due with a delivery today.

I must hurry or else my plan may begin to fall apart. Already I feel that time is slipping away from me.

I must try harder.

Today the butcher's shop is filled with blue tits, flitting to the beef, hanging upside down and sticking their bills into the white fat, all over the sheep's kidneys, nipping the suet from them. The butcher's boy does nothing about it. When he yawns I can see to the back of his throat. Saul Pinnington is bringing an uncut ham in over his shoulder from out the back. He sets it down, sweating with effort, and sees the birds.

"Get!" he shouts at the birds, enraged.

"Pests, they are," an old woman says, waiting before me. She waves her crabbed hands toward the meat. "Everywhere."

"It's that tree," Saul Pinnington says, glowering out of his shutters at the great linden tree on the corner of the street. "Harbors little beggars like these."

"Chop it down, I should, Mr. Pinnington." The old woman points out which bit of liver she is wanting from the slab.

A girl wearing a checked apron comes in. "Full of bees, that tree. Can't abide bees," she says. "Had one in my hair last summer, stang me here and here." She tilts her chin up for the butcher to examine. "You want to look out for your custom, Mr. Pinnington, do something about it." Her fingers ruffle at the lace that ties her neckerchief.

The butcher winks at her. "What am I selling to you today, young lady?"

"Sliver me up some Dutch beef, Mr. Pinnington." She widens her eyes. "They like it done finely."

"Mrs. Bray fatting her girls up, is she?" Saul Pinnington asks, smirking. His arms are bloody to the elbow. "I've got good common forcemeat ready down here. Would they not prefer a taste of that?"

"Didn't think you had that kind of money, Mr. Pinnington," she replies. Her voice is crisp. Saul Pinnington lets out a dirty red butcher's laugh. His belly shakes with it.

"Pert little madam, that one," the old woman mutters under her breath, as the girl leaves the shop. "Chop it down, I say. Doing nothing, that tree is." Her face is shriveled with crossness. "What other use is there for it, save providing somewhere tall for the likes of her associates to lean upon at night? Dirty girls."

Bray. Mrs. Bray. I cannot think where I have heard the name before.

Saul Pinnington serves me and I take the pound of mutton.

"Bray," I say, aloud this time, out on the street. What is that name? It niggles at me. I am perplexed as to the nature of the jokes he made, but it is clear he was suggesting, as no idle insult, that the girl worked in the kitchen of a bawdy house or brothel, and neither did she make a fight about it.

I turn to Lamb's Conduit Street toward the herb market to get some early onions from the skinny market woman there, whom Mrs. Blight declares the only garden trader worth the shilling. "Her things is fresh and firm, that's all I asks for in a vegetable."

The market woman has a large baby with her. It sits propped up beneath the trestle on a grubby blanket spread over the ground, playing with a spoon tied to a string. The baby's nose is running.

"I shall have to tether him, too, soon as he gains the use of his legs." The market woman laughs. Though she is young, her face is so thin that when she laughs the skin around her mouth looks stretched. Her finger-nails are stained and rough, and the silver coin I give her looks bright in her palm.

Mrs. Blight had said today as I picked up the basket, "No wasting your coinage on the first barrow boy that shoves his radishes at you. Their flavors is bound to be tainted with smoke from sea coal. Nasty, that is. You can't trust everyone, Agnes Trussel, most particularly in the way of purchases."

I go stiff with recollection.

"You cannot trust a soul," I was told, when I arrived here.

It was Lettice Talbot who had tried to send me in the way of Mrs. Bray's establishment. Mrs. Bray who must be a madam, or a procuress. Lettice Talbot's eyes were wide and blue when she spoke. Lettice Talbot's teeth were good and white. She looked nothing like a prostitute. Not like dirty Martha Cote, back home, with her long lank hair, who would lie with anyone in the fields for fourpence. Surely Lettice Talbot did not think that I could work with her?

"Get on, will you!" A woman pokes me sharply in the back where I am stopped on the pavement. I look about. The street is seething with people I do not know.

As I turn into the dead end, toward Blacklock's, I see with relief that the cart is not there. Perhaps Mr. Soul has not been yet.

I am not sure why, but at the front door something makes me turn and look back to the archway. I am surprised to see a man there, standing in the shadows. And though his head is not turned directly to me, I have the sharp sensation that it is me he looks at.

Why would that be?

I shield my eyes with my palm, against the brightness. His back is turned now, and his feet shift about as though uncomfortable or lacking patience.

How hot it is.

I blink, the sweat making my sight swim for a moment, so that I put down the basket and rub my eyes with the heel of my hand. And when I look again, the man is gone.

I let myself in and as I pass the workshop door I see two new tubs of gunpowder on the floor already. I have missed Mr. Soul.

Despite the heat, a shivery chill goes through me when I think of that strange man again. His dark clothing, the oddness of his stance, his very ordinary appearance being somehow the reverse of what it seemed.

He was a pale-skinned man taking shelter from the harshness of the sun, I reason. Or stopping heedlessly to attend to failing embers in his tobacco pipe. Or waiting to chance upon a hackney carriage. Or he mistook me fleetingly for someone else before he realized his mistake.

And yet the chill persists, even as I try to cook the meat, and only when Mrs. Blight waddles back, in the unsteady temper that tells me she has sat out an hour or more drinking at the Star, can I begin to shake it off.

"I want that oak white scrubbed, d'you hear!" She points at the table strewn with peelings.

"Beech," I say, without thinking, and bite my tongue. I do not want to provoke her crossness any more today.

"Pardon me?" She turns to make sure that Mary Spurren is looking over, and puts her hand on her hip.

"It's beech," I mutter, and try to make my voice sound sorry about it. "The tabletop is made of beechwood."

"You little—" she begins, but I do not get to hear what she has to say about me, as Mr. Blacklock has walked abruptly into the kitchen.

"Oh! Mr. Blacklock, sir, I thought you was—"

"I returned by an earlier coach from Southwark," he interrupts. "What is Agnes doing in the kitchen today? She had clear instructions to finish an order." He glares at the squat little clock over the fireplace that Mrs. Blight does her timings for meat by. "It is late."

I leave the bowl of muddy peelings at once and go in haste down the corridor. And I hear her saying, in the shrill tone that she saves for moments of crisis, ". . . just does as she fancies, sir, whatever shall I do?" But I cannot hear how he replies.

Mrs. Blight has begun to keep a bottle of gin at the back of the cupboard, which she thinks is a secret.

My own secret has grown fourfold this month. I begin to feel its weight inside me.

20

*I*n the morning Mary Spurren does not look so well.

"I feel sickly," she groans, rubbing her head.

Mrs. Blight is slouched beside the hob and flicks the greasy pages of her recipe. "A big joint like that needs to be got early, to be cooked for noon," she says loudly. "Agnes, you'll go for the meat today."

"Again?" I say in dismay. "But I have to—"

"You'll squeeze it in," she says, in a hard voice. "Just don't expect Mr. Pinnington to be so robust with you today."

"Why?"

"The hanging. You'll have heard the bell last night? They say George Nigh was his acquaintance of some long standing, fell on hard times. Served their apprenticeships together side by side like kinsmen, and shared a stall at Smithfield for close on a year before they parted company. Seems that while Pinnington's Meats to the Nobility became a fixture in the high-class victuals trade, George Nigh's luck fell on the other side of the fence and he slid into the mire of debts and turned to crime." She tuts. "Robberies is always bound to get found out. Violence like that, on the king's highway." She quivers with relish. "'Tis bound to want punishing in the end."

"But if the man had debts," I venture, "what could he do?"

"Seems a shame, I must say, when a man has to make his way by stripping well-off, middling folks of what they has and causing bodily fear."

"And did he kill a man or do injury to anyone?" I ask.

"Not as is heard of," she says. "But 'tis the principle, and besides, there's no smoke without some kind of thing ablaze somewhere. Thrusting his pistol into carriages and making threats. Loaded, no doubt, with shot supplied by the likes of your Mr. Cornelius." .

"He is not . . ."

"And two unmarried women to swing alongside George Nigh and his crowd this morning; should in all be quite a gathering. Pleaded their bellies, but when matrons examined them they found them both to be without child." She heaves herself onto her feet.

"I've heard someone's been stealing plate from churches over Westminster way. Very low, that is. You're not going to tell me that shouldn't go unpunished, neither! Crime's everywhere. These days even God has to resort to lock and key to protect what's rightly his, and that's not in the Bible, is it? *Thou shalt lock up the churches at six o'clock?* On cutting him down," she adds, "they'll take this one away to the Surgeon's Hall to be anatomized, quite took apart in the name of science. Dissecting him up to strike fear of the law throughout all of the populace." She shakes her head with a show of regret. "Disgrace for his family."

I go to the butcher's in dread.

Saul Pinnington is not there behind the counter. The shop is packed with customers and the boy is full of his story, his face flushed with talking as he tries to serve.

"Mr. Pinnington's not here, ma'am, he's off to the hanging, to lend his weight and pull on his legs to hasten the end. George Nigh's not a big man now, is he? I've seen a hanging, quite a sight." He flusters about.

"You're making a mess of that hog's cheek, young man," a woman calls impatiently. My back aches. The boy raises his piping to be heard over the hum of chatter and gossip in the shop.

"Lord, the prayers they mouth before they pull the cart from under them. I went to a hanging once, did I say that? Oh, Mr. Pinnington was in a terrible way through yesterday. Cursing and kicking the cats about all day, he was. Kept saying, 'The foolish son of a bitch' . . ."

An old woman pushes forward to the counter. "You hold your

tongue," she chastens him, jerking her crooked finger at his chest. The hubbub in the shop dies down and people turn to stare. "That's someone's father swinging on the tree this morning," she spits. "You'll speak respectful of him, if you speak at all." And she turns and pushes her way angrily toward the door.

Behind the counter the boy's face is drained of color, and I see that his hands shake as he wraps the joint for Mrs. Blight. He cannot be more than twelve years old, and looks as if he might cry, though with great effort he does not. He rubs the back of his hand on his white forehead, leaves a streak of blood. "That's one shilling and tuppence," he says in a small voice, not looking at me. The joint is as thick as a man's leg, and I feel sickened at the thought of eating it at noon.

"Lessons it is, I'd say," Mrs. Blight makes clear later, sucking her teeth. She has grown boisterous and unsteady since I saw her this morning. "They says drink leads to crime. Hah! I'm not averse to knocking back a glass or two of orange shrub," she cackles. "But you don't find me going off like a delinquent." She looks at me and hiccups. "Lessons for all of us to keep on the straight and narrow. Should be requisite to go to hangings. Should be the law."

I shift uncomfortably.

Mrs. Blight snorts. "Look at her." She points at me. "So worried someone'll make her go and see the next." She tries to explain: "It's more the . . . atmosphere you goes for. The final act itself doesn't last so long." The smell of roasting pork is everywhere.

"Sometimes there's a bit of ruckus when they cuts them down, the families fighting for the corpse to take for burial against the surgeons hoping for a bit of flesh to practice on, but 'tis never so bad as you'd think. Once you've seen a couple, well"—she shrugs—"you've seen them all. Sometimes, like today, they does a cluster all at once, say six or seven punished side by side. Daresay that would be a comfort, a bit of company in your final moments."

I put the knife into the round of the bread upon the board and slice up the whole loaf steadily. I am quite light-headed. Mary Spurren's cold is worsening and I can hear her sniffing to herself, hunched over the scullery sink, scrubbing at a dirty pot.

Mrs. Blight frowns at me.

"Hope you're hungry, madam," she comments sharply. "Wasting all that bread."

"Oh, yes, very hungry. I suppose I could be starving; any of us could, given a wrong turn here, a wrong turn there," I retort, putting the knife down. "Even Mr. Blacklock says the city's gutter is always but a step away."

Mary Spurren comes out of the scullery, wiping her nose on a crumpled handkerchief. "Don't much hold with crowds," she says congestedly, and I nod my head.

"You needs hardening up," Mrs. Blight opines. "You've been shielded from certain things in life. I don't mean you have not felt the bite of hardship or the gall of someone else's wrong, but you don't know how badness makes up half the world and how it follows that we'll rub shoulders with it in the natural flow of life."

She gestures advice broadly with an empty bottle.

"Keep out the way of trouble and lift your chin when it finds you, as it no doubt will from time to time. Evil's not something that'll be brought to account. Much of it, nigh on all of it'll slip by unnoticed, doing its willful business in due course as it fancies."

"Don't you have faith in justice?" I ask. "Why do you like your pamphlets so much?"

"Justice!" She chuckles. "Hear how the girl speaks! What is this justice?" Her eye narrows at me.

"What of divine justice, then?" I say.

"It's a whipsaw world," she goes on, "cutting both ways, and sometimes there is redress, sometimes there isn't. And you know my feelings about the Lord's House; I've said before it's not for me. Anything that's built with bricks and mortar's made by man and can't represent a higher cause. Each man to himself."

She taps her head. "I've me own counsel," she says.

"As I have a conscience," I reply, under my breath.

Aurora

21

From what you tell me," I say to Mr. Blacklock, when we come to talk of the third ingredient of gunpowder, "sulfur is a kind of latent earth." I look for his approval, to see that I have understood his meaning fully, and repeat slowly, in my own words, what he has already told me. "It is something waiting under the crust of the earth: a bright yellow under the darkness of the soil. It is old, as old as the hill that hides it. You say that sulfur comes from places where the very earth itself has bubbled out molten in cracks and craters."

He nods gravely.

"But I cannot picture this at all," I say. "It means nothing to imagine the innards of the living earth."

Mr. Blacklock raises his eyebrows. "Indeed?" he says, scratching his head. "Then consider the earth's shape to be round like that of a kernel, filled to the skin with minerals and unimaginable liquid fire."

"But how can I be sure of what you say, sir? These things seem likely when you are describing them, yet . . ."

Mr. Blacklock looks at me intently.

He goes to the study and brings back a book, and shows me on the yellow page the diagrams of little round black balls like walnuts circling the sun on strings. And I pore over them with curiosity, as one would look at marks in the mud on the edge of a pond showing that certain birds had been there, or water rats, or the dogs of poachers, yet somehow not believing in them absolutely.

"I have a thirst for *useful* knowledge, Mr. Blacklock, sir," I say.

We go on filling gerbes with common stars and silver rain. Later

Mr. Blacklock looks at me. "You are right in some ways to raise questions." He clears his throat. "But you must narrow your eyes and squint into the bright light of the world's knowledge if you are to advance in understanding what I have to teach you. Do you want to learn from me?" he asks quietly. His dark face is very serious.

I blink at him. "I do, sir."

"Then sometimes you must accept as fact some things that you cannot verify for yourself entirely." He gives his head a light tap. "Take that leap forward. Have a trust in some sources."

"I want to learn, sir," I say.

And it is true. Lately, the need to know has begun to burn inside me like a small fire.

Soon after the church clock has struck two that afternoon, at last Cornelius Soul's painted cart pulls up outside the door.

"Roll brimstone differs from flowers of sulfur," Mr. Blacklock is saying. "It can be used for making stars, as it lacks the sulfuric acid that is present after sublimation, but it is quite a labor to crush and sift." I cannot help but glance up expectantly, and Cornelius Soul opens the door and breezes into the workshop. "Can you think of anything particular about the properties of sulfur that should not be ignored, Mr. Soul?" Mr. Blacklock barks.

"It is the yellowest thing I can think of," Cornelius Soul affirms, and winks at me as he puts a tub of powder on the floor.

I try to contest his flippancy by thinking of something that is yellower. A range of yellow things runs through my head: a buttercup, the yolk of an egg slimy cap fungus, one kind of rowanberry, yellow feathers on goldfinches, wagtails, yellowhammers, the tip of the beak of a dabchick, a grain of ready wheat in summer, various caterpillars and centipedes, half the stripes of wasps, a melted butter sauce, the general sense inside a beepot, the flowers of penny rattle, and then I have it.

"The sun!" I exclaim. I am triumphant. "The sun is yellower!" I am laughing. "It is so yellow that we cannot even look at it!"

Cornelius Soul pretends to consider this. "Our own luminary," he says, stroking his jaw as though this could make him think more clearly. His pale stubble rasps. And then he counters, "But we do not know that it is not made entirely out of sulfur anyway!"

He yawns. "You see, we are undone by knowing nothing at last. I like to know nothing." He pushes at his hair. "Knowing nothing leaves so much space around one, for doing other things. I like a lot of space. I am a big fellow, am I not?" And he winks at me again, a sharp, dirty wink this time that makes my skin prickle with a kind of flush.

Mr. Blacklock stands up. "Sulfur has a bad, eggish smell that worsens upon ignition," he says crisply. "That is a portion of its ugliness. No doubt you must be done with us now, Mr. Soul. Your schedule for delivery—or should that be deliverance, God help you—must be pressing at this juncture of the day."

Joe Thomazin sits untwisting some kind of cotton for quick match.

"What is this?" I ask, holding up a length, to fill the silence when the rumble of Mr. Soul's cart has faded away.

"Nothing but common cotton, of the kind used as a wick by candlemakers," Mr. Blacklock says sharply.

I cannot understand what can have made him angry. I wonder why he finds Mr. Soul so vexing; he is too confident, perhaps, too full of life.

"And pay no heed to his licentious filthy tongue," he adds, but I do not know what he means by that at all.

Mrs. Mellin's coins inside my stays are yellow, but somehow different. I think of her face reflected tiny on the surface of each coin she handled.

How mild this sunshine is for April, and how late it shines on in the afternoon. My woollen shawl seems almost too warm about my shoulders as I go around the house, but I dare not take it off; it is covering my shape. My bodice is let out to its furthest span, but the ribbons will go no further and soon I fear I must leave off my stays. When that day comes, my condition will be clear to anyone who casts an eye upon me.

"God damn my carelessness!" Mr. Blacklock says suddenly, under his breath, and he sweeps the invoice aside on the dusty desk.

"What is it?" I ask.

"When I made out Mr. Soul's last order for gunpowder, I failed to calculate for Mr. Torré's display at St. James's. As a consequence we have only one box of powder left, which will not be enough."

"No," I say. The long list of works needed is pinned up on the wall. "We have not even started on the Roman candles." Mr. Blacklock begins to scribble on a scrap of paper.

"It is almost four and I have an appointment here with a new client in half an hour that I cannot miss," he says. He looks about distractedly.

"Joe! Joe Thomazin!" he shouts. "Where is that boy!"

"He is just out, sir, on messages already."

"Damnation twice!" he says. "There is an urgency to this!"

"Shall I go at once to Mr. Soul's lodgings and ask for more myself?" I suggest. Mr. Blacklock stands and glowers at the list as if lost in thought, and does not seem to hear me. I begin to speak again.

"Should I—"

"It is hard to say where he may be," Mr. Blacklock interrupts. "He moves between a number of places, I believe, and I admit I do not have a fixed address for him. He draws his stock from several warehouses, so there is no point in chasing him about the town." He coughs heavily into his fist. "Most likely he could be found at Child's, but I am unwilling . . ." He hesitates, clears his throat, then seems to change his mind. "No. You must go there at once and explain our position, or I will not rest easy this afternoon, knowing as I do how low that barrel's going to be."

The coffeehouse is a fug of smoke and shouting, full of men. Nobody pays any attention to me and I cannot see Cornelius Soul in among them anywhere. The only woman in here is a wan girl listlessly wiping at a table with a cloth, and I go to ask her for his whereabouts.

"Who's asking?" she says, without interest.

"Mr. Blacklock, Mr. John Blacklock," I say, and with an effort she slopes to the back of the shop and leans on the jamb. The door is ajar on to the yard.

"Cartright! Housemaid from Blacklock's here," she bawls, which makes me bristle. "Wants Cornelius Soul. Wasn't he here, not long back? Where'd he go again?"

A man replies but I do not hear it. Then he appears at the door, doing up his breeches.

"He's up at his mother's place, wench," he says, not unkindly, when he sees me standing there. "You know the way to Curtain Court, on the edge of St. Giles?" I listen to the man's directions with care.

On my way out, a man seated by the door leans forward and studies me closely, as though he has mistaken me for someone else. He is scruffier than the men around him, and has a round, stubbly face. He puts down his long pipe and seems to be about to speak, but I pull my shawl tight about me and do not catch his eye. It is a relief to close the door quickly upon his leery gaze. The sour smell of pipe smoke clings to my clothes for half the walk across the district, and then I forget about him. It is a warm day; I am glad there is no rain.

The house is thin and shabby, with a peeling front. I knock twice, until a woman's voice calls, "Will you get that!" and a girl lets me in. A small, neat woman looks up, startled, when she sees a stranger.

"I have a message for Cornelius Soul," I say.

Her eyes flick to the open door. "From . . . ?"

"From Blacklock's Pyrotechny."

"He's up in the chamber, fixing the casement again," the woman says. "That rain we had last night—came pouring in." Her voice is very quiet, so that I have to listen hard to what she says.

"Cornelius!" she calls out softly.

"He's a good son," she adds unnecessarily, in almost a whisper. A cat jumps up onto the empty sideboard and licks at its tail.

"Will you sit and wait?" she asks me. "Get up, Nat, and let the girl sit down," she coaxes, and a little boy squats politely on the ground beside the hearth, though there is no fire lit. He stares at me, winding thread upon a spool.

The woman does not say much but goes on stitching at the man's coat stretched on her lap. She hums for some time.

The room is plain and clean, though the bad, bitter smell of lye boiling at the soapmaker's comes in from the street. There is little in the way of chattels, though several garments hang across the crooked beam over the fireplace. She glances up and seems to read my mind.

"The dishes are out at pawn, though no doubt I'll get them back come wages day." She fingers the half-stitched lapel. There is a pot of something cold like stew or broth upon the table, with a fatty skin across its surface, and a quartern loaf cut into five.

"Less to wash up once supper is over," I suggest, and her face breaks into a surprising, crinkled smile, so that her eyes quite disappear.

"You could say that," she says, in almost a whisper. "One tiny blessing." She tugs at her needle.

There is a noise upstairs and Cornelius Soul clatters backward down the ladder, in his shirtsleeves. "All done, Mam," he says briskly, turning about. "Though that won't last another season."

And then he gives a start to see me in the kitchen, as though he has been caught out, and a boyish flush spreads over his face. I get to my feet.

"Your mother has explained what an attentive son you are," I say. He laughs loudly, as though he thinks that I am mocking him. "Mr. Blacklock needs more stock," I say. "More gunpowder, and more meal."

"So many surprises to be had, Miss Trussel," he replies, recovering quickly, as though from a stumble. "What a long way you have walked to tell me that."

"It is urgent," I say.

"I see," he says, and grins as if he does not believe me. "First light tomorrow, then," he says, with a dramatic bow.

As I go to the door I have a little rush of courage. "It is delivery we want, not the start of a battle!" I retort, and take my leave. My heart beats in a flutter of panic all the way down the street; sauciness does not come easily to me. Beyond the court and out of sight on Turnmill Street I check my shawl and tuck it again in the way that I have devised to cover my belly properly from view. And by a curious chance I look up to see the man from the coffeehouse who had observed me so steadily. I am sure it is the same man. But though I pass quite close to him he gives no sign of having recognized me, and steps up into the alehouse on the corner.

How warm it is.

I give the meat market a wide berth and come back instead by Snow Hill.

At the house Mr. Blacklock sits inside his study when his new client has gone, and does not come to supper. Mrs. Blight has finished up and taken herself to the Star before we are done with eating, which has stirred up some kind of grumpiness in Mary Spurren quite at odds with the way I feel today.

"Are you unwell?" I ask cheerfully. Perhaps she has her head cold back again. She gets up from the table to see to the pudding.

"Funny ideas you've got, Agnes Trussel," she hisses, unexpectedly. "Don't you know how to behave in service?"

"What do you mean?" I say, startled, but she turns back to the hob to lift the pudding from the scalding water and does not hear me, as though anger has stopped up her ears. The steam smells good. I watch her slow fingers fumble with the pudding cloth as she unties it on the plate. I am so hungry I do not care until we finish eating. My swelling belly makes my appetite a monstrous thing.

"Slipping off here and there," she adds. "Think nobody notices?" The pot she has scrubbed to the point of cruelty gleams on the side.

"But I was taking messages for Mr. Blacklock!" I protest, but she does not reply, and her mood gives a different cast to the remains of the evening. I like it better when Mr. Blacklock eats with us at supper.

What can he be working on that he misses meals so often now? Is it for urgency, or secrecy? Has he found something new? Perhaps I could ask him, I think, but I find I dare not. After all, he might not say.

Early light floods into the workshop as Mr. Blacklock pins the shutters open the next morning. "I must go down to the timber yard," he says.

"Why, sir?" I ask.

"Deal sawdust for fiery rains. Mr. Torré plans a volcanic eruption for the display at St. James's," he says. "And what Mr. Torré wants, he will have, whatever we may think about it. The sawdust must be deal, for the rosins feed the sparks in the fire." I nod. I think of putting a pine log on the fire, how it spits and whines, the gummy bubble from the end of its cut limbs. It occurs to me that Mr. Blacklock may be planning something special for this occasion, a new style of firework, perhaps one that does a loop, or shoots out a brilliant star, the like of which has never been seen before in London.

"Shall I come with you, to carry the bags?" I ask hopefully. Perhaps he might tell me as we walk along.

He scowls. "Indeed no, Joe Thomazin will do. The timber yard is crawling with rogues and foul-mouthed scoundrels; it is no place for a decent woman to hear talk. That extra powder is due from Mr. Soul this morning," he adds.

When he is gone, I make sure my cap is on straight. I have scrubbed my fingers very clean. I work diligently for a while, but my mind begins to wander and then I cannot help but scan the room for clues, just an inkling of what Mr. Blacklock is about. His bench today is uncommonly tidy and tells me nothing. The tools are laid in a row, only a worn-down sash-brush out of place. There are five one-ounce cases waiting to be filled, a short discarded length of quick match, a pot of dried-up paste. There are no scraps of paper with mysterious plans sketched out, nor unusual apparatus. But then I look again more closely at his bench, and notice a faint, bright shadow on its surface, as if a large amount of reddish powder had been brushed hastily away. I don't dare to touch, and when I sniff it cautiously, there is no particular smell I recognize.

Outside, the church clocks strike ten. I can hear the mild rasp of someone scrubbing nearby.

Turning my attention to the shelves, I climb upon a stool and lift down the dirty jars of chemicals one by one, carrying them into the light to examine them.

They are newly opened.

When I first arrived at Blacklock's Pyrotechny, all these jars of substances were sat unused, untouched for years, covered in filthy cobwebs. And suddenly, perhaps this week, the seals are broken, corks taken out, some jars left carelessly unstopped. Others lie empty, on their sides. Almost every single jar is opened now.

When did he do this? I look over at the apparatus on the far trestle. He has been using them in his experiments. He has been using all of them.

I find rose vitriol, and manganese. I find king's yellow or orpiment. *A sulfide of arsenic*, a note in Mr. Blacklock's writing says. There is yellow ochre, which is iron oxide and clay; there is telluric ochre and tungstic ochre and yellow prussiate, none of which I know and which sound like foreign diseases of the flesh.

Holding my breath, I pick up the dark jar of yellow orpiment and take out a piece upon a spoon to look at it closely. The orpiment is greasy and pearly, and brown on the outside where the air has got to it. The side that has been cut is yellower, fresher. Just looking at it tells me nothing.

"Poison, that is." Cornelius Soul's sudden voice makes me jump. "Dead in a day or so, you would be, should you have swallowed it, with a terrible purging and a sweat."

"I know," I lie quickly. "How did you get in?"

He grins. "The housemaid gave me entrance by the front door as she was there washing the step. Don't lick your fingers," Cornelius Soul says, chuckling. "Clots the blood in your heart right up. Though I daresay you've a little pink tongue I shouldn't mind a glimpse of. Very wholesome, I'd imagine." And he comes up closer and tries to fondle me about the waist.

"Oh no!" I say, stepping backward in embarrassment and knocking the stool over with a clatter.

"Good for a man to see that kind of tongue," he says, as I bend with difficulty to put it upright. "Very nourishing indeed."

I keep my mouth tight shut and do not reply, even when he asks where he should put the powder that we need. He looks at my face.

"Don't mind me, Miss Trussel," he says, and puts it anywhere. "Forgive my manners. I am a lout," he says at the door. But he does not mean it.

I do not move until I hear his horse's hooves start up. Then I return the array of jars to their places and wipe the dirt crossly from my fingers before I go to the filling-box. Why did I push him away like that? I have an uncomfortable sense inside when I think of how I am cheating him. Perhaps I had not expected him to like me. I had not thought that the plan could be effective. But it surely must. And when he finds out my condition, it will be after the marriage vows are said and done. They are all I need to save me from ruin. He will know that the child is not his—but that is another thing to think of, later.

I must work swiftly now; there is much to be done if we are to fulfill our orders. And I cannot put aside the thought of all those opened jars of chemicals. I charge eight rockets of a quarter-pound bore. I hear Mary Spurren cursing to herself as she slips on the wet doorstep when she leaves for the fruit market. The house is silent when she is gone, no sound from any other quarter. Mrs. Blight is on her half day. A fly buzzes dryly against the windowpane. I can smell the leather of Mr. Blacklock's working apron lying flat in a patch of sunlight where he left it on his bench. I charge two more rockets, until I can bear it no longer and go back to the shelves and stare at the opened jars again, as if they might tell me something. And then there is a knock at the door. A harsh, demanding kind of rapping, made with the head of a cane or stick.

My heart hammers almost as loudly in my mouth.

I do not go to answer it.

When Mr. Blacklock returns he shows me how to boil the sawdust in a kind of soup with saltpeter, then drain it of liquor with a slatted spoon. The stink it makes clams up my throat.

I do not say a word about the knocking.

Again Mr. Blacklock does not take supper in the kitchen this evening but instead goes into the study. An oblong of light from the lamp he has on the table falls under the shut door. When I pass as I retire at ten o'clock to bed I can just hear the scratching of a pen upon paper, and the chink of the nib touching the rim of the inkpot. I mean to tap and ask if he would like a bite or a glass of wine to see him through, yet somehow I cannot. The nib seems to pause as though I had already broken in upon his thinking.

At the stairs, something makes me turn around and I see that the study door is open a crack and Joe Thomazin has slipped out into the hallway. He is watching me without a sound.

"What is it, Joe?" I whisper, but his great dark eyes do not answer me.

After some days, I spread out the damp sawdust, sprinkle over equal measures of mealpowder and sulfur and stir it about.

"Now fill those candles and your flowerpots, and you have a red shower," Mr. Blacklock says. "A large enough quantity, I think, for Mr. Torré."

"A red shower?" I ask, surprised. "Really red, sir?" He nods without looking up from the bench. I close my eyes and imagine a light, brushing kind of scarlet rain, a fine drift of crimson sparkles turning on the air, flurrying out of the sweep of the sunset on the horizon's light westerly breeze, almost like snowflakes in their shape and beauty. I imagine the sweet scent of their burning, winking out as they touch the ground, and the soft resinous warmth of the smoke that would linger on their wake.

I have a fright when I open my eyes again, and see Mr. Blacklock staring at me. Most probably he cannot believe the cheek of it, just drifting off in my own dreaminess in the middle of work. His black eyes are quite fixed upon me.

"So sorry, sir," I mumble, and bend my head over my work and try to seem industrious. "Those dogs kept me awake half the night with their barking; did you hear them yourself, sir? Strays, probably. Such a racket." He does not reply. He does not like chatter, I remind myself, nor excuses. Sometimes I think it must be the child growing inside me that makes my head so apt to slide off sideways these days into its own little place of nonsense. And then again I wonder if it is the thought of fireworks. They promise so much glitter, so much magic, it is surely no surprise that they make me dreamy.

For the rest of the day I make sure my ramming at the filling-box is efficient, and when the church bells strike six I do not even look up from my bench, until Mr. Blacklock announce himself that the day's work is done.

"You must watch a full display before too long," he says, when the workshop is locked up and we are walking down the gloom of the corridor to the steamy kitchen. "To demonstrate quality."

I feel a surge inside.

I almost choke with the effort to keep my composure. "That would be useful, sir," I manage to mumble, but cannot help a smile creeping over my face as we sit down to eat the boiled beef and greens that Mrs. Blight sets on the table. *A display! Rockets, candles, squibs!* I can hardly believe it.

"Sawdust can also be used in cautious measures for silver rains and golden rains," he adds later, his mouth full of beef. "But there is no need for boiling."

I nod happily and pour some ale, and Mr. Blacklock leans over and points into my mug abruptly. "Do you see how the colors change and spin over the surface of those bubbles?"

I hold the mug up to my gaze, and with delight I can see this. "The colors are shivering across almost like rainbows, sir!"

"I thought that would please you," he says, gruffly.

Mary Spurren stares at me, and then at Mr. Blacklock. Nobody speaks after that; there is just the scraping of knives and forks against the plates. I do not have to look up to know that Mary Spurren's scowl is darkening at the far end of the table.

22

*I*t makes me proud to see the stack of rockets growing in the open crate. Mr. Blacklock allowed me to finish the batch and I'd held my breath as he examined one or two, turning them over in his hands and peering through his eyeglasses to check for flaws or weaknesses, but he gave a short grunt of approval and went out to Child's to meet with Mr. Torré. It appears he trusts me with more tasks as each week passes; increasingly he lets me work unsupervised, once he has shown me what to do. I have a good memory for all the chemicals. Each name is like a taste in my mouth that I cannot forget.

Beginning a new order, I choose two-ounce cases, set them ready and pick up the drift.

And this time, when I hear the great noise of the knock at the door, my hands become still over the filling-box. I hold my breath. We are not expecting anyone. *Suppose it is important business, and Mr. Blacklock finds out that I did not answer it. What would he think?* The knock comes again, a brisk, insistent kind of rapping, and now I put down the drift and step down the corridor toward the hall as though I were tugged by invisible string.

I open the door.

I can hardly hear what the man is saying. It is bright outside, so that I have to squint to see at first.

It is a constable, in a scruffy overcoat.

"I have come for an Agnes Trussel," he is demanding. He passes his baton from hand to hand. "Will I find her here?"

"Yes," I say, faintly.

"She is summoned on a matter of urgency concerning"—he puts the baton under his arm and consults his pocket-book—"coinage and unlawful goods." The skin on his nose is burnt and peeling, as if he had been in the sun without his hat.

"Unlawful goods? Coinage, you say?" I have been waiting so long for this question that I should be practiced, hardened to the thought of hearing it at last. He does not mention any warrant. My thief's fingers grip the door handle. They do not fly to press at Mrs. Mellin's coins, hidden in my stays.

"Let me fetch my shawl," I say, and then in a daze I go with the constable.

This is it, I think. It is happening now, and I am found out. It is Mrs. Blight's doing, surely it is.

And with discovery comes something of release, so that I am very calm and unperturbed, as though I were floating above myself as we go swiftly down the street. I hear my steps tapping on the cobbles. The constable swings his baton at his side, and whistles through his rotten teeth. He does not grip my arm cruelly, as I thought he would.

Will I go straight to jail? Perhaps this is my last walk in the sunshine before truth shows up the darkness of my fate. I watch my shadow running smoothly down there, ahead of me. Even my shadow does not care. What is that noise? It is my breath, quick and shallow, like the agonized breath of the mouse I once found caught just by the tail in the trap at home in the back chamber. We'd heard its squeaking from the kitchen, it was so loud, and in I went. Its tail proved mostly unharmed, but the mouse sat unmoving even though I held the rusty lever free for it to run, its sides going in and out with panting.

"Did you flatten its wretched skull with the shovel?" my mother had called from the kitchen, clanging the spoon on the side of the pot. "How I hate those little beasts when they dirty my flour."

"Yes, yes, all dead," I'd called, holding it in my palm to feel its quickening softness for a moment before I tipped it, scuttling, from the open window. I knew it was foolish. Outside in the hedge the catkins shivered from the alder like loose little fingers hanging down.

I am too soft.

"Er . . ." The constable's rough voice breaks into my stupor. "Perhaps you should clear up . . . er, describe . . . before we arrive at the roundhouse, what you know of Mr. Soul's hand in this affair?"

I stop dead in my tracks and blink at him.

"Mr. Soul? Dear God! None!" And I see a doubt flicker over his sunburnt face when he hears that.

"What has he to do with this?" I ask, bewildered. "Why are you taking me? I have to say, I do not know what you are talking about." He clears his throat.

"You are called by Justice Philips to speak for Mr. Cornelius Soul, to speak up for his character."

"His character!" I say.

The roundhouse is filthy and stinks of urine. The constable tells me where to stand. When my eyes are accustomed to the dinginess, I see him addressing the ear of a bulky man in a satin frock coat, whom I assume to be the justice. Cornelius Soul is there, and another man I do not know.

"Remind me again, Mr. Constable, what is the problem that we have before us?" the justice bellows.

"My name's Williams, sir, Tom Williams," the constable mutters peevishly. The judge has large, grayish lips that he presses together when others speak.

"Gentleman here, Mr. James Smith, Your Honor," the constable says, and even as he indicates the man I do not know, I begin to have a creeping sense that I have come across him somewhere before. "Has a claim against Mr. Cornelius Soul with regard to some counterfeited currency. We've been through this matter all morning, sir," he reminds him quietly.

"Yes, yes, man," the justice says. "But this woman stood before us." He waves a silk handkerchief toward me, and I smell his musty odor of stale sweat.

"Agnes Trussel, sir," I say, when directed. I am dizzy with fear. "Of Blacklock's Pyrotechny, off Basinghall Street." My voice sounds far away, like someone else's, and the lump in my stays, where the coins lie, feels burning hot.

The justice raises his eyebrow. "John Blacklock's place. The fireworks man. I like those toys. Saw some . . . huh! When was it?"

"Maybe last week, Your Honor?" the constable ventures. "At the—"

"Stick to the point, man." The constable looks at his shoes.

"How well would you say that you know this Mr. Soul?" the justice asks me.

I think of his fingers pressing my cheeks, of his hand sidling about my waist unbidden.

"I know him well enough," I say. "He . . . comes to the premises with frequency."

The justice presses the handkerchief to his mouth and coughs into the silk. "And would you vouch for his hitherto good character?" His large stomach growls again.

"I would, sir." I do not dare to glance at Cornelius Soul's face when I add, "He is a sober and industrious man, sir. I have never heard of a dishonesty connected with him."

The justice stifles a hiccup, and I see suddenly that he is fairly in liquor, though he conceals it well.

The man called Smith spits on the floor. "You should search her!" he demands. "There'll be evidence against him on her, I know there'll be, if you'd only find it!"

I have to stand on my leg heavily to stop it shaking, because I have just realized that he is the man with the round, stubbled face who stared at me so oddly in the coffeehouse. Why did he follow me?

"What kind of evidence can you be meaning, James Smith?" Cornelius

Soul mocks him. "You do not know! You have nothing on me, nothing— and you know it. They have searched my lodgings and found nothing." He turns to the justice. "This man clearly has a private campaign against me. What is his motive? Perhaps, being made a cuckold of so lately, he labors under the misapprehension that I am the cock who is pleasuring his wife so rigorously."

The justice snorts.

Cornelius Soul points provokingly at the man. "You! Known as Crooked Jim! It ought to be your own premises on Little Wild Street they should be searching with their warrants, on quite some other matter."

"I'll get you, Soul!" the man shouts. "You enrage me!" He is frothing at the mouth. "I'll make sure you piss vinegar before the year's out, you son of a bitch. I've got my eye on you and your friends. I have for months." And he points at me. "Even watching where *she* works to get some dirt on you. Bold as brass up to the door, and you was lucky no one answered."

Like the sun coming out from behind a cloud, something forms on the face of the justice. He holds up a finger.

"Suddenly you speak on naming terms, when I distinctly heard you say that you were unacquainted with this man before this incident? I sense a loosening of what is what." He draws out a watch with difficulty from his pocket. "And time is short today. They are making a fool of the law, which is inadmissible," the justice booms. "Dinnertime is pressing upon us, Mr. Constable. I have an appointment I must not overlook, and do not want more blasted paperwork."

He clears his throat.

"I sense a personal gripe in the bowels of the prosecutor here. This will not come to trial, unless costs are no object. Mr. Smith," he demands, "can you face an acquittal, should it reach the next assizes, man?"

The man spits on the floor.

"No response from the prosecutor, sir," says the constable.

"As I thought." The justice hiccups again. "Pray, how has this come so far in its proceeding, Mr. Constable?" he asks testily.

The constable sets his jaw. "My job is to apprehend those to whom I am directed as digressers, sir, not to judge the merits of a case. I present them swiftly, and take a pride in it. And the name's Williams, sir," he adds hopelessly.

"Your cause has failed for today, Mr. Smith," the justice calls across to the man with the round face, and he goes to the door and flaps his hand in our direction. "Take them away, Mr. Constable." With deliberation he pushes his hat onto his periwig, and turns about. "I do not want to see any one of you again, unless a case is watertight. Will there be a carriage to be had from here? Damn these delays, this city runs so poorly."

I am surprised to hear Cornelius Soul speak up as we come out into the brightness of the street. He edges closer to the justice.

"Need any fowling powder, my lord, at a special price?" he flatters him, with a wink at me. I can hardly believe it. "South coast quality fineness, this lot just in, fresh as a baby, for your sporting requirements."

"Get out of here, man," the justice says.

"Lead shot?"

"Are you a half-wit?" the justice barks. I pull at Cornelius Soul's arm to come away.

"Mr. Soul, this is a serious matter," I say quietly. "Try to be sensible." And thank God but a hackney carriage rolls up and the justice heaves himself in.

"Westminster!" we hear him bellow importantly, and he raps at the floor with his cane. As he drives away, the man Smith shouts from across the street.

"Damn your eyes, Soul. I've been following you. You'll slip up soon enough and I'll have you tucked up yet! I'll make it my business." And he turns away down an alley and is gone. What can Cornelius Soul have done to make this man dislike him so?

We are outside the Prince of Orange, and the smell of smoke and stale sweet beer drifts out as a man pushes his way inside.

"It was worse than a pigpen in there, in the roundhouse," I say, my legs weak with relief. My fingers press at my stays to make sure the coins are secure.

"You want to see the inside of Newgate, if you think that is bad," Cornelius Soul says.

"I do not want to see Newgate."

"It is a mistake to have enemies," he admits ruefully.

"It must be," I say. That at least is one problem I do not have.

"Drink a dram with me, Miss Trussel," Cornelius Soul suggests, touching my shoulder.

"I should get back," I say, hesitating, and he shrugs his velvet coat and takes a step closer to the tavern's open door.

"And that's it, is it!" I say, nettled, now that the immediate danger seems to be gone. "You'll just amble in there and leave me to return home at my own pace with no protection. Will you not even say sorry to me for all the trouble you have caused today?"

"You would have come to no harm there in the roundhouse, Miss Trussel," he says easily. "My clean little acquaintance in her neat working apron and fresh rosy cheeks come to save my bad character."

"You do not know . . . me," I blurt out, and stop myself. I nearly said, *You do not know what I have to hide.*

He grins as if he knows, but he does not. He lowers his voice, leans toward me and touches my chin lightly with his finger. "I would be obliged if you could refrain from mention of this matter to John Blacklock. He is a steadfast maverick, but I do not know if he would be tolerant of such . . . irregularities, inconclusive or otherwise."

"He may get to hear of it," I warn, holding his gaze. "Though not from this mouth." There is a shrill mew of a kite overhead. "We are always watched by some sharp eye somewhere, Mr. Soul."

"Let me make it up to you soon, Miss Trussel," he says as I turn away and go down the street. And he calls out suddenly:

"I am indebted to you, indebted, do you hear!" And I realize that he is right, and I cannot help but smile to myself about it. It is something in my favor.

I walk alone back to the house and come to no harm, as he predicted.

That night I heave my unbalanced bulk into bed and lie back, almost choking with the weight upon me now. In my worn cotton shift I look surely like a great sow, though when I lift my shift to my chin and turn to study my bare blind swollen belly in the cracked and spotted looking glass upon the washstand, it could not be more nakedly a shocking human sight, smooth and ripe inside my skin. I see that a faint, dark line that I did not have before is creeping up from the base of my belly. I try to remember whether my mother carried such a mark when she was bearing children, but I cannot. I look and look. It is not vanity that makes me stare so concentrated at myself I am trying to believe that this thing is happening to me, as I have realized that, no matter how hard I try, I cannot take it in.

And how sharply alone I feel when I do that, staring at my own shape. I do not even know myself now: the self I knew, was sure of knowing, being lost behind me in the past, somewhere in the hills perhaps, still running up the slope with Ann that hot afternoon not long before she left, flinging ourselves down on the short nibbled grass at the top of the ridge, at the top of the Downs where I belong.

Even the air was blissful that particular day, just before the trouble started. The sheep were lazy and made scarcely a noise. The September sun was hot and baking the grasses and thyme and the flat creeping spans of thistles by our heads. At first I thought that there were no birds singing, and then I heard a lark, winding the tidy thread of its song up and down between heaven and earth. It was higher than us. We lay with our mouths open, drinking the sun in while we could.

"What are you afraid of, Agnes? What thoughts make you shrink in terror when you have them?"

I scratched my head. The blue sky went up and up above us.

"I am afraid of the dark, and of the Devil," I said, turning and laughing at her for asking such a question. "Why, what thing scares you?"

Ann said, "I am afraid of childbed. I am afraid of being married, and of being someone's wife." She picks a stem of sorrel and twirls it about before she chews it.

"Mother is," I said. "Somebody's wife."

"I know," was all she said.

"I would like a shop," she went on, surprisingly. "Like Mrs. Langley's shop in Pulborough, selling ribbons and buttonhooks and yards of muslin." I didn't need to reply. We lay there in the sunshine on our backs, comfortable and knowing that this could never be.

"What would you like to do, in time?" Ann rolled over suddenly onto her belly and looked at me, shading her eyes against the glare of the sun.

"I don't know," I said, sitting up and looking toward the haze where the sea was a strip of blue in the distance. "I cannot see the future. There is no point in trying to; it will never be as one imagines. What dreams can women have in this life that are not battered down by experience?" I laid my fingers on the warm prickle of grasses, on the flat of the earth.

"Think harder," she urged. "Picture yourself there, ahead in the unknown, doing something—what are you doing? You are so clever, Agnes, you could do anything."

I tried this, to please her.

"No. Nothing." I laughed aloud. "It is blank. And why are you asking me?"

"No proper reason," she said, looking away.

A cloud went over the sun then, and something of the warmth of the afternoon was already gone. We picked ourselves up, brushed off the bits of mosses and made our way down the steep slope to the cottage.

At suppertime my father asked abruptly if Ann would share her intentions with the rest of the family. I had no notion of what he meant. I looked at Ann. She lifted her head and looked at the back of the room. I stared at her. There was a long red scratch on the side of her face that I hadn't noticed earlier.

She said loudly, "I'm going away. On Monday. I am going to work at Wiston House."

"You can't!" I said, appalled.

Her face looked away into the fire, so that I could no longer see the scratch across her cheek.

My spoon slammed down on the trestle.

"But you did not . . . you did not say!" I stood up. "All afternoon, it was so sunny, and you did not say!" I tried to keep my fury from bubbling up. Fury that Ann was leaving me, that she was able.

"How could you hide that from me?" I shouted out, like an idiot, and looked toward my mother in despair. I jabbed my finger at Ann, but still she would not turn her face to me.

"I don't know why you should be so upset now, Aggie love," my mother said, almost so I couldn't hear. "These things do happen. That's how it is. Finish your broth." She nodded at my half-finished bowl and wiped at spat-out broth on Hester's chin with a piece of rag.

Hester started to cry, her mouth square with misery.

"You're scaring the babies, Agnes," my brother Ab said. I could tell by his voice he was angry, too. William's eyes were huge in his head. I was ashamed. After all, I should know that nothing I could say would make a difference. The round spoon swam before me, and the flames of the fire behind grew huge and wobbling and dazzled me as I blinked back the tears and stifled them.

"You'll get those beans in tomorrow from the bottom field," my father commented into the silence that followed, picking at his teeth with his thumbnail.

"Beans?" I said.

"That's right."

"But it is a Friday!" I cried, and my voice shook. "The afternoon I have my lesson."

My father shrugged that he did not care. "They'll not keep, not in this heat."

That night when we were laid down on the ticking and trying to sleep, Ann's fingers reached out and looked for mine in the dark. How cold they were, which made her seem already far away. Selfishly, because I did not know what else to do, I pulled my hand from hers and did not speak. My unsaid thoughts rose up inside and choked me. I was afraid for her. I was afraid for all of us. I was afraid of having nobody to speak to in the way I spoke to her.

The white, fat moon shone down. The sheep bleated on the hillsides as though the brightness it was causing could be day.

Still I could not rest.

Later I turned and whispered out how sorry I was, but I knew she was sleeping and could not hear me. Her breathing was slow and even, like a vast gentle wind moving through grasses.

I am glad to go to the workshop the next morning to occupy myself in breaking stars and laying the rough little cubes to dry. Mr. Blacklock has tucked his order book into his waistcoat and gone out to Mr. Torré's. "There has been a change in the firing schedule for the display at St. James's, and there are details to discuss," he had said as he left.

"A change, sir?" I asked, looking up.

He coughed. "Some minor points. A particular addition," he said inattentively, looking for his hat.

"An addition?"

"Something over and above what we had agreed." He presses the hat on. "What you might call . . . progress."

I can't help but smile in excitement when the door closes behind him.

He must mean the red shower that he mentioned as if in passing! Perhaps he plans to reveal his achievement publicly.

I almost forget my hurt that he has not shared his endeavor with me. The stars on the drying rack in front of me take on a new significance; they seem part of something greater than they did yesterday when I mixed them. They are a part of Mr. Blacklock's quest.

Mrs. Blight had been in good cheer that morning over breakfast. She had just finished reading the latest printed pamphlet of *The Ordinary of Newgate*, which depicts the dying words of those faced with their fate at Tyburn. She'd read the conclusion aloud to me with relish. *It rarely happens, that a Man who will dare to be wicked does escape, though Punishment may not immediately tread upon his Heels.*

"Have a loan of it," she'd said, looking at me closely. "Go on." And then pressed it upon me as I went to the workshop.

Mr. Blacklock is out.

When Cornelius Soul brings his delivery, it is the first chance that we have had to speak at liberty since his unfruitful arrest. He puts down his box of gunpowder, and winks at me as he hands me the invoice, as though we have a new conspiracy together now.

"That man bore a grudge against you," I say, in a low voice lest someone should overhear.

"Jim Smith has enough temper to share out between five men," he replies cheerfully.

"What did you do to provoke him like that?"

"He hates to see my growing success," Cornelius Soul says, with a shrug. "I've known him for years." He goes to the window and looks out, up and down the street. "I detest the smugness of a wealthy merchant as much as any man, but why should Jim Smith's aversion to my steps to prosperity call a halt to them so easily? We should use every trick in the book to get where we can be."

"Then you are one of those that you despise," I say, going on with my grinding.

"I am not a wealthy merchant yet, and I will not take their notion of the law, which exists to protect property over human welfare." The stove ticks in the distance at the back of the workshop; my pestle crunches the mixture softly inside the mortar. "And I do not feel a moral duty to abide by it," he says.

I stop the pestle and lean on it. "So you would forgive a breach of the law," I say, my face hidden from him, "if it was not a crime against a person's being."

"I do not hold with violence," he agrees. "But other crimes? They're altered by who does the telling. One person's crime could be another's justice."

"Isn't it just to do with finding out the truth, and measuring it against the law?" I say.

"But the law itself is made by individuals, each with his own motives."

"These laws are ancient!"

"And their interpretation is as various as the times they occupy, Miss Trussel."

I put the pestle down. "My father had no wish to give his strips of land up to the landowner that bought them, but he had no choice in the face of the law," I admit. "Misery and damage has been done to many families like our own, though no crime was committed."

Cornelius Soul picks up Mrs. Blight's pamphlet, propped open on the bench, and flicks through it. He stops at a page and flourishes it at me.

"To kill a man of nineteen, watch him swing by the neck, with the ghastly strength of moral certainty. Or the act of trying to steal a bite to eat. Which is the more chilling?" he asks. I do not need to reply.

"If the poor had the vote, things would be different," he adds, then breaks off and laughs. "You must stop me, Miss Trussel, if you find me tedious. Besides," he says, winking, "a man amounts to more than just his politics."

"Does he?" I say. "I am not so sure. His core is his beliefs."

Cornelius Soul grins. "The change must come from beneath—like a rising tide."

I count out twenty wobbling drops of oil from the end of the pipette into the mortar, and then frown.

"But how can the poor have a will to win, Mr. Soul, when with every step they know they have not eaten enough bread to even carry them strongly to the end of the street?" I say very quietly, remembering what I saw when I came to the city. "At home we wouldn't keep cattle the way I've seen people living here. My brother Ab would be appalled. Bellies yawning for food unless numbed with gin, and their children not grow-ing or dead of neglect or sickness. Dignity of work is not a choice they have been offered."

"I had not realized how very angry you are, Miss Trussel," he says, as if surprised.

"I've got eyes in my head as I walk about," I say. He does not reply. I hope he is not disappointed in me. Our conversation lulls, and he flicks his fingers at the tools hanging from the wire at my bench, so that they clink and judder.

I try again.

"You speak so roundly of how you are part of an upsurge from the city's underbelly, but if you succeed, won't you just be like them?" I spill some sulfur as I measure more scoops into the pan of the beamscales.

"And you disapprove," he says, and something has changed. I have said too much.

I look up and try to catch his bright eye, but he will not look at me.

Out in the yard Mary Spurren tips a stream of greasy water from the bowl into the drain, wipes her wrist upon her apron and goes back inside the scullery. A bird calls in the linden tree.

"I am undecided," I say at length, trying to be honest. Then more words come out of my mouth before I have time to check them. "I do not know . . . what kind of man you are," I say, as though it matters.

He turns to face me.

"You are very direct," he says. He is not laughing, though I wish that he would. His gaze is level, but the blueness of his eyes is somehow shielded by their narrowness, as though he does not want me to know his thinking.

We hear the front door open and steps coming down the corridor, and John Blacklock strides into the workshop.

"I see you take the risk of leaving your premises unattended far more of late, Blacklock." Cornelius Soul takes up his tone of banter promptly.

Mr. Blacklock does not reply at first. He takes off his hat and puts it on the nail.

"Indeed," he says, coolly.

When Cornelius Soul takes his leave this time, he kisses his own hand and presses my cheek roughly with it. I look round hastily, but Mr. Blacklock does not see, thank God for that. It was not a caress but a challenge, I think, as though his fingertips have branded me as punishment for what I said.

My cheeks burn hotly. I have a sudden gape of shame and dismay opening inside me. How do I dare to hold forth on principles or moral ground, I with my stash of stolen guineas tucked in my stays even as I sit before him, and the lies in my heart spreading out like a canker. No, he is right to grab his chances; it is each man for himself, though it should not be. My head reels with complication.

"If that man is bothering you, you need not engage him in debate," Mr. Blacklock comments dryly.

"He was not," I say.

"But I see you are some way behind with your quota today," he adds, with a glance at the half-filled crate of rockets over by the filling-box, as he has every right to do. My guilty feeling worsens.

23

The back door of the workshop is open to the morning air. The piping of birds drifts in, and a smell of soap from the drain outside the scullery where Mrs. Nott has emptied her buckets. It is almost May.

Mr. Blacklock has a copy of the *London Evening Post* from yesterday spread out on the bench, and is scanning the pages urgently for an account of the opening season's fireworks at Marylebone Gardens. "How irksome!" he exclaims, finding it. Scornfully, he reads aloud:

"Prodigious height! Salutes that deafened the ear for hours subsequent! Glorious climactic eruption, when scarcely an inch of sky was left unemblazoned with brilliance!

"Why do these engineers inspire such hyperbole?" he asks. "Why do they pander to it? Reducing as it does the art of pyrotechny to a common battering of senses, like a blast in a tin mine. There is no room for subtleties or shaping when expectations can be predicted thus." A fly circles above his newspaper, then settles on it. He brushes it off impatiently. "Perfection of form should always take precedence over height or spread. Mere quantity is not impressive." He snorts in distaste. "Would you not say?" he demands.

"I would not know, sir," I remind him, surprised, "having never properly seen a firework."

Mr. Blacklock says nothing to this, and his face is thoughtful, as if he had not thought of that for some time.

He closes the paper, puts it aside and leaves his bench. He goes to the back door of the workshop and stares out at the yard. Mary Spurren is hanging the washed linen out to dry in the warm air. I see him looking up at the blue sky as if to judge the weather, and then he returns inside, clears a space at his table and writes quickly on a sheet of paper, which he folds and seals and gives to Joe Thomazin to deliver to an address in the Haymarket, to the west of the city.

He brings down a bundle of lengths of deal, cut into thin sticks at the carpenter's shop, and begins tying them to rockets from the box he puts at his feet.

"The display at St. James's Square is to be fired tonight," he mentions later.

"Tonight, sir?" I say politely, choosing a hollow drift at the filling-box. Of course, the crates for that order were sent out last week.

"And I have sent word to Mr. Torré, to expect us to attend." My drift pauses over the rocket's mouth. "Most of the works he intends to fire have been supplied by Blacklock's, and it would be of benefit to check the consistency in quality." I swallow. Did I hear him correctly? Did he mean . . . ?

"His cascades are on the whole of exceptional class, and also something he is apt to call the Forge of Vulcan," he goes on. "The display will be staged from a scaffold or machine outside the house, and the party in question, a private assembly, will enjoy the spectacle from within the ballroom darkened for the purpose. There would be no difficulty for us to gain entrance to the garden, to oversee the practical application of our product."

"Do you mean, sir, that I am to go as well?" I ask, and hold my breath.

He coughs into his fist. "Can you walk a distance?" he demands. "If the evening remains pleasant we shall depart at eight o'clock on foot." I squeeze my hands tightly together, so that he cannot see my fingers trembling.

"I can, sir."

"Good, good." He flicks through a box of dusty invoices and takes one out to read it. "*Two hundred honorary rockets, eighteen Caduceus, twenty girandoles, forty-five gerbes, petard rockets with brilliant fire, cascades, candles with various stars, fixed fires including Chinese fire and ancient fire, maroons et cetera.*" He waves his hand. "Also one red shower. You remember making that?"

He stops reading and looks at me over his eyeglasses. "That is what you can expect. Make of it what you will." And he puts the paper down and says no more on the subject, even in the face of questions that I dare to beg of him from time to time.

The day passes with a painful slowness.

At six when I go to the kitchen I find it full of smoke, and Mrs. Blight cursing and flapping at the air.

"Open that casement at once, Agnes!" she orders, coughing dramatically, as if it is my fault that she has burnt the meat, and she scrapes the lump forcefully away from the spit.

"Clock's broken," Mary Spurren says gloomily. The charred cinder of our supper lies on the hearthstone, smoking miserably.

"What in God's name, woman, is happening in here?" Mr. Blacklock says, striding into the room. The smell of burning is everywhere.

"Wretched object," Mrs. Blight laments, rolling her eyes at the mantelpiece. "Deplorable useless bit of mechanics." She raps at its wooden case. "Should never have got reliant on it. Never had a clock before to cook by, makes your cooking eye go blind, that does, having a clock to lean on, timewise. I'll vouch that someone's overwound it or dropped it and broken some bit of innards, but no one's owning up, sir." She shrugs, her chin wobbles with regret. "There's no one here'll say they did it."

He gestures at the smoke. "See to it," he says curtly.

"Have to go back to smelling when it's done," Mrs. Blight says, when he has gone. "Besides, timings is no use at all. When it's done, it's done, and that's exact enough. Proper time is only as long as something takes."

Mary Spurren sniffs. "That clock were handy."

"What for?" Mrs. Blight demands.

"For telling just how late Mrs. Nott is turning up these days, for one thing," Mary Spurren replies, grumpily. "Latest woman I ever knowed."

Once Mr. Blacklock and I set out for St. James's, the world seems different, walking along beside him to the fireworks. Past the great bulk of St. Paul's, past the churchyard, past the Temple, past Clifton's chophouse, past St. Clement's in the center of the street with the traffic pouring past to either side of it. I feel shy and exhilarated, walking fast to keep up with him. The Strand is bright and glassy with shopfronts; women in striped silks buying hats and Florence cordials and anchovies, gentlemen pressing tobacco into their pipes and examining swords and traveling trunks, painted blowsy women plying their trade at the mouths of courtyards, beggar boys with dirty fingers, and all the world staring at each other, this way and that, for what variety of reasons I could not say. And for all the bustle about us, I find myself glancing sidelong at Mr. Blacklock from time to time. It is a curious thing how a familiar face can appear so altered by new surroundings. How fiercely he glares at the crowd. He is taller without his leather jerkin, wearing instead a dark frock of fustian over his waistcoat, and I notice how people seem to shrink from his path as he walks through them. His long face cannot be comfortable with itself, as though thoughts and visions were constantly exploding behind his eyes. His eyes are almost too dark to see into, as if he has made them so after suffering trouble, and with his need for silence.

Away from the shops, the light fails quickly into dusk. One carriage goes by as we enter St. James's Square; the horses' hooves are crisp on the road. Mr. Blacklock stops suddenly and raps at a side door in a high wall, and presently we are admitted into the grounds of a large house that stands in the shadows beyond. The walking has tired me and I long to sit down. My belly is heavy and drags at my backbone, though the child lies still and does not push about.

It is cool and quiet in the garden. The air is blue with early darkness; bats flicker and circle unsuspecting above the tall spindly scaffold that I can just make out. There is a low, thrilling hum of preparation; shadowy figures of many men moving about, muttering. A brief flare of a taper lights up a face and is extinguished. Mr. Blacklock gruffly motions me to sit, and goes to speak to Mr. Torré. The low wall is damp under my skirts, but I am glad to rest. I rub at my back when he is gone. How hungry I am already. A bright, thin quarter moon hangs over the rooftops.

The punch of the first volley of rockets startles me, and the child begins kicking and kicking. I stand up.

It has begun.

It is so close that I can hear the hiss of the quick match rush to the lifting charge of each flight of rockets, before the pound and roar of the ignition, and then the burst, and the sky is riddled with twists of fire, feathers of fire, billhooks of light, snakes of fire and smoke. The breaks are a spill of prickling white light across my eye, crackling the glaze of the sky into bitter shards. I blink. I cannot breathe for whiteness everywhere. I am blinded by it. The sky is burnt with purple shadows when the whiteness is done, when there is a pause for darkness, though the smoke swirls about, and then more gerbes start up, pulsing sheaves of orange sparks, with stars shooting out like grains of polished light that lift, drift, stop, then fall slowly, smooth as glass, winking out into the darkness. The world is either fire, or water, or darkness, nothing else. An unformed sob gathers in my chest.

The shape of Mr. Blacklock looms out of nowhere. "The cascade!" he shouts, huge beside me.

It is a white froth of sparks and smoke that pours down the scaffold as though it will never stop. My face is hot with it. When I turn to the house the glass of the windows is white with the light caught there, as though the house, too, is maddened with fire. In the ballroom behind the reflection the white faces of the guests at the assembly throng, unmoving.

Mr. Blacklock bends down and speaks into my ear: ". . . niter, antimony." His voice is close and thrums in my head. I nod at him, speechless.

"Tourbillion!" his voice says, and I am giddy with it. Above us the tourbillion rotates wildly like a glittering muscle of fire.

There is a burst of maroons like an attack. The child inside me goes stiff with the shock of the noise. I should like to rub my belly, but I dare not. Instead I find myself clenching my hands tightly over it, as if to shield it from the flashes and blasting. The smell of gunpowder and the white clouds of sulfurous smoke fill the leafy garden to the brim.

It is over. I can hardly believe what I have seen, my heart pounding in the sudden hush.

After the display we do not speak. Mr. Blacklock crosses beneath the scaffold to talk again with Mr. Torré. The air is damp. As the smoke clears slowly I can see inside the house, where the chandeliers are lit again and the musicians have begun to play. I can just see the gleam of silk skirts turning in the candlelight as the guests start to dance. An upper window closes, as though a servant had been watching. I cannot hear Mr. Black-lock's conversation—his back is turned to me—but Mr. Torré seems to look across once to where I stand and I see his hat nodding, as though agreeing strongly with something that was said. I avert my gaze quickly when he does that.

"You are chilled," Mr. Blacklock notices when he returns to me, and we leave the garden. He adds, "Torré felt the works were good."

Pall Mall is quiet; a single horse and trap go by, then a linkboy hasten-ing, his torch flaming dirtily behind him as he runs into a lighted doorway.

We pass Suffolk Street and turn toward the thoroughfare. Mr. Black-lock stops abruptly on the corner.

"Let us take a glass inside this drinking place; then we can make our way toward Charing Cross to hail a hackney cab," he says. And as he opens the door onto the noise of the tavern and stands aside to let me pass, I realize that there was something missing from the display.

The room is crowded. The fire in the grate seems yellow and mild and ordinary compared with the fierceness of what I have seen. The girl brings our brandy. It is hot in my throat.

"Not as poor as I had feared," Mr. Blacklock is saying, his face lively.

"Mr. Torré begins to grasp the matters at his fingertips very well, and can conceive a satisfactory pattern for the eye. Things are improving. I could find fault only with the firing by the operators, which was erratic at a point when precision was necessary. Perhaps the headed rockets with the brilliant fire broke a little low. Perhaps the cascade burnt on too tediously after the gerbes played." He shrugs as though on balance these things were not significant, and swallows his brandy.

"It was astonishing," I say. "But——"

He coughs into his fist. "It was not a remarkable nor singular display, but I grant it was neat and satisfactory and well made. There was nothing to disgrace either the trade of engineer or maker of fireworks."

"What drew you to your trade?" I ask, with sudden curiosity. Mr. Blacklock leans back on the bench and looks at the fire.

"As a child I liked the clang and heat and rattle of the blacksmith's shop, but my family would not hear of such an occupation for their only son. And when I came to England at the age of ten, I studied with a Russian man of what is known as natural philosophy. My education was thorough; I received instruction in mathematics, physics, chemistry, metallurgy."

"Where had you lived before?" I ask timidly.

"My mother was Polish," he replies. "When she died, we left Poland and came to the damp tumult of Clerkenwell to live with my father's cousin and his wife." Mr. Blacklock's voice is low, as if he were talking to himself. "Surrounded by my father's books, I sat at his desk and looked out the window in a childish terror. Highways stretched as far as the mind could imagine, never-ending, filled with the darkness of houses, of poverty. It was a hard, miserable place I had arrived at. Only the fires of vagrants down there on the dirty streets suggested any kind of welcome. At night I would push open the window and lie awake, drinking in the smell of all the smoking fires about us, crying for my mother."

He coughs and falls silent, studying the hearth. His eyes glitter in his head, as though they held traces of burning.

The warmth travels through me as I finish my glass: the brandy, the fire, the easy noise of the tavern about us. Inside my head, too, the bright fireworks go on fizzing and dissolving in the dark.

"But as a wise man once said, nature abhors a vacuum. And I read the Ancients," Mr. Blacklock says. "Aristotle, Plato, Pliny. I read Theophilus, Paracelsus. I read Agricola, Biringuccio and the great man of artillery, Siemienowitz. I read Bacon, Bate, Boyle. I vowed I would be Firemaster. And then gradually I became most occupied with the way in which fireworks themselves are made. The point of source and cultivation. I purchased chemicals, tools, tutelage. As I grew older I began to experiment with new materials, to make attempts toward refining and advancing specific inquiries within the art of pyrotechny. And I kept my ear open for the merest trifle of fresh chemical knowledge that might prove expedient for my endeavor."

"Is that your practice even now, sir?" I ask anxiously. I do not want to hear that it is not. I watch the girl pouring ale for the gentlemen beside us; her arms are strong and thick. I hear her laughing as she goes into the back room, pushing the curtain aside with her red hands. The fire smokes in the draft.

"I like the stillness at the center of a firework," he says, turning the glass in his hand. "There is so much compacted silence within them; the bright flame shooting a slit of fire up into the sky, then the first silence and blackness before the sharp report and then the burst." I smile and nod, understanding what he means now that I have seen it for myself. And then he adds almost in a murmur, "The second stillness will spread from the center of all the colors—like the vast stillness at the heart of flowers."

I frown. "From all the colors?" I exclaim, remembering now how the fireworks display had lacked one thing. The brandy and the strangeness of the night make me bold. "But I saw no colors there at all. They were so white! Only whiteness and brightness. Throughout Mr. Torré's display I waited, as they went up, for the red shower, the red shower that we made with the deal." I pause. "I saw none of that. Only whiteness and bright-ness. Which in itself was magnificent, do not mistake me, but not as pow-erful as what I'd imagined. Indeed, I was hoping, sir, I had expected . . ." and then I stop.

Mr. Blacklock looks at me. "You are disappointed," he says. His voice is tight.

"Oh no, sir!" I say. "It is only that I am surprised. You see, sir, some of the explosions inside my head were rich in color. I did not know what to expect."

The girl interrupts to ask if we will take more brandy, but Mr. Black-lock shakes his head.

"It was part of the cascade," he says.

"Sir?"

"The red shower, it was the vital heart of the cascade, the volcanic eruption. Its ruddy tint was not very strong, but clearly visible. How did you not see it?"

We return to the house. In the musty hackney cab he jerks the win-dow open and stares out at the night. "I suspect we have misunderstood each other," he says stiffly, after some time. "Or perhaps the failure is all mine." The coolness of the air makes me sober. I have offended him.

And the silence worsens overnight.

"Morning, sir," I say anxiously as I slip onto my stool. Mr. Blacklock does not reply, and he says nothing for almost an hour, except once when he drops a jar on the floor and lets out a curse under his breath, making me flinch.

At last I can bear it no longer, and I go to stand beside him at his bench. He continues working.

"When you say 'red shower,' sir, I think of the fiery redness of the roots of dock, or the gloss of a currant, or the bright reddle that marks sheep," I say to him, swallowing. "I'm sorry, sir." Mr. Blacklock does not look up. "I think of things that are red, such as red hair, the iron ore that goes to make up that star we are making and even blood. That's what I meant by what I said, sir, just how lovely a fire like that would be! I did not mean . . ."

I know he is listening, although he says nothing, and continues to grind at the sulfur for stars so that I have to speak up above the noise. "Why not violet match, sir? I see the purple hue of violets in my head, of scabious, vetch, of . . . bruises. Could you make that?" Unwelcomely I see Mrs. Mellin's purple tongue stuck from her mouth.

"Purple is the nearest to darkness and blackness. It is too difficult. It has never been done," Mr. Blacklock spits out, grimly. "Anything else?"

"Well . . . what about a green fire, sir? As green and poisonous as the feathered woodpecker in the pear tree at home, the unearthly bigness of its head tipping and battering at the bark for grubs. Or as green as soap made with Barbary wax, or early gooseberries with the June sun going through them. I'd want to see yellow! Scarlet, sir!"

He coughs.

"But last night what I saw was white fire. Majestic fire, like magic. But white was its limit. I'd hoped, I'd thought . . ." Again I stop.

Mr. Blacklock lets the pestle sit idly in the mortar.

There is an agitated feeling in my stomach. Perhaps he has not been seeking new kinds of possibility, after all. No new, unrivaled recipes he has been working on in secret. Surely I cannot have been mistaken.

"Dissatisfaction breeds carelessness and bad workmanship," Mr. Blacklock says curtly. "Look at what you have, understand its benefits and work with that."

"I would like to see a blue," I persist, suddenly near to tears in my frustration. "I'm sorry, sir, but a blue as blue as milkwort, as cornflowers, as the blue sea from a distance on a bright day. A blue firework shooting up into the night sky like a . . . like a joyful spark of daylight."

"You imagine colors vividly," he says.

"I do, sir," I reply. "It is . . . almost as though I feel them as a sense of touch or taste when I am looking."

THE BOOK OF FIRES

He looks up at me beside him. I am startled to see how his eyes are tight with excitement. A hope flares up in me.

"Have you attempted a blue, Mr. Blacklock?" I whisper.

And he leans forward as though on impulse, his eyes narrow.

"When I first saw you," he says, "there on the step in the pouring rain, I thought that perhaps you were someone else. I looked more closely at your face, and there was something of somebody else within it. Not in its shape, but in its look, in its intensity."

The discontinuity of his thought surprises me. "There was something that I recognized," he goes on. "I'll admit, you reminded me of someone very close."

"Did I?" I say, and a curious feeling twists over inside me. Confused, I turn back to the bench. Did he mean that I provoked a freshness of grief in him, or did he like my face for it?

"Flowers of sulfur are soft, like a yellow soot," I say hastily, touching the jar, picking it up.

"That is because they are remade in air," Mr. Blacklock replies after a pause, as if struggling to listen properly, and when he looks at me the yellow glinting in his eyes is like shards of brightness in a pool. "Imagine the change to which they have been subjected. When the sulfur was prized out of the earth, it had been packed solid between rocks, crushed with weight and time and pressure. Then, abruptly, we have freed it from density by the application of heat, which does not reduce the substance to a liquid but gives it the freedom of an *air* to shape itself again." He indicates the jar in my hand.

"So we are given flowers of sulfur. The sublime made palpable." He speaks very quietly now. He takes the jar from me and tips a quantity into the porcelain whiteness of a chafing dish. The jar clinks on the dish. He puts a big fingertip to the flowers of sulfur and seems to lose himself in thought.

"They are . . . exalted by fire," he says, almost in a whisper.

I bend my head over them, studying them closely. I can smell his hands, the smell of skin and metal and tobacco. I look at the flowers of sulfur for some time, hardly able to breathe. Mr. Blacklock does not move away, though we are so close we are almost touching. "They are some-where between flakes and crystals," I say, eventually. I do not dare to say anything else, lest my voice should tremble. Mr. Blacklock nods. "Indeed they are," he says. And we part then, and go on with our work.

The flush on my cheeks dies down. I must not misunderstand him; that leads to trouble. I must remember my place.

24

The next day Mr. Blacklock's manner is brisk and cheerful.

"Antimony and orpiment mixed with camphor make a white flame on burning," he tells me. "Whereas a yellow flame, or," he says wryly, "what I would call a yellow flame, is made by mixing amber and cinnabar. You must understand that substances can become quite changed on becoming part of something else. For instance, arsenic presents itself in white or citrine colors, and is easily broken and powdered. But when mixed with orpiment, through sublimation they make realgar—a different, reddish substance with its own distinct properties. And in the residue of this sublimation they leave a regulus: very white like silver but more brittle than glass."

"But silver is not white," I say. "It is . . . silvery." I can think of no other word for what it is.

"You are mistaken," Mr. Blacklock says. "That is its nature only when polished. And by then you are no longer seeing the metal itself but simply what it is reflecting on its surface."

"I see," I say.

I think of Mrs. Mellin's shining coins.

I think of silverweed, growing abundantly on the lane's edge by the cottage.

"What other thoughts do you have today?" Mr. Blacklock asks me then, unexpectedly. "Was there anything else that you would find fault with, in what you saw on Mr. Torré's scaffold?" I cannot tell if he is asking me in earnest or in sarcasm, and so I answer truthfully.

"I have thought of little else since then, Mr. Blacklock, sir," I say.

"And?"

"Well, I have wondered why it had to be so overwhelming, with the loudness nearly ceaseless." Mr. Blacklock's eyebrows rise, as if he had not expected me to say that. "I would have liked to see some separate strokes of fire, sir, a chance to enjoy the rockets trailing away to nothing in the sky. To see the dipping and the darkening perhaps may have made the sense of awe I felt much stronger. I couldn't think, while it was happening. I was . . . battered by it. It was . . . too much at once, I felt, like listening to a song well-sung but bellowed out without a pause."

"Despite the efforts Mr. Torré undertook to ensure the shape of his display was built to reach a conclusion of dramatic proportion at its end," Mr. Blacklock says, dryly.

"Yes," I say, "and yet I felt there was no warning to the burst of that finishing shape. I was not prepared for it, did not have a chance to draw breath with the pleasure of the thought of things to come."

"And just how would you have shaped it, then?" he mocks. "Miss Agnes Trussel, near-six-month novice pyrotechnical assistant at Mr. Blacklock's workshop, perhaps proving to possess more than a little talent in this field? How would you shape it?"

I think about this.

"Perhaps its force could simply weaken, change and fall," I suggest. "When the ash tree drops its leaves, still green, in October without first turning ruddy, without browning, there is less delight, less feeling of wholeness than when watching the slow golden turn of the oak, say, or of the maple," I say. "A shape like this would be more . . . rounded, like the usual way of nature is."

"Perhaps you should suggest it to him," Mr. Blacklock says. Can it be that he is laughing? "Your ideas may be as quick as your fingers seem to be."

He beckons me closer and bids me watch as he pours something into a small glass vessel. "I am making aqua regia," he says. "Strong spirit of niter with strong muriatic acid; it must be freshly mixed, as it quickly loses potency." And to my surprise he drops in two shining guineas and corks the vessel up.

"Gold?" I say. There is a tube sticking from the vessel's second aperture into another jar, and even as I speak a yellowish tumbling kind of steam or air begins to pour through the tube into the jar. There is a disagreeable, choking smell that catches at the back of my throat and makes my eyes water. "Do not breathe too deeply; it is highly corrosive," Mr. Blacklock warns me.

"The coins have disappeared, sir," I say, looking at the liquid in concern. "This experiment must cost a lot."

"No. The gold, though invisible to the eye, remains within the solution, and can, with a degree of bother, be retrieved at will." He coughs. "But *this* is the substance of interest." And he holds up the jar of greenish yellow air he has collected.

He waves his hand impatiently toward the yard. "Bring me one of those little flowers out there."

"Flowers, sir? You mean the violets?" I am surprised he has noticed them, tucked away, late-blooming, between the warmth of the bricks of the outhouse. I go and pick one carefully and bring it in.

He tears the green stalk away and takes the head of petals up in a pair of pincers, which he dips inside the jar, removes and holds toward me. "See?"

"The color is quite sucked out of it, sir!" I say, shocked. The stench is overpowering.

The violet looks disturbingly dead, an eerie blanched scrap hanging limply from his grip. One petal drops to the bench, as though a piece of the skin of a ghost had peeled away.

"Where has the color gone?"

"Intriguing, isn't it," he says, staring down at it, quite lost in thought.

The church clock has already struck four when we are walking from the apothecary's shop with six packets of fresh chemicals he thinks too valuable for Joe Thomazin to bring back unaccompanied.

"Three pounds and twelve shillings and tuppence I shall add to your bill, Mr. Blacklock, sir," Mr. Jennet had calculated in a grudging wheeze, nodding his powdered wig heavily as we gathered the packets up. I saw how he had found it difficult to conceal his irritation at Mr. Blacklock's request to observe their freshness and the quality of goods in person, before they were weighed and wrapped. "I am accustomed to sending the boy out when goods are ready," he complained through his long nose, as Mr. Blacklock tilted and sniffed at the contents of each jar. "Whatever it is that you plan to do with them," he had added, with disdain.

"Another rogue, that man," Mr. Blacklock mutters when we quit the shop. "Too many times he has sold me inferior substances. He nurses a belief that it is only men of science who should be provided with those prized secrets that nature gives up to his kind in the form of chemicals. He thinks that usage such as mine should be abolished, on grounds of waste: a populist defiling of the purity of their knowledge, stained by the gaze of the common mob." We skirt a stack of barrels on the pavement. "And he is not the only one. It is a view held by many of his kind. But they do not see fire for what it is."

"What is it, really, sir?" I ask.

"Many things to many people," he replies. "To us, to pyrotechny, it provides exhilaration, a soaring pleasure, during a display. And pain, debt, guilt, grief, all these troubles, we have momentary respite from. What a gift that is." He raises his hat grimly to someone across the street.

"It transports the senses far above the moment, above happiness itself; it provides a very pure kind of change or space inside us. It quenches a thirst for rapture that we might not even know we had."

He laughs bitterly. "These men of science would not know that. And moreover," he adds, "their thoughts on fire are bound up largely in the pursuit of a nonsensical inflammatory agent they call phlogiston."

"What is that?" I ask. I have to break into a run from time to time to keep abreast of his stride.

"It is something that bends to suit their purpose in describing it. I do not know precisely what it consists of, nor do they. It is what they describe loosely as a combustible principle." He snorts. "An elastic fluid that has no actual matter attributed to it."

"Mr. Jennet did seem rude, sir," I say nervously. Mr. Blacklock's temper is rising.

"Rude? He is an ignorant chemist and his attitude disgusts me. As if they alone could have its secrets! Fire is for all who give it due regard." He stops walking.

"We have the properties of fire at our disposal, and yet we do not understand its nature, none of us. We never shall."

He blinks.

"I would like to see the craft of manipulating, celebrating fire given some respect, that is all," he adds more quietly still. He takes his hat off, turning it about heedlessly before him.

"Has your time in my workshop not given you some sense of this?" he mutters. "Have you not learnt to care for fire?" I cannot tell if he is asking me a question, so that I hesitate before replying.

"My liking for fire was there from the start," I say.

"Despite your family . . . ?" and he turns to me and frowns with recollection.

"Despite that," I say. "However that may seem. I cannot explain."

He seems satisfied with the plainness of my answer, and holds his dark gaze steadily with mine.

When he goes into the shop to buy tobacco, I stand outside. A woman selling birch brooms laid out on the paving has begun to pack up her goods into a tatty basket. She starts talking to me as she does it. At first I can barely hear her over the thoughts in my head.

"I've five sons . . . they are a great help to me . . . my husband died, you see. That happens, don't it?"

I murmur something.

"How long've you got before it comes?" she asks. I look startled at her face. Is my condition so clear to anybody now? Surely not. She has a fresh graze or sore across one cheek, like a scarlet patch. Her skin is wrinkled deeply. I do not reply.

I look away up the street, past the women selling cornflowers from their baskets, past a spaniel eating something in the gutter, past a saddle horse, and the fish girl weaving through the crowd with a wide creel of slippery flounders on her head, and I notice a tall, slender woman talking with another girl, standing with her back to me. She is like . . . As I look she makes a gesture as she speaks, the bright silk of her sleeve catching the sunlight, and I hear a peal of laughter that seems familiar. Is that Lettice Talbot there? Can it be? I narrow my eyes and try to see more clearly. This woman has her bearing, her elegance of style in dressing. Her neck is pale and long. Is it she? *Turn about, Lettice Talbot, so that I might see your face*, I think. My heart beats in fear and hope. If I had more courage I would sail past and glance directly at her, but somehow I cannot. I stay faltering and rooted to the spot and wait for her to notice me. *What will I say to her? Should I call out? Will she remember me? Will she explain that she did not want to do me harm?* How could I have doubted her, even for a moment! I am certain she would help me. The acquaintance pulls her arm as if to show her something in the milliner's. And then at last she turns and it is not Lettice Talbot at all; it is just a girl of ordinary plainness wearing a pretty cap under her hat and chewing her lip, as though deciding what new thing to buy as she stares through the shop glass.

". . . tiny little footprints, so provoking," I hear her say as they come toward me, "such a squirrel!" And she giggles to her friend. Why am I always mistaken like that? A moment later I hear the silk of her skirts whisper past me, though I do not look at her again, and gradually my disappointed heart stops pounding. I am shadowed, haunted by the lack of Lettice Talbot.

25

I saw a dead child on a rubbish heap today.

It turned my stomach to see it lying there in the early morning sunshine. Its softness, its smallness, was twisted up and soiled as though someone, some woman, had tumbled it out of a blanket in haste, in the dark perhaps, and left it alone for the dawn to chance upon it. Though the shock made me stop, I could not bring myself to stoop to look at it too closely, and I thanked God I could not see its face. The heap it lay on steamed slightly in the coolness of the air.

How could a woman leave a baby boy unclothed and dead, its waxy, bloodied limbs a muddle of perfect flesh against the darkness of the filth, one tiny arm flung sideways so that its five still little fingers were opened out as if catching something falling? The umbilical stump looked fresh at the belly. I started to shake when I saw that, and ran to a woman nearby and pulled at her sleeve.

"'Tis common enough," she said, when she saw where I pointed. "Though we may not like to see it." I saw that her shawl was riddled with moth-holes when she pulled it about her.

"A newborn, was it?" she asked.

I nodded. "It seemed so."

"Ah well," she said. She shrugged with a measure of sadness and began to move off.

"What shall we do?" I asked.

"Do?" The woman was puzzled.

"Who should we tell, what authority? So that it can be buried, so that dogs and rats cannot eat away at the corpse. So that somebody knows, so that somebody does something."

"People knows, all right," the woman said, over her shoulder. " 'Tis not the knowing that's the problem, is it? I'd say it were the stopping of it. But where would they start?"

For a moment I stood in the glare of the sunshine.

I was not brave enough to take it up and carry its dead little stranger's shape to a priest or to a constable. Indeed, they would think it were mine, as they would if I went off and brought them upon it. And so to my shame, I do what everyone else has done on this green spring morning with the birds singing all about them and the smell of fresh meat pies coming from the bakehouse, and the chandler's clanging. That is to say, I walk straight on, up Cornhill, as though I had never cast my eyes upon it, or as if I had but did not care. By the time I reached the corner of Gracechurch Street a ballad girl had set up outside the Two Bells, two women had quarreled on the pavement and the clock had chimed the half hour once more.

And I do not want to think about the sight of it again, nor the grief of its mother.

At night my lolling breasts leak milk, so that my linen shift is wet in patches when I wake. It is the rich, yellow kind of milk that comes first and quenches the thirst of a new baby in tiny swallows.

Mr. Blacklock did not come to breakfast.

And now when I go to the workshop I can see he has been working in here for hours. There is a chaos round him. Discarded all about are glass retorts and china pipkins discolored with chemical residues, traces of one frenzied experiment after another. There are opened jars everywhere, burnt piles of substances on tiles.

"What are you doing, sir?" I ask.

"Verdigris or acetate of copper is a salt of copper and produces a greenish flame," Mr. Blacklock replies, without looking up from the bench. "Copper filings have even less effect than this on burning; the color of their sparks in a fiery rain or star is disappointing." He picks out a jar and holds it up. "Steel filings for rayonet or brilliant fire. They intensify the sparks with some success, but I find little more can be achieved with them." He rubs at his face as though he has not slept. "Powdered zinc is promising," he mutters. Then he breaks off suddenly and resumes his inquiry. I try to work quietly lest I should disturb his progress. Yet even from this distance where I sit, his method seems to me to be disorderly. My fingers itch to go to his assistance.

"But what are you doing, what is your purpose?" I ask again, but he doesn't respond.

Joe Thomazin feeds the stove once, twice that morning, using the bellows to whiten the coals to a roaring temperature as Mr. Blacklock heats up pots and crucibles.

After almost four hours of clattering and silence, Mr. Blacklock turns round at the bench and looks at me directly.

"Agnes, I shall be frank," he says. "Your suspicions were correct. For some time now I have been engaged upon a search for pyrotechnic color."

"You have, sir?" I burst out, and a relief runs through my body like a gulp of fresh, cool water. "And have you found it?"

"I am looking for the sharpest kind of color," Mr. Blacklock says. "The colors that we will make one day must have the clarity and transparence of the color one sees in droplets in sunshine. The vivid green, the purple, the orange of light going through water."

"Can this be achieved?" I ask.

"Metal salts," he replies, shaking his head as though to sort and clarify his thoughts inside it. "I cannot tell," he says. "I have been looking again at the work of Hanzelet and this prompts me to think that there may be something in the application of metal salts." He indicates the little piles of burnt substance on the tiles in front of him. "They are struggling. There is something smothered about the way they burn. The colors latent in those metals are locked in; they should be freed during combustion but they are not. It is as though they need something—more air, more encouragement, more *vigor*—at that point. What could provide that?"

He looks at me grimly over his eyeglasses. "You are not to repeat a word of this to anyone outside this house."

"I shall not, sir," I say, trying to temper my excitement.

"An urgency to life and its developments has been made clear to me, and so I have decided to devote to it a greater portion of my endeavor." He coughs. "There are parallels I have discovered in my experiments with a great variety of substances, which make me think that it is no goose chase, but a path worth following."

"What kind of parallels?" I say.

He does not reply but instead goes to the coal tub beside the stove and takes up a large piece of coal, which he saws in half. On the flat, black surface he places a pinch of copper filings. He lights a wax candle, draws in a deep breath and uses a blowpipe to direct the flame of the candle upon them. I hold my breath. The provoked flame roars quietly over the filings, until they are red-hot. He puts down the blowpipe.

"But I saw nothing of note," I say, unable to keep the disappointment from my voice. "We have tried so many methods with copper filings already, and no color results from them."

"Ha!" Mr. Blacklock raises his blackened finger triumphantly. "We are not done!" He takes another pinch of filings from the jar marked copper and lays them on the coal. Then he adds something else to them that I cannot see.

"Sal ammoniac!" he says, like a conjurer, and blows the candle flame again.

The flame is a perfect blue.

It is as though we have found the elixir of life. Mr. Blacklock blows the flame until the air is spent. I feel wonder at the strangeness and the calm of it. It is like catching an unexpected glimpse of a rare wild bird in a winter hedgerow. Or drinking down a great sweet draft after a long journey.

"It is only a beginning," Mr. Blacklock says. He coughs a little so that I do not see his pride.

"There seems much promise in this," he says. "It seems to work with any of the salts of copper. But there are an infinite number of combinations I must yet try."

He spreads out his four good fingers on his right hand and looks musingly at the stump of the one that was lost. "When the atmosphere is damp I sometimes sense my finger twitching and flexing there," he says. The wind gets up.

"So have you found what you need to make the colors work?" I ask.

"No! I have not! I am leagues from arriving at an answer to this question. A rainbow of colors is not at my fingertips. Look!" He gestures at the cluttered bench, the tables. "Spread about me are broken vessels and unsatisfactory fulminations that I cannot measure or assess because I do not have sufficient evidence." He rubs at his eyes.

"I am in despair most of the time. I cannot sleep for thinking of it. And then a crack of hope opens itself in the form of nothing but a brief success. I cannot always reproduce good results. I cannot always remember to keep notating as I work. I am impatient. My methods are clumsy. I work with a minutiae of quantities as I am afraid of accidents, of losing eyes or further digits." He coughs. "I am fatigued. I breathe in fumes that make me gag with sickness, and fumes that bite my throat. My fingers burn in patches where I pick up a white-hot dish that has been in the stove." He looks out at the yard. "And I am afraid that I am too old or past the peak of life to be embarking on ambitious ventures. Still no answers come to me."

"You are not old, sir, but of course I can help you," I say eagerly. "You know that it exists, your solution, though you can't find it yet." I search for words with which I might encourage him. "It is only that you must find the way to explain it to yourself." My mind works wildly.

"You are like a jackdaw carrying a long stick in its beak to make a nest!" I say. "It tries to enter the hole in a hollow tree but the stick prevents it. After many attempts, the bird turns the stick sideways, and enters easily. After that, the nest is quick to build."

"You put these natural philosophers to shame," he says, wryly.

"In the same way, once the means is discovered, the construction of your idea might be straightforward. From what you say, measurements and stability and precision of the method are going to matter further, but, Mr. Blacklock, sir, it seems the essence of your work is already made."

There is a flicker in his black eyes as he looks at me.

"It may not happen in my lifetime," he says suddenly. "But it may be within yours."

We are expecting a small consignment of gunpowder this afternoon. It has begun to rain, and each time I hear the rumble and hiss of wheels on the wet street outside, my heart leaps in a panic and then falls when the wheels do not stop before the workshop. My ears strain. Now that I have set my mind to what I have to do, I am impatient to see Cornelius Soul again. There is so little time. What will happen when he finds out he has been tricked, I cannot think about. Perhaps he will not. Meanwhile, everything, it seems, is falling into place. He is a good man; I have seen him with his family. He would be kind with me, I am sure of it. And perhaps, just perhaps . . . No! I do not dare to think that somehow I could go on working here at Blacklock's. When the knock at the door finally comes, my heart flutters like a fresh leaf caught by a breeze. He is here! I put down my mallet and push my stool away from the filling-box. Four large Roman candles sit inside it, half completed. The knock comes again, louder this time. Mr. Blacklock looks up from the trestle at the back of the workshop and frowns.

"Agnes! The door!" he barks, and I go quickly. My hand tries to find out if my hair is tidy before I reach it. The bolt is stiff where the door has swelled in the damp weather.

I am startled to see a squat man with a sprout of ginger beard upon his chin. Red and puffed, his face is that of a man who eats too much.

He comes inside, as though he was expected, and Mr. Blacklock does not seem surprised by his arrival. The man takes off his hat and shakes the drips from it, and scratches at his beard as he talks. I do not hear much of what he says, once he has unwrapped the box of gunpowder and placed it carefully upon the floor.

When he is gone back out into the rain and the door has closed on the noise of the street, I ask, baffled, who the man could be. "Is Mr. Soul ill or indisposed that he did not come himself? Has he a new partnership that he has not thought to mention to us?"

Mr. Blacklock does not turn around from his apparatus, putting together vessels in a way that I have not seen him do before. His back is stiff.

"We have changed supplier," he says. "Mr. Hewitt is a chandler from Wapping. He has a recommended source for all grades of powder and his speed of delivery is as good as any man's."

"Why, sir?" I ask, my insides turning over, plummeting. "Is it because—" Mr. Blacklock interrupts me promptly.

"I began to find the quality of Mr. Soul's commodities a little lacking. I began to tire of it. To tire of it," he repeats, louder, as though I might not have heard him. Mr. Blacklock coughs briefly, and then there is nothing but a long silence. Could he have found out about Cornelius Soul's arrest? I hope he does not know of my involvement; surely he would have mentioned it.

Roman candles are deceptively difficult to fill.

I am clumsy today. I break stars as I knock at the drift with the mallet. I pour in too much dark fire and have to tip it out, again and again. I am distracted. At first I cannot bring myself to say a thing about the gunpowder, and then I must.

"This powder is no good," I hazard, blinking back my tears, opening the box and looking at it.

Mr. Blacklock's reply is curt. "One can hardly ascertain the quality of powder purely by observation."

I know this. It is just that I want it to be bad powder.

"But it seems . . . coarse," I suggest in desperation.

Mr. Blacklock does not look at the powder. He says, unmoving, as though it bores him to speak of it, "Mr. Hewitt's stock comes highly recommended to me. The intention to change supplier has been made upon a firm basis that does not need to be discussed today."

I am put in my place.

The anxiety eats at me now. I see the timing of my plans ebbing away from me.

Days go by.

The weather is changeable, and moves from damp to warm again. I am crossing the yard to the outhouse with the key for the safe. The sun is bright for the end of April, and beats down.

Mrs. Blight has taken herself to Saul Pinnington's to purchase sausage meat. Mary Spurren is washing pots in the scullery; I can hear the clank of copper against the sink through the open door into the yard. A wren sings from an elder bush against the hot bricks of the outhouse. Mr. Blacklock is out with the merchant in Cannon Street, which is something of a blessing because of late he has been conducting very strange experiments, sitting unflinching before small explosions at his bench. He is getting little work done toward the orders, but instead spends his time scratching notes down in the book he keeps inside his waistcoat, and muttering to himself.

And so there is no one to see when I sit down for a moment on the low wall by the elder and stretch out my legs to snatch a rest. How easily tired I am become. The sun warms my hair. I close my eyes and let the red color behind my eyelids fill up my mind like a pleasant liquid. A string of unimportant thoughts swims by: a day in spring at home, pulling the last of the leeks in the vegetable patch. I remember the wren's nest we found once in the brewhouse. William was excited. Its walls were smooth and perfect with mud and moss. He sobbed with dismay when, later that week, rats dislodged it from the beam and it fell to the floor. Five white wren's eggs were smashed outright, five tiny yolks spread out wetly in the dust.

When the baby kicks inside my belly my eyes jerk wide open to the yard. A panic passes through me. My heart beats and beats as though I have been caught off-guard. What am I thinking! I must not unwind, or sit about dreaming in the sun as though all were well, as though all were favorable, as though no ill wind were blowing over the heap of my life.

The wren flies from the elder and is gone. Without a thought I climb up to the top of the crumbling bricks of the wall and stand there as tall as I can, and I jump to the ground. I get up and do it again. I jump hard down to the earth, letting the jerk of the landing jolt right through my body. I get up again and jump down. It is exhilarating. The yard is white with brightness. I get up again and jump down; my ankles collapse a little under the strain. I make myself heavy as lead as I hit the ground. I make myself heavy as barrels of herring, as heavy as rocky flints from a cliff-side, as clay, pig iron, a sack of grain; as though I were falling fifty feet, not four feet. I do it again, staggering. As though I were creating damage to myself, to the thing inside me.

"What are you doing?" A voice brings me to my senses. Mary Spurren is standing at the back door. She is shielding her eyes with her hand and staring at me. I am panting with effort; there is dust all over my skirt. My heart beats and beats. What am I doing?

"A game, a country game," I say, weakly.

"It don't look much like fun to me," Mary Spurren says, doubt in her voice. She continues to stare at me. "More like the Devil was in you. For a trice my blood went quite cold on seeing it. Don't do it again, it's kicking up dust. I should not have to close the windows."

"I am just being silly," I say, leaning my whole spinning weight on the wall to catch my breath. "It is nothing but a country game we play, as children. The sunshine has got into my head and made me foolish." I try to laugh. "The moment has passed now. I am going to the safe to fetch more gunpowder." I hold up the key to show her. My fingers are shaking.

"What's it called?" she says.

"What is what called?"

"The game you are playing," she says, losing interest, turning back to the scullery.

"I don't know, I cannot remember," I say, and as I go to the outhouse, I am sure I see movement at an upstairs window of the house, at Mr. Blacklock's chamber, though when I look there is nothing.

When I get to the outhouse, I sob and sob, rubbing my belly. Something has to be done.

26

*S*mall portfires are the hardest, dullest work. Now that I am swift and better skilled at making them, I charge them in bundles of thirty-seven cases at a time, a kind of six-sided honeycomb of tubes, all mouths to the ceiling. The air outside is blue with smoke and a fine, blustery rain. There is a whistling, breathing sound in the chimney, as if the wind were putting its mouth to the pot on the roof, though it cannot come in.

The workshop is filled with the smell of Mr. Blacklock's experiment, and he is staring fixedly into a jar that is strapped to a glass vessel, connected to a retort over a smoking brazier. "I will have something to show you," he says, in a strange, choked voice, and I recognize the same powerful smell from the day the color was bleached out of the flower inside the air from aqua regia.

"What is that black powder?" I ask, peering at the opened pot beside the retort, but he does not reply.

"What is inside the jar, Mr. Blacklock?" I can feel a tightening of excitement about my throat that is not just from the yellow fumes leaking out.

"Stand back for the moment, Agnes Trussel, and within the hour I will show you something that I think is going to change our lives forever," he says hoarsely. "This is the third occasion on which I have been able to produce it, and I am confident that my discovery is not a stone overturned by chance."

Later, when the smell is gone from the room at last, he brings a pipkin. "See inside here," he says. "Look here and see these shiny, eager little crystals." His hand is shaking.

"What are they, sir?" I ask.

"I do not know!" He laughs, and his face is transformed. "I shall call this substance . . ." He considers. "The vital agent."

"And does it . . . ?"

He looks at me.

"I have begun to experiment with this vital agent. It seems to act as enabler or go-between, coaxing the colors out of substances when they burn."

"How, sir?"

"I do not yet know." He coughs. "The acid has driven out the air from the alkali and then I have captured it in crystal form. It is seemingly charged with the principle of inflammability. Added to powder in the place of niter, it gives astounding fierceness to the burn. It is important. I believe it is the key to my endeavor. I do not know yet if it can be controlled sufficiently to use in pyrotechny, but I intend to find out."

"Is it safe to use?" I ask. He shakes his head.

"In my experiments I have found it unstable, dangerous. It can ignite spontaneously upon exposure to friction or to unchecked sunshine. It goes rapidly from lying in a quiet state to sudden violent action."

"A snake of a thing!" I say, thinking again of the soft brown adders that soak up the hot sun on the Downs. Lying in the grasses, they begrudge disturbance from a trance and, chanced upon, they can rear up with a spiteful poison to their bite. Mrs. Porter's youngest daughter, Sarah, was bitten by an adder and did not survive a second night, although they put on adder's fat and the rector prayed for her safekeeping.

"It is capricious," he stresses. "Once coupled with sulfur, it can spring to life without warning, so that it is no simple task to establish formulations with any accuracy. This agent is highly volatile," Mr. Blacklock warns. "Never cause a tap or knock about it. Never allow any grit to be introduced inadvertently within the mortar's cavity when grinding a composition that contains it. Never even expose it to the warmth of the sunshine." He pulls at his neckcloth to loosen it. I see his neck as he does this; I cannot help it. Again I am surprised at how young it seems: the skin of his neck is smooth and supple beneath the dark stubble on his jaw. I look away quickly. "Of course, most pyrotechnic formulae should be treated with respect," he is saying. "But any containing this new substance I have created should be treated with something approaching fearfulness."

We hear the church clock strike.

"And how . . . ?"

"It is noon. Let us eat."

27

*T*he solution is close now, though it is not within my sight. Like watching a still pond, where the bank with its flaggy irises, starworts and water parsnip is reflected in the water, and you see a push, a rippling disturbance that does not break the surface. You know it is a fish under the pond's skin, a trout maybe, or perch or tench, turning its big slippery body about in the water, pushing at the water as it turns and making nothing but a fleeting ripple, but you cannot see it. You know the signs, the indications, which is enough. You do not need to see something to feel its presence there.

I say this to myself, over and over.

Mr. Blacklock counts out my wages. How many more weeks before he stops that and turns me out instead? I am seven months gone, and I have come to my senses. I begin to feel an agitation so strong that I can almost hear it rushing in my ears.

"You must fetch new apparatus from the apothecary's shop," Mr. Blacklock says. "I have to meet with Mr. Torré to discuss his needs for Marylebone next month and so I cannot go myself. You are aware of Mr. Jennet's tendency toward a bending of the honesty of things. Keep your eyes open while you are there."

I nod. And I shall go also to the herb market on my own business, I think, but I say nothing of this.

"I need new pipkins." Mr. Blacklock writes an order for me to carry. "I have broken so many. A new receiver. Some spirit of niter, manganese. Some clean spills of wood, I have no time to cut my own." In this household, spills of wood are tipped with sulfur to touch the spark in the tinderbox, though Mary Spurren does not like to use them.

"Devil's fire," she always says, pressing her pale lips together crossly.

The front door closes behind me. Out on the street with my shawl about me I have a sense that I am watched, and glance upward uneasily. Nothing at the windows, no movement, no white face staring down at me behind a scrap of curtain. And then I see a red kite circling far above the city, waiting for prey. Its forked tail is just visible against the sky.

At the shop Mr. Jennet almost snatches the order from my hand, with a tut of disapproval. His enormous wig quivers as he bends down behind the counter to reach the stacks of apparatus.

"What's he up to now that he needs so much of late?" he grumbles. "Business must be prosperous, is it? The world's gone mad, I say." He wraps the receiver and looks at the list again. "And what does he want with so much manganese? A funny purchase for an artificer."

"Just working hard, Mr. Jennet," I reply, watching him.

When I am done at the apothecary's shop I do not go back to the house with my heavy basket. At the herb market in Lamb's Conduit Street I buy a large bundle of sage. Because I am certain that the skinny market woman senses that there is something strange about my purchase, I ask her for a quantity of parsley for my basket, too. Her baby is asleep in a crate beside her. I do not look at it.

I go into a side street and I throw the parsley in the gutter, like a madwoman. It is so fresh and green. The sage, which I keep, is very soft. The tender purplish leaves are like skin or new fur. It does not seem like something that could kill a child. I secrete the sage inside my shawl, and walk back to the house. Crushed against my body, the muffled, bitter pepper smell of sage is all about me.

On my way I am surprised to see a pair of drovers with a flock of unkempt sheep heading out toward Lincoln's Inn Fields. As they bundle past I breathe in their wool smell, their savory dung smell, and I am flooded with sickness for home.

"Crabs! Periwinkles!" a boy cries out in my ear as he passes. I smell the weedy salt of his basket. The traffic closes around the sheep and then

I lose sight of them as the road bends to the right. They are gone. I am desolate and the stone steps to the grocer's are steep and regular. My legs ache with taking regular steps sometimes.

There is no one whom I recognize inside the shop. The women seem tall and grimy, filling it up with their baskets and loud voices asking for cheese and rice and fuller's earth. One of them turns when she hears my voice, and flicks a look at my belly. I almost run home and I am glad of the strange smell of the hallway as I enter.

Home. I called this place home. That was a mistake, as I know that home is a long way southward at the back of the swell of the hills on the edge of the trees, before the sea. This can never be home, surely, with its strange odors and complicated maze of corridors and outbuildings, with its old, wide, beaten-up stairways covered in city polish and city dirt. How can I call it home, when there are rooms here that I don't even know about?

When I get to the kitchen I hide the sage at the back of the cupboard.

If I think carefully about it, I find that I feel the loss of home very deep down inside, hardly noticeable now, like a tiny sob at the end of a long tunnel.

28

*A*t last, Mary Spurren has left the house to get fish from the market at Billingsgate. She will be gone for half an hour or more, and Mrs. Blight is out. I do not have much time for what I need to do.

The sage has wilted and the leaves hang limply from the stalks. I have so little time. My heart is racing with the consequence of what I am doing.

If I boil it for too long, it will fail in its purpose. Perhaps the nature of its properties will be destroyed by overheating? Or will it be increased in strength? I do not know. I can only remember bits of what my grandmother told me about herbs. Why did I not listen to her with more attention? Why does the kettle not reach the boil more rapidly! The fire is too low. I stoke the fire. I riddle the fire. I wait again. Then the water bubbles and my hands are shaking as I lift the heavy kettle away from the heat and pour. If the leaves sit for too short a time within the water, how can its qualities leak out into the brew?

I steep it for as long as I dare and pour it out hastily into a white cup. Much of the liquid spills and splashes on the table.

The water is a clouded greenish brown, like the water in ponds. Will it taste of nothing, or of all it is, boiled leaves? I begin to drink it down quickly in one gulping draft as I have so little time. It is too hot and burns my tongue and lips, which I am glad of. It is strongly bitter, acrid, unpleasant.

There is a noise at the door! I splutter and stop.

Already someone is back, turning the key, coming in down the corridor. It is a rarity for Mary Spurren to accomplish anything at speed, yet here she is, all out of breath with walking hastily, and her chest rises and falls at a pace. She sets her parcel of fish upon the kitchen table and glances about, as though the quickness of her blood beating round had made her more than usually alert.

"Mackerel, I got," she says. "Made her gut it for me, but left the heads and tails on. I like a fish to seem a fish." She trails off and sniffs. "What odd smell is that?" she asks. Her big head faces me.

I make myself look blank and busy. I look up from the sink, where I have tipped the infusion away. I dry the china cup and put it away in the back of the cupboard. "A downdraft of coal smoke?" I suggest, my heart beating. "The wind does eddy and bluster down the chimney when it comes from the northeasterly direction."

I fold a linen cloth over the drying rack before the hob. "Or perhaps Mr. Blacklock has some strong tobacco. He went to the tobacco merchant only yesterday. Mind you"—I make myself look at her—"I can smell nothing."

And Mary Spurren gives me a suspicious stare when I say this.

Girandole

29

*H*ow I wish that Cornelius Soul would bring us gunpowder again. I was not attempting to ensnare him, I remind myself. It is more that I was trying to channel the natural force of his intentions.

But if I do not see him? My thoughts were so full of fire and chemicals. Perhaps I should have prayed for a chance to present itself.

I had almost forgotten my purpose. In another week it will be too late. I have reached eight months now. I touch my belly; perhaps it is too late already. I keep waiting for a rush of blood, or waters, anything. In truth I know there is little chance that the sage will work, but, God only help me, I must try everything.

So when I open the door unknowingly and find that Cornelius Soul is stood there on the step in his gray coat, winking at me, I am both relieved and newly anxious.

"Good day, Mr. Soul," I say. I do not dare to ask why he is here. Perhaps . . .

"Just passing." He grins.

He does not come across the threshold, though his eyes dart beyond me into the workshop from time to time. He spins his hat in the air and catches it.

"You have a new hat, Mr. Soul," I say, looking at its gilt braid.

"Finest on Cheapside!" he replies. "And . . . I have an evening free next Tuesday and, alas, no lovely lady like yourself to spend it with."

"Don't you?" I say faintly, and a wave of nerves goes through me. The next moment comes swiftly.

"Could I have the pleasure of your company at the Spring Gardens, Miss Trussel?" he says, and my hand flies to my throat as if to cover it.

"The Gardens!" I say.

Behind me inside the workshop I hear Mr. Blacklock putting a tool down and pushing his chair back. Strangely, I open my mouth to decline.

"You could, but . . ." I hesitate. The Spring Gardens are a public, crowded place across the river. My heart flutters when I think of being alone there with him, in the throng of people with my baby huge inside me and due so close. But perhaps this is my only chance. I must agree.

"You could," I say, and with an effort I look up and meet his eye directly.

"Until next week, then!" he declares. "It is a gala night, there will be fireworks."

And a mixture of terror and delighted thoughts creeps quickly up on me, though I keep up a coolness to my manner until Cornelius Soul has turned smartly on his heel and gone away down the street.

"Fireworks!" I say under my breath, turning excitedly to Mr. Blacklock, and I see that he has left the room. Just dirty little Joe Thomazin sat there in the corner, always looking and listening, taking things in. His heels kick the back of the stool.

"What!" I ask him, but he doesn't reply; he just looks at me. His dark eyes are big in his thin face. When I go to the kitchen I find that I am not the only woman in the household to be beside myself with excitement; Mrs. Blight has won the lottery.

Mr. Blacklock does not seem to fully hear when Mrs. Blight waves her ticket beneath his nose at noon and squeals again, "And on my birthday! The eleventh of May for once has had an auspicious bent!" She is pink with pleasure.

"Would you, sir, be so good as to allow me to prepare the household with some especial kind of supper spread tonight?" she asks. "Nice joint of beef, perhaps, sir? A bit of topside? Saddle of lamb?"

"Yes, yes," he says, but as if he has not fully heard her.

"Tonight, sir?" she repeats as he puts on his hat.

"Yes, yes, tonight," he barks, and goes away down the corridor. When the front door bangs shut, Mrs. Blight rolls her eyes to the ceiling.

"That man," is all she says, getting on with her pastry. "Godly ungracious."

Later she makes a great show of fishing about inside her wallet and holding up a shiny guinea piece, as though she were some kind of duchess. "We'll have the beef," she announces grandly. Mary Spurren ignores her and slips out of the room. Mrs. Blight turns and tuts at me. "You'll have to go."

Perhaps the rest of the day starts to go wrong from here, at Saul Pinnington's. There is no beef topside ready, and I have to buy instead a loin of pork.

"No matter," I say, when the butcher's boy tries to explain their shortage. "It's the end of the day, miss," he calls after me, as if worried that I might get him into trouble. The streets are heaving with people and on my way back a coachman curses when I stumble in front of his horse and nearly fall.

"I could've killed you, silly bitch," he shouts down at me. "Can't you look and see what's coming?" I want to shout back angrily, "Childbirth, death, the gallows, Bridewell, take your pick!" But I clench my teeth and do not. The noise of the city is too much sometimes, I think, choking with rage. And today as I pass the church of St. Stephen on Coleman Street just behind the house, I make up my mind to slip inside for a moment's peace.

Under the great carving of the Last Judgment in the porch, I have an odd sensation, and hesitate and turn about, as though somebody is watching me from across the street. But when I look, nobody is there.

Inside, the church is dim. My footsteps echo up the aisle. Mrs. Blight's joint of pork is heavy in my basket, and with some relief I sit down and rest it on the pew beside me. I breathe the smell of stone in deeply, as if it could give me strength. Just one more minute, I think, looking toward the candles burning yellow at the altar. Outside, the world seems far away.

How close I am, it seems, to the fulfillment of my plan. Soon I will have the chance to ensure that Cornelius Soul becomes obliged to marry me. He is an honest, handsome, willful man my mother would be proud to call a son. But why is it that I feel a strong unease each time I dwell on it? Surely, in the eyes of the world, at birth it will appear to be Cornelius's child come early, conceived before the nuptials had taken place. I am not showing much, and after all, my mother always had small babies; even Hester was just a little scrap at birth.

How can that work? The voice in my head is still whispering. *Cornelius Soul will know otherwise.* But he is a good man, I reason, and perhaps if he knew my story then he might begin to understand? It is my only chance. Yet if it were a good solution surely I should have a growing sense of calm, with completion drawing near. But I do not; indeed, I fear that he will hate me for it.

I have begun to think that I should have another plan laid out. Something else to turn to, if everything else I try has failed.

At the altar, one candle gutters blackly, contracts and then winks out. It is a kind of drawing in of breath, a sudden shocking inward suck into the darkness.

If I were gone, I think, extinguished from my family's lives, then they would be blameless. Better by far that they shall never know. And in the moment of calm that I am hoping to find, I remember the orpiment. The deadly yellow poison offers me a ready answer. It will still be there if all else fails. *But it is a sin to take a life!* the voice inside me whispers urgently. It is too late now, though, to think of that. One sin leads straight toward another, and there is nothing to be done about it.

They say you do not need to swallow much.

I hear the sound of feet on stones outside the porch, and a sudden voice booms, "Anyone in?"

A hot shameful panic grips me, that someone might find me sitting here before God with my belly swollen like this, and instinctively I freeze and hold my breath. But then I hear a trundling scrape as the great door is pulled shut, and a key turns in the lock.

"No, no! There is somebody in here! I am still in here!" I call out, embarrassed, as I scramble to the porch and rap against the door. "Please come back! I am here!" But the footsteps fade away. Somewhere above me in the tower the church clock whirrs into life and I count the strokes as the bell sounds the hour. Six o'clock! How did it become so late?

A clergyman, someone, has locked up the church for the night against thieves, just as Mrs. Blight said they did. How stupid I am not to remember. I go to the north door to see if this is fastened, too, and rattle at it. I am quite locked in. It is hopeless, I think, nursing my sore knuckles. I will be here until morning. Miserably, I think of Mrs. Blight's special supper and how she will not have her joint of meat. What will they think? The household sitting down together, raising a toast, no meat, and my place at the table unaccountably deserted. The house is so close to the church, and yet I cannot even call to them.

At first there is a glow of colored light about the stained-glass windows, and then that fades. When I become thirsty I go to the font for baptisms and drink the holy water gleaming there. It tastes of stone, or something else I cannot place. I think of the fingers of priests scooping and pouring handfuls onto the crowns of infants as they are blessed and named for this world. Perhaps if I were to confess my troubles to a priest, I would feel lighter, almost forgiven.

By now, I think unhappily, they will have finished supper. I shiver with cold and as I pull my skirts tighter about me I touch a wetness, a patch of wetness on my skirt where it lies over the pew, and I feel that the pew is pooling with some kind of liquid, and then I realize that in my basket the raw meat must be seeping through the paper it is wrapped in. I almost laugh with relief. Mrs. Blight's wet butcher's meat is dripping on the consecrated flagstones.

Then I clench my knees with my arms as best I can around my belly and press my face into the cloth of my skirt. I barely hear the strokes of three and four o'clock, which means that I must somehow have slept.

I am woken abruptly.

It is light. I hear the door being unlocked from the outside and I struggle, stiff and guilty, to my feet. A minister or curate enters and closes the door behind him with a brisk flourish. He comes down the aisle with his black vestments flapping as he walks, and stops, as I knew he would, when he sees me standing there between the pews.

"In heavens, child!" he exclaims. His voice is lilting. "What are you doing there?"

"Just sitting, sir. I—"

"Sitting! Have you been there all night?"

"I have. I . . . needed to think."

"Did you now!" he says. "And you thought for a long time. I'm afraid I have resorted to locking the church doors at nightfall; there have been thefts over Westminster way, you see. Was it cold? Were you waiting for me?" he asks. "God's guidance can sometimes be slow in coming."

I shake my head, and he smiles kindly. "Well, child, if you change your mind, God waits for us in patience." The bell whirrs and clangs. "Unlike parishioners! If you'll excuse me now. But if you should need to talk about your trouble, you can find me here. Reverend Lindsay is my name."

"Thank you, Reverend," I say, and he goes into the vestry. I wonder if God might forgive me more readily if I admit to another living person what I have done. But he is busy, I reason. Starlings are chirping in the eaves. The stained glass is brighter and more richly colored by the minute with the rising sun; I make out saints walking clearly upon the stained-glass flowers between the leaded panes, St. Genevieve with her stained-glass hands pressed together in prayer. St. Genevieve was a holder of keys, like St. Peter. And I remember how, though the Devil extinguishes her candle always, an angel lights it again and the flame burns on strongly. The nave is flooded with light and color.

I step upon the stones marking the separate graves of Henry Nicholas Cuff and Catherine Pelham in the floor of the aisle as I leave the church. The stones are new and freshly laid there, the cut letters quite unworn. How close the dead are. I am glad of the sunrise.

And I am hungry. I think of telling Mrs. Blight and Mary Spurren of the key turning in the lock, and how they will laugh at me. Yet they will not know that I am not the same girl I was yesterday, when I went in. The sage has not worked, but all of me, every last drop of blood, fat, flesh, all changed, now I have remembered that there is the yellow orpiment.

I have a final choice. God help me if I have to take it, but I will, for the sake of my family.

Out on the street, chimneys are pouring the smoke of fresh-lit fires. The air is still and the smoke pours upward in bluish columns all down the street. A crowd of swifts scream past.

It is early as I approach the house and cross the yard to the scullery door, but I know that Mary Spurren will be up riddling the grate and grudgingly might flick the bolt across to let me in, if it is not indeed already open, and if the floor is not wet with mopping.

The scrape of my boots on the bricks echoes horribly about the silent yard. I glance anxiously at the upper windows of the house to see if Mr. Blacklock has risen, but the sun is blinding them with such a sheet of early golden light that I cannot tell if the curtains are still drawn or have been parted.

I am relieved to find the back door is ajar, and edge in cautiously. No one is there; both the kitchen and the scullery are empty. I look about for signs of life, for Mrs. Blight. There is an unfamiliar smell in the darkened kitchen. As my eyes accustom to the gloom I do not see anything remarkable at first: a folded pile of aired washing waiting for the flat iron, as Mrs. Nott was here yesterday; a bundle of untrimmed rhubarb wilting on the side. And then I see the bottles. A stack of empty bottles and a half-eaten knuckle of pork from the meat safe lying uncovered on the table, and beneath it a great sticky spill of liquor and broken glass where a bottle has crashed to the floor. I go back to the scullery and see unwashed plates and cutlery. And the fire is out.

I take in these details one by one. I do not know what to make of this at all. Then there is movement in a chair beside the hob and with a start I watch the shape of Mary Spurren snort into wakefulness. She looks about her in some confusion, her large, froggish eyes bulging. She is a sorry sight. Her big head appears swollen with an ache that seems almost too much weight for her neck to bear. She gives out a kind of moan.

"Are you ill?" I venture.

"Not in my person," she says, indistinctly. "And where was you last night? My neck's stiff enough to be halfway to dead." She rubs at it gingerly. "Not ill, though not . . . well, neither."

Then she presses herself up out of the chair with an effort and stands, swaying. A smell of liquor seeps from her.

"Mary," I say anxiously, "the fire is out. Mr. Blacklock is not down yet, is he? He will be angry if he sees this chaos. If I begin to clear the mess with you, perhaps we can have the kitchen clean as soon as possible!" I try to sound encouraging, and add lightly, as if I do not care, "And whereabouts is Mrs. Blight?"

But she frowns, as though I have reminded her of something she is trying to remember. She waves a forefinger. "Blacklock, Mr. Blacklock . . ." she exclaims thickly. "Now there's a man who'll . . . not be down so early as he might for breakfast."

"No?" I say, beginning hastily to clear the table.

"He did not . . ." She stops to hiccup. "He did not come back last night neither." She smirks unevenly at me and slouches back down into the chair.

"How do you mean?" I say, placing a bottle with particular care into the gape of the sack. "But there are robbers, cutthroats, abroad at night—do you know he is safe?"

"Oh, I daresay he's safe enough, if you could call it that." Her head falls back and her bleary eyes watch me with some kind of triumph.

"But he did not come to supper. Let us say he appeared to have another engagement all of a sudden, rushing in when I thought it was you come back with the meat, swapping his hat for his best one and hurrying out again without a word."

"And he did not come back?" I ask.

"No, he did not. A fine way to enjoy Mrs. Blight's lottery on the day of her birthday, no joint of meat going cold on the table, and all the sauces stiffening in their dishes."

She likes it that she has my attention now.

"Fairly striding, he was, they say." She sniffs. "Very eager, no doubt. But perhaps you would know more about that than me."

"What do you mean?"

She hiccups again, and rubs her neck. "I believe I shall join them Methodists this very forenoon. No!" She raises a forefinger. "Don't speak to me or I shall fall down in a faint like a lady's maid." I hear the clock chime nine times from the study. How late it is.

I go on alone with the thankless task. And before I can get the kitchen clean there are footsteps and Mr. Blacklock's sudden shadow blocks the sunshine falling through the back door wide open to the yard.

I look up. Mr. Blacklock has the unshaven, unkempt appearance of a man who has not slept all night, and there is a cast of something almost wild-eyed in his face. It is most peculiar.

He clears his throat before speaking.

"I must discuss a matter with you," Mr. Blacklock says, soberly.

"Me?" I whisper.

My heart begins thumping. It has happened. He has found out. He has discovered my crime or my secret and he has to discharge me. But even as he begins speaking, Mrs. Blight bursts in, as if she has been waiting for this moment outside the door.

"Morning, Mr. Blacklock, sir!" she interrupts. "A lovely day."

"I am sorry to have missed the celebration," Mr. Blacklock says distractedly. "I trust you did not wait for me."

"No, we did not, sir. Some of us indeed most certainly did not." Mrs. Blight's eyes flash spitefully at me. She is wearing a brand-new straw hat on her head, covered in carnations. "Pert little madam!" she says, smiling at me, and her dislike is polished up and glinting in her gaze.

She unties her hat, takes it off and simpers at it. "Was that Mr. Soul keeping you under lock and key that you could not return all night?" she adds.

"No, no!" I begin to explain in some alarm. "By a twist of fate I became—"

"We did so miss your presence last night, Mr. Blacklock, sir," Mrs. Blight cuts in, sweetly.

"Forgive me," he mutters abruptly, turning his back as he leaves the room. I must be brave I think, and speak up then before he closes the door. "But, Mr. Blacklock, when would you wish to talk with me?"

"Another time, another time," he says, walking away.

I can feel Mary Spurren's big head still facing me, though I do not look. "But where is that joint of meat then, Agnes Trussel?"

The pork! Left on the pew. It will be long gone now.

"I lost it," I say lamely. They will never believe me.

"Lost it? Jesus!" She pulls a face.

"You'll pay for that out of your wages, my girl, once I tell Mr. Blacklock," Mrs. Blight says, viciously. She comes up very close to me and her breath smells of fish. "There's something about the way you comport yourself about, Agnes Trussel, that gets on my nerves."

Then I slip into the workshop behind Mr. Blacklock and try to begin my day as though all is well. My hands shake as I work, as I wait for dismissal. I am faint with lack of sleep.

"Agnes, I must speak frankly with you," Mr. Blacklock starts to say again, putting his work to one side of the filling-box. And then when I look up at him, still he says nothing, and instead picks up the mallet again.

Perhaps he has financial trouble of a serious nature, and he has decided that I must go to save him money. Four shillings a week plus all my board and washing, candles; that must add up to something that might be better saved. He has been pacing the streets and has resolved that savings must be made in expenditure.

I remember when Mr. Fitton did something akin to that, and my brother Ab, who had been hoping to become herdsman's boy and learn a trade, instead found there was no longer a place for him at all with the dairy herd, as the new herdsman from upcountry had brought his own boy with him. He was told to look for work elsewhere.

It changed something in him, that discharge, which he took like a blow to the stomach that he never stopped feeling. Of course, he did not shrink nor double up—he was the sort to shoulder his new status like the burden it was—but there was a fury glistening in his eye. So when my mother said he always was an angry boy she was not right to say so. Our troubles shape our characters directly and in many ways.

Could it be another matter altogether? But there is something in John Blacklock's manner that makes me think that what he has to say to me is something quite unpleasant, and I become certain of this when for a second time he lets himself be interrupted, this time by Mary Spurren entering the workshop.

"Ah, Mary," he says, with relief.

"It's the coal, sir—will you want it for tomorrow as usual, only the cart-boy is here and he says there is some ill judgment with supply . . ."

I stop listening and sit in wretchedness.

Or perhaps, God help me, and I suppose I knew this all along, he has guessed my condition and cannot continue my employment under any circumstances for a moment longer. Has his eye been lingering on my belly as he speaks to me these past few weeks?

In the kitchen after supper, when he has gone to his study, Mary Spurren sidles up close and regards me suspiciously.

"I know where you was yesterday," she says.

"Do you?" I say.

I see her face smirking at me then.

"You do not," I say flatly.

"With Mr. Blacklock," she announces.

"Mr. Blacklock?" I frown. "Why would I have been with him? He was gone away on business, I suppose."

"Odd business it is that causes him to leave his order book idle on the desk, which leads him to go out sporting his best hat, as though he had a cause to further by it."

"You have been prying!" I exclaim.

"Not more than is needed for a simple explanation," she says indignantly, without a doubt that this is justified. She blinks at me.

"But think, Mary," I explain, more patient with her. "Why should I be with him? Mr. Blacklock does not need to take me on a business visit anywhere; my presence would never justify the fare. No," I say, "I imagine that he enjoys the solitude of journeys inside the hackney cab, his feet stretched out comfortably, sucking on his pipe and turning over ideas for formulae, uninterrupted, in his mind. Why would he want me there?"

She shrugs, as though nothing I say will dislodge her strange suspicion.

"He were seen," she persists.

"Oh?"

"At Covent Garden." She is triumphant. "And if he weren't with you, who were he with, I'd ask!"

"Why would he have to be with anyone?"

"Men go to Covent Garden for three reasons only." She counts on her thin fingers, holding them up. "One, the theater, two, the market, and three"—he lowers her voice to a hoarse whisper—"to lie with prostitutes."

"Prostitutes?" I retort. "Mr. Blacklock is not that sort of man."

Mary Spurren sniggers. "What kind of innocent are you? You know nothing of men!"

Mrs. Blight comes into the room. "Men? They're all the same, that way," she confirms, with relish. "Any man will go with a whore as he needs to."

"Mr. Blacklock would not," I repeat. "He is not that kind."

But her chance remark has set a worrying fleck of misgiving deep in my mind. It is the kind of thought that begins to fester and inflame, as the smallest of splinters can lodge in a tender skin and go bad with infection.

Why should it trouble me that he has spent the night abroad and has not told us his intentions? A man has needs; surely I heard my father slur those words enough times when my mother inclined away from the range of his unsteady grasp just back from the alehouse, forgetting for a moment her wifely duties. "Not now, Thomas," she would hiss, motioning us to get to bed at once.

And Mr. Blacklock's wife is dead. Of course he has a right to want some comfort. To choose some solace from his loneliness.

30

I am to go to the Gardens today, with Cornelius Soul.

The sky is a clear blue. Outside the city I imagine the sudden flush of growth, a silvery gray sheen on the leaves of the poplars, the soft punch of the cuckoo's call over the May blossom and cow parsley frothing like yeast in the greening hedgerows. In the meadows many buttercups must be open in the grass like yellow flour sprinkled there, in drifts.

Here inside the city walls we have the high hum of bees at the linden flowers in the yard, and the stickiness of the bricks beneath the insects' speckled misty ooze of honeydew. These days it almost seems to me as if the sap were rising in my own limbs, too.

He is late to fetch me.

"There's plenty of dogs goes barking up the wrong tree," Mrs. Blight says, sharing her unwanted opinions freely as she lifts the stockpot away from the fire. A fat, dry housefly pads up and down the table. There is a strong smell of boiling chicken bones filling the kitchen.

I pull myself up straight and act affronted. Mrs. Blight laughs out loud at me then, showing her teeth, so that I go and wait for Cornelius Soul in the hallway instead. I smooth the edge of the cap under my hat once more. It was a temptation to spend some of Mrs. Mellin's coins on new lace to trim it with, but in the end I had satisfied both vanity and conscience by washing it instead, and by pressing my clean clothes with the flat iron last night when everyone had gone to bed. I don't sit down now lest I crease my garments overmuch, and my legs begin to ache with nerves.

Joe Thomazin sidles into the hall while I wait. At first I think he has something to say, he stares at me so much. But then he sits hunched up on the bottom stair and scuffs his feet together, as if upset. "What?" I ask him. But of course he says nothing, and Cornelius Soul has come at last. I turn to wave goodbye to Joe Thomazin, but he has suddenly gone. The hallway is empty.

And then we are out of the house and hailing a hackney carriage out on the street. I can hardly look at Cornelius Soul, I am so shy. The cab is musty inside; the window is small, so that it is hard to see where we are going.

"Here," he says, grinning, "I've brought you gingerbread from Tiddy-Doll's in Mayfair." It is flat and gleaming like a brass plate, a baked shape of a woman.

"It's golden!" I exclaim.

"Gilded." He chuckles, turning it over. "Look, it's very thin. Go on," he says, "eat it." And I break off the head and pass it to Cornelius Soul. He chews and swallows it down. We eat the rest of the body between us, breaking the skirt and the bodice up into pieces. It is firm and delicious, and leaves a warm spicy taste in my throat.

The carriage rolls and jerks along.

"Where are we now?" I say. Cornelius Soul puts his head out, blocking the light.

"Gone over the river by the new bridge at Westminster," he says, sitting back on the seat in front of me. "Just going through the thicket beyond the turnpike gate." I can hear a gull crying, over the roar and chatter of wheels. "There was a robbery here of late that I saw in the papers. But you have a stout fellow beside you, no call for unease," he says, winking at me, and he holds out his hand when we climb down from the carriage. I am wearing the new kid gloves that I have never worn for working in, the ones that Mr. Blacklock gave to me.

A gaudy woman snatches Cornelius Soul's shillings from him at the gate. She is so whitely painted up and powdered I cannot see her face at all behind it. "When you're done staring, get through the turnstile," she yelps at me, rolling her eyes at the people behind us. Only when I turn away from her do I think that she must be a man dressed otherwise. How confusing the world is.

And we are here in the open air, walking beneath an avenue of elm trees so neatly ordered I can scarcely believe it. To either side of us are graveled, dusty walks, stonework, grand arches and pavilions. It is like a foreign place. A sparrow chirps.

Stretching as far as the eye can see in the evening light are beds of early roses and twisting sweet peas in pinks and whites. The earth is pale and sandy. I can see asparagus, gooseberries. Bees knock about between the blossoms and a musky, creamy scent of flowers fills my head like a spell.

I steal a glance sideways at Cornelius Soul, when I think he is not looking. His nose is small and sharp, and his silky white hair moves about in the lightest of breezes as we walk. Is it really trickery, I wonder, this trying to catch a man's attention?

"Does Blacklock treat you tolerably?" Cornelius Soul asks. He shakes a coin on his palm, flips it into the air and catches it. "Your conditions are adequate? Your victuals? Your arrangements?"

"He is a fair employer," I say. "Look at those women strolling! Their dresses are so elegant!"

"And trade is good?"

"It is," I say. I can see brocades, satins, watered silks.

"And your new supplier is a worthier man than I?" I cannot help but laugh when he says this.

"Is your trade elsewhere so bad you must be bitter?" I answer, mocking him, and he grins quickly then and takes my hand up and puts it beneath his arm. I do not pull away. I can feel his warmth inside the velvet. I see that the coat is worn at the cuffs, as though he has owned it a long time. His arm is slender for a man's, yet there is a wiry strength to it. I remember the gentle calmness of his mother, the loaf cut into five.

"I dislike losing any deal or battle. Show me a man that doesn't," he says. The ground crunches dry under our boots, and they scuff up dust. The May air is warm, and the tightly coiled springs inside my chest are unwinding like green shoots of bindweed in the sunshine. A sound of music comes faintly through the trees; then it stops and there is a drifting patter of applause. Am I in love? I am not dizzy with it. No, I know I am not, although when I think of it my stomach clenches in a nervous state of agitation at the thing that I am planning.

"You cannot pick them!" I protest to Cornelius Soul when he leans over the clipped hedge to snap off a bloom, and holds it out to me. I do not know its name—a city plant.

"I do not like those flowers," I say, shaking my head. "They have something of the smell of fresh blood about them."

"Take it!" he insists.

I laugh, but I will not take the flower from him, so finally he pushes the stalk through his own coat's buttonhole.

"That was no defeat," he says, shrugging. "The gain is mine, all mine!"

The late sun casts a bronze sheen over everything, and the shadows are long on the ground. When we stop at a fountain purling a soft jet of water, I see how it catches the light and the droplets sparkle in colors. The water looks fresh and clear.

I imagine jumping in feet first, sinking, letting the skin of the water meet and close above my head, feeling my hair floating upward like a brown silky weed. The heaviness of my swelling body would dissolve into the pool, and if I opened my eyes into the wetness of the water, all I would see, stretching on and on above me, would be the vault of the high blue evening sky.

"There is a star!" I say, pointing.

Cornelius Soul leans back against the fountain and breathes in deeply. I dip my hand near the star's reflection, and stir it about.

"Did you know, Miss Trussel," he asks, "that nightingales sing here?"

I take my hand out of the water and dry it on my skirts. "Nightingales?" I say, perturbed. "In birdcages?"

Cornelius chuckles. "No, they perch in the cherry trees, singing their hearts out to the punters until closing time." He buys sugared almonds from a booth, though I say I am not hungry. He opens the bag and holds it out, bending closer.

"There was a woman had a passion for nightingales, they say." He speaks quietly into my ear.

"What woman?" I ask, slipping the unwanted sweet about in my palm, like a pebble.

"Used an oil made from the pressed tongues of nightingales to perfume her wrists," he goes on, the sugar cracking between his teeth. "Think of that! They say she said it made the sounds of love come all the sweeter." His voice is warm, and smells of almonds. He has let out the words slowly, so that each one slides agreeably into my head. He leans away again.

"Now such cruelty would seem barbaric, wouldn't it," he declares lightly, in a different tone, as though I had imagined how he spoke before. I put the sweet into my mouth and suck its smoothness. As we walk on, his words turn over slowly in my mind, as even a slight trickle of water down from the leat will turn the mill wheel round on its axle. His hand arrives at the small of my back; his fingers climb the ridge of my spine, pressing over the crests of the bone and the flesh between.

"I hope you do not mind me complimenting you upon your healthy form," he says in a low voice. "Quite a spare and bony miss you were the first time I clapped my eye on you, and yet now you have a goodly contour. Clearly they did not feed you in the countryside." He laughs at me. "And a full blush rises in your cheek so easily! I like a rosy girl."

The sunlight dips lower and lower and then is gone, leaving only a trace of a deep redness in the sky to the west. As the air grows blue with twilight it is tinged with expectation. Hundreds of lamps, strung between the trees, begin to glitter in the branches eerily, like marsh lights, unearthly baubles. Beneath them I have never seen so many people thronged and circling together. The unfolding scene is like a tangled, many-colored cloth weaving and unweaving itself at once in front of me, the threads of their paths moving through the light and shadow, so that

I grow dizzy watching them. The noise of the crowd is like the hum of a hive. Everyone is talking, laughing. I know this world is not quite real.

He pulls me in a little closer.

"Cornelius Soul!" I say, laughing, almost losing my balance, and put him away from me.

We are swept along with the crowd to see the gentry eating in the supper boxes.

"How loud and boastful they appear," he says cheerfully. "Basking stupidly in our attention, like sheep will laze about in sunshine, plumply satisfied with their taste of the world." I watch two gentlemen cutting at cooked chickens, brandishing the pieces. They raise up bumpers of wine to each other noisily. A lady picks at salad on her plate, her wig and feathers trembling as she turns her head to listen to the shuttle of their conversation.

"Let's go to the rotunda and hear a song or two to free our spirits!" Cornelius says, winking. We find a bench. "Sit here," he says, and fetches arrack punch in a pair of thick glasses.

"What is this?" I ask him, tipping the glass to see its color.

"Rum made tasty with grains of benjamin flower," he says. I sip at its sweetness until the lights in the supper boxes begin to spin.

A woman sings like a bird from the rotunda, her voice trembling, soaring as she reaches the edge of her melody. I feel the child loop once in my belly as if it were listening, and see the glisten of a tear slip down the cheek of someone in front of me. I remember the cracked hands of Mrs. Nott.

"Imagine making a living with your own skill and magnificence, like her," I say in excited wonder when she takes her last bow and the clapping dies down.

Cornelius Soul nods. "She has a gift," he says.

The punch has made my head hot and peppery. "But I expect, Mr. Soul," I tease him a little, "you do not think a woman's place can be in serious professions, but is concerned with suckling babies and making sure of a meal on a white-scrubbed table for her husband's weary return from his work?" I have another sip of my drink. "And when she has done with mending shirts and washing the grease from the pots, if she has a head for figures, no doubt she could save herself from idle moments by totting the accounts held with the butcher, or the seed merchant, or the collector of taxes."

Cornelius Soul is frowning now.

"Wrong, Miss Trussel! There is no reason that I know of that should prevent a woman being occupied by business, if she has the head and stomach for it," he declares.

"What kind of business?"

"A man I know called Walter Johns, who owns the Abbey powder mills in Essex, inherited the business from his mother, Pip, who ran it for years as a strong concern. In peacetime that woman oversaw production of six thousand barrels of powder annually, and four times the quantity would have been needed if there was war, and no doubt she'd have had that admirably in hand." He leans forward. "It is the trading classes with the power to change things," Cornelius Soul says, defiantly. "You did not expect that, did you?" he adds. And I shake my head in frank astonishment at his ideas.

"I did not," I say. How John Blacklock would recoil at their outlandishness. "And your own mother—what does she do?" I ask.

"My mother . . . manages. She holds the house together in its shabbiness, in its falling apart." He takes out a coin again and flicks it in the air. "Heads or tails, Miss Trussel?"

"Heads," I say.

"Heads it is!"

I smile at him. How well this seems to be going. The gold tooth glints in his mouth as he grins back. The orchestra begins to play. Cornelius Soul orders ham, and a boy brings it over. And then, clean from the blue, something makes me turn my head aside and I find my gaze meets that of Lettice Talbot.

As startled as I am, she stops in her tracks for a moment, and her eye goes straight for my belly, although I try to hold my shawl to cover it. She looks at Cornelius Soul, and back to me. The gem at her neck sparkles colors in the bright light. I had forgotten how beautiful, how radiant, she is. Yet as I get up eagerly, she shakes her head, and turns stiffly away from me when I raise my hand in greeting. I am certain that I see her mouth say, *No!*

I am baffled.

She is escorted by a middle-aged man in a military uniform. She tucks her hand under his elbow, the tassels of his epaulettes gleaming and dangling like glossy catkins at his shoulders. A younger girl is clinging to his other arm. I hear her giggling, and they all move off down the walk together. Lettice Talbot giggles, too. She is pretending that she has not seen me.

Cornelius looks to see what I am doing. "You know that tart?" he exclaims, following my stare. "You do not want to associate with a woman sold to whoredom like herself!" he says in a loud voice. "How is it that you know such baggage?"

I watch Lettice Talbot's silky slippers stepping away so neatly on the gravel. It is a wonder that she does not attract more attention than she does, she is so beautiful. "We were traveling together once by chance," I say, and turn to look again at the orchestra. I blink. "But her journey was a different one to mine."

"I should hope so!"

Lettice Talbot and her companions disappear behind the bandstand. Then he shrugs.

"Pricey whore, cheap whore—all the same." He tips punch into his mouth and swallows. "You can dress a dog up in fine flounces and ruffles and charge highly for its services; yet still it has the bones of a dog, fur of a dog, foul breath of a dog." He looks down at the table in front of him. His face has a look of distaste upon it, as though he has found something rotting on his plate instead of ham.

I do not feel like eating anymore. I feel sick. I do not think this thin ham is worth the shilling he has paid for it, but do not say a word. I do not like him speaking of her in that way, no matter what she does to make her living. I can see the pattern of the china clearly through the ham's pinkness; it is like a piece of skin upon the plate. Why did she not want to talk to me just now? Cornelius folds the last slice and chews it down. He orders more punch for both of us, although I cannot finish mine, it is so strong.

"A poor way to earn a livelihood," he says with contempt.

"Perhaps that is the point," I rejoin, timidly. "It is a livelihood, not a mortal choice. God knows, we slip into our paths unchosen."

"You don't get as good as she if that way of life is not your vocation." And he changes the subject, as though it disgusts him to speak of Lettice Talbot any more. Right inside, a soft part of me I did not know I had has toughened up. The orchestra strikes up a march, and he taps his foot. The brisk, exacting notes drum in my ears. "Watch your pockets!" a man bellows nearby. A woman squeals above the thrum of the milling crowd about us.

"It is almost time for the fireworks," Cornelius Soul says. "If we take ourselves a small distance away from the crush we will have a good view. If we go now, we may even hear the nightingales before the first flight of rockets goes up. Shall we proceed, Miss Trussel?" he says, pressing me forward.

And as I go with him I have a sudden image of my uncle paddling the big pig down the lane with the flat of his ash stick, the pig breaking into a stubborn trot because it did not know where they were headed. Somehow it seems to matter whether I can remember if there was a dawning of terror in its eye as it shambled along, its view hooded by the *flap, flap* of its ears that were pink with the low winter sun shining through them, on its way to be slaughtered.

Why should I find it hard to submit willingly? It is what I wanted.

We stand away from the crowd, and wait for the fireworks. Leaves rustle in the elms behind us.

"I cannot hear the nightingales," I say, pulling my shawl about me, afraid to hear what he is about to say. Cornelius Soul seems larger in the darkness. He moves himself closer, and then closer still.

"I tell you, they'll sing, if you can wait!" he says. And he begins: "I will be honest, Miss Trussel. It made me happy when I saw that you could find some warmth inside yourself for me."

I swallow. "Did it?" I reply, faintly.

"And tonight is a pleasure," he says. "Were the Gardens as you hoped they'd be?" He puts his hand around me, and runs it slowly up and down my spine.

Confused, I keep my eyes fixed on the bright lights of the rotunda in the distance. "I did not think it would be like this," I whisper.

"When the autumn comes, Agnes," he murmurs suddenly, "should we be married?" It is the first time he has called me by my name. But that is too late, far too late. What do I do? His face widens to a grin.

"Agnes?"

I can hear a woman's voice close to us, in the shadows. "My little puggy," she is murmuring, her voice slurred with drink or fondness. "Mmm, my little puggy." Then a man's voice says something that I cannot hear, and she gives out a throaty, drunken snort.

"Need we wait until . . . ?" I begin to whisper back, but my words are drowned out by the first volley of maroons and sharp reports. I turn to look, and the firework I see is like the flash of an axe falling.

Cornelius Soul pulls me toward him and kisses my neck, which I do not like. I pull away to tell him so. I feel a panic in me. The autumn is too late, I am thinking, over and over. Too late. Too late. In the light from the lamps in the trees above us, his eyes seem as though they are lidded half-shut and his teeth look long and yellow, like the teeth of a fox or scavenger.

"I am cold," I say inaudibly against the whine and crackle of the rockets, shivering.

And then he bends suddenly and picks up the hem of my skirt, and rubs at the weave of the fabric between his thumb and forefinger. What is he doing? I know my underskirt is exposed; the chill in the air has reached the bareness of my legs. It is hard not to pull away from him. The trunk of the elm tree presses at my back. I realize that he is not the kind of man to take refusal lightly. He seems much stronger than I thought. I swallow. His big arm encircles and presses me against him harder. He is breathing fast. And then his other hand is reaching in under my skirts, pushing them back, and the air is cold on my thighs as he pulls back to unbutton his breeches. This is not what I meant. "No!" I cry, against the roar of the firing. Behind me I hear the collective pop and fizz of the Roman candles, and the admiration of the crowd.

It is happening now; I cannot stop it.

Oh, God help me, his hands are touching the roundness of my belly, the base of the undressed belly, where there can be no mistaking it for plumpness or too many garments.

"You are big with child!" he says, incredulous. His eyes in the yellow light are wide and stare at me.

And then he turns away and laughs and spits on the ground. I can see the muscles in his jaw move as he clenches it tight.

"You sly devil, Blacklock, and after all your sermonizing at me!"

"No, no—" I begin.

"Small wonder he had no appetite for whoring or gaming! He had it so cozy, so convenient at home. And what did you think, Miss Trussel, when it all went wrong and you knew you had his bastard child? That you would fob it off on to me? That I would be your saving? Did you think of this between you? As if I were some sop to be made a fool of? How he must be laughing at me, watching me take his damaged goods like the fool I am, all unawares. Damn him. Damn his eyes. Assuming it is his."

"It is not how——"

"I have a good mind to finish what I started here, but I will not taint myself," he says, buttoning his breeches and spitting again, as if to rid himself of a bad taste in his mouth. "Or God only knows what I may contract." His lips are thin. He puts his hand into his coat and brings out some coins, which he drops one by one at my feet.

"Your journey home," he says stiffly, and turns his back and in an instant disappears. I can hear the crunch of his heels on the gravel for a moment longer than I see his shape.

I am a disgrace.

I bend with difficulty and grope for the dusty shillings in the dark, for how else will I get back unless I use Mrs. Mellin's coins?

The cold lights are dazzling as I go to the turnstile. The woman who is a man leers at me as I push my way out. "Not good enough for you then, darling?" she shouts after me. "Or did he go off with another?" and her shriek of laughter fills my head.

I have made a ruin of my life.

In the carriage I realize that I had not even heeded the close of the fireworks display. My bones feel weak with distress. I did not see the fireworks. I did not see them. I close my eyes tight shut and try to think of fire pouring silver, white. And then I hardly think of anything until the carriage slows and stops, discharging me into the night.

The noise of the hooves of horses fades. The night is as black as pitch. I cannot see my hand before my face.

I make my way to the yard at the back, and enter the house by the scullery door. It squeaks open. I grope for the tinderbox on the high dresser and strike a light. There is nobody there in the kitchen; the fire is banked up for the night and the retainer put on. Mary Spurren's candlestick is gone from the shelf, so she must be in her bed.

I do not know how late it is, but I see that lamplight is still shining under the door of Mr. Blacklock's study as I go past it to the stairs. I make my treading light and even as I go by; indeed I hardly breathe at all, lest he should hear me.

When Mr. Blacklock calls out, my hand jerks with surprise, so that hot wax spills and runs down my fingers. "Who's . . . there?" he says, gruffly. His voice is strange.

"Who . . . ?" he calls again.

"Only me, Agnes," I say quietly, my fingers burning as I hesitate outside, but because his voice is so strange and the door is ajar a little already, I push it open further and look into the room.

Mr. Blacklock has fallen to the carpet before the fire.

"What is it! Are you ill?" I say, rushing to him, and then at once I see by the flush of his face and the overturned and empty bottles by him that he is deeply in liquor. He tries to get up as I grasp his shoulders and attempt to lift him to the chair, but a drunken man is heavier than someone sober twice the height, and when I let go he slumps to the floor again. His face is wet, as though he has been weeping.

I sink into the chair before him. I cannot think what else to do.

"Fireworks?" he mutters from the floor, so thickly that I have to lean forward in the chair to hear him.

"I tell you again, they were not as good as those you promised me," I reply bleakly. It is all I can say. Mr. Blacklock does not drink prodigious quantities like other men, yet here he is, quite full of liquor. How long can a man keep mourning for his wife and stay healthy in his soul?

I could fetch Mary Spurren and perhaps between us we could take him up the stairs and lay him in his bed, yet . . . somehow I do not want anyone to see him in this state. But I dare not leave him. He might knock his head on the hearthstone, or a spark could catch at his coat and flare up.

Instead I get up to put some lumps of coal upon the fire and rake the embers. The fire begins to liven up and pour out smoke. At the window the shutters have not been drawn, and in the crooked glass my disheveled face stares back at me. The reflection is so broken up, at first I do not recognize myself.

Outside I can hear the clatter of a rat or cat or vagrant knocking something over in the yard. I do not even care, and leave the shutters folded open as they are.

Mr. Blacklock has propped himself against a chair before the hearth. When I sit down once more and look at him, I see again the orange fire reflected in the darkness of his eyes as though it were burning inside his head. I lift the stopper from the decanter on the table next to me and pour more wine into his half-filled glass and drink from it myself. It is a red wine, dry and fruited and faintly metallic like blood. I drink another glass, until my body does not feel my own. I tip back my head and swallow more. I do not want to be alone with it, my ugly, swollen body that is not my own.

I let the tears I feel run down my cheeks, without a sound. I do not sob, but the tears come anyway. We are a sorry pair, I think. The fire bursts into flames beside us, and it stirs him, so that he raises himself up a little and, swaying, sits almost insensible before me at my feet. He looks up and meets my eye, and his face is gaunt with disappointment.

I cannot bear to see him so sad. I cannot bear it. I reach out and touch his shoulders. I touch his head. I hold his head, I lean forward and hold it tight against me and I rock him as I cry in sympathy for him and for myself and the ruin I have made of everything.

"John Blacklock, John Blacklock," I hear myself say, over and over.

"I have made a mistake," I whisper. "A great mistake."

I rock and rock, his head on my chest, so close to my belly. I am almost begging him to notice what is wrong with me. But now his face is pressed into my hands. His mouth is on my fingers; I can feel the roughness of his shaven skin. I have never touched a man's face before. It is large. He holds my fingers on his mouth, pressing them there fiercely with his own hands. When he speaks, I feel the heat and dampness of his words against them. I feel the tremor of his words rise through his throat.

"Agnes," he mutters. He is kissing my fingers.

"You must . . ." he says, and his voice is so hoarse I can hardly hear him. "You must . . . forgive me."

I do not loosen my hold upon him. I do not know what else to do. His head is warm and comforting against my lap. He must be quite confused with grief, I tell myself, over and over. And I go on rocking John Blacklock before the hearth until he sleeps.

The night moves on, and the fire dies down to embers once again.

A thin light creeps about outside in the yard and a wind stirs the leaves. His breathing is deeper now, stronger as he rests against me. How close he is to the child inside me, unmoving, too, perhaps asleep, inside my belly—but he does not know it. His eyelids are shut tight over his eyes, shadowed purple with tiredness.

How well I know the conduct of men in this condition. They drink, they talk nonsensically, sometimes with songs or rambling tales, then they become morose or ill, then they fall down in a stupor and take a corpselike slumber out of which they inch with a stiff neck and a bad humor in the morning, and they do not recollect a thing about the way the night before was passed. John Blacklock will remember nothing of this night.

Besides, it will be days now, I suppose, before my belly becomes impossible to hide beneath my shawl, and I will no longer have employment here.

I am finished.

Everything is coming to an end. So what do I have to lose now? Nothing.

His head is warm. The clock ticks. A coal falls in the grate. I hear the scratch and patter of a mouse in the wall behind the paneling. The shallow glorious glitter of the Gardens seems far away.

Mr. Blacklock slumbers soundly, unknowingly, against my lap. It does not matter that I touch his dark hair. Nobody knows. And nobody knows when I bend and kiss him, just once, gently, closing my eyes as I taste his skin.

I am exhausted by the time the fire is out.

I rise and untangle myself from Mr. Blacklock's arms, gone slack with sleep, ease him down to the hearth rug without disturbance and lay my woollen cloak unfolded over him. He grunts but does not stir; his breathing comes and goes with labored steadiness. I turn the lamp down but do not blow it out lest he wake in a daze before dawn. And I take up what is left of my candle and go to my chamber.

The narrow bed seems so cold after the warmth I have just had, yet as I drift into sleep, I can still feel the shape and the weight of his head in my hands. It did not seem wrong to have held it. Sometimes when I look at John Blacklock, it is as though I were looking at my own dark self, as though there were no difference between us. But then a look in his face reminds me of how he remembers his dead wife, and I am still suddenly, inside, as when a wind drops and the wrinkled surface of a pond becomes smooth like glass and shows the sky.

31

*F*or what is left of the night, I dream of nothing. When I wake, it is quiet outside. The sky is faintly blue, as when a drop of milk falls into a glass of water and spreads out gently. I am late for breakfast. Mrs. Blight is clearing the plates away and smirking, and when I go to the scullery, Mary Spurren's face is quarrelsome. All the while I am trying to work out if Mr. Blacklock has been down already. How many plates are there on the side? Mary Spurren slops the water about in the sink and makes her apron wetter than it was.

Then Mrs. Blight calls out from the kitchen, "Mr. Blacklock got a letter this morning, urging him to travel to Hertfordshire straight off."

"Oh?" I say, as if it is no matter to me.

"So he'll be gone for days, and just when I'd spent time deciding upon what to have for suppers all week. Aggravating, it is. An aunt is on the brink of death, his last remaining relative, he says, and he has gone to tie up her affairs, should that prove necessary."

"He has no other relatives?" I ask. "Not one?"

"Not so he says of," she answers, tipping coal on the fire. "Today at noon we shall have a batter pudding and no complaints."

"How did he seem?" I ask. "Before he left, what was his humor?"

Mrs. Blight does not give this question enough thought. "He had no particular fondness for his aunt, he said, when I offered my condolences, therefore I doubt his mood went either way."

"I mean, did he appear to be in any discomfort or distress?" I say.

"No, he did not. Pass me that bowl down from there," she says, pointing up at the dresser.

I find my cloak folded neatly by the hob. In private I look closely at it, but it tells me nothing, though, when I hold it to my face, it seems to have something of his person about it. I bury my face in it for a moment and breathe deeply. Tobacco, perhaps. The smell of Mr. Blacklock's garments. I wonder whether it could be his grief itself that I am smelling. I put the cloak about me, as if nothing had happened.

I go out to the grocer's.

In the shop I buy a dozen brown eggs, and do not stop to chat with Mrs. Spicer. Going back to the house I do not look at anyone I pass; indeed, I do not see Lettice Talbot until I am almost upon her.

She is leaning in the whitewashed archway where I turn back into the narrow street to Blacklock's. Her leather case is down on the cobbles between her feet, as though she had been waiting for me for some time. Her dress is very clean and fancy under her patterned shawl.

"Agnes!" she says, straightening up. "It is a beautiful morning."

"How ever did you know where I could be found?" I ask, uneasily.

"I asked about. It is not difficult to find a person, should you have a mind to do so," Lettice Talbot says. She folds her arms tightly, as if to hold herself together. "How are you keeping?" she asks. I do not need to reply to this. She can see my belly, after all. It is strange; I have looked for Lettice Talbot for so long, and now she is before me, I do not want to speak to her. I glance past her to the house.

"I'm sorry, sweetheart," she says. She puts her head to one side and smiles coaxingly at me. "I became concerned when you did not come to Mrs. Bray's at first, as I suggested, and then I thought that, unless you were in very bad hands or facedown in some ditch somewhere, robbed of your assets, then perhaps it was better. And then I forgot about you. I was thinking selfishly, of course." It is as though she has prepared a speech.

"Selfish?" I say.

"I confess I liked the look of you. There was something, I could not have said what it was precisely, but I thought there was a freshness, a pleasant candor to your manner, which might prove worthwhile for companionship, and also good for business."

"You mean you thought you could be friendly with me?" I ask. Perhaps I had not been wrong about her, after all. Perhaps she did not mean to turn her back on me.

"Of course I did, sweetheart, but I . . ." She looks at my belly again. "And then there you were at the Gardens, and I regretted it. I saw how your shape was changed—although you hide it well enough, the signs are clear.

"You do not want a life like this!" she says suddenly, looking at me.

There is something odd about her face. What that is at first I cannot see, and then her head moves out of shadow and I can see a long bruise across the base of her throat. She has tried to cover it with some whitish paste or powder but the discoloration shows through in gray and purple. I do not want to stare, but my eye wanders there again and again, until the early morning wind blows chilly down the shady side of the street and she pulls her finely woven shawl more tightly about her neck.

"You see," she says, "there is much to say for never falling out of grace."

"With whom?" I ask.

"With whoever pushes us along those paths we should have never taken. It is too hard to turn back. I know that now. It is for the best, perhaps, that you did not come and work with me. At the upper portion of the market in my trade there are gentlemen who expect . . . specialisms," she says. I feel the breeze more keenly.

"Your trade?" I say. "Is that what you call it?"

She smiles. "I would have been glad to have taken you under my wing and taught you what I know, given you tips, a little guidance here and there when your instinct didn't know which way to turn, Agnes. You are a clever girl. You would've made a good success of it, I'm sure."

"Would I?" I say. "What . . . kind of specialisms?"

"There are those, Agnes, who are not satisfied by what is enough for other men."

"And how——"

"They pay more," she says quickly. "Willing to pay above the usual price, for things, techniques, that meet their more . . . unusual appetites."

I look at her clean and lovely dress, at last grasping what the cost of it might be.

"Does it hurt?" I ask, clumsily.

She gives a pretty shrug. "Sometimes. But my power comes afterward, because they must pay handsomely for what they like to do. However, I did not come to find you to say all that. Only to tell you that there is a woman called Dilly Martinment who can help you, lodged at this address." She holds out a scrap of paper with something written on it in an untidy hand. "She does not waste much vigor on any kindnesses, but her practice is effective." As I do not say a thing, she adds, "There is often no infection, no . . . trouble, when she is done."

"I see," I say. I take the paper from her and hold it tightly this time.

"You have money, still?" she asks. "It will cost more than a little."

I nod. "The coins are here," I say, and move as if to take them out to show her.

"No! No! In God's name, child!" She looks about to see if we are overlooked. "Keep all your secrets absolutely hidden. No one must see. No one! Do you hear?"

I look at her. What if another person knew my shame? How I have longed for that relief, for some acceptance or forgiveness. My guilt is tainting the child, I am sure of it. A horrible seething mass knots and unknots itself in the place above my belly, where my heart is. My heart is choked with it. "I stole them," I burst out suddenly. "I stole those coins. And I am going to confess."

Her eyes are as round as buttons. "Confess! To whom, you crazy girl?" she hisses.

"Why are you angry with me?"

"You are so stupid!" she exclaims. "As if you imagine so simple a thing could put right all that has happened to you. I have never met such an innocent!"

"An innocent!" I say. Of course I am not.

"Now you are cross with me," she says, more gently. "You must move forward, Agnes, take up your life, just as it is. Move on. You cannot trust a soul—tell nobody."

"But I must," I say, trying to make her understand. She shakes her head.

"You cannot." She leans toward me and speaks quietly now; her eyes are narrow and very bright. "You must curb that feeling, you must knock it dead in its tracks, Agnes." Her voice is as clear as if it were shouting the words at me. "At best you would be transported at His Majesty's pleasure to some barren hellhole two months' voyage away over the high seas. At worst—you will swing from the triple tree at Tyburn."

"It will not come to that," I say stubbornly.

She puts her forefinger to my chin and raises it up lightly, almost as though she were about to kiss me, her fine face brushes so close. But she is whispering into my ear.

"How much would you care to feel that gallows breeze about you, Agnes? They say that the wind blows more freshly the higher you stand."

"The nearer to heaven," I mutter halfheartedly, though she does not hear. She is frightening me now. "Think of the roar of the crowd come to feast on your death," she murmurs. "There will be many reasons why those in the crowd are there for it; there will be many who sympathize with your crime, such as it is, and with your suffering, but with relief that it was not themselves this time around, among this crop of unfortunates. 'Poor beggar,' they will say, as they always do. 'And such a pretty face.' Remember that their sense of holiday comes not from the sight of blood cooling in its flesh so quickly before their thirsty gazes, but from the gladness that it was not a sentence dealt to them on this occasion. Think of the crack of your neck as the cart rolls forward, Agnes, your legs free to kick in the cold air!"

"But I could plead my belly," I say, swallowing. "They do not hang women who are with child."

"They do not," she says. "And after your conviction, how would you fare in Bridewell, grubbling in the dark for your waterpot, your clothes rotting from your shoulders while they wait for the child to be born so it can be removed to the workhouse? And then you will stand sentence, just as before." She shrugs.

"I know a gentleman whose fantasy it is to see women strung up by the neck. Imagine, Agnes. And there are plenty like that—men with a streak of the Devil inside them whose predilection is for cruelty—and when a handful of these men have also law and order on their side, then they will use it shamefully. They like a pale face hanging from a rope. They like it regular, at each assize, and take it for granted, like some men enjoy a stroll in the park. Believe me, even the word *execution* affords them a little shudder of delight. I have seen men moaning with pleasure at the thought of pronouncing *death* upon a woman's head."

"It was to be a priest I told," I say, thinking of Reverend Lindsay at St. Stephen's, his kind, open face.

She looks incredulous. "And you can do that at the gallows, Agnes, as you will find churchmen there to lay a cast of sanctity over the proceedings, preaching to the damned to save you on your path to higher judgment. Small shame, sweetheart, that they do not spend their breath instead on saving the blighted souls of those who wield their strength so mightily." She looks away down the street. "No, Agnes, take up your life, just as it is, and run with it."

She seems somehow thinner than on the day I met her out in the fresh air on the carrier, and she does not meet my eye so many times. The joy in her eye is gone, though it is still as blue. There seems to be less of her substance, not of her body, so much as though her spirit itself were smaller, humiliated. I do not like to see her like that. I do not know what I can say.

"And are you well yourself?" I ask uselessly, into the quiet of the lull in the traffic, and she brightens and straightens up and smoothes a hand down her silky skirts, which sheen and ripple like a tabby fur.

"Oh, I do not do so badly!" And her laugh is firm, like it was on the day I first met her. "My luck changed for the better—as yours will, Agnes—when I found a way to take what I can from life. I have no regrets about what I have done, having taught myself skills that most would shy from and applied them shamelessly, but always in command of the way I lived.

"Come and see me," she shouts over the noise of a carriage passing, and I tell her that I shall, though I know that I will not. She embraces me then, very lightly, her fine clothes just brushing my own, and when she touches my hand to say goodbye I see a line of bruising about her wrist, as though some twine or rope had been bound and tightened there. She flinches away when I reach out.

"He did this to you? That soldier man?"

Lettice Talbot shakes her head and smiles at me, as if it is of no consequence. There is too much I do not understand.

"Go to the woman," she urges me. "It is not a difficult undertaking, but neither is it easy. There is pain, and there is risk." She shrugs lightly. "But there is always risk. You are simply choosing one risk over another." She picks up her leather case and leaves me then, and goes away into the crowd gathered around a juggler on the corner of King Street. The crowd shouts and claps.

When she has gone, there is still a trace of her sweet smell in the fabric of my clothes, and it does not fade until the evening.

32

I look at the scrap of paper, over and over, until it is soft with being held in my hand. And then I go to the woman, at her address on the edge of St. Giles. It is not hard to find.

She has a dour, shuffling maidservant who shows me to a downstairs chamber. The woman is at home. "One of Mrs. Bray's girls, ma'am," the maidservant mutters as she leaves me alone with her. Dilly Martinment's jaw juts from her face in a curious manner; the flats of her hands are narrow like the paws of a stoat, and her nails are overgrown.

"You can pay me, I take it?" She turns her back as she wipes her long hands on a piece of rag and puts it aside. "I do not talk to girls unless I can be sure. Mrs. Bray's girls, they gets reduced rates. Put the coins on the table and then we can begin," she directs. There are buckets with cloths soaking by the door. "How many months?"

"It is hard to be sure," I lie. "Perhaps six?" If I tell her how close I really am to my time, I know she will not treat me with her medicine. I am good at lying now. I do not even blink.

I place six shillings on the tabletop, saved from my wages. As she gathers them up she bites each one. Her teeth are short, as though she had spent a lifetime doing that, or eating stones instead of bread. I do not like this woman. I am glad I do not like her.

"There are cheaper remedies to purchase—powders," she says. "But frankly they achieve little. They cause a bellyache that may lead you to believe yourself to be undergoing the required treatment. By all means try them, if you will, but I sense you will not find them efficacious." She eyes my belly, then unlocks a chest and takes out a squat blue bottle. She draws a quantity of liquid deftly from it with a burette, and releases the drops into a small phial. She counts under her breath, and stops when she reaches the fortieth drop.

"Oil of savine." She raises the phial and checks the level. "It is a potent stuff. I assume you do not take it lightly. Three drops, three times a day, on a good piece of sugar. Clear?" Unexpectedly, she stands up and reaches out and presses her fingers proprietarily into my belly. I do not like her doing this; indeed I am repulsed by her and have to try hard not to pull away. "Six months? I would say seven, at least," she says. "But I am guessing. You look a healthy girl."

"I have been fortunate." I mean to say that I am fortunate about my health. She looks at me and makes a tutting noise between her tongue and ground-down teeth.

"I would say you have been careless or unlucky, girl. Yet," she adds, "let's not beat about, your misfortune is my gain." And she expects me to join in as her jutting chin quivers briefly with laughter.

"I have no sugar," I say stupidly.

"Buy some, beg some, steal some," Dilly Martinment advises. "It will be a bitter thing to swallow, lacking it."

"No," I say, shaking my head. I think of the tall white conical loaf of the sugar on the high dresser. I imagine rasping off what I need with the tongs, under the nose of Mrs. Blight, and carrying a brazen bowlful of pieces right through the house to my room. It would be unthinkable.

"It would be missed," I say.

"It will be bitter, with no sweetness to offset the edge, like a dry knife at the back of the throat," Dilly Martinment cautions me. She rubs at her neck and grimaces, her chin jutting out. "Little steely raspings." And at that moment another paneled door, which I had not noticed previously, opens a crack.

"Well enough to leave us now?" she says to the small bony girl who emerges unsteadily from the back chamber.

The girl looks distinctly unwell. A strange smell has accompanied her into the chamber. Her face is as white as wax and clammy with perspiration, as though she is on the brink of a fainting fit. She grasps the back of a chair.

"Still I do not feel quite as I should." I can barely hear what she is saying. She removes one hand from the chair to touch her hair. Her fingers are red and small, and make a poor attempt at tying the ribbons of her bonnet when Dilly Martinment passes it to her.

"Wait," she says, "I am faint again," and she grips at the chair and leans over it. Her eyes are wide and blank, as though her mind were somewhere else.

"I cannot touch my stomach," she whispers. My hand strays to my belly under my cloak; it is firm and full and moves about.

"You will not need to," Dilly Martinment says, glancing over her shoulder at me.

"Wicked, I am," the girl whispers.

"I believe in neither hell nor damnation," Dilly Martinment remarks briskly. How much easier for her to say this than it is for us. "We must make the best use of what comes to us." She continues talking, but I do not listen as I am looking past her with a dawning kind of horror into the back room. I can make out a table and a pile of cloths upon it, dark with fluids. The lamplight shines upon some kind of metal instrument.

"You will find now that things will take their course," Dilly Martinment calls after the girl. "I do not ever ask for names," she mutters to me. She shuts the door, and eyes my belly again. "It has a good hold in there," she says. "It may be more difficult to dislodge than you imagine. Of course, there are other ways yet." She taps the glass of the phial with a sharp, discolored fingernail. "But the oil is a successful provoker of the catamenia, that monthly scarlet discharge that you lack and will remember now with something like a fondness, I am supposing, despite its inconvenience and accompanying aches and miseries."

"Does it take long?" I say, not being able to ask what I really need to know.

She looks at me.

"It does not."

I go away from there with a sense that it is all bad. All bad. At home in my chamber I find a strange comfort in the familiar smell of mice, a thin, pungent smell that bites at the nostrils.

I hide the oil at the back of the chest where my small linen and my Bible lie, and at night I take it out and look at it before I sleep. The baby drums on inside me, its limbs drumming and drumming at the skin of my belly. I turn the blue phial between my forefinger and thumb and watch the oil slowly coat the inside of the glass. It gleams poisonously by candlelight.

I know I cannot wait a moment longer. I take up the spoon that I have hidden for this purpose, and pour a little of the oil of savine into the spoon's bowl.

It is long after dark. Mrs. Blight has gone to her lodging and Mary Spurren is in her chamber above me. I can hear the creak of her bed as she settles.

My hand does not shake and I do not spill a drop. I put the spoon to my mouth and swallow the liquid down. It is so dryly resinous, disagreeable and bitter that my throat clamps shut. I clench my teeth and rock backward and forward in the effort not to vomit. Then I pour another spoonful and swallow it. And then another.

I climb into my bed then and I do not move or speak a word out loud, but inside me every fiber of my being shouts with rage.

Murderer, the voice inside me whispers back.

In the morning before I go to breakfast, I do the same, though it is vile and taints the flavor of the bread and ale.

Mrs. Blight notices the absence of the spoon, and my cheeks redden as I look with her into the cutlery box. I know she thinks that I have stolen it, but she does not say a word to me. Instead she exercises sarcasm to the air in general when, by the afternoon, the spoon has reappeared again.

"Would you look at this," she says, holding it up. "Always the silver ones what disappear, isn't it, Mary? Remarkable swift how they come and go, I always find," she says. She mimics the bleat of a young girl. "Oh, madam, I cannot think how that came to fall into the pocket of my apron. How shiny it is! How lucky we found it before 'twas lost at the laundry!" She bends and whispers viciously at me over the table. "Little thief! And I can't help thinking, Mary, that there is something here that Mr. Blacklock ought to know of."

How right she is. Alone in my chamber that night I drink the oil directly from the phial, and again in the morning, tears squeezing from my eyes, it is so bitter.

33

I dream of a jester performing a trick before a crowd, and the crowd is jeering. Lettice Talbot is there, too, and a man whose face I cannot see strokes the back of her white neck, and she is turning to him, her head falling back and her lovely eyes half-lidded, and then I feel a wrenching tug as if from some danger I had forgotten, and someone cries out, "Agnes, Agnes!" until my ears are ringing with distress. I wake with a gasp.

Mary Spurren is banging on the door. "Agnes?" she shouts, grumpily. I touch my face. My cheeks are burning as though I have stood too long at a bonfire. What is the matter with me? "Get up!" Mary Spurren calls through the door. "I won't say it again."

"Coming," I reply, and then I hear her stamping down the stairs. At first I do not remember that Mr. Blacklock is away, and when I do, it is a sobering thought and the house seems different.

"Feeling slow today, are we?" Mrs. Blight says, when I go to the kitchen.

How sick the oil of savine makes me feel. My mind is quite displaced with thinking of it.

"You must go to Spicer's for me," Mrs. Blight says. "I need this and that. Been rushed off my feet these last few days." I am too tired to argue that I have a pile of rocket cases to complete. Besides, Mr. Blacklock's bench would be empty beside me. I can catch up later. He would not even know.

I fetch my cloak and wrap it about me before I venture onto the street. When I pass the pump in Mallow Square, the women gathered to draw water stop their chatter and the girl at the splashing pump stills the squeak of the handle to turn to look at me. It is too warm under my cloak. It is almost summer and the square is filled with the quick flight of swallows catching flies above the water running in the open drains.

I have to walk quite slowly; the ground is not so even underfoot. Perhaps Mr. Blacklock will not be gone as long as planned. Perhaps he will be back tonight, and we can all take supper around the table as if all were well, as if nothing could ever change but could go on forever as it has been. I have to stop at a corner and cling onto the railings while I catch my breath.

When I reach the grocer's shop I find I cannot recall what it was that Mrs. Blight had needed. I put my basket down and hang back from the queue in the hope that it will come to me. The shop is full. In a daze I watch the housekeeper from the smart brick house on the high street select a piece of cheese, and the kitchen boy from the Star picks up a parcel and scuttles out again.

"Two strange men came into the shop this morning, Agnes Trussel," Mrs. Spicer shouts across, on seeing me. "I thought of you."

"Oh?" I say, and a flicker of alarm sounds, as though very far off, through the warm and sickly fog in me. "Two men?"

She wraps a chunk of cheese and hands it to the housekeeper. A slow thought struggles its way toward me as she speaks. "Up recently from Sussex, or so they said to Mr. Spicer—did not speak with them myself, as I was serving." She holds her palm out for the housekeeper's shilling. "What part of the county were they from?" she shouts at her husband. He shrugs. "Lewes? Cuckfield?" He shakes his head. "They were looking for someone, a thin maid. Like this, like that." She goes on. "Mr. Spicer sent them away with a flea in the ear, didn't you!" She looks across at him. "Nosy buggers. He does not care for too many inquiries upon his business premises. No call for poking round a district, he says, looking for trouble, stirring things up. Like I say, I thought of you, though, remembering your family was from down that way. Parish men, they could've been. Broad hats."

I am faint.

I look about me. Only the shoppers going by on the street. One dog sniffing about by the step. How large the cheese looks, and with that gaping hole cut into it there on the slab. How my heart gallops blood about my chest.

I think of Mrs. Mellin's coins pushed into my stays. I think of John Glincy's yellow hair blocking the sun above me, and the sickening, thrusting weight of him. I think of the traveling man and his bags bound up with dirty scraps of fabric. I think of Cornelius Soul spitting on the ground before me, and Dilly Martinment's ground-down teeth biting hard on the coins I gave to her. A bag of panic comes down over me, so that I cannot properly see inside the shop. It is too dark in here. Too full of strangers.

"Are you quite well, Agnes?" I can just hear Mrs. Spicer saying. Her voice is weak and faraway. "Very pale, you are." And it is hard to see as I push my way out of the shop, push my way against the light flooding through the open door. I know that I am bumping into things and people are turning around to stare as I run down the street. Out in the white light the air is warm and thick and curdled to run through. Past the orange seller, across the stretch of the endless square, left, right, and I am at the front steps of the house when I remember my basket. I have left my basket on the counter.

It is so hot.

I am doubled up, panting and panting, but the lungfuls of warm air are not enough. My legs quiver with effort. And then I feel a spread of wetness down the inside of my legs under my skirt and a twisting pain feels all wrong in the base of my belly. I hold my hand out for the railing. I can hardly stand in this heat. I can't. The stone step is heading toward me.

34

*T*he sunlight creeps around the chamber. By the time the clock has struck three, it has slid itself as a bright yellow patch onto the washstand, curved itself over the cracked jug and basin, crinkled over the blanket at the foot of the bed and then straightened out into a deep brownish yellow on the boards of the floor. It doesn't reach the other side of the room, as it rounds the corner before the church bells strike six. By seven I can still see the spires of St. Alban and St. Mary the Virgin golden with light if I raise my head, though I am weak. There is a taste in my mouth that I do not know.

I am surprised to find that my head is empty. My eyes follow the plaster cracks in the wall by the side of the bed, and I hear the sounds of things that arrive in the bedroom. The sun is silent, but there is sometimes the thin whine of flies, a carriage rumbling on the dry dirty cobbles outside, a man's shout and a reply through the warm air. Occasionally a dog barks persistently nearby like the sound of a handsaw going through wood; it becomes muffled for a while, as though a door has been shut, and then it stops. There is a spill of water onto the bricks in the courtyard below, and the clank of something being stirred in a bucket.

What is it? I remember something, but incompletely, as if the thought were behind a screen and only parts of it visible. When it becomes more whole, more clear to me, I make sure that the thought is held at arm's length, so that it slips in gradually. I look about.

There are stains on the bed, the sheet is dark with them, and there is a faint brown-sweet smell of blood around me. The pain was bad, like a wrench squeezing it all dead inside and then pushing it out in bursts. I think

I remember that, though I cannot be sure. What is that taste in my mouth? I cannot imagine what it could be. It is sweet, almost like honey.

The quiet is a nothingness. It is the feeling now that the pain has stopped, the feeling of no pain, and is it, could it also be, a quietness inside me? I hold my lungs still and listen hard, as you might if you had to check that a creature was still breathing.

Nothing.

There is nothing inside me, I think, and the emptiness is long and gray as a sky.

I do not even know what day it is.

"What is the day?" I whisper to Mrs. Blight when she comes into the room with warm water and cloths. "Did the parish men find me when I fell?"

Mrs. Blight squeezes a cloth out. When she looks up from the basin, her teeth are all covered up.

"Did who find you? It was Mary Spurren picked you up from the front step when she went out to sweep it. Half-delirious you have been these past two days," she says. "Muttering about all sorts, like a girl possessed." She tips me, and drags the dirty sheet from under me.

"God only knows how I tried to get the doctor to you, but Mary Spurren was determined that Blacklock would not have it. Just as well, as it turned out, when I saw what your trouble was. And thank God, I thought, when the fever ceased pouring out of you and I could get back to my own bed for a snatch of sleep." She unfolds a clean sheet and, grunting, tips me up again and spreads it out beneath me.

Later Mary Spurren brings me more damp cloths and a bowl of water as though she has been told to. She goes to the window and looks out at the roofs. Her head is big against the evening light.

"Mr. Blacklock has come back from Hertfordshire on the six o'clock mail," she says.

"Oh?" I say. "Does he . . . ?"

"Turned out almost a needless journey, he said, as the health of his aunt had improved to a great degree by the time he'd got there.

"He has said he will not get a doctor to you." Mary Spurren turns around and looks at me triumphantly when she tells me this, as though she suspects that I am begging for attention.

"I know," I say, and the words come slowly from me. "I do not need a doctor. I have no fever," I say. "I . . . ate bad meat."

"You ate what I ate that day," Mary Spurren accuses me, with truth, and hazily I see her shake her head. "You'll want to pull your weight a fraction harder round here, I think, before the week is through."

I do not answer this. She seems to shut the door with force on her way out.

A sparrow chirps outside. Perhaps when I feel better I shall walk and walk until I reach hedgerows. What will Mr. Blacklock think of me? Follow them deep into the countryside, follow their length like a guide leading the way. But how could I do this, with the tarnish of Mrs. Mellin's coins staining my fingers, and parish men in lawful pursuit of me?

Thief! Thief! I imagine them calling. They are not here now.

I close my eyes.

I am like a woman I read of in the *Evening Post*, who stood on the parapet of Westminster Bridge and jumped, and halfway through falling knew that she needed to live and did not die when she hit the iron surface of the Thames but was dragged out by a ferryman, sopping wet, and with both legs broken.

When I wake, Mrs. Blight is back in the chamber, putting some items down on the washstand. Though she is at my side, how far away she seems, and how fast and then how slow, like great red butterflies, her hands move about their business.

I cannot speak at all. When Mrs. Blight says something to me, I turn to her and stare because I cannot hear her very well. She tries again, coming up huge to the bed and bending down above me.

"You are all stiffened up with being anxious," she advises. "Being stiff is bad for any girl in your condition. Drink this." She holds a cup of some steaming liquid to my lips, which I swallow obediently in warm, bittersweet mouthfuls. *Why is she being nice to me?* I look at her and nod, but I am not anxious. She is wrong, I think vaguely. The liquid makes me sleepy, and gives me slippery, unformed thoughts. I am not stiff or taut beneath the shell I have created for myself. I am discovered, and my shell has been prized away to show how I am gone soft and pappy like an uncooked oyster underneath it. The room spins around and I find it is not a simple thing to keep my mind fixed into one attentive shape. I am opened up, my thoughts gone loose and soft, as when the twist in spun cord is gone, and the threads can unravel. Sleep comes easily to me then.

I dream long winding dreams of Sussex, my legs in the flow of the river Stor on a summer's day and the warm water slipping round the bareness of my legs as though I were rooted there, like willows.

It is raining when I wake again.

Mrs. Blight is stirring powder into wine and honey for me once more. The steam curls up into the morning's cool air. "Snakeweed," she reassures me this time, as though I might be afraid that she is trying to poison me. The noise of the spoon circling inside the cup is soothing.

"To staunch the flow," she says. "It works a treat. You nearly lost that baby, bleeding on and on like that."

"Nearly?" I say. And I hold my breath again. Of course, I think, the weight of it. The weight of it is still upon me.

"No need for disquiet," she says. "There's not a soul I've told and Mary thinks it's but flux and idleness. You will be better off going through with your confinement than doing away with yourself so heedlessly, and then you can leave it, if it should prove healthy, with the foundlings at the hospital in Bloomsbury Fields."

"I know of that place," I say, touching my belly with both hands under the roughness of the blanket, holding it tight. I have been wrong about so many things. Perhaps Mrs. Blight is not so bad, after all. And though she knows of my trouble now, I am sure I can trust her with my secret. Can't I?

But there is one thing that worries me. Though they seem untouched, and she has not mentioned anything about them, did she discover my coins when she loosened my stays?

35

*W*ithin a week, an appearance of normality settles on my life again like a fine skin; the kind of new and tender skin that grows quickly on the surface of a wound. Beneath the skin, though, everything is changing, transforming.

My belly is huge now under my loose clothing. I can scarcely believe that Mr. Blacklock does not see this, except that now he does not look at me directly. He is absorbed with something and does not speak freely with me as he used to; indeed he barely speaks at all once the tasks for the day have been decided upon.

"Should I begin on the half-pound rockets, sir, or the stars for Ranelagh?" I say, holding out the latest order lists for him to check. There is much to do, and I need to know which has more urgency. We are slipping behind with our stock.

"Yes, yes, the stars, then the rockets," he replies, and I know that he has barely heard.

"And then you will do the Caduceus rockets, sir, for Mr. Torré? You agreed that you would, yesterday. It says they want a dozen."

"The Caduceus, do those first, they are to be collected tomorrow," he says, changing his mind.

"Tomorrow!" I say. "I did not—"

"Quiet now!" he interrupts. "I must think, I am . . . preparing something."

That is all he ever says. Why won't he tell me what he is doing? It is as though he has withdrawn all unnecessary conversation. Nothing is the same. I am aware that these are the last few days of this new life here at Blacklock's that I have become accustomed to, that I value so much. What will happen now? I do not know. Even time itself is not as it was. The clock's tick that I hear in the study as I pass down the corridor becomes slower and slower, until every day is like a lifetime.

Mr. Blacklock did not come to see me on my sickbed upstairs. Of course I did not expect him to. And when I came down to the workshop, unsteady on my legs and too scared to meet his eye at first, he'd made very little mention of my illness.

"You are recovered?"

"Yes, sir," I'd said, afraid of what he knew of it. "Good, good," he said, brusquely, and did not speak of it again, and neither did he say a word about that night before he went away. What did I expect? It is as I had thought it would be. He does not remember.

When I stand for too long in this heat I grow dizzy. This morning I staggered on the way to the filling-box, and looked hastily at Mr. Blacklock, but his back was to me and he did not notice. He was bent, coughing, as he so often is now, over the smolder and stink of a chemical experiment he will not talk about, smoke pouring gray from a pipkin as he held a lighted taper to its contents. All the time he scratches down notes as he works, in the thin battered book he keeps inside his frock coat. I am sure there is something that Mr. Blacklock does not choose to share with me. Sometimes I have seen a flash of fire catch the corner of my eye and, though he mutters to himself about it, he does not call me over to show me what he has been doing.

Once I stood before the apparatus on his bench when he left the workshop to fetch an invoice from the study. I picked up a vessel and peered at the residue inside, turning it about in the light to get a better view, and did not hear that he had come back into the workshop. He was furious.

"How dare you touch my work!" he'd barked, and I'd jumped so much I had dropped the vessel on the ground. Broken glass was everywhere.

"Sorry, sir, so sorry," I'd mumbled, picking up the little pieces coated in substance with my fingers.

After that I strove even harder to show that I was of use to him.

I lower a fresh case onto the spindle, and tamp in a scoop of dry clay. Today I have a dozen Caduceus rockets to charge and to prepare for firing, headed with fiery rain, and stars. A dozen Caduceus means twice that quantity in cases, made as they are in a pair twined together.

I turn the mallet in my sticky palm. How hot it is, a damp, pressing kind of heat. I pour in the lifting charge and tap at the drift, which seems heavier than usual. I find that now when I charge rockets the child kicks at the sound of the thump of the mallet. Yesterday it pressed its fists or feet under my ribs unbearably, and then with a contorting lurch seemed to upend itself inside me. I could not help but cry out, it was so startling.

Mr. Blacklock glanced up at that, a dish of fulminating silver in his hand.

"Are you ill again, Agnes?" he asked me. His question was distracted, as though it had pulled him from a well of thought.

"I am not ill," I said, evenly, and went on working.

At night in my bed I have to lie on my side with one knee raised, as though I were scaling the side of a great white cliff. It is too hot to sleep right through the night. I cannot breathe, my lungs constricted by the growth inside me, and the thick air does not seem to satisfy my need for breath. In the workshop I have to hide my yawning, I am so tired.

Mr. Blacklock puts on his hat.

"Are you going out, sir?" I ask.

"I am," he says.

I glance doubtfully at the list pinned on the order board again.

"I am worried, sir, we may not complete . . ."

"You will manage," he says dismissively.

"But, sir—"

"Enough!" he barks, and the door slams behind him. He did not say where he was going.

I ease the filled case from the spindle and tap the hollow drifts to clear them of powder before I begin another. Three thousand grains troy is the weight these heads will carry. I have almost filled the eighth rocket of the batch. I yawn again. Despite the rush, I have to rest, just for a moment. I put down the tools and rub at my belly. I am quite alone; even dirty little Joe Thomazin is not in the workshop.

It is so quiet in the heat.

Sweat gathers at the back of my dress, and beneath my sleeves. At the open door I see a crimson moth or butterfly hesitate and flutter in, then out again. Outside above the yard the swifts scream, muffled in the hazy, overheated sky. How tired I am. I close my eyes, just for a moment.

I wish that . . .

And before I know it, I am jerking awake in alarm. *God help me!* I say, on hearing the clocks strike. An hour has passed. I must concentrate. Swiftly I calculate how much longer I have to complete the cases waiting to be filled, and I find I do not need to panic. If I hurry, the rockets will be done in time.

Smoothly I finish the eighth rocket, and its pair. I assemble all the boxes for the garniture, fetch common stars. The ninth, the tenth. It is going well. The first half of the eleventh. And now the mixture for the heads. Quick, quick! *Work faster, Agnes*, I say to myself. *Fulfill the order skillfully, on time. You do not want to displease John Blacklock.* All the time my ears are straining for the sound of his feet coming down the corridor. But even as I pick up the second in the pair of the eleventh rocket and put my scoop into the mixture, a sinking realization comes upon me with full force. There is not enough fiery rain to finish the batch. I have miscalculated.

At first I work on, in the hope that I am wrong, that the quantity will stretch to the twelfth rocket's garniture. Then, when I have used up the last little bit and my task is not done, I stand in front of the list again and stare at it, hoping perhaps that it asks for just eleven Caduceus rockets, or even ten, but no, *one dozen* is what it says. There is no time to grind up more. I have failed, I think, miserably. It matters so much; why did I measure out so carelessly?

I finish the others. I cut up yards of cord, and wax them thoroughly.

One by one I bind the finished rockets to their sticks, and all the time the last pair of empty cases is on the bench. In a rising desperation I cast my eye about the workshop, and I see the mixing box that Mr. Blacklock has just left unattended. What is that? It holds a quantity of composition. Of course, I remember, at first he had said that he was going to make these rockets up—this mixture must have been for them.

I sniff at it. Does it seem . . . ? *Perhaps I should not use it*, a voice of caution says. But there is so much; he will not even notice if I remove a little bit, just to finish up this job. I can replace it later. The church bell strikes the quarter now, and I know I have no choice. Quickly and gently I tip scoops of fresh mixture into the last two heads, and put in common stars. I add blowing charge, and just as I paste both heads firmly shut, I hear the front door open and then Mr. Blacklock strides into the workshop. "All done?" he asks. Hastily I push the last Caduceus rocket's unassembled parts to the back of the bench near the windowsill and hope he does not notice. I can finish it first thing tomorrow morning, before the order is picked up.

"All done, sir," I say. "Though—"

"Good," he says. "Because Mr. Torré's boy was passing by, and has come on the chance that the order is ready. He is waiting outside on the cart."

"Oh!" I say.

"Is there a problem?"

"No, sir," I say. The order will have to be short, I think. In a fluster I pack up the crate, and Mr. Blacklock beckons the sulky boy to come in and he takes it away before I have a chance to think twice.

"You are proving yourself to be reliable," Mr. Blacklock says later, unexpectedly, as we stop work for the day before supper. I look at the floor. "I hardly deserve that, sir," I say, blushing. "Shall I close up the shutters?" The days are long at this point of the year, and it is easy to forget to close them.

"I may return to work," Mr. Blacklock says. "Leave them open; the evening will be light enough to work by."

"Mrs. Blight has taken her half day," I remind him, as we go up the corridor. "She has left a cold piece of lamb in the meat safe and she says we must have more candles before the week is out."

Nobody speaks much at supper. Although Mary Spurren cuts the lamb and lays it out upon the plate, nobody eats much. It is too hot for greasy meat like this, though the flies persist in crawling on it. Mr. Black-lock seems in a state of some disorder, and gets up frequently to fill the jug of small beer at the barrel in the scullery. The bark of his cough has worsened over the last few days, as if there were a great hollow inside him, and could it be that he is thinner, leaner than he was? His skin is so white it is almost bluish.

"Have you seen a doctor, sir?" I ask uneasily.

"The burn has healed now," he replies brusquely.

"I did not mean about the burn, sir," I begin, but he ignores me. It must be the way the light is falling on his face that makes it seem so gaunt, I think, waving the flies away from the meat again. He goes to his study while we clear the plates. I can hear him coughing. Mary Spurren lights the fire for him in there, when he calls for it.

"Never known a man who must so always have a fire beside him of late," she grumbles, clattering the empty coal bucket down when she comes back to the kitchen. "It is so hot, yet there he is, hunched over his books and papers by the hearthside as if it were midwinter." She wipes her neck. "I'd swear he were shivering."

"Really?" I say, looking up. "But Mr. Blacklock doesn't feel the draft in even a cold room. He sits in his shirtsleeves and jerkin, rain or shine." She shrugs.

"It is not so hot as it was," I say, swallowing. Or at least, the sun has gone behind a haze of cloud. But the weather is close, sticky, almost unbearable. The air has a greenish tint to it, as if a storm were brewing.

Much later, toward twilight, when Mary Spurren is up in her chamber, I go out into the yard to empty a pot into the drain. How hot it is. The air presses down.

Looking across at the workshop windows, I notice that Mr. Blacklock has returned to his bench. I can just see his head bent over his work; the lamp upon the sill is catching the side of his face, and casting a lattice of shadows into the dimming yard. I cannot see his hands. What is he making? I step a little closer toward the yellow lamplight. How I wish that I knew. I draw nearer still, until I am almost at the glass itself, and watch his dark, lean face absorbed in something, something that he thinks is secret, unobserved. I do not want to trespass on his privacy, and yet . . . There is the clink of a tool as he puts something down. He presses his head with his fingers, rubbing his temples. His mouth is moving; he is muttering something that I cannot hear through the glass. His eyes glitter brightly, blackly, almost as though his eyes are filled with tears.

It looks like a lonely place to be.

As if he has heard my thought, he looks up at the window; he seems to be staring at me across the gap that has opened up between us now. My heart contracts and I shrink out of the pool of light, though I do not look away. But of course he cannot see out into the darkening twilight. He would not see me standing there; the crooked glass is between us, so he would see nothing but the room reflected back at him, and his own stricken face.

Putting his fist to his chest, he coughs deeply, as if it is causing discomfort. He mutters again, and then abruptly he gets up, pushes his stool to one side and goes out of the workshop, leaving the yellow lamp burning unattended at the bench. Now is my chance, I think, and like a thief or a spy I upturn a bucket and climb upon it to get a clearer view. I have to stand unsteadily on tiptoe, and cling to the rough brickwork with my fingertips. But what I see down there is not what I expect. It puzzles me greatly. His bench is empty, save for his usual tools laid out. Mr. Blacklock was sitting there and doing nothing. What can be occupying his mind so much that he seems so agitated?

My own place at the bench seems different from out here, as though it belongs to someone else's life and not my own. I see the last, unfinished Caduceus rocket, the two halves unbound, lying there so close upon the sill. How will I explain it to Mr. Blacklock? I hope that he does not find it before I have had a chance to tell him why I let an uncompleted order leave his premises.

Disappointed, I step off the bucket and creep back across the yard. At the back door the baby moves inside me and I stop to rub my belly. I look uneasily at the blackening sky above the roofs. It is as if the air has clamped itself around us, tight and thick. A dog barks, a distance away, and the bark sounds flat and strange, and I sense a gathering restlessness that makes me clutch my shawl about me, as though sudden, unknown changes that I cannot see are happening. There is a kind of crackling sickness on the air. "Watch out," my grandmother used to say, waggling her crabby finger at us when there was a turn in the weather, "for something afoot. You mark my words." And of course there was always an occurrence, because a hail would come, or a deluge, or a thaw. I go into the house again, bolting the door shut, and go to my chamber.

When I take off my boots, there is a flicker at the window outside, as though lightning is flashing far away. I unlace my skirts. I unpin my hair and begin to comb it, teasing out the knots until it fans out in a soft mass upon my shoulders. I pick up a handful and brush its smoothness across my lips. I look at my hair in the dirty looking glass and turn my head so that the candlelight shines glossily upon it. I am not so plain, I think for the first time in my life, and something makes me smile at the glass and my likeness there smiles back at me. There is another white spasm of lightning at the window, and then this time, a few seconds later, I hear a growl of thunder, as if the storm is fast approaching. The curtain begins to blow about as the breeze strengthens and I go and shut the casement to stop it banging on its hinges.

Lightning flashes again. And suddenly a wind bears down upon us, moaning at first and then screaming, and a rain is come, the hardest rain I have ever heard, lashing the panes. As if from nowhere, a great summer storm has got up and beats about the house.

The candle gutters. Despite the heat, I shiver. The folds of the curtain suck in and out with the violent rushes of air through the chinks between glass and leadwork. The wind howls outside in a sea of noise, pouring and crashing over the roof, as though we were the one lonely house upon the street and the wind were singling it out to be its victim. I put my boots under the washstand, and abruptly, before I am ready to extinguish it, the candle flame is blown out by a draft.

The shock of the sudden darkness makes the blackness of the night seem blacker than it is.

I grope my way to the bed, the noise of the wind and a strange smell in the air muddling me, until I find it. I think of such winds I have encountered at home, mashing the blackness of the holly trees in the thickets and whipping the hedges about like rope. After the great storm four years ago, beech trees were tipped over and scattered like dry spills of wood against the hillside. The roots of beechwoods reach remarkably shallow, and the pull and bluster of that night upturned the trees with ease, chalky great scabs ripped from the earth. That was the kind of wind that blows fishes clean out of the rivers. Men found them afterward and gathered them up so nothing was wasted; they were dead on the banks where the steep unnatural tides had left them.

A crack of lightning shows the room starkly.

I think of Mr. Blacklock sitting at his bench alone in the night, doing nothing, the despair on his face. Was it grief for his wife? Lying back in bed, my hands on the warm mound of my belly under my shift, I remember Mary Spurren's remark about the night he did not return home till morning, and a niggling unpleasant thought comes back to me. Where had he been? Lightning flashes again, and then thunder rolls.

Outside the wind batters the side of the house, and gradually drags me into a restless sleep.

I toss and turn.

A crash somewhere outside wakens me, and I lie with my heart beating and beating, my face wet with tears. Lightning and a crack of thunder seem to tear the world apart. I sob aloud. A madness that I do not recognize is boiling in my body.

I listen as the house shudders and creaks. I close my eyes. I rub at the ache in my heart, turning over and pressing my face into the mattress. It is a storm with a terrible force. Lightning blinks on and off, the thunder rumbles, but even as I listen it is passing, and now from time to time the wind drops to a light, uneven hum between gusts, as if it were taking breath.

I begin to wade through a whole riverful of dreams. It is after dusk, and the Spring Gardens are teeming with a crowd of a thousand souls or more. Their murmuring is like the noise of the wind.

Little bits of dreams lap around me.

The wind has dropped. A bell rings thinly, as sharp as a star. And at once the crowd begins to pour toward the scaffold from all directions, a dark mass chattering and bobbing among itself.

There is a pause, precisely timed like a beat of silence in music, and the first Caduceus rocket is fired.

Its tip of crackling flame splits the black sky apart, making a raw, unbearable tear inside me, and at the same time its wake stitches the wound up again with two burning threads of scrolling fire, twisting and twisting behind in an expanding helix that dissolves and opens out into the sky.

The Caduceus rocket slows further until it seems to hang above us, pauses, and explodes, bursting bits of itself out brightly across the dark and liquid sky.

It is immaculate.

The witchery that exists in fire escapes and fizzes down over the crowd.

The upturned illuminated faces are tilted into the light like flat pebbles on a riverbed, their dark mouths open and their bodies in shadow. They are tiny and similar, made perfectly still by the excitement of the spectacle, content to yield and stand and stare, drinking it in. It leaves only the memory of what they have seen on the back of their eyelids like a dark purple scar, almost the opposite of light.

Then in my dream the flat crowd disperses.

I wake to a deep and penetrating silence.

The wind has ceased and there seems to be no sound at all from any quarter. Even the house itself is strangely quiet. When I go down the stairs and walk along the hallway to the kitchen, the ticking of the clock echoes loudly out of the study, as though it were ticking in an empty room.

Mrs. Blight arrives late, and she enters the kitchen brimming with dismal tales of horror caused by last night. She can hardly speak for excitement as she unties the hat from her head.

"A great many spires and weathercocks there are blown off churches, and the masonry falling all about killing persons in their chambers, barges lost in the Thames, a wherry full with meal for Queenhithe Market was overturned and broken up at Essex Stairs . . ." She lists disasters she has already heard of, taking the newest of her horrible pamphlets out of her basket and fanning her cheeks energetically with it. I listen to her stories part in dread and part in excitement, and it is in this unsettled state of mind that I rush to put on my cloak and slip out to consider the wreckage for myself. I have a sense of fear and hope and restlessness stirred up inside me by my dream last night. I make sure that the door closes soundlessly behind me as I leave; I cannot be long, there is too much to do, as we must finish the order for Ranelagh today. I shall not be missed, as Mr. Blacklock has not yet appeared, kept up by the wind all night, no doubt, and overslept. When I return to the house I will tell him what I saw.

At the front of the house I am dismayed to see that the walnut tree has been brought down, its roots torn and stiffly grasping at nothing, a hole ripped out of the stones at the edge of the pavement. I stare at it lying there with its green leaves and unripe walnuts dashed against the ground.

The street is littered with broken tiles and pieces of glass and bricks. Bits of leaves and dirt and straw are everywhere, and the air is still and dusty, so that the light has a yellow cast to it, as when a thick snow begins to fall from the sky. My footsteps falter as I make my way toward the river, crunching on fragments. There are no carriages, and the people that I pass have a dazed, excited look upon their faces, as though a war had started.

Ancient Fire

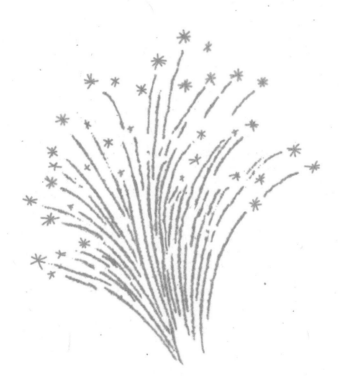

36

A child is picking the green walnuts out of the limbs of the fallen tree outside the house when I return, making a small pile in a piece of grubby calico she has spread on the ground. She points at the house as I approach. "They have been shouting, in there," she pipes defensively, as though I am about to chase her off. Her eyes are big with being hungry.

"Shouting?" I say, and I know that something bad has happened.

When I beat at the front door Mary Spurren opens it at once, as if she had been waiting in the hallway for my return. There is a foreign smell in the house, as though a stranger were here. Mary Spurren's face is flushed and her mouth is moving, her long neck hunched into her shoulders. She has a cloth in her hands that she twists about.

"What! What is it? What has happened?" I have to ask her urgently, to make her speak.

"Gone," she says with difficulty. "He is gone, and what ill luck it is for all of us."

"Who?" I ask.

Her voice sounds strange and shrill and inside out, as though it were coming from another corner of the room. She gulps. "What was I thinking of, tempting fate like that? I'd only gone to ask if he would like a bite to eat, seeing as it was so late into the day and Mrs. Blight wanted to get the breakfast plates all cleared so she could lay the dough out for it to prove. There was no answer when I knocked at the door of his chamber, so in I went."

"Gone? Do you mean Mr. Blacklock? At this hour of the day? But we have to finish up the order. Did he say when he would be—"

"No!" Mary Spurren gasps.

"He did not come to look for me? I was not out for an undue length of time, I was—"

"He is gone! Quite gone!" she interrupts, and her eyes are too big, glistening like jelly.

I stare at her. A thin crack of fear opens inside me.

"Where?" I whisper, though even as she speaks, I know.

"Mr. Blacklock—he is dead!"

I am dizzy.

I look at his hat lying there on the sideboard. He does not go out without his hat.

"Is it his chest? His cough?" I ask her. She looks at me stupidly.

"Mary!" I urge. "Is it the coughing?" I want to shake her, she is so slow. "Is he here? In his chamber? We must call for the doctor. At once!" I turn and run up the stairs.

Mary Spurren's voice babbles on and on behind me. "Not the coughing, no, no, it was not, though he was choking well enough and I thought so myself for a moment as I entered the room. He didn't know me when I went to him, he stood all bent by the side of the bed. There was something amiss, he clutched at his chest and his left arm, all doubled up, then he fell over like this, all curled up sideways and choking, he was." She tugs at my arm and tries to show me. A patch of wetness reaches down the side of her dress as though she has spilled water on it. She pulls my arm harder.

"Let me go, Mary," I say. "Let me go to him!" Why does she stand there?

"I shrieked for Joe Thomazin, we took him into his bed as best we could, dragged him in, but I knew he was gone before we lain him down. There was no breath coming from him, nor beating in his wrists or neck. I came over something shivery and Joe ran out to the Three Bells to call for help. Mrs. Blight was nowhere to be found. My palms they sweated and sweated before they came back with Dr. Kitstone." Her teeth are chattering.

"Mr. Blacklock does not care for doctors," I say faintly, my hand on the latch.

"He had been Dr. Kitstone's patient for some weeks now," Mary Spurren says, unaccountably.

I have never been to the end of the corridor up here. When I open the door into his room the foreign smell is strong. On the floor by the bed is a white bowl filled with blood, and another holding dirty water and rags soaking in it. A man is here, a doctor, here already, moving about by the bed where the outline of Mr. Blacklock lies stretched out, covered with some linen to his shoulders. I cannot say a thing. In disbelief I look and look. John Blacklock's face is shut, the skin of the lids of his eyes is purple and dark.

His pale hand is open, palm upward, on the cover of the bed, his long fingers in a cupped shape as if clasping an object.

Where have you gone? I think, disoriented. *I had so much faith in you.* It seems impossible and yet it is clear to me that Mr. Blacklock is not there inside his body. There is the smell of fresh blood in here and something bad I cannot place. I go to the casements to let in air. I open them all, counting them inside my head. *One. Two. Three. Four.* This is the largest room upstairs in the house. I breathe at the air drifting in over the sill. I can see St. Paul's Cathedral. I did not know that Mr. Blacklock could see St. Paul's from his window. How large it is. Only after some moments staring out at the pale sky do I see the faint white rind of a moon appear over the dome, and then the yellow haze covers it again.

"Agnes," Mary Spurren is saying to me. "The doctor was speaking."

He is collecting his instruments and tools, which are ranged along Mr. Blacklock's dressing table in a row. He wipes a lancet with a piece of cloth, wraps it in leather and drops it into a bag that is gaping on the bed. He presses a cork into the neck of a bottle, and cleans the rim of liquid. I am watching his hands. His face is perfectly blank.

". . . bloodletting and draining the system of bad energy," he says, "if there was to be a cure. However, in this case ... ." And he shrugs, leaving an emptiness behind his words.

"What do you believe the cause of death to be, Doctor?" I ask. I am quite light-headed.

He looks beyond me in the direction of the door, as if seeking a higher-ranking member of the household to hear his diagnosis, and, finding none, returns his cold blue gaze to me.

"Mr. Blacklock has suffered from an acute pulmonic disorder for some time now, as you may know, but I would surmise that his death was caused by a type of shock or blockage to the heart. Mortality is an unsteady thing, and never more so than when the body is under duress of any kind . . ." He waffles on. How shiny the buttons on the front of his jacket are. He is so expanded with improving the lives of others in some way. How I wish he would leave us alone now. I return to Mr. Blacklock's window and turn my back.

I imagine his coughs racking all night, but nobody coming, because no one could hear him against the wind. Would he have coughed up dark stuff into the washbowl beside the bed, as that wind howled like a great black animal against the casements and needled shudders of air between the panes? Did he draw back, exhausted, and lean on the bolsters, unable to cough because a choke was squeezing him? Was he fighting to breathe, feeling the wind taking over the air about him, pushing it away from his mouth, so that all the life began leaching away from his body?

Drop by drop, my body is absorbing the knowledge of the new world as it is now. Outside it is not so clear which part is sky and which is the space between trees, between houses. The world has slipped. Inside, a sick, sore feeling has spread sharply through my bones.

"John Blacklock is dead," I say aloud, and turn away from the window back into the chamber. Mary Spurren blinks. Dr. Kitstone breaks off his speech at last and, finding no inducement to continue, moves away onto the landing to leave us here. His hat is under his arm and he carries his physician's bag with ease as he descends the stairs.

"Pass on my bill to his executors," he calls smoothly from the hall. "The release of the certificate will not be complicated, in a case like this one."

A case like this, I think, angrily. It is a bread-and-butter day for him.

By six Mrs. Blight is drunk. She staggers about in the kitchen, sobbing with relish and stirring a pot of mutton stew that no one will eat. How I hate her for this. The brief understanding between us is over. What gives her the right to weep in that manner? Her teeth are very much in evidence. When she lurches for the gin she knocks at it and the bottle falls and spills out on the table. The overboiling pot on the hob spits and burns. I cannot bear it. There is a knock at the back door, and Mrs. Nott the washerwoman comes in to say she will not come again, under the circumstances. How swiftly news travels.

"There'll be no more work here, and I came by to offer my respects." She eyes Mrs. Blight's bottle of gin, but Mrs. Blight does not offer her a glass, and she turns to leave.

At the door, Mrs. Nott twists around and nods in my direction.

"No doubt she is more than particular saddened," she says, as though I cannot hear.

"Who?" Mary Spurren says, wiping her eyes again.

The washerwoman points.

"Agnes? Why she?" Mary Spurren looks aggrieved. I step forward.

"What are you . . . ?"

"Being his lover, and all," she says.

"His lover!" I say. "Whatever in heaven . . ."

"Oh, but I seen you," she says accusingly. "Yourself and Blacklock, inflagrantic, it were."

"What are you talking about?" I say, weakly.

"I seen you, with my very own eyes," she says brightly. "Through the winder, that time I forgot my tub was in the yard here and was in need of it early that morning and had to drag myself back for it, though 'twere the middle of the night and pitch black with it." She checks around the room to make sure of our interest. "I seen them through the lighted winder." Her boldness grows now as she watches my face. "Drinking wine they was, together. In an embrace. Very firm." She gives a little sigh. "Like I say, it must have struck her hardest."

Mrs. Blight and Mary Spurren are staring at me.

"I can explain," I say.

Their staring makes my head spin. I will not tell another lie, surely I cannot. "I had good cause!" I burst out finally. "There is much you do not know!" And in a fluster I take up a ladle and hardly see it, my cheeks burning.

"I'd say," says Mrs. Blight, dryly, "that much seems evident." Mary Spurren looks sidelong at her in some kind of knowing incredulity. There is nothing but the silence of their expectation in the room.

"You can see, but you do not always understand the whole nature of what your eye just falls upon," I protest quietly. "And your judgments should not shape proceedings if you do not know the story."

"The world is full of riddles . . . is it not?" Mrs. Blight remarks, reaching for her bottle, taking a sip. The air is alive with disbelief. The kitchen door opens a crack and Joe Thomazin slips into the room.

What must they think? I sit bolt upright in my misery and will not speak another word about it. Joe Thomazin holds out his mug for a drink from the jug on the high dresser. They can think what they will. I have admitted it, though they do not know the truth of what she saw. My hand shakes as I pour, and splashes ale upon the table. No doubt they can hear the hammering of my heart, and gain some kind of pleasure from the discomfort of the circumstances I find myself approaching. They must all see it, as I do, looming ahead of me, casting a long, desperate shadow over the muddle of my life. My reputation is plainly lost now, anyway. It would seem there is no end to the complexity of my disgrace.

"Little whore," Mrs. Blight mutters under her breath, as though she'd known that all along. At the end of the table Mary Spurren fixes me with her dead-eye stare.

Later I go upstairs to Mr. Blacklock's room to make it orderly, and find that Mary Spurren has stripped all the clothes from Mr. Blacklock's body.

"What are you doing?" I ask, appalled.

"What the doctor ordered us to do, Agnes. Can't you start on the head and work your way downward? I need it over with."

And so we wash his body between us, sharing the dreadful intimacy. Neither of us speaks a word. Mr. Blacklock's tallness ends in long pale limbs that reach to the foot of the bed. We use a new cake of pressed good soap, and the lather runs over his skin and soaks into the linen on the mattress as we work. My belly aches with tenderness to see so closely how the life has gone from him, his arms stiff, the stubble darkened on his face as if he were only sleeping here in front of us, with his eyelids pressed shut for the last time over the dark glitter of his gaze.

His ribs! I think, and when Mary Spurren goes out of the room to bring fresh water, I cannot help but put down the cloth and touch his wet, supple skin with my bare fingertips. It is marked with the physician's weals and incisions, but the inside, I sense, is still dark and tough.

We rinse the suds and blood away.

I imagine the inside of Mr. Blacklock to be like the dense untouchable wood at the heart of oak, which goes into the fire with the other fuel but the flames cannot reach it. The fire flickers around and barely touches that wood, as though the flames were made of cold instead of heat and have no strength in its presence. When eventually it chooses to catch light, it smolders on and on into the night and beyond, burning a clean smoke with unending slowness, giving out a penetrating, steadfast warmth to those at the hearth. The embers of such wood are highly prized.

There is one guilty matter that cannot be resolved, and in some ways this gives me some relief: John Blacklock will never know I lied to him about my loss of kin. Sometimes, of course, I am anxious that perhaps the dead know everything, see everything, but it is better not to think of that.

Mrs. Mellin, the man on the gibbet, the baby boy on the street, and now John Blacklock, all dead; and how easily these lives have slipped away from us. The complexity of their living was with us, was part of our own. And yet at that moment of change, and forever afterward, death is a terrible simplicity.

What I feel is like an uneven wind blowing through me: sometimes a sweet, uncomfortable hurt that seems to have settled inside like a mild dust or infection, and then at once it is a fierce, sick ache that comes at me so fast and unexpected it is like being struck in the face with something hard.

"What was it, between you?" Mary Spurren asks sadly, with her big head bowed.

"I can't say, Mary." And my eyes fill with tears. I look down at his body on the bed.

Where have you gone? I whisper when Mary Spurren leaves the chamber again, the bowl spilling soapy scum against her apron. I want to knock on his chest, press my ear to the place where his heart should be beating inside it.

And then I think of the fresh pig's heart in my uncle's open hand, how quickly we had cooked and eaten it.

Later we dress Mr. Blacklock's body, and sit in turns beside his corpse all through the night that follows, never allowing the flame of the candles to go out.

How the struts and supports of the house creak at night. It would be unthinkable to fall asleep. Now that I have seen what damage it can wreak, I am more afraid of the wind outside returning than I am of sitting here beside his body. Inside his shape laid out beside me two worlds are briefly overlapping, the now and the past, and already this moment is moving on, breaking down. I hope his soul has already left his corpse in peace, untrammeled by the doctor's clumsy cutting and prodding, unwound itself into a silvery and dusty shape above the bed and dispersed like a dry frost to another place. But of course I cannot know for sure.

Mary Spurren brings me a bowl of steaming caudle to drink before she goes off to get some sleep, but it sits untouched and cooling on the table at my elbow. I feel I am protecting him, sitting here in the guttering darkness with the night beating at the panes. It is the very least I could do. How sorry I am that John Blacklock died without me in the house.

"Did you call for me?" I begin to ask out loud, but my voice quavers in the dark and I stop. He knows what it is that I should have said; I know it also. How late, how late it is. I rub my belly as it tightens almost for a count of thirty, so that I wonder if my time has come, and then that passes and I breathe again. Downstairs I hear the study clock strike four.

In the morning Mrs. Blight does not appear. She has stolen the clock from the study and, strangely, the last of the coffee. On the kitchen table she has left the key to the cupboard in which the beans are kept, and the key to the meat safe, and the key to the door of the house. I look at them, all laid out, with a puzzled, blind relief that she has gone. How could she condemn so many for their thievery, and then help herself to Mr. Black-lock's clock as if it were her own? But it is the silence in the corridor outside the study that disturbs me most. It is like a holding of breath, not knowing the time. I do not have the patience to strain my ears to listen to the bells outside today. Mrs. Blight has taken the passing of time away from the house. But she must have gone off in a hurry, because she has left behind her stack of gruesome pamphlets on the high dresser.

37

*T*he squint-eyed undertaker comes with his measuring ribbon to draw up the size of the coffin. The knocker at the front door is muffled with crape, and the date for the funeral decided upon. "Having some measure also of the household, I have presumed there will be no need for the disbursement of gloves for the attendants," the undertaker says.

Mary Spurren blinks at that. "Plain and respectful, that'll do. He did not have much time for piety, not of the kind imposed upon one. Who will be there, I do not know; no chief mourners to speak of, no blood relatives to come and mourn his passing, save an aged aunt too infirm for travel."

I cannot speak for sadness when she says this. But ceremony, I think, he had a sense of ceremony, and also tenderness. I remember once during the planning of a display how passionate he became. Mr. Torré had been there, and a spotted clerk struggling to make notes with a badly cut quill. "It must be majestic at that juncture," Mr. Blacklock had insisted. "Those big gerbes need a dignity in presentation, their spitting has a height and trajectory worthy of substantial deference." He stood up as he spoke; he seemed like a dark giant against the light from the window. The spotted clerk, with something close to awe upon his face as he looked up at him, forgot to scratch down what was said. On their departure Mr. Blacklock sat still for a moment or two with an expressionless face, observing the yard. Then he had turned and picked up a box of tight little crackers on the bench beside him, cradled it almost in his big hands, and looked inside. I do not think he knew that I was in the workshop with him. I had to smile when I heard him softly, absentmindedly speak to them.

"Little darlings," he'd said, under his breath, as though it were a box of chicks he held.

With some shame I look down at my skirts when the undertaker is gone. In truth I had not noticed how worn they had become, and how stained with chemicals and paste and gunpowder.

"What will you wear?" I ask Mary Spurren, bleakly.

"Most every girl has a moth-eaten mourning dress, there are that many deaths in a family over a year, aren't there? Mine is tighter than it was when my mother died, of course, but still, if I keep my shawl on over the gape at the back, who's to know?" She looks at me. "You're not going to wear your rough skirts? You know that those not wearing black beside the grave can be seen by the dead?"

"I did not," I say. "Can that be so bad?"

"At the burial the spirit takes a leap for a body that's living, if it can see one. I'd not take a chance," she replies, with a shudder.

"Out of respect for the dead," I say, disbelieving, and go to Paternoster Row to buy a dress.

At first the draper will not serve me, as if he does not consider me to have the money for what I need, until I show him the shine of Mrs. Mellin's coins inside my hand. The draper makes his eyes go round in mock surprise. "And what thievery did you perform to come by such a sum?" he asks, his scornful tone made louder to ensure that his lounging apprentices can take in every word he says.

I show no response. I shall have a dress. I count spools of braid that I can see in an open drawer on my left. There are two in a bright blue and three in various shades of red, crimson, vermilion. My heart is beating with an anxiety that I will not show to him. I cannot go to Mr. Black-lock's funeral without a dress that warrants the occasion. There will be tradesmen of the higher sort, and artisans and merchants in attendance. I imagine my rough linsey-woolsey garment walking beside them to the churchyard and I am ashamed. The draper makes some kind of calculation from a piece of paper at his counter.

"We cannot do it in the given time," he drawls finally, arriving at the bottom of the page and looking up.

There being no customer at present within sight and both his tailors leaning idle at the back of the shop gossiping, I presume his meaning is more that he will not. A brief and pointless rage goes through me as the edge of a smile stirs his ridiculous mustache. He has won.

His shears lie neatly on the counter. I expect they are quite sharp, for cutting other people's lengths of fabric.

What can I do but keep my back straight as I walk across the carpet to the door, which I don't take any trouble to close behind me as I leave, with Mrs. Mellin's coins all jostled in my stays where I have thrust them. I curse the meanness of drapers.

Back at the house I am in no doubt as to what I can do. I let myself into Mr. Blacklock's chamber. It is warm and deserted, save for one fly buzzing at the window; Mr. Blacklock's body was taken away to the undertaker's shop this afternoon. I did not stay around for that. I did not want to see Mr. Blacklock's body being lumped down the stairs like a sack of meal. It is not the way I would choose to remember him.

I lift the lid of the chest with care.

Inside is a musty, shut-in smell of old lavender and tansy and laid-away fabrics. When I lift the packets of clothes out one by one and lay them on the floorboards around me, I find I am touching them gently, as though they were the clothes of someone that I had known and loved myself. Shriveled bits of herbs fall away from the paper in which they are wrapped.

The clothes I take out, one by one, are the shape of the body of Mrs. Blacklock. When they are almost all out of the chest, the room looks as though I were unpacking a traveling chest after a long journey away from home.

I am puzzled by the shape of the last two dresses I unwrap. They are the same length as the other gowns but are cut loosely and pleated at the shoulders, as if for a different, larger person.

And then I see that there is another dress with its sides unpicked, as though to make adjustments that were never completed. The bodice is in pieces, broken threads hanging down from the open seams. And I understand that they were made to clothe the swollen shape of a woman close to her confinement.

I rub my own belly uneasily where the child is pressing at it, then bend again to take out the last things at the bottom of the chest. Her pretty shoes are glossy with satin and well-kept buckles. They are too small, and I am glad of this. I would not like to wear a dead woman's shoes.

"Oh yes," Mary Spurren says, red-eyed, when she comes up to find me. "Did I not tell you? Terrible it was. I dare not give you all the details; turn your stomach now, it would. Suffice it to say that the chit was lodged within her when her time came to push it out. They couldn't deliver her. 'Too much force and pulling, perhaps,' the last doctor said that came. Too much use of tools and other new ideas, and the end result was a nasty mess. She didn't stop bleeding and the life ran away from her. Never saw blood so bright nor plentiful."

"And the child?" I ask.

"Obstructed, like I said. Never saw the daylight."

I look out at the sky through the crisscross of the window. The leaves on the linden tree move about in a small breeze we cannot feel in here.

"Don't you begin worrying yourself, though," she says. She stares at my belly openly. "I shall run for the physician just as soon as your time begins." Of course she knows my condition. Everyone knows it.

"I doubt I shall need a doctor," I say, folding the clothes.

"Well, in the meantime then, no carrying of heavy buckets, nor standing about too long at the market fussing over vegetables."

We can pretend that life at Blacklock's will go on as usual for as long as possible, I think to myself, for the next few days. And then what?

"You would do well to find a midwife," she adds, after a pause. And when she leaves the room I try on Mrs. Blacklock's good black dress.

Wearing it, I find it trails a little on the floorboards, covering my worn boots wholly, but otherwise it fits. So she was not tiny, as he had said; indeed, she was a good inch taller than myself. Perhaps it was more that he had made her so, packed her away as tiny in his heart. Tiny she would have lodged there, but persistent, shrunk to a dense dot of pain inside his chest that agonized him if he touched upon it accidentally.

I do not take the dress off when I go to my bed for the last hours of the night. I cannot bear to. Instead I lie down and sleep in it, the silk falling all over the floor, it is so full. Wearing it, thank God, I dream of nothing.

How I dread the funeral tomorrow afternoon.

I have barely spoken to anyone since the day of the storm. Mary Spurren sits at the kitchen table surrounded by the chaos of unwashed pots and piles of linen she has brought down for laundering. Her eyes are red and puffed up with crying.

"What shall I do now?" she says to me four or five times over, her head sunk into her shoulders. I do not really know why she should be despondent; she will not have trouble finding a situation somewhere as a chambermaid or housemaid soon, whereas I, with my swollen belly, will have no such choice.

"You will be fine; the world is calling out for servants," I say. Her white face stares at me.

"But with no reference," she points out, "it will not be easy. Four years unaccounted for on paper."

"Mrs. Spicer at the shop might write something for you," I say.

"She might," Mary Spurren says doubtfully. "But it will not carry weight."

"She can ask about for you, though, surely?"

Mary Spurren doesn't reply.

Heavily I climb the stairs to my chamber, where a half hour of silence turns into an hour. The mice gnaw, undisturbed, at something beneath the washstand as if I were already gone. I have been sitting motionless upon the made bed in my chamber for quite some time. I am ready to leave after the funeral this afternoon. My belongings are packed once more into the oilcloth; the dress that was my sister's that no longer fits me, my small linen, my Bible with the strip of grass between the pages keeping mark of where I am.

I have scrubbed at my boots with the blackening brush.

I have combed my hair and tied it neatly beneath my cap. Everything is washed. The lid of my hand salve is pushed in tightly so it cannot leak.

I will not take off Mrs. Blacklock's good black dress after the service, I decide; somehow I cannot. I am owed one week's wages, and though four shillings would scarcely pay for this garment's cuffs, let alone the silky fabric or the stitching of it, I reason that it was not new.

I look at the bundle. I suppose I am in a kind of shock that my life here is all over. Outside, someone whistling passes down the street. The early morning sun is shining out there.

All my learning in the art of pyrotechny, pointless now, I think, angrily. All his endeavor to advance the art toward a blaze of color, lost, wasted. I feel ill with unhappiness when I think that I will never put a taper to my own perfect rockets, candles, gerbes. My stupid face flushes to think I ever imagined I could have the luck to be engaged in such skilled enterprise. For nigh on six months I had forgotten who I am, thought myself better than I really am: a country peasant girl, the daughter of laborers. I blink to see more clearly through the tears. *Self-pity*, I say viciously inside my head, kicking my heels against the bed. *Who did you think you were, behaving in that way as if you were better than you are, than you deserve?*

My heart beats in sharp rushes of blood until I feel faint. Lying down, I do not sob but grit my teeth together as if my life depended on it.

Here on the bed my head booms with nothing.

What shall I do?

I can't turn about, return home now, the great bulk of my body brimming with impending motherhood. If I stay here I will not find work. No one will take me.

In truth, I can scarcely believe it.

Glancing up to see if the latch is tight on the closed door, I pour Mrs. Mellin's coins out upon the blanket and push them about, as if they might harbor some ideas.

But St. Mary's or St. Dunstan's strikes ten. I should go down. And before I do, I hide the orpiment that I have taken from the workshop, the little jar of yellow poison.

In the kitchen I look about the shelves and pantry, but know there is no food prepared, and we have found that Mrs. Blight also took with her the ham that was kept in the meat safe. But there is fat, and flour. I am ashamed to think of eating on the morning of a funeral but a hunger gnaws inside me, and soon Joe Thomazin will be sidling in like a shadow. I go to Mary Spurren and touch her arm.

"Make us a pudding," I suggest, because I cannot think what else to say. "When it is cooked we can arrive at a plan. It would be better to take stock of our predicament with a filled stomach, as the plans we make will prove less desperate, not so impetuous." We should eat what we can, I think; it is not stealing to make the best of what we have. It is not stealing to take a dead man's victuals, as after all the dead cannot eat them for themselves.

The muffled thump at the door startles us both.

38

A fat solicitor has come. He acts strangely at the door, bowing to me, very polite, as though he has mistaken me for someone else.

"My name is Boxall, madam," he says, removing his hat and bowing again, so that he has the mildly busy figure of a wood pigeon.

Why has he come? Does he not know that Mr. Blacklock has died? I stare at him.

Mary Spurren stands outside the kitchen, wiping the pastry from her fingers onto her apron. Mr. Boxall glances down the corridor at her, then holds his hat against his chest, as if to make his voice more quiet when he leans forward.

"Could I suggest," Mr. Boxall asks me, "that we withdraw to somewhere more private?"

I look at his hat in confusion. Perhaps he means the noise from the street distracts him here. It is a warm day to be wearing such an overcoat, and I see he is sweating at the sides of his head under his wig. Perhaps he needs to sit down. In time I remember the white flour all over the kitchen table. His overcoat is so clean that I must take him to the study.

When he closes the study door behind him, it is such a strange thing to do that for a moment I think that he is going to try to take advantage of me. It is quiet in here. But he stands awkwardly and after all he does not even sit, so I take a chair myself. It is something of a relief to take the weight from my feet. The warm air makes me dizzy and top-heavy, and sometimes my ankles feel as if they cannot take another ounce upon them. I try not to rub at my belly when the child presses on my ribs, altering the way it lies. The good dress gathers in folds about me where I sit before the unlit fire.

"With regret, madam, these melancholy circumstances . . ." he begins vaguely, shaking his head, so that the sweat glistens. "May I offer my condolences."

I open my mouth to reply, but he interrupts me. "I will be brief," he says, fumbling inside his case. "I am here to tell you of the contents of Mr. John Blacklock's last will and testament." He clears his throat and draws out some spectacles from a little pouch, and smoothes a paper he has opened in front of him. "In short, you are the sole beneficiary, Mrs. Blacklock."

"No, no, I am not . . ."

"It gives you the full meath of the business." He sweeps on, heedless of me. *"Touching such worldly estates as God hath been pleased to bless me with I do dispose of the same as followeth. I do hereby devise and bequeath unto the said Agnes Blacklock nee Trussel my said wife all my goods, chattels, money, bills, bonds and my personal estate whatsoever of what nature kind or quality soever upon this consideration nevertheless and my mind and will is that my wife Agnes Blacklock shall after my decease out of my real and personal estate pay and discharge all my debts and funeral expenses. Item I give to Mary Catherine Spurren my servant the sum of eight pounds."* He looks up. "I do not need to read on; I can see you are weary. In conclusion I daresay it is no surprise to learn that Blacklock's Pyrotechny, the house and premises, will belong to yourself, madam."

"No, no," I say again. I am embarrassed. "You mistake me! Mrs. Blacklock is dead!"

He mops his damp temples with a white handkerchief. "I am afraid you may have to speak up, madam, my hearing is not as it was once. Keen as a cat's it was; in my youth I could hear the shriek of a fishwife at Billingsgate from the site of London Stone!" He titters ruefully; the light shines on the pink of his forehead.

"What is the date of the will, Mr. Boxall?" I say loudly, attempting to disentangle the error before us.

He pushes his spectacles back on his nose and consults the document. He reads aloud again. "*This twelfth day of May in the year of our Lord God seventeen fifty-three.* Mr. Blacklock drew this up with me nigh on three weeks ago, Mrs. Blacklock. Three weeks ago." He looks down at his papers again. "Indeed, I note it is the day subsequent to the happy occasion of your marriage vows, Mrs. Blacklock." On seeing my frown he looks again. "Yes, that is correct, the certificate of marriage is here and clearly has it as the eleventh of May."

"The marriage certificate!" I say, incredulous at the turn this is taking. I refuse to look at the paper he holds out to me. "I do not know how an error of this proportion can have gathered like this!" I say. He cups his open palm to his ear. "I beg your pardon, madam? Are you suggesting that Parson Speke of Fleet Lane did not conjoin you in matrimony on the day described? That would be most irregular." He smiles in sympathy at me. "May I suggest, respectfully, that your memory has become exhausted under the strain of the circumstance? It is most easily done in a state of grief. A day lost here, a day lost there." He lowers his voice to the whisper of a man sharing a trade secret. "I assure you that it would not have been written, were it wrong. In ink!"

"But it is impossible!" I say. "Mrs. Blacklock has been dead for four years!" I am in despair. I repeat, more clearly this time, "There has been a mistake! There is something wrong with your document! A mistake!" But he does not hear me, shuffling his papers about in his ledger. What is wrong with the man! I grow impatient that he does not listen to me. "Mr. Boxall!" I say sharply, at which he turns to me.

"Madam, I understand," he says, smoothly now. "You do not wish to talk of business matters so close on the heels of your great loss, but Mr. Blacklock petitioned me strongly to come directly to his premises and speak with you upon his death."

"You do not understand," I begin. "There has been——"

"Oh, madam! But I do. My own wife passed lately away; the loss is like a sore wound in me still. Forgive my intrusion." He raises his hand before him in deference when I try to speak. "There is a deal of legal matters that we need to work through, but we do not need to discuss this here today. Of this I shall remain quite firm! You have other pressing matters to attend to." He beams at me apologetically, and looks about him for the door. *What is the use?* I think.

"Thank you, Mr. Boxall," I say.

He holds up the marriage certificate one last time and then closes the ledger. "He put the document into my hand himself," he says. "He was more than insistent that I contact you promptly should misfortune befall him; he impressed upon me its importance; indeed he wrote not once but twice about the matter, as though he thought I might not do so otherwise." He pauses.

"I am distressing you, madam, forgive me," he says, on seeing my face. "If you need to talk after the funeral this afternoon, I will be there."

Mr. Boxall bows and lets himself out. I do not move. My mind is being drummed with thoughts, like a hailstorm in April will batter the blossoms away from the pear tree.

What is it? What is that silence?

There is something wrong in here, and it is only after a while that I remember that Mrs. Blight has stolen the clock, so that I do not know how much of the hour has passed when Mary Spurren comes into the room.

"What in heavens are you doing, sitting down in that chair?" she says. "What of Blacklock's business did that man want with you? Mr. Blacklock's business is surely the concern of his solicitor."

I look at her. "That was Mr. Blacklock's solicitor," I say.

Mary Spurren stares uncomprehending. She has flour on her white face.

"I have to go out," I say.

39

*T*he stench in the street tells me how close to the Rules of the Fleet I must be. A cluster of children are scooping for fishes in the Ditch, the putrid channel that flows sluggishly along the edge of Ludgate Hill, discharging itself into the Thames at Blackfriars. It runs fitfully, and scarcely at all in the summer: a runnel of excrement and bloody butchers' waste from the Smithfield slaughterhouses. They say, among the comfortable, that there is much talk of the need to cover it over, but in the meantime the resourceful poor make what use of it they can. I heard of a man who skinned dead dogs in the Ditch for their pelts, but who drowned down there, caught out by the tide.

As I turn toward Fleet Lane, a movement catches the corner of my eye. It has been two days since something solid passed my lips. I must be faint, I think. I go to a barrow woman selling pies on the corner.

"Excuse me, madam," I say. Why do I call her madam? She will think me odd as I wear a fine dress and look like a person of some means at least, but no matter. "I am looking for a Parson Speke . . . Did I see a pig?" I add. She looks stonily at me. "Give me one of your pies," I say.

The barrow woman becomes promptly genial. "You may have caught a glimpse; there can be hogs, down on the slime. They feed on what they find there, God help them, then come up out the Ditch and run amok from time to time." Her voice is rough but easy. She leans on the handles of her barrow.

"Are they . . . wild?" I ask stupidly. She looks more closely at me and then scornfully up and down Mrs. Blacklock's mourning dress in a way that shows me that she has no more regard for ladies in good dresses than for others. Being a little too long for me it has soaked up dirt and damp from the gutter. She cannot see my shoes.

"Wild? They are as owned as you or I." She nods up the street. "Speke's wedding place is just up there, past the Hand and Pen. Business, is it?" she pries. "Or something more . . . personal?"

"A private matter," I reply.

"Ah," says the woman as though she knows, and she does not.

"He is dead. My husband is dead," I retort, to shut her up. "He is to be buried today." The ridiculous words fly from my mouth and the space that they leave behind in there floods over with a bitter taste.

There is a lull in the carriages rattling by. The coins all look the same inside my palm. When I look up I see in her face just a morsel of pity, and that is worse; it brings her too close, and lends her satisfaction. She wraps the pie and puts Mrs. Mellin's coin up to her mouth to bite at and examine it. Her teeth are black and stumpy.

"Ah well, then," she concludes with a shrug. "Some say that better off we are without a master." Mrs. Mellin's coin makes a yellow glint as it slips into her pouch.

I do not wait for any change from this woman. How heartless and exact is her presumption, and how I wish it were not so.

I do not see the pigs again. Turning the corner, I discard the revolting pie at once, shaking the contents of the packet out into the street, and rub my fingers against each other to remove the grease. Two rooks fly down noisily to fight and pull at the crust of the pie and the cooked stale meat. How I hate rooks and their black feathers dropping out. I hurry on until I see on my left the mouth of a mean alley and a faded sign that bears the image of a pair of stiff hands clasped together by the fingers. The lettering reads *Marriages Performed Within*.

Inside, the shop is badly lit by windows of thick and grubby glass.

"Parson Speke?" I call into the musty gloom, and presently an old man scuffs forward into the pool of better light coming through the open door, and looks up at me with his eyes screwed tight. His spine is bent, perhaps from a lifetime inscribing the fate of others deep into ledgers with the sharp pen I can make out in the inkpot upon his table. His wig is matted, and I see that he is troubled with a skin complaint. Clearly the business of performing Fleet marriages is not a prosperous one.

"I suppose you to be in need of my services," he rasps. "And which is it that you require?" He pushes the door shut, and inches toward his desk.

"Not a service, sir, but a confirmation of one already done, I believe." I clear my throat.

I seem to have woken him, and he will not reply until he has scrabbled about in a drawer at his desk for a candle, which he takes to light from a stove at the back of the shop. It is a poor candle, and the flame flares higher than it should, smoking and guttering alarmingly, and filling the room with the stink of sheep fat. I draw up the chair he gestures at and sit down gingerly.

"I am here to ascertain a certain point," I begin.

"If it's an annulment that you require"—his voice is thin and wheezing—"I am afraid you can be trotting on your way, my little lady; no longer can I undertake such things, the law discovers me too easily, I fear." He pretends to look cowed by the law, and coughs weakly, then snips the greedy guttering wick at last with a pair of blackened trimmers that he has beside him. The flame steadies and compacts. He clearly has not seen my belly.

"No, no," I say, "I am looking for a grasp of certainty."

"Aren't we all, young lady!" He coughs. "Aren't we all."

"Within the last month I have been made a wife," I say, "and I am unsure on which day . . ." I select my words with care. "On what date this was occasioned."

"Don't know the date?" He gathers his worn stick toward him and goes stiffly to the shelf of registers.

I look down at my gloves, my good gloves that Mr. Blacklock bought for me. I want my fate to be buried among the other weddings there, and then to come to light as if by chance, by someone other than myself: unearthed with the objective rigor of a stranger.

"And the name is . . . ?"

"Blacklock," I say, as if hearing it said for the first time.

"Two shillings, two shillings," he chants under his breath in a wheezing delight as he runs his crabbed hand along the volumes. *Seventeen fifty-three* sits at the end of the row. He takes it down and splits it open at the middle. The page is thick and stiff and does not lie flat easily. He works forward down the columns with his grimy forefinger and reads aloud. "February, April. No Blacklocks yet." He turns a page. "We have systems and filings and records in here." He taps his skull. "I can find Flintlock, Blackalphington, Blackshaw, Blackbennett. Ah! Clue, I need." He picks up the candlestick and casts the yellow light into my eyes to examine me. I blink. He puts it down again, shaking his head. "I have a memory for countenances yet I do not recall your face. Instruct me more as to the gentleman in question."

"He is . . . was a dark man, lean, with a . . . a fine look to him. He was distinguished, imposing," I say, my throat tightening.

"Ah, May," he says eventually. "He wore no wig." The parson screws his face up as if in pain as he struggles to remember. "There was an *air* about him. Yes, a smell I could not place. Not far from vinegar, the smell of him was, very sour and odd. I put it down to being some drops or physic he must be taking for that condition causing him to cough prodigiously our conversation through. Wicked deep, twisty cough, it was; the kind of cough the Devil gives you to suffer on a damp day in boggy country without spirits in your flask.

"Ha! It is here." With effort, Parson Speke pushes the volume around to face me and holds a finger against the entry so that I may see.

At first I can make neither head nor tail of the swarms of letters arranged in rows across and down the page, there are so many lines. And then it detaches itself from the others; the meaning floats toward me like smoke as the letters unfurl and become clear. The thing is there, in a black ink that slopes and curls along the page. With amazement I read *John Blacklock, widower,* and beneath it is written *Agnes Trussel, spinster.*

"That is not my hand," I say plainly to the parson.

"It is not," he verifies, and he indicates an inky cross beside it on the page. "That is your mark."

I look at it.

"After all, you cannot write." He says this as a fact, not as a query.

"I cannot." I look again at the mark on the page that I am said to have made. It is a mark altering my course of life, and yet what a black, shaking, twig of a shape it is, lying there on the white page. It is like a mark made by a bird's foot on a path, after a thin powdering of snow has fallen on a cold day and frozen there. I touch its raised surface as though I were blind. The ink must have flowed thickly from the nib as it pressed onto the paper. I begin to believe that I could have made it. I shall choose to believe it.

I put one of Mrs. Mellin's coins onto the desk and he gropes for it blindly and drops it into a box in a drawer beneath the table. He must think it's a florin, and gives me nothing back.

"The law is changing," he remarks. "In a month I will no longer be able to undertake such matrimonial joinings as that." He pauses. "The more *costly* joining requiring more than the customary benediction. I mean the riddlesome, make-no-bones, ask-no-questions sort of matrimony that brings in a little supplementary benefit for me."

"You mean that he bribed you?"

The parson shrugs. "I did inquire if the lady concerned was absent due to some grave illness or indisposition," he says, as if to defend the strangeness of the settlement. "But he replied that no, she was not ill. And said nothing more about it.

"Well, I did think, here's a situation. And then I took his guineas like they was quite, quite, ordinary." He shrugs. "What could I do? I have an earning to be made. There is no crock of gold to dig for under rainbows." He narrows his eyes at me as if he expects me to say otherwise, then wheezes with regret. "I should have taken on more darkly business. Life would have been most profitable should I have had more requests that were lacking a bride."

A spark flies from the candlewick into the dark.

"There will be a flurry of business like the brief falling of leaves in autumn toward the end of the year, a little gold finding its way into the pot, and then I shall close my door for the final time; unlawful this, unlawful that. Banns will need to be read before any wedding can take place. It will mean the end of all Fleet marriages.

"I recall your gentleman quite clearly now. When he left I followed him to the door, and saw him leave. He had ordered no carriage and walked solitary down the street. I watched him till he turned the corner toward Holborn Bridge."

A great ache washes through me.

For a moment I am too sad to stand up, although I know I must be on my way.

A coach rumbles by. Parson Speke talks on through the noise. "It was an odd business, that day. Very odd. I said so to my wife in the evening when the shop was shut up and the dinner dishes was laid out on the table."

"You believe in marriage for yourself!" I say, relieved. "Are you a religious man?" I ask hopefully.

A sad, uncomfortable look passes over his face, like a man who has remembered the loss of something dear to him. "I was a full-fledged churchman once. They do say that once the faith is planted in you it will grow and sweeten healthily, with time becoming easier, then effortless. I did not find it so. Occurrences transpired to my disadvantage and I found a need to continue my endeavors here in a different district of the city. I have discovered little magic since.

"Do I consider myself a religious man?" He leans on his stick and looks down at his dirty vestment. "I wear the cloth still." He seems perturbed by such a question.

"I looked for things to demonstrate the purpose of it all to me, young lady; occurrences evoked by prayer or distinctive stillness in my thought. Not miracles or tricks, but something that once I would have called religious change."

His eye lights upon my belly as I stand up to leave. He seems to rouse himself, blinks behind his spectacles, bows and stands aside. "I see you are about to be congratulated, madam, on a delicate matter. I wish you well."

I think of the slight, uncertain mark where I made my cross by proxy in his ledger.

"The greatest thing of wonder can come out of the smallest changes, Parson," I say, and I cannot help but smile at him as I go out, because a bubbling strangeness of content has begun to realize and open up inside me.

"How glad I am to hear it, Mrs. Blacklock. There is much refreshment in that thought." He glances at my belly once again, as though he cannot help himself, and a puzzled look is dawning in his face as he bids me goodbye. I can feel his gaze upon me as I walk down the street.

I hardly know how I find my way home; my feet move of their own bidding, and my heart goes above them as though a bird is flying in its place. Not with the heavy, suspicious, greedy flight of crows or ravens, but fluttering and soaring like a wood lark.

Thoughts tumble through me: I am a grieving widow carrying a child that is to be born into wedlock. I have no need to conceal the grotesque swelling of my shape, and I have no need to be ashamed. Indeed, the sudden loss of shame surprises me. The relief I feel is something like the physical shock upon straining to lift a heavy basket and finding it as light as an empty wicker. My great burden has been removed, and every day can come now as it will.

I look down at the good dress I am wearing. I must go to the cobbler's shop, as my mended country boots look strange and dirty when I lift its hem.

As I walk to St. Mary the Virgin for Mr. Blacklock's funeral, the bell begins to toll. Outside the church the undertaker's bier is already empty.

Beyond the porch the nave is black with mourners, so that I stumble on the step in fright to see so many gathered, like a sea of crows. Who can they be? I catch a glimpse of Mrs. Spicer at the back, in a black crape hat, and the merchant from Cannon Street with his wife. Other clients must be here, I realize, distinguished-looking people, colleagues, acquaintances. Mr. Boxall takes my elbow and guides me to a pew at the front of the church. A dry flutter of sidelong glances follows me along the aisle, and I feel the sharp beadiness of their gaze fixed on the back of my neck throughout the sermon, which I can scarcely hear. Surely they do not know already? It is all I can do to sit up straight, my mother would have told me to. Behind me Mary Spurren sniffs into her handkerchief. And I cannot take my eyes from the sleek coffin that four strong men carry away from the altar and through the great door toward the light.

Outside, the bright air is filled with the buzzing of insects and swifts screaming over the crooked rows of tombstones. The grass is tangled with daisies and speedwell, like an uncut meadow around the rawness of the open grave.

"Ashes to ashes," the rector says, firmly and smoothly, because he buries people every week. And John Blacklock's body is lowered back to the earth where all things come from. I watch the old sexton take gritty spadefuls from the mound like a slow workman, and the steady, falling soil crackles on the coffin's lid.

When the ceremony is over, the man at my side turns to me and starts to speak, and it is Mr. Torré, though I hardly recognize him without his hat.

"When they say that Prometheus himself brought fire to the people packed in a fennel stalk, I think they meant John Blacklock, madam," he says. I do not know how to reply. Most of the mourners have dispersed to the street, gone off already to their lives and occupations, though a huddle are stood talking by the gate, and their pale faces glance across at me from time to time.

"He was a brilliant man, a thinker. London is a poorer place for the loss of him," Mr. Torré says. He takes his wife's arm and turns to leave.

"I would be pleased to offer my advice," he adds. "Let me know what I can do to help once you are ready." And I smile ruefully at his kindness through my tears, because I can almost hear John Blacklock objecting how that man had always itched to get his hands upon his business.

I look back once when I get to the lich-gate, at the old man bent over the weight of his piled-up spade, and at the space between the headstones where the body of John Blacklock lies. The breeze is mild, and I see that there is a clear view of the sky above the graves.

There is no wake.

40

*M*y dearest Ann,

Please come at once. There is too much to say. My husband is dead and the time of my lying-in cannot be long now. I will repay your fare on your arrival in London. Forgive my haste.

I am taken aback when Mrs. Spicer suggests, and writes, *With deepest regard, Agnes Blacklock*. I look at the new shape of it upon the page. Mrs. Spicer's hand shakes with a trace of palsy, and little spots of blackness speckle the page.

"All very extraordinary it is, too," Mrs. Spicer says, admiring her work and shaking the castor over it to soak up the ink. "There's no lack of gossip, mind, but I've no time for that." She smiles kindly at me then, and leans out and puts her shaking hand over mine for a moment.

And she folds the page until it is small and square, with my sister's name at Wiston House faced out on the top surface and a hardening waxy seal holding its edge fast. I am shocked at the letter when it is done, at seeing the facts laid out so baldly upon the page. It is not a selfish letter. My proposition to her is a good one, I believe.

"And the postage is threepence," Mrs. Spicer says, waiting patiently for me to come to my senses and leave the shop.

I find that the light-headedness I feel is also a curious, misplaced kind of anger. I have no right to be angry, I say. I reason that this ingratitude will do no good, yet I do not understand why he has done this. I am angry because he is dead, because he did this thing and did not tell me, did not ask me. Why did he not shout for me instead of dying? Why did he die when we had so much work to do together?

I suppose there was a point in time when the shape of life could have unfolded differently.

I do not think I loved John Blacklock. I do not know what it is to be in love. I do not know what it was that John Blacklock felt for me. And yet I have a sense that there was something not quite arrived at, not quite formed, nor spoken of, nor finished. This something, this unformed love, is within me still: a kind of bright, unhappy warmth that may dim slowly as the years go by, or it may not.

At the moment I am so sad that I can taste sadness in my mouth; when I breathe, I breathe in the smell of sadness.

Mary Spurren just looks at me when I tell her I am married, and to whom. "You are not surprised," I say. She blinks.

"I rarely find surprise in anything," she replies. "Only sometimes what my poor mother called perplexity." She sighs. "Besides, I knew it. I knew it from the very first. He was different from the day you came here, all sodden with rainwater. I must say, it made me mad." She wipes her nose across her cuff. "Little spots of color started up on his cheekbones and didn't die down."

"What did you know?" I ask.

She looks at my belly openly again. "It accounts for things. I did suspect it, not in this peculiar way, but there was something afoot. How could a body not notice! My mother always said I were not stupid, though there's plenty of folks may have said otherwise.

"At dinner he would sit and stare at you, stare at your hands as you ate. He'd never talk no more at table, just kept glancing, over and over. Mrs. Blight said that you should act upon it, very slow she thought you were, cool as custard you sat there, shoving your spoon in and looking at your platter saying nothing like you was an untouched milkmaid. *Clever*, Mrs. Blight said at first; playing at being all unawares and fresh up from the country.

"And then it became clear your belly had more inside it than Mrs. Blight's loaves and gravies. *Not so clever then*, she said. *Agnes Trussel is quick with child, if I am a day*. She said in truth that she were sorry for you. I was not, though I was surprised at Mr. Blacklock. I wanted you gone. Easier it was before you came, with your distraction. He had had a kind of gratitude toward me I were happy with. I was here the day his wife died, after all. I was here when he had trouble with his business and with his apprentice Davey Halfhead, who had a rage on him like a mad dog in a crate, and here when Davey Halfhead ran away. And then Mr. Black-lock did not take on any other people. It was for a long time very plain and simple, just the way he liked it. I could get on steady as I pleased. Then all of a sudden came Mrs. Blight one day, and the next day you, too, was there, though I could not for the life of me think why."

"He stared at me?" I say. I am baffled by this. Her watery eye meets mine and holds it briefly.

"Like . . . like you was gold dust come to the table." She sniffs. "So angry he was when Cornelius Soul began to pay you more attention than he should have. Mind you, plenty of us foresaw disaster lying there." She scratches the back of her head and shakes it, as if to dislodge something of her confusion. "But marriage in May! And nobody knowing, I can't fathom it all quite," she says.

"When were you wed?" she asks.

"On the eleventh of May."

She frowns. "Why does that stick in my mind as a date of note?" I can see the thought struggling to the surface of her face, and at last she breaks out with a burst of recognition. "Oh, yes, the day that Mrs. Blight won on the lottery." She rubs her head. "That were a funny evening, now that I comes to think of it again. What with her making all that good sauce and it going to waste as no one came to eat it. Mr. Blacklock not turning up at all, and you not coming neither . . ." She trails off.

"Ah," she says. "I gets it."

She blinks.

"I don't know." She shakes her head again. "There is a missing bit, I don't know what."

I do not tell her that I did not know myself; it is something that I will not tell a soul.

I am a widow before I am a bride, I think.

There is a silence as we spoon in broth that Mary Spurren has made.

"Do you miss your home?" she asks me. "Can you go back to where it is? Your fortunes have changed so; you could do anything!"

I cannot answer straightaway. I think of Sussex, and the lane to the cottage flooding over with whiteness when the rains pour down the slope of the scarp onto the clay. I imagine the wind blowing the green leaves of the beech about. I imagine bits of myself caught all about there, in the way that the sheep leave scraps of wool on the thorns where they rub or push through, going from patch to patch of ground.

"No," I say. "I will not go back to live in Sussex." And then I laugh aloud and say, "I have come to like the taste of water from the pump in Mallow Square too much!" And she smiles at this, her big pale head grinning open with the thought of it.

"What will you do yourself?" I ask. "You know you can stay here, with the same arrangement as before."

She nods. "Plenty of dirt still," she says. "And what is dirt but work, and where there is dirt there is work for me or anybody." She takes her bowl to the scullery and knocks about in the cupboard there. "Talking makes my head hurt," she mutters, rubbing at it. She pauses by the door.

"Pushed me out, she did," she says.

"I'm sorry?"

"Alice Ebbs. That woman whom my father married, after my mother died. I heard her once, nagging my father in his own kitchen: *That great girl, eating and eating.* I had to leave."

"Where did you go?" I ask curiously, thinking of my own flight.

"Came straight here, I did. Never been nowhere else except my father's place and here. Dirty, it was then. Till I came." And she looks about her with a touch of pride.

"I'll get on now," she says. And she goes off up the corridor with her dustpan and brush.

The kitchen is quiet when she has gone. A fly comes in through the open door from the yard and settles on my emptied dish. I can hear the brush knocking the risers of the stairs as Mary Spurren sweeps. I push back my chair and go to the workshop for the first time in seven days.

Joe Thomazin looks up, startled, as I enter.

"Good morning," I say to him, and he nods his head shyly, though he does not look at me. He is perched on a stool close to the lit stove, despite the warmth of the day. I sit down heavily before the filling-box and look about, touching my belly. The baby is asleep inside me. Sunshine is flooding the sills and benches, and when Joe Thomazin gets up and begins sweeping beneath the benches, dust spins in the beams of light. The hiss of his brush is regular against the boards.

"Joe Thomazin," I say. "You will stay with me." The sweeping pauses and then goes on, as if that was expected. In time, I think, he will be more than useful. He has watched John Blacklock at his work for years.

How hot the sunshine is, streaming in through the windows, all over the benches. Little beads of sweat run down my face. It is almost midsummer. Shouldn't this baby be born before midsummer? The summer is making it lazy. How warm it is. I shall open the door to the yard, I think, and I get up slowly, turning my back on the sun.

The blast shatters the window.

A searing crackle rips the air, and shards of glass are everywhere, a taste in my mouth . . . and a plume of choking, blood-red smoke begins to pour from the bench. The ground vibrates. I gag, panicking for breath as white and fiery explosions pepper the air, a river of redness streaming over the bench, overturned stools, scattered . . . it is a violent, pulsing arc of fire.

"What in God's name! Help, somebody, help!" I scream.

I wade retching in sparks and colored fire and smoke, bent doubled up, and then I see half of the Caduceus rocket, my unfinished Caduceus rocket, trapped and fizzing against the floor in a corner like a dying, furious animal.

"Joe!" I cry. "Joe Thomazin!"

The second head of the rocket explodes and leaps up and recoils beneath the bench and is trapped again, miraculously, kicking violently and spewing a rush of sparks out sideways into the middle of the room. I am astounded. It is the pulsing red of the back of the eyelids closed against the sun. It is the red of passion, rage, of fear. It is a haze of crackling insects. The smell of the red is everywhere. And Joe Thomazin is lying on the floorboards.

Abruptly, it seems, the drowning is over. The hiss of sparks, dying down, gives out a last spurt of fizzling and comes to an end. The dim, ruby, choking air quivers with silence.

"Are you hurt? Where are you hurt? What were you doing?" I shout, the sulfur, the red smoke catching my throat. "It is over! There is no fire!" I am shaking him. And, thank God, he is not hurt. He struggles free and jumps in distress from foot to foot, tears streaming runnels through the blackness on his face. There is a strange noise coming from somewhere close. It is not the smoking carcass of the rocket's parts. I have to stop and look. When I see that the noise comes from him, my own breath stops for a moment as I strain to hear it.

"I didn't, I didn't," he is saying, over and over, in a hoarse, thin wheeze. "I didn't. Didn't touch." His blackened lips hardly move as he says the words.

"You didn't touch?" I say, in astonishment.

"Didn't touch," he says. And I believe him. I pick him up and he clings to me, his scrawny knees bent into my side, his head pressed into my neck. His body shakes with the force of his sobs, long after the crying is over. It is so calm, and so desolate. I collapse onto the scorched boards with my legs out and hold Joe Thomazin against the bigness of my belly.

My ears are ringing. They are hearing the boom of the explosion's echo again and again, the tinkle of jars breaking, the rolling tools in disarray. The air is loosening now, slackening. And the red smoke has vanished around us like a mist eaten up by sunrise, leaving barely a trace, as if it had never existed, and through the broken window I see Mary Spurren running from the scullery across the yard.

"Agnes!" she pants. "Are you in there? I heard a . . ." Her big head stops by the window and stares in. "What is it? I heard . . . I thought something bad had happened, I thought . . . I thought we had exploded." I can hear her feet crunching the glass. "Has it finished?" She coughs. "Oughtn't you to come away from there?" she adds uneasily. "Your face is bleeding."

"It is lost," I say, sat there on the floor, quite unmoving.

"Lost? What is?" she says, bewildered.

"The knowledge is lost, Mary . . . all gone. He did not trust me."

"Trust you with what?"

"He discovered the color. He knew how to make it. He did not share his precious secret with me."

It has gone to the grave, buried with him. And still the crickets go on chirping in his yard; fresh summer air drifts in.

41

I am waking earlier and earlier as the time for this baby to be born grows near. Today I find I cannot sleep and cannot lie still, so I rise and dress, go down to the study and sit at Mr. Blacklock's desk beside the open shutters in the first light. Looking through some papers lying there I see there is still another order to fulfill. Yesterday I had been surprised to receive a formal message of condolence from Mr. Torré, repeating that he would be pleased to offer his assistance, if he could be of service to the business at this difficult time. The world is not all bad.

Dawn begins coloring the sky long before the sun rises, and a black-bird starts to sing from the linden tree outside. The weight of the child inside me shifts about as though it is waking, too. Does an unborn child close its eyes when it sleeps? I allow myself now to imagine what its face may look like. Sometimes it pushes at my ribs so that I cannot breathe freely or sit still, so that I have to get up and pace about. Of course, now I do not wear my stays.

I think of those rocket heads, pouring out redness. What a waste of beauty, what a waste of knowledge a sudden death can inflict, like spilling something vital away into a dry soil. How will I manage here without his guidance? I do not know enough. I hope the stock we have will last awhile.

I go to the shelves and take up a book and open it at random. I turn a yellowed page. And another. And I see that great masses of written notes in Mr. Blacklock's hand have appeared in the body of the book, notes that were not there when I looked into these same books on that day so many months ago. The notes spill all down the margins. I go to the early light from the window and try to look at them more closely. There is an

urgency to their inky sprawl, unclosed pothooks, hastily crossed letters, dark threads of knowledge poured out all over the printed text, but I
cannot read these scribbles, so blackly tangled that they are unreadable.
I open another and find that the same has been done. I cannot read his
handwriting; it makes neither head nor tail of sense. I open another, my
hands trembling. Mr. Blacklock's shelf of books on pyrotechny have all
been annotated for me. I am certain of it. His secret is in here, and yet I
cannot read a word of it.

And then I reach the end of the shelf and see another volume that I
think, at first, I have never seen before. Smaller than the others, with a
pale calfskin cover. I realize it is the battered notebook that Mr. Blacklock
kept inside his coat. I look again and open it. It is more than a notebook—
it is a manuscript. And as I start to read a tiny gasp comes from my throat,
because I see what I am holding.

Not in my lifetime, but perhaps in yours, he had said. And it strikes me
that perhaps John Blacklock knew that he was dying, and that when I
turned up so strangely and so insistent on his doorstep in the rain, reminding him of something that he had known and lost, he saw a chance, a
glimpse into the future that suggested a way to pass on the artistry that
was his core. If he saw later that I was with child, perhaps it drove him to
act with the secrecy and urgency with which he made sure I was his wife:
sanctioning the birth, protecting me because I was the key to the conti-
nuity he sought so keenly. Without marriage, his plan could not work.
But why did he not tell me? I suppose that he had to be sure I was capable
of the task in store. It was an experiment. Haphazard, not without risk.
Perhaps he was afraid I would refuse. There was so little time. He would
have known that I could only gain from the arrangement, but once done,
he could not bring himself to tell me of it. He must have suffered dismay
when he saw how Cornelius Soul paid me attention, but perhaps he did
not believe it would come to anything.

This is what he worked on, late into every night, trying to complete
everything he needed to pass on to me, making these fine, swift drawings,

listing formulae, assembling instructions, quantities, measurements, conversions, queries, solutions . . . discoveries. My heart leaps. I know it is for me. My book of fires.

So much of what we do in life stays unexplained. Probably I shall never understand his motive for acting as he did, though I will think of it often, but I know for certain that a strong thing had started up like fire between us.

I turn to the beginning of this precious work that I have in my hands, sit down at his desk and begin reading in earnest. There is much hard work to do ahead of me. I like that, I think. I am sure my dream of color is somewhere before me in the darkness of the future, between these pages, as though the bright thread of my story is running on ahead of me and I have only to catch up with it. It is the presence of fire that is constant, and as I have said, my liking for fire has been there from the start.

The door opens and Joe Thomazin slips into the room. He looks at the book lying open in my hands, and a wide, jagged smile breaks out across his face.

"You knew about this?" I ask him.

"All . . . the time," he stammers shyly.

Reading for hours, I become late for an appointment with a banking man in Lombard Street, who is to give me advice as to the nature of the investments that I now possess. My investments! I almost laugh aloud at the absurdity.

I am shown to the waiting room when I arrive, where I sit down. It is strange how the sudden wearing of a good dress makes one sit up straight and put one's feet together. I suppose that is the power of gold and fortune, even in small quantities like those I have. It is at once mysterious, wondrous, and distasteful. Surely now would be the time to straighten out one final matter. I cannot live with something pricking at my conscience all my life, and this is why I have the rest of Mrs. Mellin's coins wrapped up in oilcloth on my lap, in readiness to show him.

The banker is a crisp, neat man called Mr. Dunn, wearing a brown velvet coat the color of horses. His face is smooth with politeness as he discusses my affairs. I try to attend to what he says. It seems I am wealthy, having money here and there. His wig is impeccable.

"And the best for your family," he concludes.

My child! I think, and I vow to put its welfare before all other matters. Which is why I do not feel the remorse that I should when I say in a rush, "And these gold pieces I have, can I leave with you also?" I tip them out of the piece of oilcloth in front of him like a confession, and my hands shake so much I hide them beneath the table. Mrs. Mellin's coins shine against the polished wood.

"Certainly," Mr. Dunn says at first. But as he picks up the first coin his mild face suddenly narrows with attention, and he reaches for an eyeglass to look at them more closely.

"Is there something wrong, Mr. Dunn?" I venture anxiously. He turns the coins over in his clean white hands as he examines them. He clears his throat, and puts the last one down. The table between us is vast.

"Have you had these long?" He lowers his eyeglass and looks at me keenly. I shake my head.

"How much . . . is there, altogether?" I ask, and my voice sounds small in the big room. Could he know that they are stolen? That is surely impossible.

He replies, very slowly, "I am afraid to say that I cannot take these for you, Mrs. Blacklock."

"Why?" I ask, and my heart beats in my mouth.

"These are illegal coins. They have no value; they are nigh on worthless." He puts one or two onto a small brass scale. "They are defective in weight, and have been tampered with to disguise their shortcomings."

"Do you mean to say that they are forgeries?" I ask, swallowing. This is not at all what I imagined I would hear. *Mrs. Mellin's coins have no lawful value?*

"They are not counterfeit so much as tampered with." He pushes a coin to me. "See how the head of King George II has been added inexpertly to the original mint. This particular Spanish coin holds no value here." He holds another up to the light from the window, and it flashes fiercely. He looks at me again, very directly. "Someone has scoured at them, to wear away at the evidence. But they are quite thin; it is clear to the experienced eye that they have been meddled with."

"So they are not gold, even?" I manage to say, faintly.

"They are gold, but they are not legal tender and severe penalties exist for carrying such currency. Naturally, I cannot take them." I drop his gaze. "You are taken aback, Mrs. Blacklock. I am sorry to embarrass you, but you have been the unlucky victim of a fraud. There are many rascals out there. I am only sorry that you will have trouble getting rid of them." I begin to gather them up. "I am not sure how I can advise you," he goes on, "but you may be lucky. There is a shortage of good coins and no lack of unscrupulous traders who may have them off your hands for wares or services."

I take a deep breath, and stand up to leave.

"I am sorry about your husband, Mrs. Blacklock," the banker says. "He was a good man. Do not hesitate to call on me again, should you need to consider other business matters." He holds the door open, and I thank him and make sure I do not run as I go out onto the brightness of the street.

I do not need to try to spend the coins, I realize as I turn toward home. My secret solution is neat and strange. At last I have the perfect end for Mrs. Mellin's coins, knowing as I do how some freshly mixed aqua regia will dissolve the gold quite readily. In the workshop there will be one jar of liquid on the shelf that has no label, and when I glance up at it from time to time it will remind me of how very fortunate I have been this year.

And life goes on.

Not as normal, but the tilt of time keeps us rolling onward. Eating, sleeping fitfully at night, going to the butcher, the grocer.

"How are you keeping, Mrs. Blacklock?" Mrs. Spicer asks, wad-dling over. "In your state, these hot days must be causing you a deal of nuisance."

"Oh, not so badly," I reply.

"There is just one thing I meant to ask you," she says, drawing out the lid on a glass jar. She dips the ladle and the pale heads of artichokes nod slowly in the oil as though they were drowned in there.

"There is something in the matter of your marriage and its secrecy, I can't say what, that seems a puzzle." One after the other she drags up artichokes, drains a spool of oil back to the pot and lays them glistening on a dish.

"There are folks out there who cannot comprehend the need for such concealment, nor what purpose did it serve. Does it even cast a doubtful light on its authenticity? It is just that it confounds them." She looks at me. "I hope you do not mind me speaking frankly, Mrs. Blacklock."

"No, no," I say, biding for time.

"It's just that the very abruptness of his death caused some tongues to wag. You are excessively"—she pauses—"big with child, after all. Folks do not like to feel misled in what is what."

"How do you mean?" I ask.

"Discovery of hidden facts gives them excitement, and a crossness that they did not know the facts themselves. They fret that other folks might have heard before them, not liking to be the fool who has not heard the news. And then, of course, disclosure causes them to rub their hands together with the flavor of their knowledge. Aggrieved by the existence of other people's secrets when they come to light, their chatter springs up like flames from a tinderbox when the flint has struck."

"Faster than that," I say ruefully. "Like quick match!"

"Well, they feel hoodwinked by the not knowing of a whole affair, as though it were their right to have the details of a body's business, and it must be said that that fuels a certain speed to its delivery from mouth to ear." Mrs. Spicer pushes back the wide cork.

The child kicks and my hand goes to my belly. I look hard at the bottles on the shelf above the counter, my eye lingers on the syrup glow of empress peaches and, may God forgive me, a neat little lie comes out of my mouth.

"It was for the sake of Mr. Blacklock's relative," I say. Mrs. Spicer puts her webbed hands on her hips.

I pitch my voice as if in confidence. "I'm sorry to say that his aunt is stubborn. It was the conditional nature of his inheritance. In her old age she has become a little shaky in her grasp on the customary ways of things, and announced John Blacklock should not remarry if he was to receive her legacy. It was as if she laid the blame for his first wife's death at his feet, though she did not say so. She has theories brewing in her head about the world and the way it should be run."

Mrs. Spicer digests this, weighs it up. "In short, she is a little odd but well-to-do; and he complied with an old woman's unreasonable request."

I shrug, as if to say I did not disagree with what he did. *May all concerned forgive me. There is a need for these untruths.*

"I do recall he had an aunt," Mrs. Spicer admits, wiping her oily fingers on her apron. "More than once I have been occasioned to pack up a crate of oranges for carriage, or Rhenish wines. A solicitous nephew, I always thought, sending gifts to his old aunt to brighten the darkness of her days, her twilight days in the heart of winter. How lonely that can be in old age, and how long.

"And yet it was the money all along. Still, I don't know, to keep a thing like that, like marriage, under wraps." She shakes her head. "I did not have him down as a man of such cupidity, putting material wants before vital matters of the heart. Before matters of decency."

Then her face clears, and she glances at my belly in relief.

"Yet of course, I am forgetting that he had the future of his child to think of. His progeny. I daresay he did not care for the muddification of it all himself, but he suffered it for his child's safekeeping. How restrained of him, and how forbearing."

"He was an honorable man," I say.

"Of course he was," she says. "There is a lot of talk. I must say, I do not care for it." She shakes her head. "Pay on account, at the end of the month when your affairs are settled. The chatter will pass, Mrs. Blacklock, like a shower in summer. Plenty of other things for them to think about soon enough, when someone else's life takes a twist and turn out of the ordinary. I should not trouble yourself overmuch on its account." And she puts an additional package on the counter. "Here is a little titbit for you to savor for yourself. A gift, we shall call it, toward the concentration of your strength." Her brow wrinkles in sympathy. "You must promise you will eat it, mind. Cakes is good for you."

"You are a kind woman, Mrs. Spicer," I say as I go out. She did not suggest that it might have been wiser to enjoy a spot of married life before his time in this world was up. Of course she did not. No one can see into the future like that. If we could, how differently we would all conduct ourselves.

42

*M*y confinement must be days away. The baby is huge inside me. It does not kick now very often, it is so squeezed up in there. It seems, as I am, to be simply waiting.

The kitchen is quiet this morning. The kettle of tea I have just made is steaming lightly as it brews beside the hob. I look about the room. My kitchen, my house, now, and it hardly seems possible. I put a finger to the objects on the table, a spoon, a pair of bowls laid out for breakfast. I pour some tea, blow on it gently, and take a sip. I turn to the high dresser, and my eye falls on Mrs. Blight's stack of pamphlets there. I shuffle through them; there are a variety of publications—*Last Dying Speeches, Proceedings of the Old Bailey, Ordinary of Newgate's Accounts.*

I remember the conversation we had only a month ago, on the evening she said that I should read some myself to gain some understanding of the wicked world. Uncomfortably, I went to them and picked one up.

"What is the Ordinary?" I asked.

"The prison chaplain," Mrs. Blight said, warming at once to her favorite topic. "Put upon to give spiritual care to those condemned to death. His perquisite being the right to publish their final confession at the scaffold, with accounts of their lives. I like the *Ordinary's Accounts* best," she'd said, nodding at the one I held, "as it gives the unfortunates a little bit of a chance to put their side of things."

Some of these are from many years past, I note. She has been collecting them a long time. I thumb the yellowing pages idly. But this one, for instance, that I hold in my hand, is very new. *The Ordinary of Newgate. His ACCOUNT of the Behaviour, Confession, and Dying Words of*

the MALEFACTORS Who Were Executed at TYBURN, on FRIDAY the
25th of MAY, 1753.

Just two weeks ago; I must have heard the bell myself for this very execution. I take another sip of tea. I turn the pages absentmindedly, and am not prepared for the great and icy shock that I receive from it. A chill spreads through me, like a drench of cold water.

"Oh God, no," I whisper, my flesh creeping with a sudden understanding. And I read: . . . *indicted for stealing one Diamond Locket,* 13th November 1752.

LETTICE TALBOT, *aged* 23, was born in the parish of St Anne, Westminster; *of Genteel and Pious Parents, possessing handsome Property*
in the City and beyond; she was afforded the best Education available,
the particulars of either not proper to mention; and seemed to be set
upon a Life gliding along the esteemed paths of Virtue and reputable
Content. The seed of her Undoing lay in her great Beauty, attracting
as it did the attentions of many; including those of one wealthy Baronet
owning a sizable manse near Chelmsford *in the County of Essex, and*
whom with more innocence than wise counsel her Parents had thought
eligible. At the first opportunity he proved untrustworthy; violating her
most shamefully and lewdly, and she became with Child. When she
could no longer conceal her vulnerable Condition she was turned out by
her mortified Family and, though soon afterwards she suffered a Mis-
carriage, was forced to accept support extended by her seducer's associ-
ate the notorious Courtesan Sally Bray, *and fell quickly into a Life*
of Vice. Claiming some of the most learned and respected Gentlemen
among her Voluptuaries and Admirers, she could command high prices
for her debauched and particular Services and lived in a style of fash-
ionable Elegance. She claims as her final Downfall a singular inti-
macy with one Charles Kettering, *of* Dorking *in Surrey, Husband*
to the prosecutrix Elizabeth Kettering, *and declares that her Error*
was to have succumbed to the temptation of Love itself, and its unreli-

able and wily accomplice Trust. *In this incautious state of illicit Love, she maintains herself to have been in receipt of the Gift of a Diamond Locket,* val. thirty-five guineas, *from the said* Charles Kettering, *proven subsequently to be the Property of the prosecutrix* Elizabeth Kettering *his* Wife, *who made the discovery that her Loss was adorning the neck of her Husband's Mistress and ran to him with the threat of public Disclosure, whereupon he denied all acquaintance and falsely accused the defendant a Thief.*

Lettice Talbot *denied to the last the Fact for which she was Convicted; not blaming the court, but imputing it to her Lover* Charles Kettering *for such a weak and dishonest Betrayal.*

As the executioner tied her to the fatal Tree, she cried out to the crowd that her Heart was full of Grief, and that she would not Rest. And then the Cart was drawn from under her, and the Execution was done with as little Noise and Disturbance as the Nature of so tragical a Scene may be.

A hot coal slips in the grate and a small, bluish flame starts to play over the surface of the embers.

I take a breath. Lettice Talbot is dead. She has been dead for days.

43

*M*y sister Ann has come, brimming with questions that I will not answer yet.

But pieces of news arrive with her. I have a new sister, as my mother's child is born.

"She is called Clemmie, she came on time, slipping out readily like an easy calving," Ann says. "Nevertheless," she goes on, "Mother has put her foot down firmly and says it is the last one. 'No more babies I am having, Thomas,' she announced to Father, with Clemmie hanging off her milky pap as she stirred at the pot. 'Not one!'" Ann giggles. "His face was such a mixed-up sight, not knowing if she was saying this in full solemnity.

"But look at you, look at you!" she says, reaching for my hand and rubbing it. Her eyes glisten with tears in the candlelight. "Lil said that Father was too angry to speak when you disappeared. All through December with barely a word from him, even when I turned up at home on my half day from Wiston. Much later on your brother Ab went all the way to London looking for you. He asked around everywhere but had to come back empty-handed, and they said it near broke Father's heart, he missed you so sore. And old Mrs. Mellin died!" she exclaims. "It was about the time that you left when the corpse of a traveling man was found all twisted on the lane outside her cottage. He was dead from being beaten about the head—it was a horrid sight, they said. There were signs of a scuffle in the muddy path and his bale of fabrics was unfolding and flapping round him. It was thought that he was attacked for a quantity of gold it seems he must have had upon his person, an amount having gone missing from Mrs. Mellin's cottage, or so they said. There was no gold upon his corpse, of course, so how could this be proven? At least that was what we said when we heard of it, considering how mean she lived, but it turns out she had quite a hoard according to Amos Cupper who knew her husband well enough when he was alive. Mind you, some people said that Amos Cupper was sporting a new overcoat made of good woollen stuff all of a sudden, but I have not seen it."

I cannot remember who Amos Cupper is, but I do not say so; I am too busy thinking that the traveling man's misfortune means that the finger of blame for the theft of Mrs. Mellin's coins will never point at me.

"What is it?" Ann has stopped her talking and looks at me. "Are you surprised to hear of so much incident in so short a space of time? I thought you might be sorry to have missed it!" She laughs.

"And the Common!" I look up quickly at this. "The scrubby common is to stay. So William lets out a big fat porker every day to snout up roots and the crisp white tubers of earthnuts. A fatting hog. He finds a sheltered spot. William goes to sleep when it is sunny and returns to the house covered in bits of gorse and dried mosses. It is such a big pig."

Ann cannot stop talking.

And then another tightening comes and I am closing my eyes and awash with an agony that rises and rises like a spring tide rushing in. There is nothing now but the swell of the water. Then it is draining away and I remember that I must breathe again.

All is quiet.

The old woman who is the midwife sits down with a creak on the wooden chair beside my bed in Mr. Blacklock's chamber. She takes a sip of something she has in a jug. She tries to put more brandy to my lips, but I turn my head away as another tightening comes and I cannot bear the jug to touch my mouth.

All through the night Ann tells me over and over that I must not be afraid, but I am not and she need not say so. She touches my forehead, my hand. She puts a wettened rag across my lips, which are hot and dry. The tightenings are faster now, and fiercer. I cry out under my breath. I must not cry louder. I must save up my vigor. When I close my eyes the pain is a thing pressing inside me: a thing made of chalk and flint and the mineral whiteness of the bones of the earth that we are all made of, our flesh wrapping around it. And the pain is the weight of the earth upon me, the earth that is made up of bodies, our bodies, my body; my own body is squeezing me open. Hours and hours go by like this, gathering pace. Bones. Hours.

And they say, "It is coming, it is crowning, here is the head!"

Pushing against the rim of myself, it is almost free. It could be anything, any creature being born in the field. I wait till the agonizing thing rises again inside me, redder and redder when I close my eyes, and then I push again. I am pushing uphill, it seems, and then turning inside out. I am split. I am ruptured, broken, burnt. I can take no more of it. I shout out from the redness and my voice is strange and harsh, but they do not hear.

And yet it is over, it is out of me. There is just the dripping of some fluid on the floorboards. They tell me they are cutting the cord. They say that the child I have carried all these months is a daughter. She cries once, thank God, a healthy cry quavering with shock and life.

"Bring her," I say, in my strange voice.

She is dried of blood and put to me.

I am astonished at her heaviness. She is all weighty, softened limbs. Her bluish eyes are open as she stares at me, the most open they could be, and how strange and how familiar her gaze seems, coming from a damp, ancient place where the light is different. Her hair is dark with a waxy substance from the womb, as though she had some vestige of the darkness that she has come from clinging to her still. Her eyes squeeze tightly shut. Her mouth moves. Her lips are fine and supple, and they part and then contract again around her tiny, perfect tongue, as if tasting the air about her for the first time. Her fingers flex. And then she turns in my arms and finds the breast blindly and sucks from me, forcefully knocking her mouth against the teat as though she had come from a desperate hunger of nine months' length, as though there were no time to lose. And there is not.

"That is a big baby, Agnes," Ann says. "For one come so early."

"It is," I say, and when I look at her, I see she knows enough.

But she does not know the wholeness of the story, how I have acted like a woman half-asleep. Nobody does, though one day I may have the chance to fully share my secrets. There is one person in particular to whom I owe an explanation: someone who may understand, even if not quite forgive. I know nothing of the future, but for today at least I am grateful to be safely delivered of my child. My mother always said that childbirth is the closest a living woman comes to death within her lifespan, if she is lucky.

The baby calms and sucks more slowly now.

Mary Spurren sits falling asleep on a chair by the window. Her head tips forward onto her chest from time to time.

It is close to the height of summer. At home on the Downs the sunrise would break over the forest at this point of the year, a liquid pink spilling out and broadening across the milky sky and unfurling slow, brilliant beams of light that warm the eastern sides of the hill and burn up the night mists that have collected in the dips and valleys. Sometimes then the sun will slip up behind a blanket of cloud and proceed concealed by it for a good part of the day, and only later will it burst out low in the sky to the west, casting a golden clarity on everything.

One by one Ann puts out the candles that have gone on burning unattended as the blue daylight grows brighter. The smell of smoking wick travels about the chamber like an incense; it is so sweet, I am almost drunk with it. She asks if I need to sleep, whether she should take the baby from me and place her in the cradle, but I will not leave her for a second, despite her strength and her regular breath as she lies, sleeping now in the world for the first time. My body is alight with a fierceness of purpose, needing to hold my child and begin to know her.

"What is she to be called?" Ann asks me, into the silence.

I look down at her, my chance-born daughter in my arms, finished at the breast and gone furled up and tightly snug like a snail or a fresh shoot, and the early sunshine begins to spill into the chamber as I speak.

"Her name is Lucy," I say. "For light, for newness, for nothing that has gone before. She is the beginning."

And how new she is, I think; so new that I can see her heartbeat pulsing in her head.

ACKNOWLEDGMENTS

My first debt of gratitude is to my agent, the late Pat Kavanagh, for her support and enthusiasm, and who I'm so sorry isn't here to see this to fruition. I was also very lucky to have had such rigorous, insightful and sensitive editing from Sarah Ballard, now also my agent; Clare Smith and Essie Cousins at Harper Press; and Pamela Dorman at Viking U.S. I would like to thank Sophie Goulden, Becky Morrison, Anne O'Brien, Taressa Brennan and everyone at Harper Press; also Zoë Pagnamenta, Carol MacArthur and Julie Miesionczek. I am grateful for funding from South West Arts, and indebted to the Royal Society of Literature—in particular to Maggie Fergusson, Julia Abel Smith and Piers Paul Read—for the time and space in which to write. Among the many books, places and people I was able to consult during research, certain resources were invaluable and I am particularly grateful to the staff at the British Library, and to the Weald and Downland Open Air Museum in Sussex. Special thanks to the expert pyrotechnician Maurice Evans for taking the time to talk to me about his work, and to the science historian Dr. Simon Werrett at the University of Washington for so kindly showing me chapters of his forthcoming history of fireworks. Other people I would like to thank for their help in a variety of ways are Chloë Hill, Jon Hill, Valerie Hill, Annie Hunt, Sam Hunt, Peter Beatty, Marie-Thérèse Please, Paddy Greaves, Sidney Greaves, Lillian and Maurice Hill, Alice Oswald, Peter Oswald, Christopher Burns, Dr. Tom Hutchison, Robert and Maria Pulley, Helen Whittle at Storrington Museum, Danae Tankard, the late Vincent Woropay, Tom Widger, Catherine Beckwith-Moore and John Eric Drewes at *American Fireworks News*. Last and heartfelt thanks to my husband, Sean, for being my anchor light and litmus test. This is to him and the boys, for their love and patience.

SOME REFERENCES

This is a work of fiction, but many contemporary and later publications helped me toward a fuller understanding of fireworks and their chemistry and history, including *The History of Fireworks*, Alan St. Hill Brock, Harrap, London, 1949; *Fireworks: A History and Celebration*, George Plimpton, Doubleday, New York, 1984; *The Chemistry of Fireworks*, Michael S. Russell, Royal Society of Chemistry, Cambridge, 2000; *The Incompleat Chymist*, Jon Eklund, Smithsonian Institute, Washington, D.C., 1975; *The Pyrotechnist's Treasury: The Complete Art of Firework-Making*, Thomas Kentish, American Fireworks News, Pennsylvania, 1993; *Artificial Fireworks: Improved to the Modern Practice*, Robert Jones, London, 1776; *The Great Art of Artillery*, Kazimierz Siemienowitz, trans. George Shelvocke, London, 1729; *The Art of Making Fireworks*, Frederick Bruhl, London, 1844; *Pyrotechnia, or A Discourse of Artificiall Fireworks*, John Babington, London, 1635.

Web resources included Old Bailey Proceedings Online, Ordinary's Accounts, and Manuscript Sessions Papers, at oldbaileyonline.org; and Carmen Giunta's Glossary of Archaic Chemical Terms at web.lemoyne.edu/~GIUNTA/archema.html.

Reading about eighteenth-century life included *The Diary of Thomas Turner 1754–1765*, ed. David Vaisey, Oxford University Press, 1984; *London Life in the 18th Century*, M. Dorothy George, Peregrine, London, 1985; *Dr Johnson's London*, Liza Picard, Phoenix, London, 2001; *Lichtenberg's Commentaries on Hogarth's Engravings*, trans. I. and G. Herdan, Cresset Press, London, 1966; *The Family, Sex and Marriage in England 1500–1800*, Lawrence Stone, Penguin, London, 1990; *English Society in the 18th Century*, Roy Porter, Penguin, London, 1991; *English Dialect Words of the Eighteenth Century*, ed. N. Bailey,

London, 1883; *Housekeeping in the 18th Century*, Rosamund Bayne-Powell, John Murray, 1956; *The Art of Cookery*, Hannah Glasse, Prospect Books, Totnes, U.K., 1995.

   Peter Lineburgh's *The London Hanged*, Verso, London, 2006, was a particular inspiration, as was *The Psychoanalysis of Fire* by Gaston Bachelard, Beacon Press, Boston, 1968.